LITTLE WHITE SECRETS

What the critics said about *An Evening with the Messiah*:

'What a joy. A contemporary Australian novel so artful it soars like the highest notes of Handel's *Messiah*. Catherine Jinks has a mastery of dialogue and understanding of human behaviour that puts her in company with writers like America's Anne Tyler or, in Britain, Anita Brookner.'
Penny Debelle, *Adelaide Advertiser*

'This is a rare and enormously refreshing book. It is unpretentiously light, but it is also beautifully observed, cunningly constructed... and written with wit, style and great assurance.'
Katharine England, *Australian Book Review*

'... a novel that succeeds, as do the early novels of Kingsley Amis, in being both lighthearted and profound, moving the reader alternately to sadness and to mirth.'
Jamie Grant, *Who Weekly*

'... a sparkling white comedy, tolerant, mature and benign, and it deserves to be widely read, not least because it is funny.'
Alex Buzo, *Sydney Morning Herald*

Catherine Jinks was born in Brisbane, Queensland, in 1963. She grew up in Papua New Guinea and later spent four years studying medieval history at the University of Sydney. She has had seven children's novels published: *This Way Out*, *Pagan's Crusade* (shortlisted for the 1993 Children's Book Council of Australia Book of the Year Award), *The Future Trap*, *Pagan in Exile*, *Witch Bank*, *Pagan's Vows* (winner of the 1996 Children's Book Council of Australia Book of the Year Award) and *Pagan's Scribe*. Her first adult novel, *An Evening with the Messiah*, was published in 1996.

She now lives in Sydney with her husband and their baby daughter.

LITTLE WHITE SECRETS

*

catherine jinks

PENGUIN BOOKS

Penguin Books Australia Ltd
487 Maroondah Highway, PO Box 257
Ringwood, Victoria 3134, Australia
Penguin Books Ltd
Harmondsworth, Middlesex, England
Viking Penguin, A Division of Penguin Books USA Inc.
375 Hudson Street, New York, New York 10014, USA
Penguin Books Canada Limited
10 Alcorn Avenue, Toronto, Ontario, Canada M4V 3B2
Penguin Books (NZ) Ltd
Cnr Rosedale and Airborne Roads, Albany, Auckland, New Zealand

First published by Penguin Books Australia Ltd 1997
1 3 5 7 9 10 8 6 4 2
Copyright © Catherine Jinks 1997

Designed by Jo Hunt, Penguin Design Studio
Cover illustration by Anna Wilson
Typeset in 11/15 pt AI Prosperall by Post Pre-press Group
Made and printed in Australia by Australian Print Group

National Library of Australia
Cataloguing-in-Publication data:

Jinks, Catherine, 1963- .
Little white secrets.

ISBN 0 14 026354 3.

I. Title.

A823.3

To Ann Dockrill,
the perfect mother-in-law

PROLOGUE

October

Oakey Marshall lived in his grandfather's house, on Marshall Street. Like most of the houses in Sable Cove it was a nineteenth-century monster, three-storeyed and multi-gabled, expensive to heat and maintain. Only its ground-floor rooms boasted storm windows; its shingle walls, which were innocent of aluminium siding, had the sand-scoured patina of driftwood. Oakey had erected a brand new, forest-green, prefabricated shed for his Ford pick-up, and used the old barn as a workshop. He stacked his fuel near the back door of the house, in a bulwark of kindling that stood one metre high and eight metres long. He grew no vegetables, and let the fruit trees take care of themselves. He never went near the boathouse. It sat on the stony shore at the bottom of Oakey's garden; its stanchions were slowly rotting away.

Alice McDonald, who lived next door to Oakey, knew very little about him. Unlike his brother (whose recent death had deprived the community of an active volunteer), Oakey was neither sociable nor opinionated. Upon Foster Marshall's death, Oakey had taken his brother's place on the Curling Club Committee, but was otherwise uninvolved in local affairs. During the winter he drove a municipal snow-plough; occasionally, in the summer, he would mow people's lawns. Alice knew this because she had seen him doing it. Whenever he crossed her path he would nod, or raise his hand to the brim of his baseball cap, which bore on its crown an advertisement for Moose Head beer. She had exchanged perhaps ten words with him during her five-year sojourn at Sable Cove.

But his call, when it came, did not entirely surprise her. As editor of the *Kempton Gazette* she had received many such calls, and was only surprised that he had chosen to pin her down at work, rather than in her own front yard. People in Sable Cove would often invade her kitchen with their hockey team results or their advertisements for used boilers. The fact that Oakey had not done so testified to a certain delicacy, on his part, which was quite unexpected. For this reason - and because she was running short of copy for the next issue - Alice agreed to drop in on her way home.

She left the office with her camera, at half past four, after checking the batteries in her flash. It was a twenty-minute drive from Kempton to Sable Cove, and when she pulled into Oakey's driveway she was greeted by a volley of barks as his three-legged Jack-Russell-cross surged towards her. Tripod was notorious throughout the neighbourhood - in fact Oakey's one failing was held to be his refusal to tie up his dog. Although Tripod was more Foster's dog than Oakey's (Oakey had inherited him, along with Foster's chainsaw and .243 Winchester), everyone felt that this was no excuse for letting a badly trained dog run free.

2

The sound of Alice's engine drew Oakey on to the front porch.

'Goan! Gerroot!' he cried, but not at Alice. He only ever raised his voice to Tripod; otherwise he was a soft-spoken individual, a man of few words, who swallowed his vowels and mumbled into his moustache. Most of the people around Kempton swallowed their vowels. It was a speech pattern characteristic of rural Nova Scotia.

Alice smiled at him briefly, over the steering wheel, before turning to collect her camera and notepad.

'Hi there,' he mumbled, opening the driver's door. 'Thanks for comin'.'

Alice inclined her head. 'Thanks for calling.'

'You gonna use that?' he asked, with a nod to the camera, and she raised her eyebrows.

'Is there a problem?'

'No.' He began to rub at his chin, which was long and scrubby. A lean man of average height, he had the gingery Marshall colouring and the pale, unblinking Marshall stare. 'Only I don't wanna give anyone a pattern. To work off.'

'Then I won't,' said Alice. 'I won't show the whole thing.' Dusk was beginning to fall; she looked towards the house, squinting into the wind that blew off the bay. 'Where do you keep it? Inside?'

'In my workshop,' said Oakey, and led her towards his barn. It was an enormous structure, as grey as granite; it smelled of oil and glue and sawdust. Oakey flicked a switch as he stepped through the open door, and Alice – who was just behind him – found herself in a familiar clutter of oil-skins, paint cans, broken picture frames, petrol drums,

3

kerosene lamps, antique lobster traps and rickety, spindle-backed chairs: the usual contents of a nineteenth-century Sable Cove outbuilding. Coils of wire were heaped on an old sewing-machine table. A ruinous pianola supported an electric jug.

'Here it is,' Oakey declared, his hands in his pockets. He stood back, as if eager to disassociate himself from the object on his workbench. Cautiously, Alice approached the thing; it looked like a breadboard, except that its flat, square surface was decorated with an intricate pattern of silver wire. The wire had been arranged in a double whorl that put her in mind of a couple of giant fingerprints. A voltmeter stood nearby, in a space completely cleared of clamps, pliers, drill bits and soldering equipment.

'So this is it?' said Alice.

'Yup.'

'And what does it do, again?'

'I'll show you.' Oakey stepped forward. 'See them?' he said, touching the ends of the wire. Instead of being fastened to the board, they quivered in the air like antennae. 'There's power comin' through them - you can measure it. Not much, because it's only a small unit, but enough for the job.' He fastened the antennae to the voltmeter; Alice saw its needle register a slight current.

'That's it?' she inquired. 'That's what you're talking about?'

'That's it.'

'If it was bigger, I suppose you'd have a bigger current.'

'Sure would.'

Alice studied the elegant arrangement of wire. She studied the voltmeter. 'You're not pulling my leg, Oakey?'

'Nope.'

'This is the real thing.'

Oakey shrugged. 'See for yourself,' he rejoined. 'No plugs. It's not wired up to nothin''.'

'How did you figure it out?'

Another shrug. 'I've thought about it,' he murmured. 'Read some books . . .'

'So it's got something to do with magnetic fields. Is that right?'

'That's right,' he said, and proceeded to explain. Alice flipped open her stenographer's pad; she made hurried notes about the arrangement of the wire – about the way in which it imitated patterns made by the earth's magnetic fields. 'Magnets are what you use,' Oakey declared. 'When you want an electric current, magnets are what you use. You get your two magnets, you pass 'em over each other, and you've got your current. That's what turbines do.'

'But not what this does.'

'No.' His moustache trembled, as one corner of his mouth lifted in a smile. 'I don't know how this works.'

'You don't?'

'Not really. I just had a hunch.' He surveyed the mys-terious generator with a slightly pensive air, tugging at the breast of his flannelette shirt. 'I was wonderin' what would happen.'

'But this sort of thing . . .' Alice waved her hand. 'You must have some kind of training. You're retired now, aren't you?'

'Yup.'

'And you used to work for . . . ?'

'Maritime Tel & Tel.'

Alice nodded. Maritime Tel & Tel was the provincial telephone company. 'So was that where you picked up all your training, or . . . ?'

'I did a year at university,' Oakey mumbled. 'Dalhousie. Long time ago.'

'Did you?' Alice tried not to sound surprised. 'And how old are you now, Oakey?'

'Sixty-five.'

'Early retirement, was it?'

He grunted. Alice jotted it all down: *Tel & Tel, sixty-five, Dalhousie*. 'So you went for an engineering degree?'

'Don't put that down.'

'But -'

'I never got my degree,' he said, in firm, flat tones. Alice shrugged. Her hands were cold.

'Have you told anyone about this?' she asked. 'Anyone at Dalhousie?'

'Fellow up at Wolfville. The university there.'

'Acadia?'

'Showed him how it worked. Said he'd get back to me.'

'And what did he think?'

'Didn't,' said Oakey, with another wry smile. 'Didn't know what to think. He'd never seen nothin' like it.'

Alice copied down the professor's name. She positioned Oakey beside his workbench and took a photograph - in which only one corner of his invention appeared. Then she asked him what his plans were.

'This is pretty remarkable stuff,' she pointed out. 'If you can create electricity from thin air . . . this could change the world, Oakey.'

'Could do.'

'You don't sound very excited.'

Oakey made a long, drawling, incoherent noise that word-lessly conveyed his scepticism. 'It's a long way from this bench to that bulb,' he observed. 'A long way.'

'But if it takes off, you'll be a billionaire.'

'Hope so.' He grinned. 'I could do with a new TV.'

It was a good quote; Alice quickly transcribed it. She also recorded his vague, disconnected remarks about the need for 'investors' and 'venture capital'. The words fell awkwardly from his lips, but she gathered that without more money he would be unable to build - or market - a bigger prototype. When Alice suggested government subsidies, Oakey snorted.

'Catch Ottawa payin' out good money to a retired linesman from Sable Cove?' he said. 'Some crazy guy who thinks he's solved everyone's problems? That'll be the day.'

'You could try, though.'

'Mmmmph.'

It was almost dark. Alice tucked her notebook into her camera bag, and thanked Oakey for his time. She promised that his story would appear in the very next issue. 'I'll call Acadia,' she added. 'Get a few quotes.'

'Sure.'

'And you'll keep me informed? About what happens?'

Oakey nodded. He accompanied Alice to her car, and stood watching until she had completed the short trip from his driveway to her own.

Six months later, his barn burned down.

January

David said goodbye to Gus on Wednesday afternoon.

It was poignantly romantic. Gus arrived at half past twelve, hot and tired from a job in Punchbowl; he headed straight for the shower, filling the bathroom with clouds of scented steam from which he emerged like the Christ of Raphael's *Transfiguration*, his limbs swathed in clinging folds of white terry towelling. He was warm and damp, all flushed skin and black hair, and David almost wept at the sight of him. After a vigorous session in bed (Gus was always vigorous), they dressed and went out, walking up to the restaurants on Victoria Street, where they ate lunch at one of the less popular Italian cafes. David ordered a focaccia, Gus a large plate of spaghetti followed by salad and a slice of cheesecake. (He loved his food.) Over coffee he told David about his cousin's latest renovation disaster; about a customer who had asked him to spray the S-bend in her toilet ('because those beasties can swim up the drains'); about the way his yellow tulip refused to die. The others had died, but not this one. 'According to the instructions, when they're on the ground dead, you dig up the bulbs,' he observed. 'So I'm waiting and waiting, all the rest are dead, but this one's still hanging on – looks pretty sick – and I'm saying, for Christ's sake, get a move on, man, you're not a bloody perennial!'

'Identity crisis.'

'Yeah.' Gus laughed, displaying a double row of strong, white teeth. He had a loud and joyous laugh. 'Needs a psychiatrist.'

'I never could understand the attraction of bulbs,' David remarked, a little vaguely, distracted by Gus's heat and by the movement of his stubbled jaw as he chewed. 'So much effort, for a two-week return.'

'You're just lazy,' said Gus, through a mouthful of cheese-cake. 'I've seen your pot plants. Poor little fuckers look like they're dying of cancer. You don't even water them.'

'I do! I do water them!'

'Whenever you need a slash, you water them.'

'That's not true. That's a vicious rumour,' said David, for whom Gus's interest in gardening – like Gus's interest in cook-ing, and opera, and David himself – was a perpetual source of awe and gratitude. In many ways the quintessential bloke, Gus had somehow escaped the cripplingly narrow-minded outlook that turned so many blokes into unadventurous bores. David often wondered if it was Gus de Souza's Portuguese back-ground which had rescued him from such a fate.

'Augustino,' he murmured, savouring every syllable.

'Not in public, thank you.'

'It's a beautiful name.'

'Shut up and finish that wog sandwich.'

After lunch they wandered back down to the park in Rushcutter's Bay, where they played cricket with a couple of schoolboys who claimed that their teacher was on a 'development course'. Both boys admired David's style of bowling: they could appreciate his speed and accuracy, although his grace was something that only Gus seemed to notice. He had noticed it from the very first, that day at Lidcombe, during a B-grade match which had attracted only wives and children and Gus de Souza, whose taste for cricket was even more impassioned than his taste for Australian Rules football. Gus had marched straight up to David after the match and complimented him on his skill.

It was only later, in the privacy of a hotel bedroom, that he had also complimented David on his appearance in white flannel. 'Wiry guys like you,' he had said, 'look so good in those floppy daks. Those floppy shirts. The way you moved - it was driving me up the wall.'

David never forgot that Gus had used the word 'wiry', rather than 'skinny'. It was exactly the right word. Gus used compliments fearlessly, frankly, without sparing a thought for their possible effect, and this was one reason why David loved him. Other reasons included his accent, his muscular build, and his brave, happy, careless attitude towards things like road maps, car engines and heckling drunkards. Gus would tackle anything, and he would do so with zest; when playing cricket he invariably reverted to primary school behaviour, yelping and whistling and jumping up and down. 'Go!' he would cry. 'Go, go, yes, out!'

David loved to watch him playing cricket.

At about two o'clock the game broke up, because Gus announced that he had a two-thirty job in Ashfield. David bowed to the inevitable; they returned to the flat in silence, and it was only as they reached the front steps that Gus found the courage to look at David, fixing him with the breeziest of smiles. 'So,' he said. 'Are you going to keep in touch? Tell me what's happening?' David's heart almost died within him.

'Would you care?' he rejoined, and saw Gus's heavy eyebrows come together.

'Don't start that again.'

'I was just asking.'

'Sure you were.'

'It will be interesting to see how much you miss me. Not half as much as I'll miss you.'

'God, you're a prima donna.'

'God, you're macho.' Through a film of tears, David saw Gus snatch the keys from his own fumbling hand and unlock the front door. There was a dim, confused interval; after tripping over the welcome mat, he suddenly found himself in Gus's arms.

'Come on, Dave. Cheer up. This was your idea, remember?'

'I know. I know that. I just wish you'd . . .'

'What?'

'Nothing.' What David actually wanted was some sort of declaration, some sort of commitment. But he knew that it was never going to materialise, if things continued along their present course.

'I love you,' he whispered.

'Take care,' said Gus. 'Be good.' They kissed, and clung, and made various promises about letters and phone calls.

Then they said goodbye, and Gus returned to his wife and baby.

'You mustn't brood,' David's mother declared the next morning. 'Try to be positive. You're going to Canada, for God's sake! Think of all the lumberjacks!'

'Oh, please.'

'You're doing the right thing, David. I know you are. He's got to make a decision.'

They were sitting at her kitchen table, writing out a shopping list for the farewell party - which was scheduled for Thursday night. David had insisted on Thursday rather than Friday, because he had no wish to board the plane with a hangover. He was also worried about Maureen Lawrence; she would be arriving on Friday, and would be in no state to deal with his mother's friends. He was barely able to cope with them himself, at the best of times.

'I've asked Ron to fix up a lobster salad,' Clara informed him. 'So we won't have to worry about that, or about the stuff I've ordered from Felice. We'll just have to get the bread and the cheese and the dips and the booze -'

'I'll do the drinks,' said David firmly, because his mother was inclined to force strange and inflammatory mixtures on people if not carefully supervised. 'You can do the food. I suppose you'll want me to clear out the front parlour?'

'Oh yes. And you'll take care of the music, won't you, my love?' Clara's tone was vague; her mind was already on something else - costumes, perhaps, or flower arrangements. She was a last-minute planner when it came to social events, but somehow her parties always worked, even when the caterers arrived halfway through the proceedings. Even when toilets failed to function, or cars to start. Her house, her friends and her sheer uninhibited energy combined to produce one memorable experience after another.

Her friends did annoy David, sometimes, but he had to admit that they were very good at parties.

'We'll have to get everything cleaned up before Maureen arrives,' he said, knowing that the wreckage would not be confined to his mother's own space, but would surge across the garden into his flat - which occupied what had once been the stables. Clara lived in her grandmother's house, a huge Victorian terrace with marble fireplaces and four-metre ceilings, servants' quarters, cedar woodwork, picture rails, sculptured cornices. The stables had been converted into an artist's studio during the late 1960s, so that David's father would have somewhere in which he could grapple with his muse. Now David's father was back in England, and David himself occupied the four-room studio, which was entered from a lane at the rear of the house. 'What do you think, Mum?' he said. 'Should I leave all the roach traps or not? Would they make a good impression or a bad one?'

'Don't ask me.' Clara was squinting through the smoke of her cigarette. 'My only advice is to clear out all your porn.'

'I had no intention of leaving it.'

'Maybe I'll pop up to the Cross and get something a bit more suitable. Something for the mature woman.'

David flashed her a warning glance.

'Don't you dare.'

'David, she's - what? Fifty-nine? She's only four years older than I am.'

'Mum, give the poor woman a break. She's from the country.' David knew that his mother was teasing; he also knew that Maureen Lawrence - school teacher, churchgoer, champion quilt-maker - would prove an almost irresistible target for someone like Clara French. Poor Maureen. She was going to have a very tough year.

Not that David's year was going to be much more enjoyable.

'Ms Lawrence will have to take me as I am,' Clara announced. 'I'm sure we'll get along very well - I always get along with people. Now, what about lights? Shall we put up some fairy lights in the garden? What do you think?'

They did put up fairy lights; they also put up paper lanterns and mosquito coils. David bought a lot of champagne. He swept paths and moved furniture and changed handtowels and listlessly selected dance music, knowing that the party would have no effect on him, one way or another, because Gus would not be attending. He had invited a few friends of his own (fellow teachers, old university chums, cricketing enthusiasts), but most of the guests would be from his mother's circle: art dealers, choreographers, consultants, columnists, all noisy, all well dressed, all hopelessly addicted to a certain incestuous brand of gossip. Even his mother's osteopath - even her hairdresser - had been sucked into the maelstrom.

As it happened, David was quite pleased to see this hairdresser, who was more than just a friend. Steven Simmons had changed David's life; at the age of twenty, David had been transformed from a pale, skinny geek into a lissom mop-top, and five years later he was still marvelling at what a simple haircut had done for his image. Steven was certainly no Albert Einstein, but when it came to streaks and styling gel he had the touch of a maestro.

'Steven! Hi!'

'G'day.' Steven was the only member of Clara's circle who could pull off this form of greeting. He was the only one who could say it without sounding awkward. 'How are things with you?'

'Fine. Good.' David knew better than to air his emotional problems at one of his mother's parties. 'You're looking very fit.'

'New gym,' said Steven, cryptically. He had a solid build and a blank, blunt face that was almost hidden by his elaborately careless coiffure. 'I hear you're off to Canada.'

'That's right.'

'On a holiday, or . . . ?'

'No.' As usual, Clara had neglected to make the situation clear. 'It's an exchange program. Weren't you told? I'm changing places with another teacher. You know – her job, her house.'

'For how long?'

'Twelve months.'

Steven made a startled noise, but his gaze was already wandering. He had a very short attention span. David filled his glass and moved on, from the rich-red dining room to the yellow kitchen, past booming actors and shrieking editors. Pat Cairns, the design consultant, had brought a stunning new boyfriend along; the boyfriend was very young and angular, and he smiled as he caught David's eye.

'David!' Pat roared. 'The Man of the Moment! Come and tell us all about Canada.'

'I can't tell you all about Canada. I haven't been there yet.'

'They'll lap you up. Look at him, Matthew, isn't he a knockout? He's my godson, you know.' Draping an arm around

16

David's shoulders, Pat beamed at the angular young boyfriend. 'I was at his christening.'

'Oh yeah?'

'Of course Clara's mother was alive, in those days. She was the one who wanted Davey christened.' Pat snorted into her chablis. 'That's why I couldn't give him that silver-plated nipple clamp as a christening present.'

David grunted. He was growing tired of Pat; she never stopped teasing and probing and trying to set him up with various members of his mother's circle - middle-aged men, friends of the family - who had all been mildly interested since David's haircut. Some of them were quite attractive, in a leathery sort of way, but David shrank from that kind of exposure; since his childhood he had repeatedly heard them discussing each other's love lives, comparing notes, exchanging intimate details. Everyone in Clara's crowd slept with everyone else, and no one ever kept anything a secret.

'I've got to circulate,' he declared, and retreated into his mother's workroom. Here he found Stella and Jim, who were trying to construct a sign with Maureen's name on it. ('So she knows who you are at the airport,' Stella explained.) Upstairs, someone was going through Clara's wardrobe, pulling out evening dresses, trying on shoes. A husband and wife were talking quietly, seriously, in one corner; they glared at anyone who approached them. People were lighting up illegal substances. The bathroom door was locked.

Viewing all this, David decided that he would be better off drunk. It was that kind of party, and he was in that kind of mood: a morose, feeble, uncooperative mood. 'Gus,' he murmured, as he tipped the last of the Chivas Regal into a teacup.

'Gus, Gus, Gus.' By eleven o'clock he was pouring his sorry tale of thwarted love into Gwyneth Schaumann's ear; at midnight, or thereabouts, he found himself lying in a warm bath, naked, while Max Valance sat on the toilet seat, droning on and on about astrological compatibility. It was all very odd. Very confused. At last Max wandered away into the night, and David dragged himself off to bed.

He woke up hours later, with a punishing headache and sticky hands, wondering where the party had gone. Could he have slept through most of it? He was, at least, in his own bedroom; for that he was grateful. The sun beat down through the skylight – the air smelled of incense – it was very warm. Conscious of some vague, looming difficulty that he had no wish to confront, he buried his face in his pillow and tried to will himself back into a state of unconsciousness.

But the sound of knocking soon drove him to his feet.

'Oh, for fuck's sake!' he groaned. 'What *is* it?' He was wearing a T-shirt and nothing else; dragging on a pair of track pants, he stumbled into the bathroom, relieved himself, and went to answer the front door. Through clouded eyes he noticed that the flat was not looking its best, littered as it was with empty glasses and dirty paper napkins. I'll have to clean up, he thought, tripping over a bottle. What the hell time is it, anyway? There was a red wine stain on the carpet and an overflowing ashtray on top of the fridge; most of his father's paintings were hanging crookedly. Kicking aside a pair of running shoes, he unhooked the chain (why was it up?), released the deadlock and dragged the door open.

Whereupon he found himself face to face with a grey-haired woman in a lilac twin-set.

'Oh - ah -'

'Hi there.' She spoke through pursed lips, her expression-less, pale-blue gaze sweeping over him. She had a North American accent. 'Are you David French?'

'God - you must be - sorry.' He had overslept. They had both overslept, he and his mother. Unless . . . perhaps . . . 'Did my mother pick you up?'

'I didn't see anyone at the airport. I waited for an hour.'

'Oh - look, I'm so sorry -'

'You *are* David French?'

'Yes -'

'I'm Maureen Lawrence.'

* * *

Every morning, Alice would check the tide from her office window. She worked in a shabby old weatherboard structure that was built out over the mudflats of Kempton Gut; twice a day, the Bay of Fundy's colossal tides would surge across these mudflats, flooding them with metres of water or leaving them exposed to the attention of strutting, quarrelling gulls. The gulls were always there because of the fishing fleet; the fishing fleet came and went like the tide. Alice had a good view of the fleet from her office, which contained only a desk, two chairs and a bookshelf (her employers did not believe in spending money on decor - or, indeed, on anything else), and she was often heard to remark that the view of Kempton wharf was all that her office had to recommend it. In saying this, however, she was not doing justice to the central heating, which was really very good. The staff of the *Kempton Gazette* never went cold during the winter.

From her desk Alice could also see (if her door was open) the back of the paper's receptionist, Erica Wellwood, who sat facing the front entrance. To Erica's right lay the darkroom, and the office of the advertising manager; to her left Raylene Tibbett was holed up in a foul little den stuffed with back issues and filing cabinets. Alice sometimes worried about the unhealthiness of this arrangement, but Raylene seemed perfectly content – perhaps because she spent more time on the road than in the office. Although her writing was of a fairly low standard, Raylene's appetite for news was insatiable. She went to almost every concert, fundraising dinner, memorial service and Municipal Council meeting held in the Kempton district. She would have gone to them even if she had worked for Scotiabank, or the Liquor Commission. Alice had come to realise that Raylene was worth her weight in gold; it was very fortunate that the paper employed a woman who was not only a chronic small-town gossip, but who was related to almost everyone in the county.

Alice could think of no one else, for example, who would have driven for miles through a blinding snowstorm just to attend a meeting of the Curling Club Executive Committee.

'So,' she said, as Raylene clattered into the office the next morning. 'How was it?'

'Oh – you'll never guess.' Raylene removed her coat, her mittens, her gloves, her scarf. She threw her bag into one corner and headed for the darkroom, where the tea-making equipment was stored. 'You'll never guess what happened to Walter Rudd.'

'What?' said Alice and Erica, simultaneously. Erica was a tall, gaunt, fifty-year-old Anglican nun; she dressed in woollen skirts and hand-knitted sweaters, and she lived with two other nuns in a farmhouse that had become known as St Mary's. Raylene was twenty-five, a thickset girl with beautiful brown eyes and a pugnacious jaw. Although very firm and outspoken in her views, she tended to favour submissive shades of pastel, lacy collars, and childish patterns of sailboats and ducks and teddy bears. When she emerged from the darkroom, holding a steaming mug of tea, Alice noticed that she was wearing her red angora top - the one with the appliqued cows on it.

'He's been dismissed,' said Raylene. 'He's off the committee.'

'Who is?' Alice frowned. 'You mean Walter?'

'That Oakey Marshall is a sneaky man. I always said he was sneaky.' Raylene propped herself against the wall, sipped her tea, and grimaced. 'Do you know what he did? He went and read up the rules. I bet nobody's done that for a hundred years.'

'Wait.' Alice lifted her hand. 'Start from the beginning. What's Oakey got to do with this?'

'He's on the committee. You know. When Foster died -'

'I remember what happened when Foster died.'

'It's that whole problem with the liquor licence,' Raylene continued, and Alice grunted. She knew all about the liquor licence controversy: it had been cluttering up the *Gazette*'s front page for almost eighteen months. Kempton's Curling Club occupied premises within the town's ice rink, and had always been in charge of the bar on those premises. But the liquor licence had originally been taken out by Kempton's Recreation Commission, which owned and operated the rink; the new Rink Manager, on discovering this fact, had insisted that the bar should be run by the Commission. Since this meant that any revenue raised by the bar would also go to the Commission, Kempton Curling Club had refused to cooperate.

'Walter's always been on both committees,' Raylene pointed out. 'He was the only one in the Curling Club who wanted to do the right thing. Foster Marshall called him a spy. Don't you remember? You must remember.'

Alice nodded. 'But Foster was an old busybody. Oakey's not like that.'

'Oakey's a Marshall. Marshalls always back each other up.' Raylene sniffed, but before she could elaborate she was interrupted by Erica, who was smiling her crooked little smile.

'If Foster had a last wish,' said Erica, 'it would have been to get rid of Walter Rudd. Perhaps it was a deathbed promise. Perhaps Oakey didn't have much choice.'

'Perhaps.'

'Anyways, Oakey read up all the by-laws,' Raylene interjected, 'and he found out there was some rule about how long a person can stay on the executive committee. No more than four terms in a row, he said.'

'Oh, my.' Alice blinked. 'Don't tell me Walter Rudd's been on that committee for twelve years.'

'Fifteen.'

'*Fifteen?*'

'It practically broke his heart,' Raylene concluded, in somewhat sententious tones. 'There were tears in his eyes.'

'Mmm. Yes. Well - it should make a good story,' said Alice, and looked up as the front door creaked open. With a sinking heart she saw that Delbert Wheelhouse was wiping his enormous snowboots on the mat; at the sight of him Raylene instantly disappeared into her office. (She and Delbert were not on speaking terms.) Alice was about to follow Raylene's example, but Delbert's hearty greeting forestalled her.

'Hi there! Cold, out. How're you, Sister?'

'Fine thanks, Delbert.' Erica carefully refrained from asking after his own health; to do so would have elicited a detailed account of his latest prostate troubles. 'What can we do for you, this morning?'

'Well, I've got a letter, here.' Delbert fixed his strangely vivid, strangely innocent blue eyes on Alice's face. 'About the closures. For you to print.'

'The closures?'

'All of them schools.'

'Oh yes.'

'I'm callin' a meetin'.'

Alice sighed. Delbert's meetings were as ineffective as they were numerous, and were always preceded by endless changes of date, time and venue. He haunted the *Kempton Gazette* like a cloud of blackflies; it had become his official mouthpiece. Alice lived in fear that he would start to harass her at home, as well as at work. She would often publish his letters just to stop him from turning up on her doorstep.

'Okay, Delbert,' she said. 'We'll do what we can. You give it to Erica - Erica will take care of it. I've got to make a phone call.' And she retreated into her office, closing the door behind her.

It was shaping up to be a typical Friday morning at the *Kempton Gazette*.

* * *

23

When Maureen moved in, David moved out. He spent Friday night in his mother's guest room, from which (because it overlooked the back garden) he could hear the sound of his own vacuum cleaner, humming and whining as Maureen put it through its paces. He was willing to bet that it had never been worked so hard; in fact he found himself wondering if there would be any carpet left, by the time he returned from Canada. Maureen was evidently one of those women who could not relax until every tile, every cupboard, every mirror around her was spotless. She had barely entered David's flat before she was hunting around for sponges and disinfectant - although she took great care not to allow a single reprimand to pass her lips. Only by the slightest pinching of her nostrils did she convey her thoughts on the condition of David's handtowels, and crisper, and microwave oven. She really was very polite.

'No, no,' she would say, as David apologised for the congealed fat on his garbage bin. 'That's not a problem. Don't worry about it.' *Doon't w'rry aboat it.* She had a soft, slow drawl and a charming accent; her mouth barely moved when she spoke. Her face was long and placid, her frame heavy, her smile bland. But she attacked the bathroom floor like a tornado.

'I don't know how she does it,' David remarked, awe-struck, as he returned from his flat with two bulging suitcases. 'She just spent twenty-four hours on a plane, and now she's defrosting the freezer.'

'Mmmph,' his mother replied. She was not looking her best; she never did, after a party. 'What are those boxes in the hall?'

'I'm taking them with me. They're full of books.'

'Oh.'

'Should we ask her to dinner tonight? It's the least we can do.'

But Maureen refused the invitation, professing herself to be 'tired out' and 'not hungry'. She said that she planned to turn in at six. The fact that she was still up at nine, vacuuming, did not offend David - on the contrary, it filled him with wonder and relief. He went to bed feeling that Maureen and Clara were pretty well matched, at least in terms of energy output, and that Maureen might actually have the strength to cope with life in Sydney after all.

The next morning she was hanging out her washing before David had even shrugged off his pyjamas (he and his mother shared a rotary clothes line), humming a little song that David recognised - with a shudder - as something of Tammy Wynette's. Then she disappeared again. But at half past six, shortly before he was scheduled to leave, she tapped on the glass door of the kitchen as David and his mother were bolting down their muesli.

'For you,' she said, presenting David with a small, beautifully wrapped parcel. 'You can put them on when you get there.' The parcel contained a pair of mittens, a woollen scarf and sixteen disposable foot-warmers - little plastic packets which, when opened and tucked into his socks, would generate heat for three or four hours. 'You're going to need 'em,' she added. 'It's been a hard winter, so far.'

'Oh, Lord,' said David. 'You shouldn't have.'

'It's nothin'.'

'How very kind.' Stricken with guilt, David glanced at his mother. Neither of them had thought to buy a gift for Maureen. 'Um . . . can we offer you breakfast, or - ?'

'No, I've had mine. I got up real early.' Smiling and nodding, Maureen held out her hand. 'So I'll wish you good luck,
and have a nice trip -'

'Thanks -'

'And I guess I'll hear from you in a little while.'

They shook hands. Then Maureen made her way back
across the garden, and David went to load his luggage into
the car. His mother had offered to drive him to the airport; no
one else - not even Gus - had felt energetic enough to brave
the airport so early on a Saturday morning.

'I'm going to be such a wreck when I get there,' he muttered,
as he rubbed his bleary eyes. 'Such a wreck.'

'If you look any worse than you do now, they'll be pushing
you into Canada on a wheelchair,' was Clara's response. She
backed out of the driveway, changed gears, and headed west
towards Victoria Street. The traffic was very light, even at the
Oxford Street intersection; pretty soon they were bowling
down Anzac Parade. 'I meant to give you my nausea pills,' she
added, after a long and sleepy silence. 'Do you want to stop at
a chemist?'

'There'll be one at the airport,' David replied. He was feeling distinctly odd in the stomach, but knew that this was a
symptom of his emotional rather than his physical state. He
wanted Gus. He *needed* Gus. And his mother was being so
sweet - so uncharacteristically organised - that it brought a
lump to his throat.

'You'll be all right, won't you?' he said, whereupon Clara
grimaced.

'Don't start.'

'Sorry.'

'Just let me concentrate. If we get into the wrong lane, we'll end up at Sutherland.'

'It's the International Terminal –'

'I know, I know.'

Sydney Airport was a chaotic gridlock of double-parked taxis and screaming children. The check-in lines stretched on forever. David chose the shortest, then saw that it was for business-class passengers only; he had to drag his luggage over to the next one, which immediately stopped moving. He and his mother stood speechless, too glum even to exchange remarks about the American tourists in front of them, until at last he was relieved of his overweight baggage.

Then it was time to pass through customs.

'Well,' he said. 'So this is it.'

'This is it.'

'I'll write.'

'I'll phone.'

'I'll miss you.'

'I love you.' She clutched him fiercely around the chest. 'You're a darling boy.'

'Be nice to Maureen.'

'You have fun, okay?'

'I will.'

'And bring me back a Mountie!' she cried. He left her standing there, a slight figure in a baggy blouse and trailing Indian skirt, her wild red hair tied up in her favourite Pucci scarf, her creased, yellow face enlivened by a slash of scarlet lipstick.

He was still sniffing when he boarded his plane.

'Dries you out, doesn't it?' the woman next to him remarked. She was wearing a pink tracksuit and carried her knitting in a bag. 'The airconditioning, I mean.'

'Oh. Yes.'

'Always does terrible things to my sinuses.'

David grunted, and astonishingly - miraculously - she seemed to take the hint. Throughout the entire first leg, from Sydney to Honolulu, she barely said a word; she merely smiled as she passed him his meal-trays, and murmured incoherently when she had to squeeze past his legs on her way to the toilet. After Honolulu, during the darkest, grimmest portion of the trip - when the long hours crawled by like snails and the movies all seemed to merge into one distorted dreamscape - the sound of her clicking needles would penetrate David's nightmares, as he drifted in and out of consciousness, his head full of clocks and crickets and the tapping of typewriter keys.

Although she did not appear to sleep at all, she managed to consume a hearty breakfast of eggs and tomatoes - offerings which David was unable to touch.

'Are you getting off at Toronto?' she inquired, as he sipped his tea.

'No, I - no.'

'Because even if you're not, you'll have to go through customs. Immigration. First port of call.'

'Oh,' said David. The prospect was unappealing. 'You mean - with the bags and that?'

''Fraid so.'

'Jesus.'

It was every bit as bad as he had feared. First came the interview with Immigration; then the wait at the carousel;

then the endless walk across the terminal, to check his luggage on to the plane bound for Halifax. He felt as if he had survived a long night of illness; groggy and confused, he stumbled from seat to seat, from lounge to gate to cabin, until he finally found himself gazing out of an aeroplane window on to a wide expanse of snow-capped evergreens.

He realised, with a start, that he was looking at Nova Scotia.

'Beef jerky?' said the man next to him. David turned, and blinked.

'What?'

'Beef jerky.' The man was proffering several long, reddish sticks of dried meat. 'You're welcome to try some.'

'Oh - no thank you.' David tried to conceal his horror. 'Thanks very much, though.'

'Where're you from?'

'Australia.'

'Australia!' The man nodded and beamed. 'I'm from Saskatchewan. Guess you've come further than I have.'

'Guess so.'

'You'll like Nova Scotia. It's a pretty place,' the man said, and entertained David with an account of his trucking business until the plane had come to a standstill. Then, in mid-sentence - long before the seatbelt signs had been extinguished - he shot to his feet and began to haul coats and briefcases and wardrobe bags from the overhead locker. He was halfway down the aisle when the door opened; David had a feeling that he would be first off the plane or die in the attempt.

'Goodbye ... goodbye ... thank you, sir ...' The bright, smiling faces of the flight attendants flowed past (quite attractive, some of them, but David was in no mood for dalliance). He shuffled out of the plane and along a narrow, carpeted corridor, past dull little photographs of Nova Scotia's numerous attractions, into the baggage retrieval area. It was a very small airport. David noticed a souvenir shop and a vending machine; he saw French signs as well as English ones. Canada, he thought. I'm in Canada.

Then somebody tapped his arm.

'David French?' a voice remarked. It belonged to a thin, whiskery, middle-aged man in a baseball cap.

'Yes,' David said. 'That's me.'

The man nodded. He had pale, protruding eyes and a red nose. He wore a bulky vinyl jacket over loose trousers. His boots were lined with fake fur.

'Thought it was,' he announced. 'You're late.'

'Oh . . .'

'I'm Oakey Marshall. Maureen's brother.' He tugged at the front of his cap, peering up at David from under his ginger eyebrows. 'I'm gonna be taking you down to Scotsville. Should be two, two-and-a-half hours - more likely three, in this weather. You wanna use the bathroom, before we go?'

* * *

On Friday night, Alice attended a special public session at Kempton's Town Hall. The meeting had been called by Municipal Council, to discuss a new amendment to the regulations of the provincial Litter Abatement Act; normally Raylene would have covered it, but Raylene was at a Royal Canadian Legion turkey supper, in Watervale. So Alice was obliged to sit through two hours of angry debate concerning

Council's right to demand that bags of garbage be placed in garbage cans, before being collected.

'I object to you tellin' me I have to put my garbage in cans!' (Delbert Wheelhouse, as usual, had a lot to say on the subject.) 'I don't have enough room to store cans. Does this mean I'll have to take my garbage to the dump myself?'

'It seems to me that Council hasn't considered what effect this new by-law will have on our elderly and handicapped citizens,' Alberta Belliveau pointed out. 'Also, what happens in winter, when the cans are blown about during storms, or get covered in snowdrifts?'

'I want to ask the Mayor if he's looked into the extra cost incurred because garbage placed in cans will take longer to collect,' Kendall Tibbett rumbled. 'Will the rate-payers be expected to foot this bill, as well?'

Sighing, Alice dutifully recorded all these remarks, and then commiserated with the Mayor after the meeting had closed. 'Anyone would think we were asking them to sacrifice their first-born sons,' he exclaimed fretfully. '*They're* the ones who complain when their garbage bags are attacked by raccoons.'

'I know.'

'Next thing they'll be wanting to leave it all in a heap on the side of the road. So they don't have to waste money on bags.'

Alice nodded sympathetically. Then she said goodnight, pulled on her overcoat, and plunged into the bitter cold (minus twenty, according to the forecast – a very chilly winter, this year), taking great care with her car keys. Only last week she had dropped her keys into a snowdrift, and had ended up with a frozen ignition lock.

'Goodnight, Alice!'

'Goodnight.' Alice lifted her hand to Alberta Belliveau.

'Take care, now.'

'You too.'

Alice had bought herself a big, secondhand Chevrolet with all-weather tyres – a good, solid car. She drove it back to Sable Cove via Watervale, a slightly longer route than the direct one (through Scotsville), but the off-ramp to Scotsville was dangerously steep in this weather. Alice always worried about black ice.

She reached Sable Cove at nine forty, and noticed that Oakey Marshall's pick-up was missing. There were no lights on in his house. This was unusual, because Oakey was an early-to-bed, early-to-rise sort of man, and Alice made a mental note of his absence. As she got out of the car she paused for a moment, her attention caught by the calm, shining expanse of Sable Cove: the moon was full, the night very clear, and the snow reflected a soft, unearthly radiance.

But it was too cold to stand still for long.

'Damn!' she said, slipping on a patch of ice. Cautiously she climbed the front steps, fumbling with her keys, and let herself into the tiny, crowded vestibule, which smelt of old boots and rain jackets. Her house was a 1960s bungalow, very plain and straightforward, with lots of pale-orange tiles and a carpet the colour of nutmeg. The most beautiful thing about it was the view from her living-room window; she would often sit on her chesterfield and watch evening fall over Sable Cove, because her garden stretched all the way down to its shoreline. She loved this view. She had taken pictures of it, pictures which she had framed and hung on the walls among other pictures of other views – for she had surrounded herself with photographs. Hundreds of mounted photographs covered every available surface; only the floor and ceiling presented uncluttered visual fields.

Even so, the atmosphere of the house was very tranquil - very serene. Silence reigned in every room except the kitchen, where the refrigerator hummed and the oven clock ticked remorselessly. Sometimes the furnace would clank and belch, as its thermostat registered a drop in the temperature. Sometimes the roof would creak under the weight of falling snow. But for the most part this was a silent house, silent and still, and much too big for Alice - three bedrooms, as well as an unfinished games room in the basement. It cost her four hundred and eighty-five dollars a month, but was worth every penny just for the peace. And the view. And the heating, of course, which was excellent.

Alice made herself a cup of tea, conscious of the unwashed dishes on the draining board. She had dashed off to Kempton right after supper; her egg-stained frying pan had been left to soak. 'I'll do it in the morning,' she announced, her voice echoing strangely in the empty kitchen, and went out to the dining room. Here she settled down at one end of the table, with her cup of tea, her fountain pen and a large, cloth-covered notebook.

Half of the notebook had been filled, so Alice turned to a fresh page. She wrote the date in the upper left-hand corner. Then, after a moment's thought - and a sip of tea - she began to transcribe her day's activities in a neat, cramped, royal-blue script.

Overcast, but clearing. No snow. Minus ten to minus twenty. I went to Foodland this morning and saw several people: Fairlie McNeil, Gwen

Wylie, Paul Anderson. Paul seems to be settling in – he is looking to buy a house on King Street. He told me he'll be testifying in that Longshaw child abuse case. Fairlie McNeil told me he's going to hospital next week, for a gall bladder operation . . .

* * *

David woke with a start as the engine died. For a moment he thought that he was back on the plane; then he realised that he was slumped in Oakey Marshall's pick-up, his head propped against the frosted window. In front of him, through the windscreen, he could see the facade of a house illuminated by Oakey's headlights – a long, white, weatherboard house, circa 1970. It would have been quite unremarkable if not for the fact that it was festooned with Christmas decorations: a fir wreath on the door, glowing plastic candles in the windows, coloured lights arranged around every eave, every shrub, every handrail. The adjoining houses were similarly decorated, one of them boasting a giant fretwork Santa's sleigh in its front yard, the other an illuminated sign that said 'Jesus is the reason for the season'.

'Bloody hell,' croaked David, rubbing his eyes.

'We're here.' Oakey was looking at him. 'You'll have to help me with your stuff.'

'Oh. Yes . . .'

'Bonnie'll look after you,' Oakey added, and pushed open the door. David flinched as a cold wind struck the side of his face; when he followed Oakey's example and alighted, he nearly fell flat on his back.

'Watch your step.' Oakey's drawl was unperturbed. 'There's a lotta ice about.'

'Is there?'

'Walk slow. Dig your heels in.'

David did as he was told. They managed to unload the truck without further incident, David conscious only of his aching, stiffening fingers. He had never been so cold in his life. They carried his luggage, piece by piece, up to the front porch, and Oakey was searching his pockets for the keys when someone came tripping towards them, leaving a trail of footprints in the snow.

'Hi there!' she exclaimed. 'I didn't hear you arrive – that damned washing machine makes such a racket. Are you David? I'm Bonnie. I live next door.'

'Hello . . .'

'Go on in, and I'll make you something to eat. You must be starved. What about you, Oakey, you hungry?'

Oakey shrugged. 'Stopped for a hamburger at Kentville,' he replied.

'That's not a meal. I'll heat you up some of my chowder.' Bonnie waved a piece of Tupperware under David's nose; she was a plump little woman in her fifties, quick and spry, with dyed blonde hair cut short and a round, snubby, small-featured face. She led them through an entrance hall into a large room that made David wince, despite its air of comfort. One of the walls (the feature wall) was panelled in walnut-stained pine; the shag pile was dense and textured; the lounge suite was upholstered in some kind of carnivorous-looking, flower-print velveteen. There were a great many brass pokers and coal scuttles arranged around the fireplace, which had been constructed from a bland grey stone like putty. Every available surface was decorated with framed needlepoint pictures, Mexican souvenirs, hideously expensive mail-order porcelain and rather nice pieces of quilting.

It was as hot as a sauna.

'For God's sake, woman,' Oakey growled. 'What're you tryin' to do, boil us?'

'I turned up the furnace. I knew David wouldn't be used to the cold.'

'It's all right,' David assured her, gasping. 'I don't need it this hot.'

'Well, you can fix it up yourself, if you want, and I'll get supper. This is the kitchen in here. Bedrooms are down that way. Why don't you show him, Oakey? I won't be a minute.'

Oakey was adjusting a switch on the wall. When David asked him what it was he looked surprised, but explained (civilly enough) that it was the control for the furnace - or rather, for the oil furnace. 'You can take your pick,' he informed David. 'Maureen's got two of 'em - oil or wood. She hasn't used the wood furnace in a long time, but it's up to you.'

'Is it . . . I mean, is the wood furnace less trouble?'

'Nope.'

'Then I'll use the oil furnace.'

Oakey nodded. He showed David the bathroom, the master bedroom, the guest bedroom, the laundry: everything was spotless, and shrouded in fluffy mats or frilly coverlets. (Oakey himself looked oddly out of place among the silk flowers and decorative rag dolls.) He then led David down a flight of stairs and into a large, leathery room which he called the 'den'; it contained an elaborate bar, more pine panelling, and any number of sharp-shooting trophies - some of them wall-mounted and arranged around a coloured print of *The Monarch of the Glen*.

'John won these,' Oakey remarked.

'John?'

'Maureen's husband.' Oakey sniffed reflectively, eyeing the rifle that was sitting in a bracket above the bar. 'He's been dead twelve years.'

'Oh,' said David, who knew nothing about a husband. He followed Oakey into another basement room, which was very different from the first: its walls and floor were of concrete, and it was bitterly cold. 'Wood furnace, oil furnace,' Oakey pointed out. 'And that's the ping-pong table.'

'Is there - I mean, what are you supposed to do with an oil furnace?' David eyed the thing fearfully. 'How often do you have to put oil in?'

Oakey lifted an eyebrow. 'You don't,' he replied, after a brief pause. 'Woodmans does it for you.'

'Woodmans?'

'Woodmans Fuel. They come along, top you up. The tank's outside. Just keep your eye on the gauge, and give 'em a call if you're runnin' low.' As David opened his mouth to speak, Oakey added: 'Bonnie can show you the gauge. Tank's full now - I made sure of that.'

David thanked him in a low, groggy voice. They went back upstairs and tucked into Bonnie's chowder, which was a creamy fish soup, rather too rich for David's stomach. But he managed to eat half of it, as Bonnie prattled on about the arrangements. 'There's some food to get started with,' she informed him. 'Just a few things - bread, cheese, milk, tomatoes. Maureen says that if you want to use the frozen blueberries, you're welcome. One of the hotplates on the stove doesn't work too well - you'll have to keep it on "high".

Tomorrow I'll show you where the mailbox is. This is the front door key, the back door key, the car key, the mailbox key . . .'

David nodded and smiled, absorbing perhaps one word in ten. He was utterly exhausted. At last Oakey got up to leave, wiping his mouth and pulling at the brim of his cap. 'I'll see you later,' he announced, turning to Bonnie. 'Thanks for the meal.'

'No problem.'

'They say it's gonna snow tonight. If it does, do you want me to –'

'Oh, yes. I'd appreciate that.'

'Tomorrow? Early?'

'I'll leave the money with Floyd.'

After this cryptic exchange, Oakey put on his coat and departed. David heard his engine coughing, firing, roaring; he heard the crunch of wheels on frozen snow.

Next thing, Bonnie was shaking his shoulder.

'David?' she said. 'Come on, now – you can't go to sleep in here.'

'Wha–?'

'Which room do you want? Maureen's? I'll just turn down the bed for you.'

She bustled away, and David groaned as his head sank into his arms. It was so embarrassing. Maureen had put in a full day's work after her epic plane trip, and Maureen was fifty-nine years old. David was only twenty-five, but he had to have his bed turned down. What other indignities were in store? Would he have to be washed? Dressed? Would he have to have his teeth cleaned?

I'm so bloody feeble, he thought. How am I going to man-age in a place like this? I wouldn't know what to do with a frozen blueberry if it hit me in the eye. Ice scraper? What's this ice scraper Oakey was talking about? God, it's all too much . . .

He was asleep again before Bonnie returned.

February

Alice had heard about David through her contacts on the school board. She gave him two weeks to settle in before requesting an interview; his voice, over the phone, was very young and light. 'Me?' he said. 'You want to write a story about me?' He seemed astonished, and tickled. 'Well, yes, I suppose so. If you really think it's worth the effort. You can come around here - do you know the house? It's -'

'Yes,' said Alice. 'I know the house.' She was familiar with most of the houses in Scotsville, and had spoken with Maureen Lawrence at any number of public events. A strange woman, Maureen. Although she indulged in no behavioural quirks - like most other women of her age around Scotsville she devoted her spare time to cooking, gardening, shopping, quilting and making some sort of contribution to the local spring fair - she did have more than her share of the characteristic Marshall reticence (aggravated by a slightly formidable, schoolmarmish demeanour). And of course there was the question of her husband. Her husband's suicide was still shrouded in mystery, if only because Maureen had never spoken of any personal or marital problems. Not that Alice would necessarily have expected her to do so, being just as protective of her own privacy. But she had often wondered what lay behind that calmly cheerful, neighbourly facade. Surely it was not the sum total of Maureen Lawrence? Sometimes, when talking to Maureen, Alice was overcome by the strangest feeling - as if she were talking to one of the robotic Stepford Wives.

The interview with David was scheduled for Sunday morning at ten o'clock; Alice decided that she would drop in on her way to the office. (She frequently visited the office on Sundays, to develop her photographs.) David preferred a weekend appointment because, he said, he was still rather tired during the week. Perhaps that would change as his jet lag wore off. 'It's all very different,' he confessed. 'The school, I mean. It takes a bit of getting used to.'

'Good.'

'Good?'

'You'll have a lot to talk about.'

Sunday morning was clear and cold, and the wind off the water seared Alice's nose as she climbed into her car. On her way to Scotsville she stopped to photograph a cascade of ice - a frozen waterfall - that decorated one of the man-made cliffs near the off-ramp. It was very beautiful. The sand on the road looked like brown sugar; the snow glistened under its film of ice, dirty and brown along the side of the road, clean and white in the woods and paddocks.

A treacherous day. So pretty, but so deadly. A bad day for driving.

41

When Alice reached Scotsville, she noticed that Maureen's front door was impassable, buried behind a metre of frozen snow. Apparently David French had neglected to clear his porch; there had been a thaw, and a cold snap, and now he would have to wait until the snowdrift melted. His driveway, however, was navigable. Alice parked beside the oil tank, gathered up all her equipment, and made her way to the back door, which was obviously the main point of access. She knocked and waited.

Presently she heard footsteps. The doorknob rattled; somebody cursed.

'Hello?' she said.

'Hello!' It was David's voice, muffled. 'Hang on a second, I can't . . .' The doorknob rattled again. 'I can't get this open.'

'What?'

'It's stuck! I can't turn it!'

'Oh dear.' Alice's breath was emerging in great clouds of steam. 'It's probably frozen.'

'What?'

'It's probably *frozen*.'

A stunned silence.. Then: 'Frozen? What do you mean, frozen?'

'Have you got a hairdryer?'

'Who?'

'A *hairdryer*. Can you thaw it out with a hairdryer?'

'Jesus . . .' Alice heard his footsteps, fading as he retreated; she herself went back to the car. It was too cold to stand around on a doorstep. She turned on the radio, and after a long wait (five minutes, by her watch), she was startled by the sound of David's voice. He was heading towards her, waving a little red appliance.

'I did it!' he exclaimed. 'Thank God for that!' He was tall and slim, with a dishevelled mop of pale-brown hair and a bright, appealing face. He wore a gigantic sweater over narrow jeans. 'I would have been stuck there, otherwise, because I can't get out the front door –'

'Yes. I noticed.'

'Nobody told me how hard it can get,' he observed in a plaintive voice. 'The snow, I mean. It's like rock, now – you'd need a pickaxe. I just thought I'd let it go for a bit, and shovel the whole lot at once . . .' He was holding the back door for her. 'Come in, and I'll make you some coffee. Or would you prefer tea?'

'Coffee will be fine,' said Alice. In the laundry she took off her coat and her snowboots; from there she passed into the kitchen, which was big and warm and cluttered. A cook's kitchen, she thought, eyeing the range of pots and cake pans.

'Now . . . the one thing Maureen doesn't seem to have is a percolator,' David remarked, fishing around in a cupboard. 'So I can only offer you instant. Is that all right?'

'That's all right.'

'She's got every other appliance on the face of the earth,' he continued. 'I've never seen anything like it. Half this stuff . . . it's like being on an archaeological dig. Like this, for instance. Any idea what this might be?'

He held up a long, stainless-steel object with a curious tangle of wire at one end. It looked like a surgical instrument.

'Some kind of egg whisk?' Alice suggested. 'A potato masher?'

'Who knows?' David discarded it. 'I bet she's the only person in the world who actually *uses* a fish slice.'

'She's a very good cook,' Alice agreed, thinking of Maureen's contribution to various fundraising bake sales. As David fussed around the kitchen she watched him intently, fascinated by his flowing movements; his dense, sculptured sweater; his effortless hospitality. He was so articulate - so eye-catching. He had a kind of urban gloss, a mobility of feature and ease of expression, that reminded Alice of her years in Toronto.

She wondered how he was getting along at Kempton Elementary School.

'I'm just not used to snow,' he was saying. 'I never thought about locks, before. Like with the letterbox, for instance - milk? Sugar?'

'Milk. No sugar.'

'I went to open my letterbox the other day, and I broke the lock.' He shook his head. 'It was frozen, and I forced it. Had to ask Oakey for a bolt-cutter.'

'Oakey?' said Alice. 'You've met him, have you?'

'Oh, yes.' David handed her a steaming mug. 'He picked me up at the airport. Do you know him?'

'I live next door to him.'

'Do you? Then perhaps you can tell me . . .' Leaning forward, David fixed her with a wide-eyed, curious look. 'What's the deal with his name?'

'His name?'

'Oakey. Is that a real name, or - ?'

'Oh.' The penny dropped. 'Oakey. Yes. That's a nickname.'

'I *thought* so.'

'His father was a champion woodcutter. They used to call him "Oakey", too. Oakey was no champion, but he won a medal when he was in his teens.' Alice cast her mind back, frowning. 'It was some kind of joke, I think, but it stuck.'

'What's his real name?'

'I've no idea.'

'It's probably something like Cyril,' David laughed. 'Or Julian. Something he doesn't want anyone to know about.'

They carried their coffee into the living room and sat down on the chesterfield, which was completely covered in quilts. There were quilts and throws draped all over the easy chairs. Alice wondered if this was Maureen's idea, or whether David had arranged it; she suspected the latter.

But the craft books were definitely Maureen's.

'So.' With an embarrassed grin, David set his cup down.

'What do you want to ask me?'

'Spelling,' Alice replied. 'Let's get the spelling right, first.' Having established that his name was spelt in a straight-forward fashion, she went on to ask him about his background, and why he had decided to come to Canada in the first place. He told her that he was from Sydney, that he had been teaching for three years, and that Canada - well, Canada had been one of several choices.

'Basically, you take what you're given,' he said. 'But that's fine with me. I mean, Canada's fine.'

'Even the weather?'

'The weather was a bit of a shock!' He grinned again; his teeth were slightly crooked, but very white. 'It's mid-summer in Sydney, right now. And of course we never get snow there.'

'Never?'

'Never.' He regaled Alice with an account of his attempts to find thermal underwear in Sydney during the hottest month of the year. He talked about trying to referee an ice hockey match ('the kids were very understanding') and about his North American spelling problems ('they're very nice about that, too'). He named a few of his fellow teachers ('Do you know Sam Peck? Jill Comeau?'), who were trying to introduce him to the mysteries of baseball and gridiron, if only because he would be unable to function socially without some sort of grounding in the rules of those games. 'It's bad enough in the classroom - I can't pick up all of the TV show references,' he confessed. 'Thank God we get *The Simpsons* back in Australia, or I'd be *completely* lost!' He chattered on about the hardihood of Canadian children, and their willingness to play outside in sub-zero temperatures, and having to make sure that they put on their hats and scarves and mittens before they were dismissed for lunch. It all added a different texture to the day, he said. 'Playground duty. Crossing duty. You could die of exposure! But if I grouse enough, the other teachers think, "Oh, that poor Australian", and they very kindly swap duties with me.'

There was no need to prompt David; the words came pouring out, vivid, breathless, emphatic. It occurred to Alice that he might be a little lonely. 'Of course I'm starting to feel isolated,' he went on, as if reading her mind. 'You don't get much Australian news. The only thing I've heard about so far is that giant clam business.'

'Giant clam?'

'Didn't you see that? The Australian Navy has relocated thirty thousand giant clams.' He laughed. 'Really puts things in perspective, doesn't it?'

'I suppose it must.' Alice glanced down at her notes. 'And what do you hope to gain from your year in Canada?' she

46

added, her pen poised. David's eyes veered away from her; a pensive look settled over his features.

'Oh . . . I don't know. Fun. Excitement. Confidence. New ideas. New friends. The usual.' He seemed oddly discomforted by her question, his gaze flicking from corner to corner. Alice was about to proceed to the country-city issue when he suddenly leaned across the coffee table and looked her straight in the eye.

'Can I ask you something?' he said.

'Of course.'

'It's about Maureen's husband.' He hesitated, as if choosing his words. 'Do you know about him?'

'I know he killed himself.'

'But do you know *how*?'

Alice tried to remember. 'He shot himself, didn't he? It was before my time.'

'Pardon?'

'I'm not from around here,' said Alice, and he blinked.

'Oh - aren't you? Where are you from?'

'Well . . . P. E. I., originally.' Seeing the blank look on his face, she felt compelled to explain further. 'Prince Edward Island.'

'Oh, yes?'

'But I've moved around a lot.' To prevent him from pursuing the subject, she reverted to his original question. 'So what did you want to ask me? About Maureen's husband?'

'Her husband. Yes.' David cleared his throat. 'The thing is . . . I've been told that he shot himself with one of his own guns. He was a champion shooter, apparently (whatever that means), and now she's got all his guns - all his trophies - lined up on the bar downstairs.' He grimaced. 'Don't you think that's a bit . . . well, you know. A bit *weird*?'

Alice smiled, more at his expression than at what he was saying. 'I guess so,' she said.

'I mean, obviously some people don't. Bonnie doesn't. Do you know Bonnie? Bonnie McNeil? She lives next door.'

'I know Bonnie.'

'You must know everyone around here.' David nodded, as if something had been confirmed. 'Bonnie told me about John in the first place. I was just sitting there - you know - with my mouth hanging open. We were right there in the den. But she didn't seem to think it was peculiar.'

He stopped, and peered across the table. Alice saw that he was waiting for some kind of reaction.

She took a deep breath.

'There are different ways of looking at it,' she observed, cautiously. 'Perhaps you've never had much to do with guns. Have you?'

'No.'

'No. Well, around here, people use guns all the time. A lot of them have guns in their houses.' Alice thought for a moment. 'They'd probably say: "If my husband slit his wrists, would you expect me to get rid of all the kitchen knives?"'

David frowned. 'That's not quite the same thing,' he said.

'No. It isn't. But it's what they'd say.'

At this point the conversation stalled, so Alice returned to her country-city questions. Were city schools different from country schools? What advantages did he see in country living? To most of these queries David's response was somewhat

48

guarded: he had not, he said, been in Canada long enough to answer them. (Alice also fancied that he did not want to offend anyone.) At last she put down her mug, shut her notebook, and glanced at her watch. Eleven thirty! How quickly the time had passed.

'Would you like to stay for lunch?' David said. 'I can warm up some pizza.'

'No thanks.'

'Or a fried cheese sandwich?'

'I'd like to, but I have to develop some photographs.' Alice smiled at him, touched by the rather forlorn droop of his neck. 'Maybe another time.'

'It must be interesting,' he continued, as he followed her out to the car, 'being the editor of a local paper.'

'It can be.'

'You must find out a lot of stuff about people.' He watched her pull in her legs, slam the door, and fasten her seatbelt. 'Good gossip.'

'I do,' Alice agreed. She looked at him for a moment - at the speculative tilt of his eyebrows - and found herself smiling again. 'But I'm no tattle-tale,' she said. 'When people tell me a secret, it stays a secret. There are things I know that no one's ever going to find out.'

And she turned the key in the ignition.

* * *

For three years running, the Scotsville Blueberry Carnival Executive Committee had been holding its monthly meetings in Maureen Lawrence's den. Bonnie informed David of this fact just a week after his arrival; she also explained to him that in Maureen's absence, she herself had been elected Chairwoman.

'If you want us to go somewhere else,' she added, 'that's not a problem. We don't want to get in your way.'

'You won't. Really.'

'Are you sure? Because there's always my house. Floyd can go bowling.' Floyd was Bonnie's husband: a large, morose, moustachioed man. As a logger, he was generally out of work during the winter months. 'It wouldn't be any trouble.'

'Bonnie, I'm quite happy to have you here. It'll be interesting.'

And it was. For a start, Bonnie felt constrained to provide David with the backgrounds of all the committee members. (There were six of them, including Bonnie.) Keith Hughes, the Fire Chief, represented the local fire department, which received a large cut of the profits. He was 'a nice man, a really nice man, very quiet', and it was a pity about his autistic son. Bob Wheelhouse represented the Royal Canadian Legion; he was a bit of a whiner, everything was always so difficult for him, and he and Raylene Tibbett - another committee stalwart - were constantly at each other's throats.

'The Tibbetts and the Wheelhouses,' Bonnie sighed. 'There's been a lot of bad feeling since Bob's son Watson went off to Vancouver. He left Raylene's cousin behind, you see.'

'They were married?'

'No, not married. But the baby was his - at least, that's what *she* says. The Tibbetts say that Watson isn't giving her enough child support. The Wheelhouses say it isn't Watson's baby, and they won't give anyone his address. None of them will make any kind of concession.'

Then Bonnie told David about Raylene Tibbett, a 'funny girl', who lived with her lobster-fishing boyfriend in a house that he was building himself. 'But it's lobster season now,' Bonnie said, 'so the poor girl's got no proper kitchen. He still hasn't put any of the cupboards in.' As for Raylene, she worked on the *Kempton Gazette*.

'Oh!' David sat up. 'I know the woman who edits that. Alice McDonald. She interviewed me.'

'Alice. Yes . . .' Bonnie pulled a wry, thoughtful face. 'She's a strange woman, Alice.'

'Why?'

'Oh, just the way she lives. All by herself. No family.' Bonnie waved Alice aside, returning to the matter of Raylene Tibbett. 'Raylene's a smart girl. She could do a lot better than Gary. A lot better.'

The other two members of the committee were Walter Rudd and Gordon Blanchard. When David heard Gordon's name he uttered a little yelp of surprise, because Gordon was the Deputy Headmaster of Kempton Elementary School. 'I know Gordon,' he said. 'At least, I've met him. Does he live around here?'

'Up on Brook Road. That big old grey house.'

'Really?' The big grey house was an impressive structure, newly renovated in the best possible taste. 'But that's quite a spread.'

'Mmmm.'

'Well, I'll be damned . . .' David pondered for a minute, wondering if he really wanted to see much of Gordon Blanchard. People tended to exchange veiled looks when Gordon was around; he was a bit of a know-all, a bit of a prima donna.

David had heard that he was divorced. 'And this other guy? This Rudd person? What's he like?'

'Oh, Walter's nice enough. He's a good person to know, Walter – he's on the Town Council. If you want something done, you should ask Walter.' Bonnie was full of such sage advice: she was always telling David where he should shop, what he should buy, when he should shovel his driveway. She had shown him how to operate Maureen's washing machine, and where to put his rubbish for collection. David clung to her; lonely and bewildered, he depended on her for company, as well as for information. The people he worked with were friendly, but not overly hospitable; even Jill and Sam, while they made an effort to talk to him – and sometimes even questioned him about Sydney – never asked him to dinner or invited him to go tobogganing with them. As for most of his neighbours, they seemed to live like hermits or hibernating bears. Occasionally they would scurry out to do some shopping, but for the most part they remained holed up behind their double-glazed windows, consuming load upon load of wood or fuel oil. Many of them seemed to be unemployed; David could not imagine how they occupied themselves, day in and day out.

'Oh . . . quilting,' said Bonnie vaguely, when asked. 'Woodwork. There are some very good carpenters in Scotsville.' She explained that timber and tourism were seasonal industries (as, indeed, was fishing), so that many people only worked during the summer, drawing on Unemployment Insurance when winter rolled around. She herself was lucky to have a twelve month job with the Employment Centre.

'We get by,' she said. 'And there's always something for Floyd to fix around the house.'

In the face of such stoic reserve, David had tried to be more self-sufficient. He had bought a few jigsaw puzzles and written several letters home. Maureen's music selection left a lot to be desired (she favoured the Rankin Family, Rita McNeil and various other local folk artists who were unfamiliar to David), but fortunately she had cable TV, so he was able to indulge himself in thirty-three channels. Nevertheless he found his evenings very long, so long that he was even, in desperation, considering the drastic measure of accompanying Bonnie to a church-based anniversary salute to some famous hymn writer.

Consequently, he was only too delighted to host a committee meeting every month.

The first took place on a Tuesday night at seven o'clock. Bonnie arrived early, with muffins; she piled them onto a plate and then fussed around, arranging furniture, until Walter Rudd made his appearance. Walter was a large, solid, grey-haired man with a slow, slightly pompous way of speaking. He cleared his throat a great deal, and barely opened his mouth. David found him difficult to understand.

'Hrrmm . . . settling in . . . rmmbrrm . . . Bonnie's help?'

'Oh - um - yes, I think so.'

'Brrllmm . . . find it cold . . . rrfffrrm . . .'

No one else made much of an effort to converse with David. Keith Hughes tried to be sociable, but was hampered by his overpowering shyness; he produced a few strangled words ('Nice to meet you . . . From Sydney, eh?') before retiring, red-faced, to a chair in one corner. Bob Wheelhouse - who was small and flabby and fretful - simply nodded in

53

David's direction, while Gordon looked positively alarmed when David let him in.

'Oh. That's right. I forgot you were living here.' Gordon was in his forties, and favoured tweedy jackets with leather elbow patches. He looked slightly decayed, somehow: his features were battered and lugubrious, his wispy curls thinning on top. An air of dissatisfaction hung about him like a bad smell, giving a sardonic edge to all of his remarks. 'You don't know what you've let yourself in for.'

'Oh?'

'By the time July rolls around, you'll be cleaning blood off the furniture.'

'Really? Is it that bad?'

'You watch,' said Gordon, nodding at Raylene. 'Watch her close in for the kill.'

David was surprised; he thought that Raylene looked singularly harmless, in her rose-print dress with its white collar. She was talking to Bonnie about Christmas decorations, complaining that Gary had yet to take theirs down. Bonnie was reassuring. 'We only just got ours in the other day,' she replied. 'Floyd couldn't do it, because his back is bothering him, and of course the boys won't help. We had to ask Oakey - he didn't charge a thing.'

'Oakey!' said Raylene, with a sniff. 'I saw Oakey in Sable Cove yesterday. Down by the convenience store. He's got some funny friends, for a man his age.'

'Oh, those people. They're not his friends.'

'I saw him talking to one of them.'

'Oakey was brought up right,' Bonnie declared firmly. 'If someone talks to him, he always answers.'

'Well, he'd better watch out,' said Raylene. 'It doesn't do any good, to get involved with those people. My Mom won't even shop at Sable Cove – she never goes near that convenience store.'

'Why?' David asked, and the two women looked at him.

Bonnie's face twisted. Raylene sighed. 'There's a bad crowd, down at Sable Cove,' she said. 'Lots of fishermen.'

'Oh, Ray . . .'

'Well, it's true! They're the ones, they always have been.' She lowered her voice as she leaned towards David. 'Drugs,' she breathed.

'*Really?*'

'Cocaine.' Raylene nodded. 'Everyone knows about it. They take it when they're out on the job. Long hours, hard work . . . it keeps 'em going. Not Gary, of course,' she added. 'Gary wouldn't take that stuff.'

'Gary wouldn't dare,' Gordon murmured, *sotto voce*. At this point Walter cleared his throat, and suggested that they all sit down; Bonnie, as Chair, was asked to call the meeting to order. She did so, then requested that Raylene read out the minutes of last month's meeting.

Listening to them, David was left with a confused impression of blueberry-pie-related activities: a blueberry pie bake-off, a blueberry-pie-eating competition, a blueberry-pie-throwing competition. There had been much talk about the general absence of blueberries around Scotsville, and the need to find a supplier before the big day.

'Used to be a whole stack of blueberries up behind the Ryans' place,' Bob Wheelhouse remarked, once the minutes had been confirmed. 'But then they put that road through. Haven't seen a berry since.'

'And they were nice ones, too,' Bonnie agreed. 'Not like the ones at Foodland. Smaller, but tastier.'

'You can't expect people to go *picking* blueberries,' Gordon objected. 'Who's got time to go picking blueberries? I certainly don't.'

'I would,' Keith offered. 'My kids love picking berries. Even blackberries.'

'Well, if we ever manage to find any blueberries, Keith, you can pick them.' Gordon rubbed his eyes in a long-suffering manner. 'The question is, did Bob ask that friend of his about ordering some punnets? Did you, Bob?'

'Well – I asked him, but you didn't tell me how many we wanted, so he couldn't give me a final answer on the price. He said it would all depend on the volume, and what the market's doin' then. He said July's not the best time for blueberries. Maybe we should move the carnival into August.'

There was a general outcry. August was impossible; every weekend was taken. Kempton's Haddock Festival was on the first weekend, the County Exhibition on the second, Watervale's Children's Parade on the third . . .

'Don't be a fool,' said Raylene, contemptuously. 'We've already set the date – we've already announced it.' She turned to Walter. 'Let me take care of the berries. That can be my job.'

'Okay,' said Walter. 'Everyone happy with that? Yes? Good.' And they moved on to the next item.

When the meeting adjourned, at nine o'clock, David had more or less worked out where everyone stood. Raylene hated Bob, and respected Walter; Bob was jealous of Walter and rather taken with Bonnie; everyone liked Keith, but tended to disregard him. Gordon seemed to elicit the same reaction from all of them (except Walter) - a mixture of veiled resentment and grudging approval.

Walter was the only one who baffled David. He was such a pillar of the community - such a Grand Old Man - that he was unreadable. Opaque. He was like some kind of Victorian monument, heavy and immovable and always exactly the same. Even when Raylene asked him about Oakey's dog, his features remained undisturbed.

'I hear you've got Tripod in custody,' she remarked, as they were climbing into their coats and scarves and snowboots. 'It's about time, too. That dog is a menace.'

'What's that?' Bonnie pricked up her ears. 'What have you done, Walter?'

'Hrrrlmm . . . followed up complaints,' he replied. 'The Dog Control Officer hasn't been doing his job . . . rrhlllmmm . . .'

'Oh, but Tripod hasn't bitten anyone,' Bonnie objected. 'Has he?'

'Hrrllmmrr . . . public nuisance. If it isn't restrained . . . lffrrggrmm . . .'

Bonnie caught David's eye, and grimaced. After her fellow committee members had gone, she forced the last of her muffins down his throat and told him about the great Marshall-Rudd feud.

'I knew something like this would happen,' she said. 'After Oakey got Walter thrown off the Curling Committee, I told him: you're playing with fire, doing this. Walter Rudd is on practically every board and council in the whole province. I knew he'd get his own back.'

'Is it true, what Raylene said?' David inquired, through a

mouthful of muffin. He had been listening carefully all evening. 'About those guys in Sable Cove?'

'Which guys?'

'The ones that Oakey was talking to. She mentioned drugs –'

'Oh, that.' Bonnie wrinkled her nose, scornfully. 'That's a load of trash. Oakey's got nothing to do with those people. He wouldn't know what a drug was.'

'But is it true about the fishermen? And the cocaine?'

Bonnie replied with a guarded comment about the police, but refused to elaborate. She insisted on washing the dirty teacups before she left, saying that they were her responsibility; she also promised to bring over more muffins, next time the church had a bake sale – and some brownies, as well.

'It was very kind of you,' she said. 'We're very grateful.'

David smiled. He was loath to tell her that the evening had been his most enjoyable so far. If he did, she would only feel sorry for him.

* * *

Alice had been asked to judge a limbo competition at the annual St Valentine's Day dance. It was Raylene, in fact, who had asked her; Raylene's Dad had helped to organise the event. 'You're a bit of a celebrity,' Raylene urged. 'And Dad's running out of people.' Sighing, Alice agreed to do her bit for the Lions Club, but insisted that the competition be held no later than ten o'clock. She had no wish to spend the early hours of Sunday morning in the hall at Kempton High.

When she pulled into the school grounds, at half past seven, she could hear the throb of music through her sealed windows. Large, pink, cardboard hearts had been taped to every accessible wall; streamers fluttered, balloons bobbed. There was a lot of activity around the entrance. Alice saw various familiar faces (Bonnie's son Eric, Raylene's brother Cluny) as she passed from the icy schoolyard into the hothouse atmosphere of the hall. It was very noisy and dim - only the stage was illuminated. Raylene had mentioned that the band hailed from Yarmouth.

Alice found Kendall Tibbett in the throng, and tapped him on the shoulder. He greeted her absent-mindedly.

'Gimme half an hour,' he said. 'I'm just sorting out this karaoke stuff.' He was surrounded by people waving cash boxes and faulty electrical equipment.

So Alice headed for the bar, which appeared to be the centre of a small riot, but which was simply undermanned. Raylene Tibbett was serving. When she saw Alice's face, wedged between the shoulders of two large fishermen, she paused.

'Hello!' she exclaimed. 'What would you like?'

'Just a Coke.'

'Coke. Okay.'

'On second thoughts, make that two Cokes.' Alice had no intention of returning; one visit to the bar was more than enough. She took her Cokes to the back of the room, and sat down at an empty table which had a good view of the dance floor. It was always interesting to watch the dancers. Sometimes they formed the most unlikely combinations.

Enos Ruggles, for instance, was dancing with the young, red-headed and lively Angela Wheelhouse.

'Hello.'

59

Alice looked up. She saw David French looming above her, a bottle of beer in his hand. He was wearing a very elegant black jacket over a white shirt.

'Hello.'

'Mind if I sit down?'

'Go right ahead.'

'I don't know anyone,' David confessed, sliding into the seat next to her. 'I came with this couple - I work with them, Jill and Sam - but they haven't stopped dancing.' He pointed to an energetic pair clad in semi-formal attire, the male tall and heavy, the female small and brittle-boned. 'Unfortunately, I don't like dancing.'

Alice looked at him. 'Then why did you come to a dance?' she asked.

'Well . . . there isn't much else to do, is there?' He made a face. 'I spend most of my time watching television. And even that's not as good as I thought it would be.'

'No?'

'No.' He sighed as he examined the label on his beer. 'When I first came, I thought: thirty-three channels! Bull's-eye! But if you take away the weather channel, and the news channel, and the shopping channel, and the four French channels, and the sports channel - because I don't know anything about baseball or gridiron -'

'And the religious channel,' Alice remarked, with a smile, but David's response was unexpected.

'Oh no,' he said. 'I *love* the religious channel. Do you know what I saw the other day? I saw this amazing sixties program, modern Biblical stories, and they were doing Cain and Abel. Only Cain and Abel were called Chuck and Andy. It was *hilarious.'*

'And of course there's the local channel,' Alice continued, with gentle humour, at which point David rolled his eyes. (The local channel featured classified ads, Municipal Council meetings, and a shot of Kempton wharf.)

'Spare me,' he said.

'Maybe you should join something.'

'Do you think so?' David took a swig of beer. 'The trouble is, they all seem to be Christian things. Or women's things. I mean, I can't very well join the Stitch and Chatter Club, can I? I can't even sew.'

'How did you find out about the Stitch and Chatter Club?'

'Watching the local channel.' He laughed. 'You can see how I spend my weekends.'

'There's always curling,' Alice suggested, lifting a hand to Paul Anderson, who was passing by. 'Or cross-country skiing.'

'What *is* curling, anyway?' David asked this question in the manner of one who had been puzzling over it for a very long time. 'Is it some kind of sport?'

'Sure is.'

'What do you have to do?'

'You slide a stone along the ice, and sweep the ice in front of it to make it go faster.'

David blinked. He scratched his neck. 'Oh,' he muttered.

'Or there's the Historical Society. Or the County Hospice Society - they always need volunteers.' But David had withdrawn his attention; he seemed to be thinking about something else. Alice, for her part, was conscious of curious looks from all over the room - guarded, speculative looks. Many were aimed at David, because he was such an attractive prospect, lounging there in his stylish clothes, and the women of Kempton County were not well supplied with eligible bachelors; the poor things were waiting for him to make a move, because none of them had the strength of mind to approach him without encouragement.

As for the other curious looks, they were directed at Alice, who understood exactly what was going on. Ten more minutes with David, and the gossip would start. *Saw Alice McDonald at the dance, last night – making eyes at some kid. Young enough to be her son, poor sap.* She would never hear the end of it.

'I don't want to join the Curling Club,' David suddenly declared, frowning. 'It sounds too rough for me.'

'Rough?' said Alice, who knew some of the club's sexagenarian members. 'Rough' was not a word that she would have employed. 'How do you mean, "rough"?'

'All that business with Oakey and Walter.'

'Oh. I see.'

'Bonnie told me about it. She told me that Oakey blocked up Walter's driveway. Is that true?'

'Apparently.'

'But how? How would he do that?'

'With a snow-plough,' Alice replied. 'Oakey drives a municipal snow-plough. You've seen them, haven't you? They push the snow off the street, and it has to go somewhere.'

David winced. At first Alice thought that this might have been in response to what she had just said, but then noticed that he was shielding his face, and hunching his shoulders. 'God,' he muttered. 'How ghastly. You come to a dance, in a place like this, and you're surrounded by your own students.'

'Who?' Alice glanced around. 'Oh. You mean Owen Tibbett?'

'Don't get me wrong. He's not a bad kid, even if he does get

Australia mixed up with Alaska. It's just that I'd rather not spend *all* my time in his company.'

Alice, who lived her job twenty-four hours a day, simply smiled. 'At least the dance isn't being held at your school,' she observed, and this time his wince was unmistakably her doing.

'At Kempton? I'm safe from that, thank God – there's nowhere to hold one. You'd have to march everybody around the corner, to the church hall. That's what we always do on Friday mornings.'

'Yes,' said Alice. 'It's not a very big school, is it?' As she swallowed the dregs of her second Coke, she saw Kendall waving at her, and wiped her mouth. 'I'm sorry,' she added, 'but I have to go and judge something. I promised I would.'

'Oh.' David looked blank.

'It's the limbo competition. That's why I'm here.' Alice hesitated; they were both on their feet. 'There's going to be karaoke, after this,' she continued, and laughed as his features rearranged themselves into an expression of exaggerated horror. 'I thought you might want to leave before it starts.'

'Thanks for the warning.'

'If I were you,' she advised, 'I'd look in the paper. There are lots of things you can do. You could learn how to line dance.' She nodded at the clusters of women ranged along the walls. 'Then there'd be some point in coming to a thing like this.'

'Alice?'

'Yes?'

'Do you fancy a cup of coffee, some time?' His tone was casual; Alice eyed him sympathetically. Poor kid, she thought. He's that lonesome.

'Sure,' she said. 'We could have supper, if you want. I'll fix it.'

Then she went off to grapple with a crowd of drunken limbo dancers.

＊　＊　＊

One morning, when David turned on his kitchen tap, nothing happened. No water appeared. The bathroom taps were working, but not the kitchen or laundry taps. So David called Oakey Marshall.

'I can guess what it is,' Oakey muttered. 'Your pipes're frozen.'

'What?' David could hardly believe his ears. 'But I've been keeping the heat turned up! I've been doing exactly what you said!'

'It's not your fault.' From the odd sounds at the other end of the line, David judged that Oakey was eating his breakfast. 'I'll come and see.'

'Could you make it soon, do you think? Because otherwise I'll be late for work.'

'Gimme ten minutes.'

I can't believe it, David thought, as he hung up. First the padlock, then the doorknob, then the car, then the eaves – the eaves had been particularly trying. A recent rainstorm had left the kitchen flooded; Oakey had been forced to bring a ladder, and chip half a tonne of ice off the eaves. 'Eaves are always the last to thaw,' he had explained. 'And the water's gotta go somewhere.' It seemed as if daily life in Canada was always one long, debilitating struggle.

Nibbling a piece of toast, David wandered restlessly from

room to room, from window to window. Most of them were covered in condensation. 'I love a sunburnt country,' he murmured, glancing at his watch. It was all such an *effort*: getting up, getting dressed, getting to work. Even making friends was an effort. But perhaps things would improve during the summer – perhaps the people would thaw, along with the landscape.

Or perhaps he would just have to join one of those clubs. One of those societies. He liked the idea of learning to quilt, but sensed, somehow, that it was not the done thing for men of a certain age. Although no one in Kempton had heard of the AIDS quilt, there would undoubtedly be a certain stigma attached to the traditional women's crafts, and David was keeping a low profile. For the time being, anyway. Until he found his feet.

With a sigh he finished his toast and washed his plate in the bathroom. Then he called the school, warned the receptionist that he might be held up, and sat down to mark a few exercise books. In defiance of the season – and to create an illusion of heat in a classroom whose windows were frosted over – he had initiated a 'desert' project involving many vivid red and yellow drawings, a bookshelf garden of potted cacti, and a great big papier-mâché sun. He had also asked his students for a story about camels, and while many of the compositions submitted to him were frustratingly illiterate (*Caml s hamp got water in, but teh camlik osis tooo*), he could at least warm his hands over the colours used in the illustrations, which were as bright as Ken Done tea-towels.

He was enjoying Amanda Burgess's dramatic little

65

account of the kidnapping of 'Sarah, a baby camel taken away to sea even thohg she love the desert' when Oakey Marshall arrived.

'It's an old problem.' Dressed in layers of dingy work clothes, Oakey never failed to inspire confidence. He wiped his feet very carefully before crossing the threshold. 'It's always the same pipe.'

'Really?'

'Right under here.' They were in the laundry; as David watched, Oakey kicked aside a straw mat and pulled up a section of the floor. 'There's no heat in this room, so I put a light down here to stop the pipe freezin'.' He pointed. 'Bulb's blown,' he added, laconically.

'Can you fix it?'

'Sure can.' From the pocket of his anorak, Oakey produced a brand new bulb. 'If I stick this in, it'll thaw in no time.'

'Good.' David went to make some coffee; he never quite knew what to say when Oakey was around. The older man made him feel terribly inadequate. He knew he cut an unimpressive figure, screaming for help every time something froze, but what else could he do? He had never been good at physics. And Oakey was such a difficult person to talk to - so brusque and expressionless.

David lacked the courage to ask him about his latest offensive against Walter Rudd.

'I heard from Maureen,' Oakey remarked, as they stood in the kitchen, waiting for the pipe to thaw. 'She called me last night.'

'Oh yes?'

'Complained about the heat.'

'Oh dear.'

'And the traffic.'

'Yes, the traffic in Sydney is pretty bad.'

'And what your mother puts in her washin' machine.' Oakey threw David a sly, sidelong glance. 'She says your mother doesn't know how to wash.'

David winced. He had always shared his mother's laundry, and they had never clashed over detergents or line-space or whose clothes were in what load, but he could see how a perfectionist like Maureen Lawrence might object to scraping sodden bits of tissue off her underwear. In fact it surprised him that this particular bone of contention had not been raised in his mother's last report on the state of things at home. She had been keeping him well informed (perhaps *too* well informed) on every noteworthy incident that had taken place so far: Maureen's stunned reaction to the Gay Mardi Gras street parade; her futile calls to various welfare services regarding that poor old man who slept in the St Vincent's Hospital bus stop; the time when one of David's more irrepressible friends had pounded drunkenly on her door at three o'clock in the morning. Maureen was proving to be quite an entertainment, for Clara - although they did clash occasionally over things like noise levels, garbage disposal and the health of certain cherished plants. Now, apparently, there was this new disagreement about laundering techniques.

'Maureen's got her own way of doin' things,' Oakey continued. 'She's real fussy about her whites.'

'Yes. I'm sure she is.'

'She passed on a message for you. She said: be sure and clean the filters on the range hood once a month.' As David blinked, Oakey slapped his shoulder. 'Cheer up,' he said. 'I'm not gonna spy on you.'

It was an unexpected remark, and David was still turning it over in his head when he heard a sharp rapping noise. Someone was knocking at the front door. Murmuring his excuses, he went to answer it - and found himself face to face with a hungry-looking man in a leather jacket.

'Yes?'

'Is Maureen Marshall around?' The man's voice was gruff; his hair was long and untidy. David could smell smoke on his breath. 'I'm looking for Maureen Marshall.'

'If you mean Maureen Lawrence, I'm afraid she's not here.'

'When will she be back?'

'December,' said David, and felt instantly contrite as the man's shoulders slumped. 'She's in Australia, right now.'

'Are you her son?'

'No. I'm just looking after the house.'

'You're not related?'

'No.'

The man's intense gaze veered off towards the line of vehicles in the driveway: Maureen's Daihatsu, Oakey's ute, his own yellow sedan. 'She got any family?' he inquired, and ran his tongue over his cracked bottom lip. David judged him to be about forty years old; a seamed and battered individual. One of Oakey's dealer friends? But a local would have known about Maureen.

'Her brother's in the kitchen,' David confessed, reluctantly, and the man swallowed.

'Brother?' His voice sounded strange. 'Which brother?'

'Oakey. Would you like -'

'Tell him to come here. Tell him I want to see him.'

Weirdo, David thought, and decided not to leave the door unattended. 'Oakey!' he cried. 'Someone to see you!' The man stepped back; he was breathing quickly, through his nose. When Oakey appeared he squared his shoulders.

But Oakey remained silent.

'You Maureen Marshall's brother?'

'Yup.'

'Foster Marshall?'

'Nope.'

'I want to talk to you.'

Oakey waited. The man waited. Then he said: 'In private.'

'Oh!' David flushed. 'I'm sorry.' He retreated into the house, and heard the door close. From the front room he saw them walking towards the driveway; he saw them getting into Oakey's truck. They stayed there for so long that he finally lost interest, and went off to check the taps - which were running, at long last.

With a silent prayer of thanksgiving, he packed his brief-case, pulled on a parka, and went out to tell Oakey the good news.

'Oakey?' Standing in the snow, David watched Oakey's friend climb down from the ute. Without even glancing at David, he headed for his car as Oakey leaned out of the driver's window.

'Is it workin'?' he said.

David nodded.

'Good.' Oakey turned his ignition key, and the engine roared. 'Now you know where it is,' he added, 'you can fix it yourself.'

'Thanks very much.'

'No problem.' Oakey looked in his rear-view mirror. 'I'll get outta your way, now.'

'Oakey -' David began. But his voice was drowned by the noise of the yellow car, which was beginning to back down the driveway. Swinging on to the road, it sat there in a steamy cloud of exhaust while Oakey's truck rattled after it. Then, with the truck in the lead, both vehicles rolled off towards Sable Cove - leaving David to draw his own conclusions.

March

There were ninety-eight fishermen all together. They sat in the bingo room at Scotsville Fire Hall, arms folded, legs crossed, as they listened to Glen Burgess, representative of the Maritime Fishermen's Union.

'Now you all know it's rough,' he was saying. 'And it's gonna get rougher. You say you need a one-thousand-pound-per-trip limit, if you want to survive. Well, the Department of Fisheries and Oceans has just announced the total haddock quota for fixed gear boats in this area, and you know what it is, and it's not good.' Raising his voice above the murmur of protest, he added: 'But it could get worse. If we don't fight this, it could mean the end of the fixed gear haddock fishery.'

Glen was a small man with a strident voice; after years of weathering Atlantic gales, he had the dogged persistence of a worker ant - the ability to hammer away at one point until it pierced even the thickest of skulls. His focus was absolute, his energy remarkable.

'Now the MFU stopped the lobster restrictions from gettin' worse,' he continued, 'and we've also made some progress on handlines -' He paused as someone's arm went up; Alice recognised it as belonging to Enos Ruggles.

'We should look at all of them damn National Sea Products boats,' Enos declared. 'The way they fish on the Seal Island grounds, it stops the fish from gettin' into the bay.'

'Haddock is your problem,' Glen replied crisply, but was interrupted before he could continue.

'It's not the problem it was,' Fairlie McNeil observed. 'Used to be you couldn't catch enough haddock to eat, let alone sell. Now it's different. Must be the way they cut the dragger quota.'

Alice yawned discreetly, and checked her watch. Everyone always had to have their say at such gatherings; despite Glen's iron grip, she calculated that the meeting still had at least an hour to run. Various people voiced their support of the MFU, applauding the fact that it represented only inshore fishermen with boats of forty-five feet and under. There was much talk of strength in unity, and 'being told what's really going on'. Glen made a point of mentioning the Department's recent attempts to rescind inactive licences. 'When the fishermen rose up, the minister backed down,' he said. 'Not all the way - there are still some people who are gonna get screwed - but he did back down some.'

At last the fishermen voted unanimously to join the union, and an executive was elected. By this time it was eight forty-five. As the meeting broke up, Alice went around collecting quotes from various people who could be relied upon for a colourful turn of phrase. Young Hardie Garron urged people to 'get their ass in gear'. Fairlie spoke of having someone big on their team.

'How are you, Fairlie?' Alice eyed his sturdy frame and relaxed, genial expression. 'I haven't seen you since you got out of hospital.'

'Oh, I'm fine, now. Just fine. Have to take it easy, though.' He removed his cap, and ran a hand over his balding scalp. 'Can't get out on the boat much, yet.'

Alice shrugged. 'Looks as if you're not the only one,' she remarked. 'There won't be many people out on their boats if it keeps up like this.'

Fairlie shook his head, solemnly.

'It's a bad business,' he agreed. 'A bad business.'

'Going to be a tough year.'

'Uh-huh. Sure is.' He kept nodding, but his eyes narrowed. A smile tweaked at one corner of his mouth. 'Did you go to the Council meetin', last night?' he asked.

'No. No, I didn't. Raylene did.'

'But you heard about Oakey Marshall?'

'Of course.' Everyone had heard about Oakey Marshall. Incensed at having his driveway blocked, Walter had managed to have Oakey barred from the municipal snow-plough. During the four-hour meeting he had dwelled not only on Oakey's 'criminal carelessness', but on his unauthorised use of the plough for 'private purposes'. It appeared that Oakey had been running a little business on the side.

'Hell, I've called him in myself,' Fairlie grinned. 'Does a good job - couple of dollars cheaper than the regular snow-ploughs. No overheads.'

Alice muttered something noncommittal.

'It's a real war,' Fairlie added. 'First that Curlin' Club business, then Tripod, then the snow, and now this. I wonder what's gonna happen next?'

'I guess we'll just have to wait and see,' said Alice, who was sick and tired of the whole subject. As Oakey's next-door neighbour she had been questioned repeatedly about this latest development, despite the fact that she knew no more than anyone else. 'Seems to me that there are bigger things to worry about than the latest Marshall-Rudd skirmish. Like the fisheries, for instance.'

'Oh, sure,' said Fairlie – but he was still smiling. Alice decided that she had had enough; she said goodnight and went out to her car, which was covered in a light dusting of snow. A few large, fluffy snowflakes settled onto her hair and shoulders as she brushed down the windscreen: they melted when they touched her face.

A cheerful chorus of car-horns followed her out of the parking lot.

She drove home past acres of scrubby forest, past dense, dim screens of spruce and birch and maple. The weather was softening up. Soon the ugliest part of the year – the slushiest part of the year – would be upon them, and after that, summer. Alice thought about summer. She thought about university vacations. Turning into her driveway, she saw that Oakey's lights were on, and wondered how he was going to fare without his snow-plough job. Not that it would make much difference, at this point; winter was losing its grip.

She parked her car, retreated into her house, and called Ottawa.

'Hello?' The voice on the other end of the line was a male one. Alice did not recognise it.

'Hello. May I speak to Louise?'

'Hold on.' There was a scraping sound; Alice heard the voice yelling 'Louise!', and another voice replying. There was a long pause. Then someone picked up the receiver.

'Hello?'

'Louise?'

'Oh.'

'It's me. How are you?'

'I'm fine.'

'Are you busy?'

'Why?'

'Oh . . .' Alice took a deep breath. She could hear music in the background. 'I just don't want to interrupt anything.'

'You're not.'

'Good. That's good. So everything's going all right, then? I mean - you're enjoying yourself?'

A sigh. 'Not especially, no. Why? Are you expecting me to?'

'Louise -'

'Is there something you wanted to ask me, or what? Only it's my turn to cook supper, and I've got to keep an eye on the chicken.'

Alice's heart sank; the signs were not encouraging. 'Well . . . as a matter of fact, I was thinking about May,' she said, with failing courage. 'I was wondering if you had any plans. Do you?'

'If you're talking about holiday plans, no, I don't. I'm going to look for a full-time job.'

'Oh.'

'One of my professors mentioned something. A kind of research assistant. It wouldn't pay much, but it would give me a bit of experience.'

'I see. Good. That's wonderful.'

A pause. When Louise spoke again, Alice fancied that she could hear a trace of apprehension in the quiet, well-modulated tones.

'So what about you? Will you be going anywhere, this summer?'

'Not on my salary.'

The relief at the other end of the line was palpable, despite Louise's efforts to disguise it. 'Why on earth don't you get something else?' she said briskly. 'Something that pays better?'

'Because there is nothing else.'

'You should go back to Toronto.'

But not to Ottawa, Alice thought. Never to Ottawa. She listened to her own breathing for a few seconds, then asked Louise if there was anything she wanted.

'No thanks.'

'Are you all right for money?'

'I'm fine.'

'Well . . . that's all I wanted to know.' Suddenly Alice's voice failed her. She swallowed, and struggled, and finally found the breath to say goodbye. 'Take care now.'

'You too.'

And the dial tone intervened.

Alice put the receiver down. She sat for a while, staring at it, as the oven clock ticked away.

Then she buried her face in her folded arms, her eyes

closed, trying to block out the images that were pushing their way into her consciousness.

＊　＊　＊

'All right, everyone . . . settle down, please . . . that's enough.' David clapped his hands as he surveyed the restless group of children in front of him. Hilary Shipright was chewing gum. Andrew Johnson was fighting with Owen Tibbett. 'Hilary! Spit that out, please. Andrew! Stop it. Stop it, Andrew!'

Andrew stopped. Hilary placed her gum in David's outstretched hand; transferring it to the rubbish bin, he was conscious of her reproachful stare. He was also conscious - highly conscious - of the two visitors hovering nearby, both of whom were having a disruptive effect on the children. Alice McDonald, though inoffensive enough to look at (with her short, mousy hair and mild, intelligent face), was carrying a notebook and camera, while Keith Hughes was dressed in his full fire-fighting outfit, complete with axe and oxygen tanks. He looked like something from outer space.

'Now, as you know, this week is Fire Prevention Week,' David continued, fixing his eyes on the toughs down the back. 'And that's why Mister Keith Hughes, who's the Fire Chief from Scotsville, has kindly agreed to come and talk to you about what you should do if you're caught in a fire. So I want you to listen carefully, because if you don't, and your furnace explodes, Mister Hughes won't come and rescue you. He'll just leave you there to burn.'

Keith looked shocked, but the children roared with laughter. (There was nothing they liked more than a good, bloodthirsty joke.) David flashed the fire-fighter an encouraging smile, and went to stand beside Alice, who winked at him. Then Keith began to talk about a little girl he had once saved from a burning house; she had been a clever little girl, who, instead of hiding under the bed, had closed the door to her room, gone to the window, and waved a red scarf.

'I wonder if your house has a fire escape plan,' Keith observed, in a slightly jocular voice. 'Has your mom and dad told you where to go, if there's a fire? Because it's very important that you should know something like that . . .'

David's attention started to wander. He thought about furnaces, and the wood stacked outside every second house in Scotsville. He thought about the characteristic Nova Scotia dwelling, with its shingle walls and wooden framework. He thought about the size of Scotsville's Fire Hall.

Then he pricked up his ears, as Keith referred to the importance of changing batteries in smoke detectors.

Batteries?

'Do all smoke detectors have batteries?' he asked, raising his hand. Keith shrugged.

'Pretty near all,' he replied.

Oh shit, thought David, who had never laid eyes on a domestic smoke detector until he had moved into Maureen's house. Oakey had been forced to tell him what the things in the ceiling were. And now he was supposed to change the batteries? How the hell was he going to do that?

'It's no big deal,' Alice assured him, after Keith's talk had become a demonstration, and the kids were lining up to try on his oxygen mask. 'I'll do it for you, if you want.'

78

'Would you? That would be terrific. I can't ask Oakey again - he already thinks I'm a complete moron.'

'Why would he think that?'

'Because I never know what to do about anything,' David sighed. 'Amanda! Leave Josh alone! I'm a complete klutz, you see, I can hardly change a fuse. Hang on a second . . .'

He hauled Amanda out of the line, and made her stand by the window. (No oxygen mask for Amanda.) Keith went on to explain why the mask was making a hissing noise, and to point out that an alarm went off when the oxygen level was low: he was doing his best to 'demystify' the apparatus. 'So many children are terrified of firefighters in full gear,' he had told David at the last Blueberry Carnival Committee meeting. 'Sometimes they run away when you try to rescue them.' David had found this difficult to believe, at first - Keith, after all, was a singularly harmless-looking individual - but there was no doubt that the oxygen mask transformed him. With his mask and helmet on, he reminded David of the villain from *Star Wars*. What was his name? Dark something?

'Well . . . I hope you all remember what the Fire Chief told you today,' he said, when Keith had finished. 'And I want you all to show him how much you appreciate his coming here, and bringing his wonderful equipment. Thank you, Mister Hughes.'

There was a round of applause, followed by photographs; the honour of appearing in the *Kempton Gazette* went to six of David's more nicely behaved students. 'You see what happens when you're good,' he declared, as Keith backed out of the room. (He still had several other classes to visit.) 'Owen, if you do that once more, I won't let you sit next to Andrew ever again. Now, I want all those desks put back, please. On the double.'

Then he joined Alice in the hallway for a moment, shutting his classroom door on the noise of moving furniture.

'I hope that was all right,' he said. 'Did you get everything you need?'

'I think so.' Alice looked up at him through her spectacle frames. She was smiling. 'You're very good.'

'Good?'

'With the children.'

'Oh.' David shrugged, embarrassed. 'It's not so hard.'

'And how are things with you? Any better on the social front?' Before he could reply she frowned suddenly, and put her hand to her chin. 'Wasn't I supposed to organise something? Dammit!'

'Don't worry –'

'No, I promised. I didn't even think . . .'

'It's okay,' said David, who had, in fact, been wondering when to expect her invitation. His nights were still lonely; Gus had neither written nor called. 'When you're organised.'

'How about this evening?'

'This evening?'

'For supper.' Alice adjusted her glasses. 'It won't be anything fancy, but –'

'That's okay.'

'I'll give you my address.' She scribbled it on a piece of paper, suggesting that he come around at seven o'clock. Then she inquired about allergies ('Fish? Garlic?'), told him not to bring anything, and apologised again for her lapse. By this time the noise behind the door had reached an unacceptable level; David bade her a hurried goodbye, and went back into the classroom feeling a good deal happier.

'All right, you people! What do you think you're doing? Jenny, pick the desk up - now. Owen, I'm losing my patience. Good girl, Paula . . .'

It was his second dinner invitation in as many months. Jill and Sam had finally made an effort, receiving him into their nice little turn-of-the-century farmhouse for a meal of chicken cacciatore and chocolate cake, but the evening had not lived up to his expectations; the other guests had been fellow teachers, and they had mostly bitched about Gordon Blanchard's financial mismanagement and playground duty rosters. Knowing what fun Maureen Lawrence must be having (according to Clara, Maureen had been invited out on a cruise boat for a tour of the Hawkesbury, and she had enjoyed everything about it except the 'terrible glare'), David was beginning to feel a little ill-used. Of course Maureen was throwing away most of her opportunities, turning down Clara's invitations to gallery openings in favour of picnic parties with teaching colleagues, but at least she had been given opportunities. David had received nothing but some chicken cacciatore, unlimited access to the Blueberry Carnival Committee meetings, and now this dinner invitation from Alice McDonald. It was hardly what you would call a busy social life.

That afternoon, on his way home from work, he took a detour past Alice's house to make sure that he could find it again in the dark. It was a disappointing suburban bungalow in a panoramic setting; behind it stretched the grey, choppy waters of Sable Cove, and the bleakly beautiful headland of St Andrew's Ferry. David noted the green shutters, the carriage lamp, and the huge, dilapidated barn next door. Then he turned around and went back home, stopping at Foodland to pick up a box of chocolates.

He even wrapped it, in some of Maureen Lawrence's red cellophane, before heading off at six forty-five.

'What's this?' Alice said, when she answered his knock. 'I told you not to bring anything.'

'They're not for you, they're for me. I need my after-dinner chocolates.'

'Well . . . all right. You can have the chocolates, and I'll have the ice-cream.' Stepping back, she ushered him into her living room, which was all white and beige and brown. The furniture was dull, but the view was spectacular. The walls were covered in black and white photographs.

'Are these yours?' David asked, eyeing an accomplished shot of Kempton wharf in the mist. 'I mean - did you take them?'

'Yes.'

'*All* of them?'

Alice smiled; she was wearing an apron over her trousers, and there was a smudge of food on her nose. It was shocking, somehow, to see her in such disarray - normally she was as neat as a pin, self-contained and unruffled.

'It's my hobby,' she said, in her soft, dry voice. 'Can I offer you a drink? Wine or beer?'

'Wine, thanks.'

'It's in the kitchen.'

There were more photographs in the kitchen - and in the

dining room, as well. David recognised several familiar faces: Gordon Blanchard, Oakey Marshall, the man from the video store. He saw a circle of seagulls; a child on a rock; two fishermen, staring. He saw a little girl on a city street, licking an ice-cream.

'Where's that?' he asked. 'That's not around here, is it?'

Alice glanced over her shoulder. 'No,' she said. 'That's Toronto.'

'Have you been to Toronto?'

'Yes.'

'I'd like to go to Montreal,' David remarked, and began to describe his withdrawal symptoms as he wandered about the room, examining landscapes, portraits, still lives. He missed the city; he missed Asian food and department stores and cinema complexes. He compared Australian breakfast cereals with Canadian breakfast cereals - there seemed to be so many junk cereals in Canada, so many multi-coloured sugary shapes. Of course the cookies here were better, but he was hanging out for a decent meat pie. Or a Chiko Roll, even.

'Have you tried our rappie pie?' Alice asked.

'No.'

'You should. It's a regional delicacy.'

David stopped in front of another picture. It was a picture of a little girl with a dog - a family snap. He recognised the little girl. 'Who's this?' he asked. 'Isn't this the girl from Toronto?'

'Yes,' said Alice. She was stirring goulash in a large pot. 'That's my daughter.'

'Your daughter?'

'Her name's Louise.'

'Oh.' David hesitated; he could feel a slight tension in the air. Could the daughter be dead? But as he cast around for another topic, Alice volunteered more information.

'She's twenty-three. About your age.'

'Where is she?'

'Ottawa. She's studying science.' Alice dumped rice into a colander. 'She's a clever girl.'

'I'm sure,' said David, politely. Avoiding the subject of Louise's father, he asked if there were any recent photographs.

'No,' said Alice. She scraped rice on to two plates, then picked up the pot of goulash. 'I'm divorced, in case you're wondering.'

'Oh.'

'Ready to eat?'

Over dinner, Alice asked David questions about his own family. She listened as he described his mother, his mother's business, his mother's boyfriends. 'You probably haven't heard of Paul Kotter,' he said. 'Paul was quite a famous Australian artist - he died about ten years ago. Mum was in some of his best paintings. She's even in the National Gallery. If he hadn't already been married, he would have married her. He had this kind of tortured relationship with his wife -'

'He's your father?'

'Oh no!' David laughed. 'I wish. No, Dad was just passing through. He's back in England now. He was only around for six years.'

'Do you see him much?'

'Never.'

'That must be hard.'

David shrugged. 'I don't even remember him. It's like he

84

never existed. My uncle Alan was more of a father to me.' Poking at his goulash, David stifled a sigh. 'He's been dead for three years now.'

'I'm sorry.'

'He was a nice man.'

They finished the wine and cracked open a bottle of Bailey's Irish Cream. David insisted that they sample the chocolates. Sitting in Alice's lounge room, gazing out at the lights of St Andrew's Ferry, he began to talk about Nova Scotia: about how incredibly gloomy the economic outlook seemed to be; about the poverty of some of the children he taught at school (startling domestic stories of kids sleeping three to a bed, to save on heating); about the reticence, the reserve - he had never met with such reserve, not even in Australia.

'Thank God for the Blueberry Carnival,' he said. 'And Bonnie. Thank God for Bonnie. Otherwise I wouldn't know what was going on.' He explained that the Blueberry Carnival Executive Committee was meeting in his den, every month, and that he was therefore well placed to hear much of the local gossip. 'Bonnie knows everything about everyone,' he added. 'And if Bonnie doesn't, Raylene does.'

'Ah yes. Raylene.' Alice smiled. 'Raylene is certainly a mine of information.'

'Do you know her? Oh . . .' David slapped his forehead. 'Of course. She works for you, doesn't she? I keep forgetting.' He was already inebriated - not sloshed, just a little tight. He felt pleasantly relaxed. Pleasantly mellow. He began to giggle. 'It's so funny,' he said. 'Bonnie hates Gary so much - Raylene's boyfriend, I mean. She's always saying he's not good enough . . . dropping little hints . . . she's desperate for me to get together with Raylene. Make an honest woman out of her.' He shook his head, still laughing. 'It's such a hoot . . .'

'Why?' said Alice. Her voice was as dry as woodchips; David noticed it at once. He saw her beaky face harden, and realisation dawned.

'Oh - I'm not saying she's not attractive,' he said quickly. 'It's not that. It's just that . . . well . . .' He paused, wondering if he should take the plunge. But he trusted Alice. He liked her careful manner and clear, dispassionate gaze. 'It's just not my sort of thing,' he concluded. 'Girls, I mean.'

Alice looked at him for a moment. 'Ah,' she said, and her expression relaxed.

'Anyway, I'm already involved. At least I hope I am, but . . . oh, I don't know. I don't know what to think any more.' David unwrapped a piece of chocolate, and popped it into his mouth. Hazelnut. 'You know, I actually came here to teach him a lesson. Isn't that crazy? I must have been out of my mind. Because he's married, you see -'

'To a woman?'

'Oh yes. Wife, house, kid, everything.' Thinking of Gus, David felt an ache deep inside. He wanted Gus so badly. 'I thought I'd show him how awful life would be without me, for a year. You know? But he hasn't called once. Not once.' Suddenly David realised, with horror, that his lip was trembling. Jesus, he thought. Don't be such a *wimp*, French! The poor woman! 'Sorry,' he muttered. 'I'm sorry, you don't want to hear this.'

'It doesn't bother me.'

'I miss him so much. That's the problem. And he doesn't seem to miss me at all.'

86

Alice blinked like a cat in the lamplight. 'I bet he does,' she said.

'You think so?'

'I think you're the kind of person whose absence would always be noticed. You're a noticeable kind of person.'

'Really?' David flushed, then frowned. 'In what way?'

'Oh - the best possible way.' Alice smiled as she sipped her drink. 'If he doesn't seem to miss you, David, then he's not worth missing.'

They lapsed into silence. David heard the click and throb of the furnace. He heard the wind pounding against the big, glass panes. He heard a clock ticking.

'It's very quiet here, isn't it?' he said.

'Very quiet.'

'Would you - I mean - I hope you don't mind . . .' He looked at her. 'I'd rather you didn't spread it around. That I'm gay.'

'Of course not.'

'I mean, it's no big deal, it's not a problem, but I'd rather do it in my own good time. When I've sussed things out.' He flapped his hand, and grimaced. 'Things can get a bit dicey, when you're a teacher. In some schools.'

Alice nodded. She stared out the window as David unwrapped another chocolate. Caramel fudge, this time.

'Talk about cutting off your nose to spite your face,' he remarked gloomily. But Alice said nothing.

* * *

Slowly the image began to appear. A dark patch on the right, another on the left. The delicate, fretted shape of a leafless branch. A headstone. A picket fence. White snow on black ice.

87

It was always an exciting moment for Alice, even after so many years. She felt as if she were attending a birth, and the surroundings somehow lent themselves to this impression: the small, damp, pungent room; the red light; the airlessness. And the picture, of course - the picture that appeared gradually, miraculously, spreading across the paper like dawn spreading across the sky, growing darker and stronger, more solid, more distinct. A lovely one, this one. Beautifully framed. Nice composition. Alice removed it from the developer tray, placed it in the fixer and checked her watch.

Then someone pounded on the door.

'Alice?' It was Raylene. 'Alice, I'm back!'

'Good.'

'Are you done in there? Because I need a coffee!'

'Just five more minutes.'

'Okay.'

Alice studied the dripping photographs pegged on a string that stretched from wall to wall. Some were for the paper (a hockey match, a fish plant) and some were for her own collection. She particularly liked the shot of David: he stood knee-deep in children, his arms outstretched, like a saint blessing the multitudes. She liked the resigned, patient, slightly ironic look on his face - not a look she had often seen there, but one which added weight to his delicate features.

Her graveyard shot was ready, at last. She rinsed it off, hung it up, and opened the door.

'Sorry,' she said. 'I'm finished now.'

Raylene was sitting on Erica's desk. She had just returned from a school board meeting, and her cheeks were still red with cold. She jumped up as Alice appeared.

'Have you heard about Walter Rudd's mailbox?' she exclaimed.

'No. What about Walter Rudd's mailbox?'

'It happened last night. I was just telling Erica.' Leaning forward, Raylene lowered her voice melodramatically. 'Somebody shot it right off its post.'

'Oh, dear.'

'You can imagine how Walter's reacting.' The mailbox in question was a perfect miniature of Walter's own house; he had spent almost a year of his life building it. 'Everyone's saying it was Oakey.'

'Oakey?' Alice frowned. 'Oakey wouldn't do a thing like that.'

'Are you sure? He must have been pretty mad when Walter got him fired.'

'Oakey wouldn't do a thing like that,' Alice repeated, firmly, and Erica backed her up.

'Plenty of young fools with guns who get smashed at night,' the nun said. 'I've seen 'em out on their snow-mobiles, shooting at barns.'

'Anyways, I didn't hear Oakey leave last night.' Alice gave the matter some thought. 'No, I didn't hear a thing. He couldn't have gone out, I would have heard him.'

'But you might have been asleep,' Raylene objected. 'He might have done it early. Real early.'

Alice shook her head. 'There was snow on his truck this morning. Hasn't snowed since five - maybe six o'clock yesterday afternoon.'

'Still . . .'

'Are you saying he borrowed someone else's car? I don't think so, Raylene.'

'Maybe it was one of his friends. His junkie friends.' Raylene sat up. 'Maybe they wanted to teach Walter a lesson!'

'Oh, come on, now. That's just stupid.'

'He's got some pretty funny friends, Alice.'

'And you've got some pretty funny ideas.' Alice made for her telephone, which was ringing furiously. 'You'd better watch it, Raylene, or you'll get yourself into a whole heap of trouble. Hello? *Kempton Gazette.*'

'Hello? Alice?'

'Speaking.'

'It's Walter Rudd, here.'

'Oh. Hello, Walter.' Catching sight of Raylene's eager face and frantic hand movements, Alice shut her office door. 'What can I do for you today?'

'Hrrlmmbmm . . . school board. I don't know if Raylene's told you . . .'

'About your mailbox?' said Alice, without thinking. There was a brief silence at the other end of the line.

'No,' Walter growled. 'About the condom machines.'

'Condom machines?'

Walter began to explain. It appeared that a student council executive had approached the district school board with the suggestion that condom dispensers be installed in all secondary schools. Thanks largely to the support of the Superintendent - and against the wishes of several other board members - it had been decided that a survey should be conducted to see how parents felt about the proposal.

'Grrrbllmm . . . encouraging sexual activity among our children -'

'Do you think so?'

'All these ridiculous classes they're running at school . . . ffrrblmnn . . . bad enough,' Walter grumbled. 'No wonder it's putting ideas in their heads . . .'

'Walter -'

'Lrrggbblm . . . day care now! Day care! At school! For girls with babies!'

'Walter, I'll be running a story on it. And I'll take everyone's views into account.'

'But something's got to be done . . .'

As Walter vented his frustration, Alice swung around in her chair and gazed out the window. It was high tide; the fleet bobbed at its moorings and the rain-dimpled swell lapped against the pier.

'Walter, they haven't even asked the parents yet. You don't have to worry unless the parents agree - and frankly I doubt that they will.'

'Mmmbblm . . . editorial . . . ffmmbll . . .'

'I'm sorry, I can't do that.' The clouds were low and misty. Alice shut her eyes, and took a deep breath. 'If I did write an editorial,' she added, 'it would probably be in favour.'

'What! But grllmbffnnn . . .'

Alice let him rave on for another three minutes. Then, as a squall of rain pattered against the window, she turned around to face the door. 'I'm sorry, Walter,' she said, cutting him off. 'There really isn't anything I can do. If you want to stop this, I suggest you talk to the school board, or the parents. Or write us a letter. What? Yes, we can run an ad . . . Well, if that's what you want, I can let you talk to our advertising manager . . .'

She transferred the call to Ian's line and put her receiver down. More fuss about nothing. Children were dying of strangulation in schoolyards, because the drawstrings on their hoods and coats were catching on playground equipment, and Walter Rudd was worrying about condom machines. Alice tried to remember the statistics. Was it thirty per cent of grade nine children? Something like that. Thirty per cent of grade nine children in Nova Scotia were sexually active, and –

Hmmm.

'Erica!' she cried, rifling through her in-tray. 'Do you remember that AIDS report that came in a few months ago? Do you remember where we put it?'

She had thought of a topic for next week's editorial.

* * *

It had been raining for three days in a row. Not torrentially, with the semi-tropical drama of a Sydney downpour, but lightly, continuously, with the sullen persistence of a Melbourne drizzle. David had been told several times that Nova Scotia was one of the wettest Canadian provinces; this fact had been offered to him by way of comfort, perhaps to reassure him that he was experiencing not a rogue weather pattern, but a genuine slice of Maritime melancholy.

His response (like that of many Nova Scotians) was to purchase a large bottle of scotch, wrap himself in a quilt, and settle down in front of the TV with the phone in his lap.

'Hello?'

'Hello? Mum?'

'*David?*'

'How are you?'

'Is everything all right?'

'Yeah. I guess.' David swallowed. 'It's raining. It's been raining for three days.'

'It's very muggy here. Maureen's been on at me about her heat rash.'

'Oh.'

'And she's been complaining about the stereo. If I don't turn it off at eleven o'clock sharp she's over here bashing down the door. Can you believe that? She's been getting stuck into the Lochards, too, whenever they put on their African music. I told her to buy some earplugs like everyone else, and she sucked in her bottom lip, the way she does . . .'

David listened morosely as Clara enlarged on her favourite topic - Maureen Lawrence. Apparently Maureen had been seen hosing dog shit off the footpath, not only outside Clara's place, but all along that side of the street. She had been asked to give a lecture on quilting by a local church organisation, and was now fighting off suggestions that she should hold a series of quilting classes in the church hall. She had summoned the police three times, so far: once to arrest a couple of junkies shooting up near the garbage skips in the alley, once to report very loud music at a party across the road, and once because someone had set fire to a motorbike parked near her bedroom window. 'She told me she sent little letters to the police afterwards,' Clara gabbled, 'thanking them for their quick response. I bet she used pink notepaper, with kittens on it.' Clara had been making futile attempts to draw Maureen out on the subject of her dead husband, and was irritated by her lack of cooperation. There was a knockout story there, if only Clara could get to it. As far as she could see, Maureen's relationship with the opposite sex was guarded to the point of paranoia; she was calm and firm and faintly disapproving with all Clara's male friends, just as she was with the children in her class. She even had a gentleman admirer – some church fellow – who had turned up one day on Clara's doorstep by accident, bearing (of all things) a jar of jam. Didn't he know, Clara said, that Maureen had been experimenting with new kinds of jam for weeks now? Mango jam. Star-fruit jam. Papaya jam. But Maureen must have given him short shrift, because Clara had never laid eyes on him again.

'I asked her about him – you know, with a wink and a nudge – and she screwed up her mouth and told me that she "didn't like what he said about the RSPCA",' Clara crowed. 'Isn't that marvellous? Of course it was just an excuse. What she really doesn't like is men. Period. She's probably a closet lesbian.'

It was some time before Clara had exhausted the subject of Maureen, and moved on to the latest gossip about Max and Simon and Yollande. David found it hard to concentrate. He was not in the least bit interested; it all seemed so irrelevant. So far away. 'Any mail?' he finally inquired, cutting short his mother's account of Earl's latest chin-tuck.

'Mail? Oh – hang on – let me get it.' There was a pause as she scampered off to the kitchen. When she finally returned, David could hear the crackle of paper. 'Are you there? Yes? A couple of bills, but I've paid them. Something from the union – some kind of magazine –'

'Chuck it.'

'A postcard from Italy, signed *Mark* –'

'What does it say?'

'Not much. *Dear David, Remember what you said once, about the "stupefying wealth" of Baroque? "Too rich for me", you said. Well, I was in the Museo Medici today, and your words came back to me when I was standing in the chapel, looking at the extraordinary marble inlays – spinach green and spaghetti-bolognese red. Made me feel quite queasy. Yours with love, Mark H.'*

David grunted. 'Anything else?' he said.

'That's all. Why? Were you expecting something?'

'No.' He had wondered, with failing hope, if Gus might have lost his address in Canada. 'Thanks for your card, by the way.'

'Have you already got it? That was quick.'

'I got one from Pat, too.'

'We're all missing you, my darling. We'll be throwing a birthday party *in absentia*.'

'Gee, thanks.'

'What's wrong? You don't sound too bright.'

'I'm not.' David swirled the ice cubes around in his glass. 'I haven't heard from Gus, you know. I've written him three letters, and he hasn't called once.'

Clara sighed. 'Well . . . I hate to say it, Davey, but –'

'Yes, yes, I know!' She was supposed to reassure, not denigrate. 'You've told me often enough.'

'Aren't there any nice lumberjacks over there? Any nice Mounties?'

'No,' said David. 'And even if there were, they'd be holed up in cabins with their wives and kids.' He went on to complain about his desolate social life; about the layers of clothing that everyone had to wear; about the general absence of gay pornography.

'Just as well I brought my own,' he grumbled.

'Poor baby. Perhaps it'll get better in the spring.'

'Perhaps.'

'Didn't you say something about the personal section? In that newspaper?'

'The *Chronicle Herald*?' David snorted. 'Yes, you see a few lone cries in the wilderness. They sound so desperate it's scary.'

'Poor boy. Never mind. I'm sure you'll stumble across something one of these days.' He could almost hear her frowning into the phone. 'They've got to be there, Dave. They're just very, very quiet.'

'Mmmmph.'

By this time they had been talking for ten minutes; conscious of the mounting expense, David said goodbye and hung up. The postcard from Florence had shaken him. Mark had been out of his life for three years, so why this sudden message? Was it loneliness? Perhaps Mark was lonely the way David was lonely, stuck in Florence (on sabbatical?) with no one to talk to, no one to mould and teach and woo with classical quotations. Sitting cross-legged on Maureen's couch, David thought about his one-time tutor, whose love life was founded on a steady flow of students that would almost certainly have dried up in Florence. No students, no nookie. Graduation was like divorce, for Mark; he hated to see his partners succumb to the lures and pressures of the outside world. In fact he hated the outside world. He preferred to remain in his academic hothouse, soaking up the adoration of wide-eyed young innocents like David and that bit of fluff who had succeeded him - what was his name? Russell? Rory? Something like that.

David sipped his drink. He had identified the exact moment at which Mark had turned away: that time on Oxford Street - they had been heading for Ariel Bookshop - when the boy from the music store had stopped and given David a long, groping kiss. It had meant nothing, surprised no one, but it had been too blatant for Mark. Too brutal. The outside world in its lewdest form. Besides which, of course, David had already graduated, and Russell (Rory?) was waiting dewy-eyed in the wings.

Fuck this, David thought. He wondered why he always fell for secretive types: first Mark, now Gus. Mark's excuse was professional - he claimed that he was breaking an unwritten rule, by sleeping with one of his students, and that once David graduated they would be free to flaunt their love. But Mark's interest had never survived graduation, so he was never obliged to keep his promise. And as for Gus . . .

Gus. David pictured Gus in bed: the tousled hair, the white loins, the broad, furry chest and sleepy smile. God, he felt horny. It was unbearable. Gus was like Mark - he kept David in a little compartment, away from the rest of his life, refusing to invite him home or to the pub with his mates. 'You wouldn't get on,' he always said. 'They're a bunch of yobbos, Dave, they don't have a clue. You'd be bored shitless.'

'Fuck that,' David said aloud. Gus was a coward; he was afraid to be labelled - tagged - condemned. They were both afraid, he and Mark, for all their fancy excuses. But where did that leave David? Why did he put up with it?

Is it what I want? he wondered, thinking of the flagrant

97

pairing in his mother's circle. None of that lot could keep a secret; every tweak, every birthmark, every telephone call was examined minutely, in public, over and over and over again. Death by exposure. David had a certain modesty - his feelings were too delicate to survive such handling.

So where did that leave him now?

'Gus,' he said, and reached for the phone. He was going to call. He had promised not to call, but he was going to. He had to. He dialled the number and waited, his heart beating wildly.

'Hello?' It was a woman's voice. 'Hello?'

'Is - is Gus there?'

'No, he's out. Can I take a message?'

She had a slight accent - an accent like Gus's. David could hear a baby screaming in the background.

'I'm just . . . could you tell him . . .' It was impossible. Impossible. Gus would be furious. 'That's all right, I guess I'll . . . I'll call back later.'

When she broke the connection, David felt as if she had punched him in the head. He thought (briefly) about the guns in the cellar, but the very idea made him wince. No thank you. Things were never that desperate.

After all, he still had three-quarters of a bottle of scotch to drown his sorrows in.

April

It was the noise that woke Alice - the noise of sirens. She opened her eyes, and knew instantly that something was wrong. The light was wrong. The shadows were wrong. And there were other noises, faint but ominous: crashes and shouts, and the tinkle of breaking glass. Confused, still half asleep, she staggered to the window. She could see nothing but a reddish glow above the roof.

Fire, she thought.

The sirens were growing louder; Alice began to feel alarmed. Pulling on her jeans, locating her spectacles, she remembered the story she had written, that very week, about Scotsville Fire Department's new Automatic Foam Injection System. They would be needing their Class A foam, now. She threw on a coat, stepped into her boots and grabbed her camera. (No point in missing a good story.) On her way out she picked up her car keys, but realised, even as she fumbled for the door, that they would not be necessary. The vestibule smelled of smoke.

'Judas Priest.' From her porch, Alice could see the leaping flames, the showers of sparks, the clouds of ash. Was it Oakey's house? No; it was Oakey's barn. With a dying howl, the first fire engine bumped across his winter-brown lawn, its red light flashing. Another followed close behind. People were already running up the road; Alice recognised Fairlie McNeil, wearing a plaid jacket over his pyjamas. She waved at him, and he waved back. He tried to say something, but his words dissolved into a cough as the smoke tickled his larynx.

'Alice?' It was Keith Hughes, lumbering towards her in his space-age gear. 'You'd better get out of here, now.'

'Why? You don't think –'

'No, but it's best to be on the safe side. Just go and wait down the road, some.'

'Where's Oakey?'

'He's fine.'

'Don't you want me to –'

'Please, Alice.'

At that instant, the barn's roof collapsed. It made the most tremendous noise. Keith gave Alice a little nudge, and jogged heavily back towards his engine as she trained her camera on the barn's disintegrating silhouette, which was now black and jagged like a hollow tooth, its gables and windowsills gilded with flame. Some of the firefighters were wrestling with a hose; as Alice watched, the first stream of water arched across the garden.

'Alice!' Puffing and blowing, Fairlie McNeil almost ran into her. Behind him, his wife Adelia was holding up the skirts of her blue chenille dressing-gown. 'You okay?'

'I'm fine.'

'Where's Oakey?'

'I'm not sure . . .' Alice peered through the haze; her eyes were beginning to smart. 'Keith said he was all right. Is that him?'

'That's him. *Oakey! Hey, Oakey!*'

Oakey stood near his pick-up, which had been moved to the bottom of the driveway. His head was bare, his arms were folded, and he appeared to be fully dressed.

When he heard Fairlie's voice he looked around, his attention diverted from the fiery spectacle in front of him.

He raised a hand.

'Come here!' Fairlie cried, beckoning. Adelia muttered something about fetching a Thermos, and Alice became aware of two cars, their headlights ablaze, hesitantly converging on the scene. They stopped some distance down the road, as if unsure of their welcome. A handful of people got out.

Alice identified them as sightseers, drawn from afar by the urgent wail of the sirens. There was so little happening in Kempton County that people would come for miles to see a good fire. One man had even brought his kids along.

'I think it's dying down,' said Adelia. 'What do you think, honey?'

'Could be.'

'I think they've got it under control,' Alice declared, as Oakey advanced towards them. Even through the smoke she could see Keith and his crew; the cuffs and hems of their yellow suits were trimmed with fluorescent stripes. 'They don't seem to be running about so much.'

'I wonder what happened.' Adelia's voice was unsteady. 'Did Oakey have a stove in there?'

'You ought to go back, Dell. You're shiverin'.'

'They're lucky it's not too cold,' said Alice, who knew what could happen to water pumps at minus twenty degrees. She smiled at Oakey, her gaze wandering over his sooty face and hands. He was wearing a pyjama top under his parka.

'You okay?' Fairlie inquired.

Oakey nodded.

'What caused it?' By this time Adelia's teeth were chattering. 'Was it a kerosene lamp?'

'Dell, for God's sake, will you go inside?'

'I dunno.' Oakey's glance strayed back to the barn; only two of its walls were still standing. 'I heard a noise. Woke up. It was already far gone . . .' He shook his head. 'That barn's real old. Burns like a torch.'

'But it was empty, wasn't it?' Fairlie asked, and Alice suddenly remembered.

'Your thing!' she exclaimed. 'Oakey, your invention!'

Oakey grimaced.

'What invention?' Adelia was stubbornly resisting her husband's attempts to dislodge her. 'What are you talking about?'

'God damn, Oakey.' (Fairlie, it seemed, had read the paper - even if his wife had not.) 'Was that thing of yours in there?'

'Sure was.'

'God damn.'

'But you can rebuild it, can't you?' Alice queried, and Oakey shrugged.

'Took me a long time,' he said, his eyes on the ruins of his workshop. 'And it might go up in smoke all over again.'

Alice blinked. She had noticed, beneath the smudges of charcoal, a very curious look on his face. 'What do you mean?' she said, but he just sniffed and scratched his jaw.

Back towards his house, the barn's last wall had crumbled.

* * *

'So!' Bonnie exclaimed, as she wiped her feet on the mat. 'What do you think about Oakey's fire, eh?'

It was half past six; she had arrived early, as usual, bearing the customary plate of muffins. As he helped her out of her coat, David observed that she was wearing what appeared to be a brand new denim jacket, heavily studded and appliquéd in the best country and western tradition.

'New jacket?' he inquired.

'Oh!' She preened herself a little. 'It's cute, isn't it? I got it at Frenchy's. Only cost me three dollars.'

So it's not new, David thought. (He was familiar with the chain of secondhand clothing stores known as Frenchy's.) Following her into the den, he helped to rearrange furniture as she babbled on about Oakey's fire: how it had threatened both the Marshall house and Alice McDonald's, how it had been fuelled by exploding paint cans, how Keith Hughes had almost been crushed by a toppling beam.

'It must have burned like sawdust,' Bonnie declared, with something that bordered on relish. 'There's nothing left there now, just a pile of ashes.'

'So I heard,' said David. He had, in fact, heard everything there was to hear; Oakey's misfortune had been the main topic of conversation at school that day. People had been talking about it, not only in the staffroom (where it had lent animation to the usual dry, unemphatic recitals of ice hockey statistics and furnace problems) but also in the class-room. At least half of the children in David's class had been so desperate to relay their parents' opinions of the accident that David was forced to turn it into a 'discussion topic', attempting, as he did so, to channel the discourse away from Oakey's personal habits and towards Keith Hughes's visit the previous month. 'A lot of people reckon it was arson,' he observed.

'Could be,' said Bonnie, with a wise look. 'But I know what Oakey thinks.'

'Do you?' David pricked up his ears. 'You mean you've talked to him?'

'I have.'

'And?'

Bonnie frowned at the arrangement of chairs. 'I think that'll do,' she murmured. 'Those people over there can put their cups on the bookshelf.'

'Bonnie.'

'Well, it sounds strange,' she admitted, 'but Oakey seems to think it had something to do with his invention.'

'His what?'

'His invention,' Bonnie repeated, looking up. 'Don't you know about that? It was in the paper - though I guess they ran it before your time . . .'

'What invention?' David asked, fascinated, and Bonnie wrinkled her nose.

'Something to do with electricity,' she said. 'Some new way of creating electricity. I never did understand, but Oakey always said it would change people's lives. He showed it to a professor, up Wolfville way. I don't know what happened after that.'

David sat down. It all sounded very unlikely – a world-beating invention, in Oakey's barn? Doubtless Oakey was spinning some kind of tall tale. 'Did you ever see it?' he inquired.

'No, I never did. But there must have been something to it, or Alice McDonald wouldn't have run that story. She's a smart woman, Alice.' Bonnie put her hands on her hips, which were encased in a very tight pair of jeans. 'Oakey went to university, you know. He studied engineering.'

'I still don't understand,' said David, with a frown. 'What's the fire got to do with Oakey's invention? Does he think it short-circuited, or what?'

'I'm not sure.' Bonnie cast up her eyes. 'Is that the doorbell?'

'I don't know. Is it?'

'I'll go and see.'

'Whoever it is, they're early.'

It was Raylene Tibbett, and she apologised; she was on her way back from Kentville, she said. Anxious not to be late, she had overestimated her travelling time. 'The roads are real good,' she observed, pulling off her gloves. 'They've fared well, haven't they? It was such a bad winter, I thought we'd be seeing potholes as big as buses. But there are just a few cracks here and there . . .'

'What were you doing in Kentville?' Bonnie asked, whereupon Raylene dropped a few vague, disconnected remarks about shopping for a cousin's wedding present. Having disposed of that topic, she admired Bonnie's new jacket, greeted David with a smile, and turned her attention to the far more thrilling subject of Oakey's barn, her brown eyes gleaming with excitement.

'It's the drugs,' she said, ignoring Bonnie's protest. 'Those friends of his have turned against him. I told you, didn't I? They're trouble, all of them. Once they've got you, they've got you for good.'

Bonnie clicked her tongue. 'Oh, now that's not true, Ray, you're making that up.'

'Well, who else could it be? You don't think Walter did something like that?'

'It was probably an accident. It was probably Oakey's invention.'

'His what?'

'You know. Alice wrote that story.'

'Oh, that.'

They discussed Oakey's mysterious generator, and whether or not it had - for some inexplicable reason - suddenly burst into flames. Bonnie was unconvinced; Raylene frankly sceptical. Then Keith Hughes arrived, and was asked for his opinion.

'Oh . . . well . . . I dunno . . .' He was barely out of his coat when pounced upon by Raylene Tibbett. 'It's hard to say.'

'But was it an electrical fault, or did someone get in there and torch the barn? What do you think, Keith?' Raylene followed him into the living room. 'Do you think it had something to do with Oakey's invention? Bonnie thinks it was Oakey's invention.'

'I didn't say that. I was just telling you what Oakey told me.'

'Ah,' said Keith, lowering himself on to Maureen's recliner. There were dark smudges under his eyes. 'So you've talked to Oakey, have you?'

'Only in passing. He mentioned that machine of his.'

Keith grunted, and Raylene folded her arms. David could see that she was determined to get an answer from the Fire Chief even if she had to drag it out of him.

'You can't believe that story about the invention?' she said, in tones of withering scorn. 'You can't believe it sponta-neously combusted, or whatever it's supposed to have done?'

Keith's surprise was obvious; he looked up, blinking, his hand arrested in mid-air.

'Who told you that?' he asked. 'Did Oakey tell you that?'

'As far as I know.'

'He didn't tell *me* that,' Keith confessed, knitting his brows. When pressed for details, he mumbled something about oil companies, and Nova Scotia Power. Bonnie and Raylene exchanged a puzzled look.

'I beg your pardon?' said Bonnie.

'Oh, hell.' Keith ran a hand through his hair. 'I dunno. It sounded pretty crazy to me . . .'

'What did?' Raylene demanded, but Bonnie was ahead of her. Bonnie had already filled in the pieces.

'He's not saying it was *sabotage*?' she exclaimed, in such a bemused, high-pitched voice that David burst out laughing. Keith shifted uncomfortably.

'Well . . . I mighta been mistaken. It was hard to get the drift.'

'Oh, for God's sake,' Raylene snorted. 'He can't be serious. Some kind of *plot*? Is that what he's saying? Nova Scotia Power torched his barn? I never heard anything so crazy.'

At this point Bob Wheelhouse arrived, smelling of tobacco, and the conversation became more heated. In Bob's opinion, the culprit was almost certainly Walter Rudd; Oakey had shot Walter's mailbox to pieces, so naturally Walter had responded by setting fire to Oakey's barn. It was a simple matter of retaliation. Tit for tat. 'I'da done the same thing myself,' he remarked, oblivious to the red flush on Raylene's cheeks. 'That mailbox was a landmark. The tourists used to stop and look at it.'

'You'd better watch yourself, Bob Wheelhouse. You could be arrested for saying things like that.'

'Like what? What are you talkin' about?' Bob eyed Raylene fretfully. 'I'm just sayin' what everyone's sayin'.'

'Yeah, and it's garbage. Walter Rudd wouldn't do a thing like that. He's got too much self-respect.'

'Is that so?'

'Yes it is so.'

'I've got to say she's right, Bob,' Bonnie interjected. 'If Walter wanted to get rid of Oakey's barn, he wouldn't have to burn it down. He'd get it demolished for safety reasons. He'd get Keith to go and inspect it, wouldn't he, Keith?'

'Well . . . maybe . . .'

'Walter always does things through the official channels. It's what he's best at.' Bonnie disappeared into the kitchen, and emerged with a laden platter. 'Muffin, Keith?'

'Oh. Thanks.'

'Well, I'm just sayin' what everyone's sayin',' Bob repeated, in sulky tones. 'Maybe it's right and maybe it's wrong. But if someone lit that fire, then I don't know anyone with a better motive than Walter Rudd. That's all I'm sayin'.'

Even as Raylene opened her mouth to object, there was a knock at the door. Keith nearly choked on his muffin; Bonnie sprang to her feet. 'That's probably Walter now,' she said, bustling into the vestibule. Sure enough, Walter's low rumble soon reached David's ears, and he looked up to see Walter's large, looming shape on the threshold.

It was an irregular shape, ill-adapted to the suits he wore. David often considered raising the subject of double-breasted jackets in Walter's immediate vicinity; he also wondered if anyone had ever told Walter that the end of a man's tie should always touch his belt, instead of dangling somewhere above his navel. 'Suits are a skill,' Clara had always said. 'Just because you're wearing one, doesn't mean you're well groomed. Half the time,' she added, 'it could mean exactly the opposite.'

'Ffrrgghmm . . . sorry I'm late. Where's Gordon? Not here?'

'Gordon's got something on at school,' said Bonnie, glancing at David - who knew damn well that Gordon Blanchard was nursing a migraine. But it seemed that Walter had little sympathy for men who weakly succumbed to their indispositions. Bob's gallstones, for instance, received very short shrift, when Walter was around.

'Gfflglrrr . . . Keith. Bob. Raylene.'

'Hello, Walter.'

'Hello, Walter.'

'How's it going?'

Looking around, David saw nothing but heightened colour and downcast eyes. He heard Keith clear his throat, and saw Bob reach silently for a muffin. Evidently no one had the courage to raise the subject of Oakey's barn.

Even Raylene was speechless.

'Well,' said Bonnie, after a long pause, 'now we're all

here, why don't we go down to the den? David's bought a new percolator, and he's offered to make us some of his coffee.

'Unless anyone wants tea?'

* * *

Overcome by a sudden craving for donuts, Alice stopped at Tim Horton's. It was a miserable day, grey and sodden and lashed by violent winds; the warm, bright, sugar-scented eatery was crowded with people who sat with their numb fingers wrapped around their coffee cups. Tim Horton's had been created for just such a day - it was so bleak outside, so cold, that no one felt any shame in laying down another stratum of insulating fat over the kidneys.

Alice studied the board above the counter, savouring every word: *Honey dip, Apple crisp, Walnut crunch, Chocolate glaze, Chocolate fudge, Double chocolate* . . . She smiled as she remembered David's first visit to Tim Horton's, just a week before; his eyes had nearly popped out of his head. Thirty-five donut varieties! He had written them all down on a paper napkin . . . *Cinnamon sugar, Maple dip, Toasted Venetian, Toasted coconut, Old-fashioned plain, Sour cream, Strawberry delight, Strawberry Bismarck* . . .

'Yes please?'

Alice ordered a cherry donut and a cup of coffee. She took them over to a table by the window, and sat down; her hair was wet, her nose running. She plied her handkerchief, staring out at the scurrying figures in the parking lot. The children were being blown about like dead leaves.

'Alice?'

Looking up, she saw Oakey Marshall. His hands were buried deep in his pockets.

'Hello, Oakey.'

'Mind if I join you?'

'Go right ahead.'

It occurred to Alice that she had not spoken to her neighbour since the morning after the fire. He had been picking over the ashes and she had asked if there was anything she could do. Breaking up the glowing embers with a broomhandle, he had solemnly shaken his head.

Half an hour later, the Mounties had arrived.

'Aren't you going to eat something?' Alice queried, as he slid into the chair opposite. With gentle humour, she added: 'They might throw you out, if you don't eat something.'

'I just ate,' said Oakey. He sniffed, and wiped his mouth on the back of his hand. Alice thought that he looked tired; the pouches under his pale, expressionless eyes were heavier than usual.

'So how's it going?' she said. 'Have you sorted everything out?'

He looked at her.

'Sorted what out?' he asked.

'Oh - the fire. You know.'

One corner of his mouth lifted.

'Lotta questions,' he said. 'Everyone wants to hear about that fire.'

'Not much excitement around Kempton, Oakey.'

'Think so?'

'Well . . .' Alice shrugged. She knew what he meant. 'Maybe not at first glance.'

'Matter of fact, I want to talk to you about that fire.' Oakey began to fiddle with a sugar packet, his eyes downcast. Alice waited. She knew that he was like a squirrel, or a raccoon; if you were still and silent, he was more likely to expose himself.

'Remember that story?' he said at last. 'You came around, and took a picture.'

'Sure.'

'Do you have any copies of that?'

'We should.' Alice nibbled her donut. 'We always keep copies of every issue for a year or two.'

Oakey grunted. 'I kept a copy,' he said, 'but it was in the barn. Got burned up, like the rest of my stuff.'

'You want another one?'

'It's for insurance,' he explained. 'There's a lot of fuss and bother. Thought it might help.'

'Oh.' Alice raised an eyebrow. 'It was insured, was it?'

'The barn. Not the generator.'

'For much?'

'Hard to say.' Shrugging, Oakey let his gaze wander across the windswept parking lot. 'Like I said, there's a lot of fuss and bother. Looks like I'm gonna be waitin' a long time.'

'For the money?'

'For whatever they decide to do.' He snorted. 'If there's a loophole, they'll find it. Don't matter how long it takes.'

Alice regarded him with interest. He was being uncharacteristically outspoken. She sensed that, in his present mood, he might be encouraged to divulge a little more than he normally would.

'Do they pay up, if it's arson?' she inquired delicately, and he shifted in his chair.

'Hell, I dunno.'

'Did you *tell* them it was arson?' Seeing him frown, she hastened to add: 'I've heard people say you've got a theory. Something about your generator. You know what it's like around here.' She was waiting for him to speak - watching the play of muscles in his forehead - when all of a sudden she heard her name, pronounced by a high, happy voice that pierced the background murmur like a siren.

'Alice! Hello!'

It was David. People around the room fell silent and stared; he looked very large in his heavy suede parka, which added bulk to his height and was cut in lavish, sweeping folds. Beneath it he wore one of his extraordinary sweaters, so thick and ropy that it could have been knitted out of tree roots. A four-metre scarf was wrapped around his neck and shoulders.

But it was his manner, rather than his clothes, which excited attention. His face was radiant, his stride buoyant, he bobbed and swayed to the music that issued from some concealed radio behind the counter. He was carrying a chocolate dip donut in his left hand, and a cup of coffee in his right. When he reached Alice he flourished them as if to say: Look! I'm a native!

'See?' he laughed. 'See what you've done? I come here all the time now.' His teeth flashed - his eyes sparkled - he swooped down to kiss her cheek. Alice flushed, conscious that they were attracting an audience. Oakey, she observed, was sitting very straight, his long neck extended like the neck of a deer caught in somebody's headlights.

'Well,' he muttered, 'I guess I better be goin' . . .'

'Oh no! Don't leave!' David's garments seemed to billow around him as he threw himself onto the seat next to Alice. 'I'm sorry - am I interrupting something?'

Oakey's reply was incomprehensible. He was on his feet by now, and pulling at the brim of his baseball cap. Alice surmised that David's dazzling, almost excessive display of high spirits had rung alarm bells for Oakey.

I wonder if he knows, she thought, but immediately dismissed the idea.

'Be seein' you,' Oakey growled, as he sidled out the door, and David's brow puckered.

'Oh dear,' he exclaimed, vigorously shaking his tiny packet of sugar. 'Is it something I said?'

'Don't worry.'

'I didn't realise - if you want to go after him, don't mind me, I shouldn't have sat down without permission -'

'No harm done.'

'I'm so rude.'

'You're not rude.'

'You didn't *look* like a pair of conspirators,' David pointed out, his festive mood overcoming any feelings of remorse. 'I didn't realise you were arranging drug shipments.'

'You what?'

'Oh, I'm just quoting Raylene. She seems to think that Oakey has a Colombian connection.' He was still bobbing along to the music as he emptied sugar into his coffee. 'Don't you love this song? I love this song.'

'I've never even heard it before.'

'Haven't you? Really?' But his mind had already veered off down another path. 'So,' he continued, 'have you managed to worm the truth out of him? What does he really think?'

'Who?' Alice was losing track. 'You mean Oakey?'

'Who else?' David sipped his coffee, and grimaced, and flapped a hand in front of his mouth. 'Hot,' he said, by way of explanation. 'Does he really think it was an oil company, or is that just his way of putting people off the scent? Bob Wheelhouse seems to think it was Walter Rudd.'

'Are you talking about that fire?' Alice queried, catching up at last, and David rolled his eyes.

'Come on, Alice, it's been the *number one topic* -'

'Oakey doesn't confide in me, I'm afraid.' Even as Alice spoke it crossed her mind that if the barn was insured, Oakey himself might have burned it down. He had, after all, lost his snow-plough job.

But the possibility seemed so remote, so out of character, that she instantly rejected it. If Oakey needed a little spare beer money (and there was no indication that he did), then he was smart enough to find an easier and safer way of earning it.

'You seem very happy today,' she remarked, in an effort to steer the conversation towards less delicate topics. David beamed at her. He really was an extraordinarily attractive boy, when caught at the right moment.

'Gus rang,' he said.

'Gus?'

'My friend. You know.'

'Ah.' Alice nodded. She found herself lowering her voice. 'And he obviously said the right thing.'

'Did he ever! I mean -' David checked himself. 'He still hasn't proposed, but . . . oh, well, he made me feel good.'

'So I see,' Alice murmured. She had formed her own opinion of this so-called 'friend'. If only I could find him a nice, steady man with no encumbrances, she thought – and then smiled. It was the kind of thing her own friends were always saying about her.

'And your social life?' she asked. 'Has that been improving?'

'Oh – listen – I've been helping at bake sales.' He made a wry face. 'I've been getting involved, just like you told me to.'

'Bake sales?' said Alice, running through the calendar in her head. 'For the Animal Shelter, you mean?'

'Bonnie roped me into it.'

'Yes. She's a keen volunteer.'

'Shit it was funny,' he said, and proceeded to recount his 'stall-at-the-mall' experience. His retailing efforts had been severely hampered by a complete inability to distinguish one kind of cake from another. 'We never had those cakes at home,' he said plaintively. 'It was always Lebanese sweets, and French pastries. How am I supposed to know what a ginger sponge looks like?' He went on to describe his first ever baking effort (chocolate chip cookies, using Maureen's flour and chocolate and recipe book), concluding with an open-ended invitation to dinner.

'It won't be very exciting,' he warned. 'Probably steak or spag bol. I can't do much else.'

'Neither can I,' said Alice, wondering what 'spag bol' was.

'I'll fix up a date,' he continued. 'Is there anyone else you want me to ask? Any special friends?' He contorted his features into a suggestive, exaggerated leer. 'Oakey, perhaps?'

Alice suppressed a smile. 'Not on my account.'

'Sure? You were looking very chummy.'

'It was business, David. Purely business.'

'Oh, *business*, was it? In that case I'll order a couple of grams of cocaine, if you please. And something a little exotic for my next committee meeting.'

'You,' said Alice, 'are being very, very silly.' She rose to her feet, smiling. 'I've got work to do now. I'll see you later - when you've calmed down a bit.'

'Think this is silly? You should have seen me at the bake sale!'

'Goodbye, David.'

Alice headed for the door, pulling her rain-hood down over her eyes. She had just reached the threshold when she heard David's voice, loud and clear and confident, ringing across the room.

'So Mum's the word, eh, Alice?' he announced, and she turned to see him dissolving into suppressed giggles. Around him people were exchanging pointed looks.

Another piece of gossip for the rumour mill, she thought, acknowledging the joke with a raised eyebrow. It was childish, of course, but you had to give him his due.

He was picking things up very quickly.

* * *

David had given up on his colleagues. After nearly four months, he knew little more about their private lives than he had in the beginning - and now the Great Rift had frozen out every sign of a spring-related thaw (such as talk about summer holidays, for instance). The Great Rift was a direct result of budget-pruning measures that had deprived the school staff of certain privileges: free milk, various postal facilities, and unrestricted access to the photocopier, to name just a few. Gordon Blanchard, while staunchly upholding these changes, had come under attack by a rival group; it blamed Gordon and the headmaster for the sorry state of the school's finances, claiming that together they had pulled a great deal of wool over the School Board's eyes. What had all their expensive and impractical programs come to? Nothing. Except that there would be no more milk for the teachers' coffee.

As was to be expected, the entire teaching staff was split over this issue, and the atmosphere at work was tense. Discussions withered when certain people entered the staffroom. Other people were being difficult about the milk-purchasing and photocopying rosters. If it hadn't been so cold outside at lunchtimes (for the weather was still unsettled), David would have spent them all as far away from the staffroom as possible. As it was, he hid himself in a book, or occupied himself with his students' homework. He knew that there would be no more socialising with fellow teachers - not for the time being, at any rate. And even if there was, it would be a sour, carping, uncomfortable kind of entertainment. The kind of entertainment he could do without.

As for Bonnie's attempts to amuse him, they were well-meaning but unsuccessful. The first bake sale had been an experience; the second had been a bit of an effort; the third had been, quite frankly, a bore. There was only so much he could say to, or learn from, the coterie of faithful, middle-aged women who devoted their spare time to the Animal Shelter, the fire station and the local Baptist church. He admired them, of course - he found them remarkably energetic, and almost frighteningly public-spirited – but he couldn't really talk to them. And they all assumed that he was leading the sort of riotous, busy life natural to every young man, no matter how much he might assure them that he was at a bit of a 'loose end' in the evenings.

That was why he became so interested in the bobcat. According to Bonnie, Keith had seen a bobcat wandering around the back roads behind Watervale. They were unsealed roads, in that region, and no one had logged any timber there since the turn of the century. Keith had been forced to stop for the bobcat, which had sauntered into the blaze of his headlights with an almost suicidal lack of concern. Although small, and rather bedraggled, it had definitely been a bobcat.

David, who had driven nearly thirty kilometres one weekend to see a beaver dam (but no beaver), was thrilled by Keith's story.

'Where did he see it? Which road was it on?'

'I think they call it Scots Road,' Bonnie said. 'It's that one off Thibault. The dirt one.'

'And what time was this?'

'He didn't tell me the time. It was dark, though. Late.'

'I wonder if bobcats cover a lot of ground? Or do they stay in one spot?' David was determined to find the elusive cat, if only because he had nothing else to do. He knew that his letters home were becoming very dull (they were full of staffroom gossip and descriptions of the weather) and he had always prided himself on being an entertaining correspondent. Perhaps his quest for the bobcat would add spice to his next account of life in Scotsville. It would, at least, be something new to tell Bonnie.

So he set out one evening with a map, a torch and a survival kit, which consisted of two footwarmers, a cheap cigarette lighter, a candle and a flask of hot coffee. Someone (Raylene?) had once told him that a candle would emit just enough warmth to keep one person alive during the depths of winter. Not that it's winter now, he thought, as Maureen's car bounced and shuddered over the lumps of frozen snow in her driveway. But it's best to be on the safe side. He made a mental note to tell Clara about the survival kit, because she enjoyed little details like that; with a few embellishments it would arouse much interest among her friends. She had loved his stories about the frozen locks, and the bake sale. Such anecdotes were highly prized, in her circle.

David drove carefully, conscious (as always) that he was driving someone else's car. A somewhat unseasonal but in no way freakish snowstorm had surprised everyone just a few days before, and subsequent low temperatures meant that many roads were still sheathed in a crust of hard-packed snow. Concentrating hard, David kept to the more frequented routes; gradually the familiar churches and inlets and intersections yielded to unexplored territory - farmhouses, gas stations, convenience stores, clusters of golden windows that marked the location of humble trailer homes. Every so often David would stop to consult his map. Sometimes he would reverse to check a road sign. At last he found himself bumping along between stretches of thick, dark forest, and realised that he must have reached his destination.

It was the sort of place you would expect to find a bobcat - or perhaps even a moose. (He was desperate to see a moose, before he left Canada.) The road was very narrow, its shoulders heaped with hard, dirty snow; leafless branches almost blocked out the moonlit sky overhead; the occasional wooden bridge, built across a little frosted stream, would slow him to a crawl as he passed over it – because road signs warned him repeatedly that bridges always freeze first. Ice sparkled in the glow of his headlamps. A tumbledown fence seemed to spring out of the darkness and lurch drunkenly towards him before being swallowed up by shadow once again.

David wondered what he should do. For some reason, he had expected to see the bobcat as soon as he reached this particular stretch of road; he realised now that he had not given the matter enough thought. Bobcats, after all, were not hitch-hikers. Any bobcat with half a brain would keep away from the roads, unless they had something to offer – like food, for instance. David remembered the steak sitting in his fridge. Would a bobcat eat steak? He realised that he would either have to keep driving around these unpopulated backwoods, in the hope that he and the bobcat might intersect, or stop somewhere and wait silently for the animal to show itself.

Then it occurred to him that to wait somewhere, silently, would involve turning off the ignition – and that turning off the ignition would mean turning off the heat.

'No thanks,' he murmured, having no intention of providing the bobcat with its next frozen dinner. Or would bobcats eat people? Only babies, perhaps; Bonnie had said that they were quite small animals – smaller than cougars – and that they tended to live on little things: rats and mice, chickens, lambs, squirrels, ducks, even fish. 'It's a bad season for bobcats,' she had said, 'but I guess this one must have found a nice coop, somewhere. Or a careless fisherman. Something like that.'

David turned left, on to a road that bore no signpost, and realised immediately that he had made a mistake. No courageous snow-plough had ever ventured down this track; it was barely wide enough to admit David's car. Cautiously he braked, and tried to reverse - but nothing happened. His wheels spun impotently, as the noise of his engine mounted to a frantic, high-pitched note.

'Fuck, fuck, fuck,' he said, changing gears and stamping on the accelerator. The car behaved like a dog on a leash, straining forward to no effect. Again nothing happened. The wheels moved; the engine roared; the car remained where it was.

'Fuck!' David unbuckled his seatbelt, and got out. A cold wind punched him in the face. Shivering, he squatted down and peered at the back wheels, which had dug themselves a little trench in the snow. Removing his glove - feeling around the tyre - David touched something hard and slick, and realised that he was parked on top of a large patch of ice. A large, slippery, unforgiving patch of ice.

'Oh, shit,' he said. It had happened once before, in his own driveway - but Floyd had been around at that point, to help him push his car on to firmer ground. Floyd had been within hailing distance.

This time he was on his own.

'Shit! Shit, French, you fucking idiot! You fucking idiot!' He kicked the mudguard, before remembering who it belonged to. No dents, please. 'I have to think,' he said, and climbed back into the car. He had his anorak. His footwarmers. His Thermos.

He would have to walk to the nearest house, and ring Oakey Marshall, and ask for help. Or perhaps someone would come back and shift the car with him. Some kind-hearted Christian with big muscles. Preferably tall, dark and Portuguese.

You wish, he thought.

After slipping his Thermos into his pocket, he read the instructions on the footwarmers: *Remove from package. Do not place next to skin.* He had to tuck them under the arches of his feet, where they nestled like bits of bunched-up sock. (Rather uncomfortable to walk on.) Then he pulled his mittens over his gloves, removed the key from the ignition, locked the door and slammed it behind him. The sound was like a gunshot. The beam of his torch seemed thin and pale.

He began to pick his way back up the road.

What a stupid thing to do, he reflected. I bet that bobcat's having a good old laugh. He found himself listening for the bobcat, through the hiss of his breathing and the crunch of his footsteps; surely no bobcat in its right mind would attack a six-foot cricketer? Everything was so quiet - too quiet. It was like a scene from a horror movie. David had walked down many streets at night, but never one so dark or deserted. Clara's anxious warnings about gay-bashers seemed to ring in his ears. Not that many gay-bashers would be hanging around the woods behind Watervale, but still . . . there were a lot of people with guns, out there.

The road was hard to walk on, slippery and uneven. David's steamy breath turned to water on his lips. He found it hard to abstract his thoughts; his physical discomfort was too immediate, too pressing, to allow for the relief of daydreams. The cold was nipping at his ears and his cheeks, and burrowing down the neck of his anorak. His nose was running.

Finally, after a twenty-minute walk, he spotted lights in the distance. Electric lights.

'Hooray!' he said - out loud - and quickened his pace. Almost immediately he lost his footing, slipped, and fell; he landed heavily on one knee. It was the ice, of course. The ice was always there, ready to take advantage of any lapse in concentration.

Picking himself up, he limped towards the friendly glow, which (when traced to its source) turned out to be the product of somebody's living-room lamp. The lamp was sitting in a window, and the window belonged to an old, dilapidated house with a smoking chimney. Even in the dimness, David could see that the house needed a coat of paint. It was shingle-built, two-storeyed, and surrounded by rubbish: piles of kindling, rusty paint cans, a tricycle, a bath, a tyre, a broken washing machine. There was an Oldsmobile parked in the driveway.

David went up to the front door and knocked. He had to knock again before he received any answer.

'Who is it?' The voice was shrill and fearful - a woman's voice. David tried to sound harmless.

'I'm sorry - I know it's late -'

'What do you want?'

'My name's David French. I live in Scotsville -'

'What?'

'*I live in Scotsville!*' He put his mouth to the keyhole. 'My car's broken down, and I need help. I need to use your phone.' He heard a child snivelling, and added: 'I'll pay for the call.'

Silence. At last the woman said: 'You can't come in.'

'But -'

'I've got a gun in here!'

David blinked. Then it occurred to him that the woman was probably alone; that she lived a long way from her closest neighbour; that it was nearly nine o'clock, and the people of Kempton County were generally in bed by ten.

'Look,' he offered, 'I don't mind if you make the call. Just so long as somebody calls Oakey Marshall. I don't know his number, but –'

'Oakey Marshall?'

'Yes.' Encouraged by her tone, David continued: 'I'm living in his sister's house. I'm a teacher. My car's stuck in some ice down the road –'

The door opened a fraction; one round, blue eye regarded him over the chain.

'You were at that dance,' the woman said. She was quite young, a little younger than David. 'I saw you.'

'Oh.'

'I'll call Oakey first, and then you can come in.' The door clicked shut; footsteps receded. David heard a child wail. He heard the woman raise her voice. After a long, cold pause, the woman returned. 'Oakey's on the phone,' she told David, as she admitted him. 'I said you were here.' The rifle she carried was almost as tall as she was.

'Th-thanks,' said David. Gingerly he slid past her into the living room, which was big and sparsely furnished. David noticed bumpy floral wallpaper and a sagging grey couch. He had to tread carefully, to avoid the bits of Lego that were scattered all over the carpet. A brown-eyed toddler stared at him from behind the TV.

'Hello,' he said, and the toddler's bottom lip trembled.

'The phone's over there.'

'Thank you.'

'I told Oakey you're at Linda Tibbett's house.'

Linda Tibbett! Raylene's cousin? David eyed the woman with renewed interest, but failed to see any family resemblance. Linda was small and slight; her shoulders were narrow, her features more delicate than Raylene's. She had dark hair, and wore a dispirited green cardigan over a shapeless tracksuit.

'I know your cousin Raylene. She's a friend of mine.'

'Oh.'

'She'd be very annoyed if you shot me,' David joked, still worried about the rifle, although its barrel was dragging on the floor.

Linda grunted. 'Aaron,' she said, 'get away from that television.'

David picked up the receiver.

'Hello? Oakey?'

'I'm here.'

'Look - I'm so sorry about this, but -'

'You've broken down.'

'Not exactly. I'm stuck on some ice. I just need a push.'

'Where are you? On Scots Road?'

'Right now I'm at Linda Tibbett's house -'

'Yeah, but the car. Where's the car?'

David explained. Because Oakey was one of those people who never make reassuring noises when other people are speaking, David found himself confessing to everything - the bobcat, the Thermos, the ill-considered left turn on to a goat track - just to elicit some kind of response. At last, having finished his sorry tale, he fell silent.

'Mmph,' said Oakey. 'Well. You'd better stay put till I pick you up.'

'This is so embarrassing –'

'Shouldn't be more'n half an hour. You can show me where your car is.'

'I'm so sorry –'

'Guess I'd better bring a tow-rope.'

Click. The dial tone intervened. Startled, David turned to Linda, who was still hovering with her gun.

'Oakey's coming to fetch me,' he said. 'Would you mind if I waited? I can wait on the porch.'

'You don't have to.' She shrugged, in a listless fashion. 'You can stay in here.'

'Are you sure? Because –'

'It's okay.'

She sat down, the gun propped between her knees, and looked at the television. Some kind of American sitcom was in progress. Reaching for the remote control, she began to flick from channel to channel until she alighted on a home-shopping program; the item for sale was an exercise bike.

'You don't have to stand up,' she said, punching the keypad. A talking head appeared on the screen. David lowered himself on to a rocking chair and smiled at Aaron, who was drooling down the front of his sweatshirt. Encouraged, Aaron promptly presented him with a wet piece of Lego.

No one said another word until Oakey arrived, some twenty minutes later.

'Hi there.' He stood on the porch, his hands in his pockets, his eyes on the trailing barrel of Linda's gun. 'What's with the Ruger? Isn't that Cluny's?'

Linda glanced at the weapon as if she had never seen it before. 'Cluny lent it to me.'

'What for?'

'Protection.'

Oakey snorted. 'You gonna trip someone up with it?' he said. 'That gun's too heavy for you. Too heavy for Cluny. I told him he needed a lighter gun - might as well drag a rocket launcher around.' Gently he removed the gun from her slack grip; David noticed that he held it comfortably. Appraisingly. 'Cluny get himself a new huntin' rifle? Can't beat a Winchester featherweight.'

'Don't ask me.'

'If you want a gun,' Oakey continued, squinting pensively down the barrel, 'you oughta do the right thing. Bet you don't even have a small game licence, do you?' As Linda turned and walked back inside, Oakey checked to see if the gun was loaded. He shook his head. 'Don't go borrowin' other people's guns, eh? Get one of your own. Learn how to use it.'

An inner door slammed; Oakey shrugged, and placed the weapon carefully against the wall.

'Do you think you should leave it there?' David asked. 'What about the kid?'

'It's not loaded.'

'Yes, but . . .' David's objections died on his lips as Oakey looked at him. It was a perplexed, quizzical look. It made David feel like a creature from outer space.

'Better show me where you left that car,' Oakey said. They trudged back down the steps towards his pick-up, David moving carefully, to avoid mishaps. (He knew that if he fell again, in Oakey's presence, he would die of embarrassment.)

The twenty-minute walk was reduced to a five-minute drive; they found Maureen's car easily, without exchanging more than a couple of words, and Oakey got out to survey the damage.

'No problem,' he said. 'You trying to go forwards or backwards?'

'Backwards.'

'Won't need the rope. Just a coupla feed sacks. Get in and start it up - won't take a minute.'

It took about three minutes; with a few judiciously placed bits of hessian, and a push or two, the car was coaxed forward just enough to clear the ice. Oakey then emptied half a sack of sand over David's tyre tracks, reversed the pick-up, and waited on Scots Road as David carefully steered his car back down the trail.

The manoeuvre was completed without difficulty.

'We did it! Oakey, we did it!'

'Sure did.'

'Listen . . .' David climbed out of his seat, and approached the pick-up. 'Let me buy you a drink. Please.'

'No thanks.'

'Please, Oakey. Or a meal. Let me buy you a meal.'

'That's okay.'

'Would you - would you like to come to dinner? I've asked Alice to dinner. Maybe you can come too.'

Oakey shook his head, and changed gears. David could see him biting his moustache. In anger? Surely not - although there was a slight tension in the muscles of his jaw.

'But I owe you one, Oakey! Isn't there something I can do?'

'You can keep out of the woods,' Oakey replied. 'That trail's for a snow-mobile, not a sedan.'

Then he pulled at his cap, adjusted his wing mirror, and roared off into the night.

M a y

❄

It had been a difficult day. To begin with, the paper had arrived - hot off the presses - with a typo right under the masthead. (*'Fish Wokers Vent Anger Over DFO Decision'*.) Then Glen Burgess had called, claiming that he had been misquoted. At lunchtime Walter Rudd had appeared, to air his views on Alice's latest coverage of the condom machine controversy, and Delbert Wheelhouse had turned up shortly afterwards, with another incoherent contribution to the letters page. By four o'clock, Alice had dealt with so many complaints that she decided to go home early. 'I've got a headache,' she told Erica. 'If anyone has a problem, they can call me tomorrow.' Nobody in Kempton seemed to understand that correspondence had to be edited before it could be published.

Eight hours in the stuffy little office had left her stale and dispirited, so she took the scenic route home, stopping at St Andrew's Ferry. She drove all the way to the lighthouse and got out of the car; the breeze soon revived her, for although it was cold, it was not too cold. A few wreaths of cloud were soaking up the late-afternoon colours - all the pinks and golds and lavenders and maroons. The tide lapped gently against her rubber soles as she trudged along the shingle, past an abandoned lobster trap, a bleached and fretted bone, a long trail of dead seaweed. She thought of the people who sold dulse out of their cars, near the Watervale turn-off: she had tried the stuff once, and found it unpalatable. An acquired taste, perhaps. Like that awful black sandwich spread of David's . . . what was it called? She had sampled it on her last visit to Maureen's house, after the discussion had turned to fiddleheads. David had never seen fiddleheads before. He had asked how they were cooked, sounding faintly suspicious, although they were just like any other green vegetable. Perhaps more delicately flavoured than most. Certainly prettier. Alice had promised to serve them up the very next time he came around for a meal.

Turning right, she left the shore and began to climb back towards the lighthouse, her wandering gaze caught every so often by a rock or a branch or a dead leaf. The grass was no longer brown; a green mantle had spread across it, but the trees were only just beginning to bud. Soon, she thought, the lupins will be out. David will like those. She remembered what Delbert Wheelhouse had said about his garden that morning: 'It's comin' along fast,' he had said. 'We were lucky, last winter. It was cold, but the snow came down before the ground froze.' According to Delbert, the wildflowers would be early this year.

Of course, Delbert had also said in October that the winter would be a warm one, because the beavers were putting less mud on to their dams. He had some very funny ideas, did Delbert.

Alice returned to her car in a much happier frame of mind, and as she drove through St Andrew's Ferry she was cheered still more by the sight of young Hardie Garron, sitting on the launch outside his boathouse and fish store, mending a net. Nice to see a man of Hardie's age mending a net. Not that there was much point, if things continued along their present course; nets were useless without fish. Alice began to think about the Fisheries Resource Conservation Council, and her mood promptly changed. By the time she reached Sable Cove her spirits were so low that not even the pretty pink blush of sunset could lift them. It really had been a depressing sort of day.

But like every other day, it had to be given a page or two in her journal.

Early spring weather. Paper came in – prominent mistake. How does it happen? Erica received a belated birthday present by post: a video, Sister Act. *She says she has a whole library of videos, sent to her by well-meaning friends and relatives, and they're all about nuns:* The Sound of Music, Nuns on the Run, The Singing Nun – *I can't remember the rest. It was quite funny. Walter called about the condoms, again . . .*

Sighing, Alice paused for a second. She would have liked to gloss over that particular conversation – she was so sick of the whole damned business – but knew that she had to recount every detail, or why keep a journal at all? There had to be detail, and lots of detail: detail on top of detail, until the pattern emerged. Until everything else was blocked out, including those forbidden paths down which her mind (unless occupied) would be tempted to wander. She had made herself a promise.

He said the results had come back from that survey they conducted, and most of the parents seemed to want condom machines, but not in St Andrew's Ferry; he said the whole thing should therefore be decided on a school-by-school basis . . .

At this point the phone rang.

'Hello?'

'Hello, Alice?' It was Raylene. 'How are you?'

'Oh . . . not bad.' Alice felt guilty; the nonexistent headache had simply been a ploy - an excuse to get out of the office. 'What's up? Don't tell me you're still at work.' It was half past six.

'No, no. I left at five thirty. Just checking to see you're all right.'

'I'm fine.' Alice was touched, but at the same time slightly suspicious. 'Is something wrong?'

'No, nothing's wrong. Don't worry, no one's threatened to take us to court.' Raylene laughed, and babbled on for a few more minutes - in a neighbourly fashion - as Alice waited silently for her to come to the point. At last she said: 'I was just wondering, Alice . . .'

'What?'

'You know David French, don't you? I mean, you're a friend of his.'

Alice stiffened. Damn, she thought. Don't tell me someone's worked it out.

'Yes,' she replied, cautiously.

'Well . . . do you know anything about him and Linda?'

'Linda?' Alice's mind was a blank. 'Linda who?'

'Linda Tibbett. My cousin.' A pause. 'Do you know what I'm talking about?'

'No I don't know what you're talking about,' Alice sighed, tapping her pen on the table. She could sense the rapid approach of a large, juicy piece of gossip. 'What are you getting at, Ray?'

'Well, you're not going to believe this, but Bob Wheelhouse said he saw David French going up Linda's steps with a big bunch of flowers . . .' Raylene launched into her account of David's movements, not with relish, but in the indignant tones of someone who smells a rat. Alice listened patiently. She noticed that it was already dark outside. ' . . . and now they're saying Linda's a whore, because she's got all of these men coming and going, and why should Watson send money to support a whore?'

Her breathless, panting voice abruptly stopped; Alice knew that some kind of response was called for. But what kind of response? Certainly not that David was gay.

'Isn't the money for Watson's child?' she observed at last, whereupon Raylene shrieked: '*Exactly!* That's exactly what I said!'

'If Linda's seeing somebody, that doesn't mean Watson has a right to abandon his child.'

'How do you mean?' Raylene sounded subdued. 'You mean she really is involved? With David French?'

'No.' Alice frowned. 'And that's not the point. The point is that whatever she does is her own business.'

'But they're saying she's a whore, Alice!' Raylene's cry was so piercing that Alice winced, and held the receiver away from her ear. 'You know she's been seeing Eric McNeil! Now they're saying she's loose, and she always was, and Aaron isn't Watson's kid at all.'

'Oh, for God's sake.'

'I've been saying it isn't true, but Bob was with Keith, and Keith says it was definitely David. Why would David be giving Linda a bunch of flowers? And a box of chocolates, Bob says. Why would he do that?'

'I don't know,' Alice replied. 'But I do know that if he's seeing Linda, then it's purely as a friend.'

'Has he told you that?'

'No he hasn't told me that!' Alice let her temper show. 'For God's sake, Raylene, if you're so interested, why don't you ask him yourself?'

'He probably wouldn't tell me. Linda wouldn't want anyone to know.'

Alice took a deep breath. She let it out slowly, rolling her eyes and reminding herself that there was very little to do, in this part of the world. Unless you hunted or fished or sewed, unless you played hockey or kept a journal, what else was there but gossip? Besides, she was in no position to carp. She made a good living from recording news of other people's activities - and more than that, she made a hobby of it. Busying herself with other people's affairs was one way of keeping her mind off her own.

'Raylene,' she said kindly, 'as far as I know, David French is not involved with your cousin. But if you want to find out what he was doing on her doorstep with a bunch of flowers, then I suggest you ask him for an explanation. Because I can't give you one.'

Judas Priest, she thought, as she put the phone down. You can't take a pee in private. She wondered what David had been doing on Linda's doorstep, but then pushed the question aside with a flap of her hand. It was none of her business. It was nobody's business, despite Raylene's belief that she had a God-given right to interfere in everything that concerned the Tibbett family. Raylene was quite obsessive about her clan. When she wasn't collecting gossip, she was running around making sure that her relatives had the support they needed – and since she was related to almost everyone in town, that kept her pretty busy. Sometimes Alice almost envied her. With an extended family like Raylene's, there would be little time for introspection or regret.

Picking up her mug of cold tea, Alice wandered back out to the kitchen; it was time for supper, but she had no appetite. Maybe just enough for some soup, or a sandwich. Or a boiled egg. She glanced out of the window and saw that there was a light on in Oakey's garage. The doors were standing open, but from her kitchen she was unable to see inside. Suddenly Oakey himself emerged, heading back towards the house, and Alice waited, nursing an idle interest, lazily rinsing her mug, until he appeared again.

This time he was carrying something – something large and long, wrapped in a blanket. It looked very heavy. He carried it into the garage, treading carefully and deliberately, and Alice heard several loud noises that were muffled somewhat by her storm windows: a bang, a thud, a creak. Presently he returned to the house, and by this time Alice's interest had sharpened. What on earth was he doing? After a few minutes the screen door flicked open and Oakey shuffled out again, carrying what appeared to be a camp stove and a fishing rod. A camp stove? He entered the garage; there were more thumps and bangs; then he retreated into his house to fetch a large cardboard box full of unidentifiable objects. Peering hard, Alice could just make out a glint of metal before Oakey and his box and its mysterious contents vanished into the garage.

How interesting, she mused. He's never gone fishing before. He's gone hunting before, but never with a camp stove. And what was that thing in the blanket? It looked like a pair of skis. Why would he be needing a pair of skis, on a spring fishing trip?

All at once she blushed, as she realised what she was doing. Look at me, she thought. I'm as bad as Raylene Tibbett, sticking my nose in where it's not wanted. And she pulled down the blind, firmly, before focusing her attention on the refrigerator.

* * *

The postcard depicted an enormous pile of tropical fruit: mangoes, bananas, pineapples, paw-paws cut open, their black pulpy seeds gleaming like caviar, shaggy coconuts, crumpled passionfruit, halved melons, avocado pears. A brief legend - 'Greetings from the Gold Coast' - had been embossed (in gold) on its shiny surface. On the back, Gus's salute was just as laconic.

From one fruit to another. These family holidays are over-rated. Count your blessings. G.

Shit, David thought, as he let himself into the house. I hope the postmaster didn't read this. He was annoyed with Gus for sending something so blatant: would it have killed him to use an envelope? Or even to write a letter, for once? But it was a miracle, really, that he had sent anything at all - after four and a half months, this was only the second piece of mail that David had received from Gus.

Laying it reverently on the kitchen table, he returned to the car and collected more bags of shopping. So Gus was having fun in the sun? He could picture that pale, muscular body stretched out on the sand. Black hair disappearing into red swimmers. A white grin beneath dark Ray-Bans (Gus was very fussy about his sunglasses). David had never actually seen him at the beach; they had never sauntered along a seafront together with a bucket of hot chips, sand in their shoes, salt on their fingers. David, in fact, had never much liked the beach - not since puberty, anyway. Embarrassed by his scrawny build and inappropriate erections, he had steered clear of the seaside. Nevertheless, he begrudged Gus's wife every drop of sweat and sunscreen.

On the other hand, how much billing and cooing would there be, with the baby around? It occurred to him that his mental image of leisurely days on a beach towel was probably very far from the truth. A more realistic vision was the one that suddenly popped into his head as he dumped a bag of oranges into the crisper: baking footpaths, rippling exhaust fumes, and the baby screaming as melted ice-cream trickled down its chest.

He smiled grimly. *These family holidays are over-rated.* Serve the bastard bloody well right. He pushed the last packet of cookies into the pantry cupboard and cracked open a beer.

But when he went to fling himself down in front of the television, he realised that something was wrong. The television was wrong. A perfectly strange TV had been substituted for Maureen's twenty-one-inch Sony.

'What the hell . . . ?' He started up, and looked wildly around. Everything else seemed to be in its proper place: the lamps, the clock, the record player, the expensive porcelain figurines. Only the television had somehow been replaced by this dusty old antique, with its primitive channel changer, its vertical hold, its woodgrain case and protruding chrome knobs. It was as if some bizarre metamorphosis had occurred - as if the gleaming Sony chrysalis had burst open to reveal this sad, wizened old Hitachi.

With mounting dread, David turned the thing on. (There was, of course, no remote control.) For a while nothing happened. Then slowly the picture appeared, as if from a dense fog; it was, as David had expected, a black and white picture.

'Oh, for . . . !' He was almost speechless with horror. A black and white TV! It had to be twenty - maybe thirty - years old. But who was responsible for its abrupt manifestation? Someone with a key to the house, obviously: either Bonnie McNeil or Oakey Marshall. He rushed to the telephone.

'Oh - hi - Floyd. Is Bonnie there?'

'No.'

'Has she - I mean - do you know anything about this television? Did she come into my house today, and switch TVs?'

There was a long pause.

'What?' said Floyd, at last. But David's hurried explanation only seemed to confuse him further.

'I'll get her to call you,' he said, cutting David off in mid-sentence. 'You'd better talk to her. I don't know nothin' about it.'

So that was that. David hung up, and called Oakey's number; it was some time before anyone answered the phone.

'I was downstairs,' Oakey explained, by way of apology. 'I was fixing Maureen's TV set.'

'Oh.' David sat down. 'So it was you!'

'Yeah, it was me. I looked in today, to check if the grass needed a trim. Turned on the TV. Wasn't workin'.'

'Really?' David frowned. 'But it was working perfectly well last night.'

'Tube blew.'

'What?'

'Tube blew.' Oakey's voice was even gruffer than usual; he sounded as if he was speaking through a mouthful of rolled oats. 'Needs to be replaced.'

'The tube?'

'Don't worry. I'll take care of it.'

'But . . . you mean I'll be stuck with this black and white? Until you've fixed the other one?'

Oakey sniffed, and cleared his throat. 'It's a good set,' he rejoined. 'I've been usin' it for twenty-five years.'

'Yes, that's pretty obvious.' Any older, David thought, and it would have had a stained-glass screen. 'So how long will this take, this repair job?'

Oakey mumbled a few vague words about ordering in a replacement tube – about warranties and spare parts and driving to Kentville. David tried to pin him down, but without much success. 'Won't be long,' was the only assurance offered. 'Won't be long, I'll do it as fast as I can.'

David, however, was not completely satisfied. He wanted to check with Maureen. After all, it was Maureen's television. 'Why don't you call a repairman?' he asked, and Oakey made a derisive noise.

'Out here? Cost a fortune.'

'But how does Maureen feel about this? Have you spoken to her?'

'Oh, I always fix her stuff.'

'Yes, but TVs are different -'

'Fix 'em yourself, do you?'

That silenced David. He found it impossible to argue from a position of complete ignorance. Nevertheless, he decided to ring Maureen as soon as possible; he refused to take the blame for giving Oakey a free hand. If the repairs were botched, then Maureen herself should assume responsibility for them.

He calculated that if he was to catch her before she left for school, he would have to ring in about half an hour. But because he felt quite strongly about the whole business, he called Alice almost as soon as he had finished speaking to Oakey.

'Hello? Is that Alice? It's David . . .'

'Hello, David.' She was at work; he could hear other people talking in the background. Her tone was cool and formal. 'How's it going?'

'Well, as a matter of fact - are you busy?'

A quiet laugh. 'I'm always busy.'

'Yes, but can you spare me a minute? Or should I call back?'

'No, no. You go ahead.' She lifted her voice: 'Erica! Will you shut the door please?' Then, as the chatter subsided, she addressed herself to David once more. 'What's up?' she asked.

David told her. He described the feeble Hitachi. He aired his misgivings. 'I mean, it's all very well, but what happens if he breaks the television? She won't blame me, will she?'

'There's no reason why she should.'

'I'm going to tell her. I'm going to tell her tonight. If she doesn't like it, she can talk to him herself.'

'Yes. That's probably the best plan.'

'And it's a black and white set, for God's sake! Next thing I'll be crapping in a deep-pit latrine!'

Once again, Alice laughed. 'Cheer up,' she said. 'You can always rent another one.' Then she asked him how he had come to meet Linda Tibbett.

Startled, David sucked in his breath. How on earth -? Who had told -? Unless it was Oakey.

'Ah. You know about that, do you?' he mumbled, and she expelled a noisy sigh.

'You were seen,' she confessed. 'With a bunch of flowers. You know what it's like around here - people are talking.'

'Talking?'

'They always talk, David. They've got nothing else to do. We just have to nip it at the bud.'

'You mean . . .' Slowly realisation dawned. 'You're not serious?'

'I'm afraid so.'

'Oh, but that's a hoot! That's such a hoot!' David was quite tickled. So he was having an affair with Linda Tibbett, now? 'Who saw me? Was it Raylene?'

'It was Bob. Bob Wheelhouse.' Alice paused. 'I didn't mention that you were already . . . involved,' she added, delicately. David realised that she was not going to ask him for an explanation - that she was determined not to pry. So he told her about the bobcat incident.

'Afterwards, I felt so bad about scaring poor Linda,' he concluded, 'that I thought I'd drop in and apologise. Give her a bunch of flowers.'

'And chocolates?'

'Chocolates?' David frowned. 'No, I didn't give her chocolates.'

'Bob mentioned chocolates.'

'Then Bob has a pretty vivid imagination.'

'His eyesight isn't the best,' Alice admitted, and went on to inquire about school. Was everything all right? Was he settling in? After discussing the school system for a while, Alice said that she had to go. 'But if there's anything you specially want to see in colour,' she remarked, 'I'd be happy to lend you my living room. Just give me a call, okay?'

David promised that he would. Then he broke the connection and rang Maureen - whose response could not have been more phlegmatic. No, she said, that was fine, just fine. If Oakey wanted to fix her TV, then Oakey was welcome to fix it. She sounded a little strange, David thought, but when he questioned her, she denied that anything was wrong.

'I'm fine. Perfectly fine. It's wonderful weather.'

'Mum's all right, is she?'

'Oh yes.'

'And the toilet's working? It hasn't blocked up again?'

'No, no.'

'How are you getting on at school?'

Fine, she said. Everything was fine. The children could be a little trying, but they responded well to firmness. Yes, she was finding her way about. No, the car was not giving her any trouble. The Baptists in this part of the world were rather different from the ones at home, but there was a very nice woman called Joyce, who had taken Maureen to her nephew's wedding. Although Maureen related all this in her usual quiet, unemphatic manner, David could sense that her thoughts were elsewhere.

He asked her about some of the incidents that his mother had recently mentioned: a parking ticket, an obscene phone call, a run-in with the local drycleaner, who had done something unforgivable to one of Maureen's suits. Still her voice remained calm. Those were all little things, she said. There were so many other things to be grateful for – such as the ease with which her clothes dried, in the Sydney sun. And the cheapness of the lamb chops. And the lovely sheepskin products so freely available.

Listening to her, David was struck for the first time by her resemblance to Oakey. Her delivery was softer, and more conventional, but she shared a similar sort of reticence – even though it was disguised somewhat by domestic platitudes. She really seemed averse to admitting how she felt, or what she thought. He wondered suddenly if this was a Nova Scotian characteristic, since it was evident to some degree in Alice, as well. But then he remembered that Alice came from Prince Edward Island.

'And what's up in Scotsville?' she said at last. 'Is Bonnie takin' good care of you?'

'Like a mother.'

'And there haven't been any problems?'

'Only with the TV –'

'And the carnival? It's all full steam ahead?'

'As far as I know.'

'Good,' said Maureen. 'That's good.'

Then she reminded David that her car was due for a tune-up, inquired about her African violet, gave careful instructions regarding the mould in the bathroom, and bade him a gentle - but firm - goodnight.

* * *

It was Alice's birthday. Although she would have preferred to let it pass without comment (she was, after all, forty-six years old), she submitted without protest to Erica's gift of delphiniums and Raylene's plans for a night on the town. Nothing too wild, of course; just a drink and a meal at the Crow's Nest, with Raylene and Gary and Erica and anyone else who wanted to come, and then maybe a bit of dancing afterwards, at Club 66. If people felt up to it.

'Not Club 66,' said Alice, plaintively. Club 66 was a singles bar - the only one in Kempton - and on Friday nights it tended to be the backdrop to many an ill-fated coupling (although there were generally more people at the video gambling machines than on the dance floor). Alice found it a most depressing place. 'Please,' she murmured. 'Not Club 66.'

'Well . . . whatever.' Raylene flapped her hand; there was a crusading light in her eye. 'Do you want to ask anyone? Anyone else, I mean.'

'We'd better ask Ian,' Alice suggested, glancing towards his office, but Raylene frowned.

'Oh, he won't come, he never comes.' Ian, in fact, lived an hour's drive from Kempton, and could rarely be persuaded to stay after work. 'I mean anyone else. Like your friend David.'

My friend David, Alice thought. There had been several references to David recently: bright, casual references. She would have disregarded them if not for the fact that they were being made by such a wide variety of people.

'Yes, ask David,' she said. 'David's got cabin fever. And ask Paul and Sue.'

'Paul and Sue?'

'Anderson.' Paul Anderson was the new doctor in town, a clever young man with a quirky sense of humour. But like most recent arrivals he was struggling to establish some form of social life. 'And Gwen. You'd better ask Gwen. And Keith Hughes.'

'Oh, not Keith.' Raylene screwed up her nose. 'I don't mean people like Keith.'

Alice smiled. 'Why not?' she asked. 'What's wrong with Keith?'

'If you ask Keith, you might as well ask Fairlie McNeil. Or Delbert Wheelhouse. This is supposed to be a fun evening.' Noting her boss's raised eyebrow, she quickly changed tactics. 'Anyways, we can't have too many people. There won't be enough room.'

According to Raylene, ten was the limit - any more, and the whole affair would become unwieldy. So on Friday night ten people gathered beneath the suspended fishing nets and lobster traps of Kempton's only seafood restaurant: Alice and Erica, David, Paul and Sue, Raylene and Gary, Gwen, Gwen's husband Mike, and Ian the advertising manager (who had, unaccountably, accepted Raylene's invitation). Like Alice, Ian was divorced; he was in his mid-thirties, a short, neat, rather touchy redhead with a well-groomed moustache and a passion for golf. Alice had always felt sorry for Ian, when she was not furious with him. He had an unenviable job - a job that would have soured anyone's temper - and seemed to spend most of his time sulking. Even his jokes had a trenchant, morose edge to them.

Mike, in contrast, was very loud and jovial. Alice had interviewed him several times, because he was the Rink Manager, and rink managers are important people in places like Kempton. But she had never exchanged more than a few words with him at any social event, and was unprepared for his insistent, rollicking humour. She was surprised by it. Gwen was such a quiet person, so subtle and delicate in her manner, so gently witty, so proper, so careful. She was a pharmacist, and had a sweet, bland healer's face; a sweet, soft healer's voice; a tranquillity that served to disguise her formidable commonsense. Yet she was married to this clown. This bigmouth. This clumsy raconteur. Alice was terrified that he would launch into a series of nun jokes: not nun jokes as Erica told them (good, clean, religious jokes), but the cruder variety that would cast a pall of embarrassment over the whole table - if not the whole restaurant.

She was relieved when he and Ian began to argue about the local recreational facilities.

'That Australian boy,' Gwen murmured into Alice's ear. 'I'm sorry - what did you say he was called?'

'David French.'

'David French. How old is he?'

Alice thought for a moment. 'Twenty-six,' she said. 'He just turned twenty-six.'

'Really? He doesn't look it.'

They both glanced at David, who was listening, wide-eyed, to Paul Anderson. He and Paul seemed to be getting on well; Alice hoped that, by introducing them to each other, she had enriched both their social calendars.

'He seems like a nice boy.'

'He is.'

'Bonnie certainly thinks so.' Gwen was regarding Alice with an intent, slightly quizzical gaze. She lowered her voice. 'Bonnie tells me he's a better prospect than poor old Gary, over there.'

Gary was sitting forlornly at the end of the table, poking at his molars with a toothpick as Raylene chatted with Erica and Sue. He was wearing a denim jacket over a checked flannelette shirt, but not his customary baseball cap. He had the distinctive, chinless Ruggles profile.

'Bonnie thinks David and Raylene would get along just fine,' Gwen continued, and Alice remembered that she and Bonnie McNeil were both on the Animal Shelter committee. Noting the archness in Gwen's voice - registering the twinkle in her eye as yet another manifestation of bubbling, subterranean gossip - Alice shook her head and studied the menu.

'Bonnie's an incurable romantic,' she rejoined. 'I think I'll have the lobster.'

'I'll have the lobster too,' said Mike. He was evidently one of those annoying people addicted to eavesdropping on other people's conversations. 'That's if Gary recommends it. What do you think, Gary? Would you recommend the lobster?'

'Never ate it, here,' Gary retorted.

'Yeah, but don't you know who they buy it from?'

'Not from me,' Gary growled, and Gwen quickly, gently, intervened.

'I'll have the lobster too,' she said. 'Might as well go the whole hog.' Alice wondered if she often had to clean up after Mike's more unsuccessful sallies, but at that moment the waitress arrived, and her train of thought was interrupted.

The waitress was Linda Tibbett.

'Oh!' Even Raylene looked startled. 'Are you working Fridays now, Linda?'

'Mum's mindin' Aaron.'

'Doesn't she have bingo, on Friday night?'

'Not any more.'

'Why not?'

'I dunno.' Linda began to look sullen. As for David, his cheeks turned a curious, mottled shade of red as he glanced around the table, and caught Raylene's eye. But the flush faded quickly; pulling himself together, he ordered the scallops with an airy, unselfconscious grin.

Alice decided to help him out.

'How long have you been here now, Sue?' she inquired, creating a gentle diversion.

'About seven . . . eight months.'

'But it feels like forever,' Paul added, and Sue hastened to explain.

'He's been very busy. We hardly ever see him.'

'Oh my.' Gwen seemed genuinely concerned. 'That's no good. And you have children, don't you?'

'Three.'

'*Three?*' Sue was small and blonde and waif-like. She looked about seventeen. Alice had shared Gwen's surprise, on first encountering the Anderson brood.

'Three and a half,' Paul amended. 'The cat misses me more than the kids.' He was about to say something else, but Raylene forestalled him.

'Speaking of cats, did Walter's turn up yet?' She looked around. 'Has anybody heard?'

Alice sighed, Erica grimaced, but everyone else just stared - everyone except Gary. He was gazing out the window, at the lights reflected on the choppy expanse of Kempton Gut.

'Walter's cat has disappeared,' Raylene revealed. 'It's been missing for three days.'

'Walter *Rudd's* cat?' said Ian, and Mike guffawed.

'Oakey strikes again!' he remarked. 'What do you bet it's been kidnapped? Catnapped, I mean.'

'Oh, rubbish.' Alice fought a rising sense of irritation. 'Raylene, you're stirring the pot again. Leave that poor man alone.'

'Yeah, but Raylene's a journalist,' Mike pointed out, with lumbering humour. 'She's got to get to the bottom of these mysteries, eh, Raylene?'

'The only *mystery* is how people can be so stupid.' Alice realised, even as she spoke, that she should have eaten something before sampling the chardonnay. 'Oakey and Walter are two respectable, middle-aged Nova Scotians. Anyone would think they were mafia hoods.'

'But -'

'There isn't one *shred* of proof that Walter had anything to do with Oakey's barn, or that Oakey had anything to do with Walter's mailbox. They've never once accused each other of malicious damage. The whole thing is a fantasy dreamed up by people who don't have anything better to talk about.'

'Yes,' said Paul, 'it's amazing how these stories get started. I heard the other the day that my car was stolen, and I never even knew it was gone. God knows what I've been driving around in, all this time. Some sort of hologram.'

'Maybe someone else's car was stolen,' Erica suggested. 'Maybe someone got the names confused.'

'No, I don't think so. I think these stories just blow in from somewhere. Like high-pressure systems.'

'I think people make them up,' said Ian, but David shook his head.

'They don't make them up. They misconstrue. They put two and two together and they end up with six.'

'It's not even that. It's more than that.' Alice was thinking of the waves of gossip that ebbed and flowed across town like the tides in Kempton Gut. 'It's the pattern. The structure. The patterns are laid down . . .' She realised that people were staring at her, and quickly changed the subject. 'So . . . has everyone ordered? No one's missed out then? Good. Okay. Thanks, Linda.'

The food turned out to be adequate, though David was obviously dismayed that his scallops were deep fried in breadcrumbs, rather than lightly sautéed in butter. The conversation drifted gradually from the fishing industry to domestic violence to censorship, diverted occasionally by Mike's inappropriate and ill-timed party jokes. As alcohol consumption increased, Mike grew louder and louder, until finally Gwen - by some cunning form of manipulation that was not readily apparent - forced him out of his seat and into their car. ('Thanks,' she said, kissing Alice on the cheek. 'It was wonderful.') Erica left with them, after being offered a ride home, and Ian bade everyone a brusque goodbye soon afterwards. With the departure of these four, a certain feeling of constraint was lifted.

'Let's go dancing!' Raylene cried. 'Let's go to Club 66!' Alice protested, but was overruled; having tipped the unresponsive

Linda (who received an especially large contribution from David), they all spilled out of the stifling restaurant and into the crisp, bracing air of Main Street. Kempton's waterfront, though well lit, was almost empty of pedestrians - it was still too cool for loitering on the promenade, and very few people in Kempton ever walked if they could drive. So Alice and her party had the street to themselves. Chased by a stiff, salty breeze, they clattered past Lawton's drug store, past a window full of Sears appliances, past McNeil's pizza parlour and the post office, until they reached Club 66: a grey weatherboard facade under a red neon sign.

Sue was beginning to worry about her children.

'No, no!' David protested. 'Don't go yet! Safety in numbers!' (He was, Alice decided, more than a little drunk.) Inside, the illuminated dance floor was completely deserted; Alice recognised Hardie Garron sitting in one corner with Eric McNeil, and another moustachioed fisherman. Glen Burgess was drinking with one of the Wheelhouse girls (Angela, by the look of things). Three or four people were hunched over the gambling machines. Paul fumbled at his hip pocket.

'What can I get for you, Alice? I wouldn't recommend the margaritas, in this place.'

'Oh - an orange juice, thanks,' Alice said quickly. Gary ordered a beer, Sue a mineral water, David a vodka and lime. Raylene was torn between bloody Caesar and bloody Mary.

'I'll get both,' said Paul, wandering off to the bar. David laid a hand on Sue's wrist; he was flushed and bright-eyed, and his hair was fetchingly tousled.

'You,' he said, 'are a very lucky lady.'

'I know.'

'You can always tell a gentleman by the way he offers to buy the first round.' Releasing her arm, David turned to Raylene and added: 'Don't tell me you're just going to sit there and wait.'

'Huh?'

'This is the nineties, Ms Tibbett! You don't have to be a wallflower! You must ask your partner if he wishes to dance.'

'We're not dancing by ourselves,' Raylene declared. 'Someone else has to get up too.'

'Paul will get up. Didn't I say he was a gentleman?'

Raylene, however, had a better idea. 'We'll get up if you get up,' she smirked. 'You and Alice.'

'Oh no, not me,' said Alice, and David said, 'I don't dance.'

'Sure you do.'

'No I don't. I can't. I get dizzy spells.'

But David was forced to his feet, in the end. As Paul bobbed about with Sue, and Raylene with Gary, David swung Alice into a facetious tango, deliberately ploughing through the other couples like a torpedo through a destroyer escort. He was surprisingly strong, Alice found. Half the time he was lifting her off her feet.

Inevitably, they all finished up in a tangled heap on the dance floor. Then there was more drinking, and more laughing, and several song requests, until at last the Andersons tottered home (they only lived up the street) while Gary dragged Raylene to his car. David fluttered a handkerchief at them from the threshold of Club 66. 'Hurry, Cinderella!' he cried, in a shrill tremolo. 'Before you turn into a pumpkin!'

'David –'

'O, brave seafarer! My heart goes out to that apple-cheeked lad.'

'*David.*' Alice shook him. 'I'm taking you home, now. No - *no*. You're not going to drive. You're not fit to drive.'

'But my car!'

'You'll have to come back for it.'

'Yes, mother.' As they moved towards Alice's Chevrolet, he suddenly said, 'Did you get any presents?'

'No.'

'Not even from Louise?'

'Louise sent me a card.'

'Well, I got you a present.' He folded up like a deck chair to insert himself into the passenger seat. 'I wrapped it and everything. But I forgot to bring it with me. I left it at home.'

'Then I'll collect it tomorrow morning,' Alice replied, fastening his seatbelt. 'I'll give you a lift into town, so you can get your car. I've got to come in anyway.'

'You're such a pal.' Even in the tank-like Chevrolet, David's knees were almost jammed against his chest like a kangaroo's. 'You're such a nice person, Alice.'

'Tell me about it.'

'Will you help me get my television back?'

'Your television?' Pulling into Main Street, Alice checked her mirror and accomplished a neat U-turn. Then she headed for Scotsville, as David moaned and fretted about his TV. 'It's been two weeks, now. Two *weeks*, for God's sake!'

'So rent another one. I told you to rent another one.'

'But I can't tell him off,' David continued, as if she had never spoken, 'because he fixes everything else. I'd be lost without him. Shit, shit, shit, why am I such a goddamn *blouse*?' Grumbling and muttering, he turned on the radio; someone with a deep voice was talking about Palestine. The next frequency featured a wailing country and western croon. David swore, and flicked from station to station - there were five of them, all told.

'Stop!' he cried suddenly. 'Stop the car!'

Alice swerved. She pulled over. 'What?' she exclaimed, genuinely frightened. He was groping for the door handle.

'This is the kind of thing,' he said. 'This would work, wouldn't it? This music?'

'*What?*' It was a Rankin Family song: 'Johnny Tulloch'. One of their non-Gaelic productions.

'For step-dancing,' said David, already out of the car. 'Don't you know how to step-dance? I thought everyone did, around here.'

'For God's sake, David!' Alice could have hit him. 'You scared the life out of me!'

'Quick, quick! Before it finishes!' He bounced into the glow of the headlights; beyond him stretched the glossy black waters of Kempton Gut. They were up on a headland, not far from the Scotsville turn-off - Kendall Tibbett's convenience store was just down the road. 'Come on, Alice, please? Just teach me a couple of moves.'

'I haven't done any step-dancing for years,' Alice growled. She was still feeling shaken. 'Get inside. Don't be an idiot.'

'Oh please! Please, please, *please*.' He began to prance about, clumsily, like a long-legged wading bird, flapping the loose folds of his parka. Alice rested her forehead on the steering wheel.

'*Please*, Alice -'

'Oh, all right!' It had suddenly occurred to her that if David was determined to dance the night away, there was nothing

156

she could do about it. He was far too big to push back into his seat. 'Just a couple of steps, and then we get going.'

'Johnny Tulloch' was succeeded by something crisp and edgy, on a Cape Breton fiddle. It took Alice right back to a certain night in Georgetown, some twenty-five years before – to a typical McDonald clan gathering, held to celebrate her cousin's engagement. They had brought that fiddler all the way from Cape Breton, and piped everyone into supper, too: a supper of Malpeque oysters, squash pie, planked salmon and her mother's own Dutch Mess.

It had been Alice's last step-dance, just a year before she was married. She had danced for hours, under a starry summer sky, with Bernard beside her, awkwardly imitating her movements. Bernard, fresh from Toronto – he had never step-danced in his life.

'Okay,' she said, shaking off this recollection. Images from the distant past were all very well, but they tended to lead to more recent memories. And there were things about her husband that she wanted to forget. 'You don't have to worry about your hands so much,' she continued, positioning herself on David's right. 'It's more like Irish dancing than Scottish dancing.'

'I thought it was like line dancing?'

'That too. Now watch me. Step, step a-a-and step, step. Step, step-step, step, step . . .'

In the glow of the headlights, on the edge of Bay of Fundy, Alice neatly and steadily went through her paces, while the fiddle soared and squawked and stuttered.

June

Although David knew where Oakey lived, he had never set foot inside the old Marshall house. It was such a forbidding structure, despite its manicured lawns - so large and grey, with such a morose, untenanted look - that he had never found the courage to walk up to the front door uninvited. But four weeks of black and white television can change a man; one afternoon, on his way home from work, he was suddenly filled with a sense of righteous indignation, and made a left-hand turn on to Bay Road instead of following his usual route via the Scotsville off-ramp. Bay Road took him right to the end of Marshall Street, where Oakey's great ancestral pile stood, dark and menacing, against a vivid blue backdrop of sea and sky. It was a fresh, clear, sunny afternoon, but the house seemed to absorb the light, retaining its haunted appearance even amidst a froth of golden dandelions.

David was halfway up the front path when a dog came lurching towards him, barking hysterically. It had three legs and was tied to the porch with a very long rope. David paused, and retreated a short distance; when the dog reached the end of its tether it stood there, growling, its tail lashing back and forth. These mixed signals confused David. If he extended his hand, would the dog sniff or bite?

Fortunately, he was saved from having to find out, one way or another.

'*Goan! Gerroot!*' Oakey was standing at the nearest window. '*Tripod!*' As the dog looked around he disappeared, emerging from the front door moments later with a cup in his hand. 'Git! Gerrootofit! Dumb dog. Come here!'

The dog stood its ground, but it was grinning and panting. Oakey made a wordless, threatening noise. 'Dog won't hurt you,' he informed David. 'Wouldn't hurt a fly.'

'Oh?'

'Hardly got any teeth left.' By this time the dog was sniffing at David's ankles, its brown eyes limpid under knitted brows. 'He's not mean, he's just dumb. One dumb dog. Tripod! Come here!'

The dog ignored him. Fending it off, David inquired about the television. 'I was just driving past,' he said, 'and I thought I'd drop in and see if you were done.'

'No.'

'No?'

'The parts're still comin'.'

'But it's been four weeks, Oakey!' David made no effort to conceal his impatience. 'How long is this going to go on?'

Oakey shrugged. 'Depends,' he said.

'But - I mean - can't you . . .' In the face of Oakey's imperturbable expression, David began to feel that he was over-reacting. 'Look, if there's a problem, why don't we call the manufacturers?' he offered. 'Get them to fix it? I'll pay.'

Oakey shook his head. 'Too late now. I've ordered the parts.'

'But surely you can send them back? I mean - shit, Oakey, I really need that television.'

Oakey rubbed his chin. He looked uncomfortable. 'Sorry,' he muttered, with a sidelong glance that aroused David's suspicions.

'You haven't broken it, have you?' he demanded. 'Where is it? Can I see it? Show me what's wrong.'

'It's just the tube,' Oakey rejoined, and proceeded to blind David with science, lapsing into a fog of technical terms. Fidgeting, David eyed the front door; somewhere in there his TV languished, held hostage by an obsessive handyman.

'It's in a million pieces,' Oakey observed, noting David's speculative gaze. 'Down in the cellar. It's a mess.'

'Can I see it?'

'Why?'

'Because . . .' David faltered. Why indeed? Because Oakey was so obviously reluctant to let him in?

Maybe Raylene's right, he thought. Maybe the whole house is full of illegal substances.

But the very idea was so preposterous that he almost laughed out loud.

'Well . . . how much longer?' he asked, effectively admitting defeat. 'Is it going to be days or weeks or months or what?'

'Soon as I can.'

'Yes, but how *long*, Oakey?'

Oakey looked up at the sky. He looked down at his boots. He reached for his cap, then remembered that it was inside, and tucked his thumb into his belt instead.

'As soon as the parts come,' he replied at last. David surrendered. He returned to his car and drove back to Scotsville, wondering if anyone was ever invited into the Marshall house. And what was Oakey trying to hide in there? A corpse? A bad smell? Perhaps a stockpile of old tin cans and newspapers. Perhaps one of his fancy inventions: a miniature atom bomb, perhaps. Or a death ray.

That evening, before the Blueberry Carnival Committee had gathered, he asked Bonnie if she had ever been inside the Marshall house.

'No,' she said. 'Why?'

'Oh . . . I was just curious. It's such a spooky-looking place.'

'The Marshall boys never wasted a penny on housekeeping,' Bonnie informed him, arranging her banana muffins on one of Maureen's serving dishes. 'I've seen 'em buying curtains at Frenchy's, and linoleum at yard sales. I don't expect the house is anything special, inside.'

'It's a nice house, though,' David mused. 'I bet it would clean up well - oh!' He suddenly remembered the other question he had been meaning to ask Bonnie. 'You know that place next to Gordon's? The big white place?' He was referring to an enormous, nineteenth-century edifice on the hill above Scotsville's Baptist church: it had its own tennis court, a grove of fruit trees, and an imposing pair of carved gateposts. 'Gordon said it was empty, but I saw someone in the driveway this afternoon, unloading a whole bunch of suitcases.'

Bonnie grunted. 'It's June,' she remarked, and, as David stared at her, added: 'I guess Mister Beaton's in town, again.' She went on to explain that the house was owned by an antique dealer from Toronto, who spent the whole summer in Scotsville but who left his house empty for the rest of the year. Gary Ruggles earned a little extra cash as part-time care-taker, draining pipes in the fall and mowing grass in the spring.

'You mean this guy - this antique dealer - only spends three months here?' David exclaimed, and Bonnie shrugged.

'Two or three months. Lots of people do that, in Nova Scotia - people who come from Toronto and Montreal and the US. It's a popular place for summer houses, if you've got a bit of money.'

'Money! I'll say. He must be worth a *fortune!*'

'He's a rich man,' said Bonnie, pursing her lips. 'They say that kind usually is. No wife and children. No responsibilities.' Glancing at David, she screwed up her nose in a fastidious fashion. 'Sometimes he brings his boyfriends to stay with him,' she revealed. 'You know.'

'Ah.'

'I've got nothing against homosexuals,' she continued, enunciating all five syllables of the word very carefully. 'What they do in their own homes is their own business . . .'

('But,' thought David.)

' . . . but it's not very nice to whistle at people on the street. Or walk around half naked, smooching and pinching in front of young children.'

David said nothing - there was nothing much to say. Presently Keith Hughes arrived, and the conversation turned to summer activities. They discussed baseball and fishing and canoe trips through Kejimkujik National Park. Bonnie remembered John Lawrence's old fishing tackle, which was normally kept in a downstairs closet with his skis; the closet, however, was empty. 'It's bound to be somewhere,' she told David. 'Maureen can't have taken it with her. You should have a good look around the cellar, one day, and see if you can find it.' She went on to speculate about the mysterious disappearance of Maureen's electric waffle-iron, which Bonnie occasionally borrowed in exchange for free access to her own rice cooker. If Maureen had taken the waffle-iron to Sydney, she was in for a disappointment: Canadian appliances were not adapted to Australian currents or wiring.

Then Raylene appeared, and there was a quick, earnest exchange on the subject of Gordon Blanchard's latest fling with the redheaded Angela Wheelhouse. The subject had been well and truly aired by the time Gordon himself arrived, close on the heels of Bob and Walter. Coffee was distributed, chairs rearranged, and the meeting was declared open at five past seven.

Raylene was the first to make her report.

'I've ordered the blueberry pies,' she declared. 'Dad's going to put 'em in his cold store, and I'll take 'em out on Friday. All the square-dancers are booked in. Fairlie's agreed to call the auction.' She was counting off points on her fingers. 'Gwen Wylie's offered to take care of the face painting – she says she's done it before. The Shriners are giving us some prizes, but we haven't worked out what they'll be, yet. The *Gazette*'s donating a year's subscription. St Mary's is organising the

Bake Sale - we don't have to worry about that.' Suddenly she bent an accusing gaze on Bob Wheelhouse. 'What I want to know is: what's happening with the beer garden? Is Moosehead going to sponsor it, or not?'

All eyes turned to Bob, who was sitting with a plate of muffin crumbs balanced on his stomach.

'It's in hand,' he said, and Raylene frowned.

'What's that supposed to mean?'

'We're still in the process of negotiation.' Bob spoke slowly and thoughtfully, concluding with a nod of the head. But if he was trying to impress Raylene, he was unsuccessful.

'Now look here,' she snapped, 'we have five weeks left - *five weeks*, Bob. We don't have time to fool around! What exactly have you been doing, for the last month?'

'Gfffrrmmllnn . . . calm down. There's no need to panic . . .'

'Yes there is.' It was Gordon. 'Raylene's right. We've got to know *now*. Is there going to be a beer garden, or not?'

'There is,' Bob replied, with great dignity.

'Then who's going to sponsor it?'

'I told you. That's in hand.'

Another explosion. Finally Walter intervened: to settle the matter, he offered to help Bob with his negotiations, providing that Bonnie would, in turn, help him with the quilt display. Bonnie agreed. Then Keith was asked to present his report on the rented equipment - which was received with wordless approval until he touched on the supervision of the dunking machine, to be undertaken by Bonnie's son Eric and Delbert's unfortunate nephew Dwayne.

'Dwayne!' said Gordon. Then he flushed, and glanced at Walter, who was knitting his brows.

164

'Ffgglrrmphmm . . . manage it?'

'Oh, sure,' said Keith, quietly. 'Dwayne can manage it.'

'When Dwayne puts his mind to something,' Bonnie added, 'he's as thorough as anyone else. You know how well he sweeps the station.'

'He's very excited about it,' Keith observed, with a firmness that forestalled dispute. Later, when Bonnie had declared the meeting closed, David asked (in a low voice) who Dwayne might be.

'Dwayne?' said Bonnie. 'You must know Dwayne. He's always hanging around the fire station.'

'He's retarded,' Raylene supplied. 'He's got those bottle glasses and he rides his bike all over the place -'

'Oh, *him*.' David recalled the long, misshapen face - like something out of Munch's painting *The Scream* - with its vacant, distorted stare. 'So he's Dwayne, is he? I saw him wandering about in your garden the other day. Talking to a stick.'

'He's a nice fellow,' Bonnie insisted. 'He doesn't mean any harm. And he loves to help out.' David noticed that her attitude towards Raylene was rather stiff; as she turned to address Walter, he glanced at Raylene with a questioning look. 'Is something wrong?' he murmured.

'Oh . . .' Raylene drew him aside. 'She's mad at me because of the story I wrote. For Alice.'

'About what?'

'About the Animal Shelter. You must have heard what happened.'

'No. What happened?'

'Didn't you know?' Raylene brightened at this chance to relay a fresh piece of gossip. 'There's some money gone missing,' she said, in a whisper. 'Donation money. People are saying that Eunice had something to do with it.'

'Eunice?'

'Eunice Wheelhouse. She's the Chairperson.'

'Oh! Right.' David remembered being introduced to a charming old lady before his stint at the bake sale. She had very kindly told him what gingersnaps were, and had donated a lemon meringue pie. 'Oh dear.'

'It's not as if I said she did it. I said she couldn't provide any information. And Gwen is the secretary, and she doesn't mind, so why should Bonnie?' Raylene shook her head, as if to free herself of such unpleasant thoughts. Then she peered up at David. 'Incidentally,' she remarked, 'I've heard a rumour about you and my cousin. That isn't true, is it?'

David blinked. 'Your cousin?' he said - and suddenly the penny dropped. He smiled.

'My cousin Linda. You know.'

'Oh yes. I've met Linda.'

'But you're not involved with her, are you?' Raylene sounded so anxious that David toyed with the idea of an eva-sive, indefinite response. But he resisted the temptation.

'No,' he rejoined. 'I am not involved with Linda, and I never have been.'

Honestly, he thought, do I look that desperate? As soon as the question had crossed his mind, he felt ashamed of himself: just because she was a waitress, and a single mother, he had no right to dismiss her out of hand. Waitressing was an honourable pursuit. A springboard for many talented young actors. A job requiring great speed and coordination.

All the same, it was surely quite obvious that Linda was not his type. Even if his tastes had run to the opposite sex.

It was enough to make him worry about his public image.

* * *

The lupins were out. They filled the ditches and cascaded down the hillsides, white and mauve, pink and yellow and crimson and purple, the pride of the province, the queen of the wildflowers. (Some of them were as long as Alice's arm.) Slightly outclassed, but equally pretty, were the daisies, big white discs with golden hearts, which lined the roads and fought the dandelions for a place in the sun. The mallow-flowers, too, were unfurling their tissue-thin, poppy-like petals; Alice was happy to see them, because she had always had a soft spot for mallow-flowers, which were as stubborn as they were fragile. Climbing into her car, she noticed that a few of them were blooming around her mailbox.

Good, she thought. I'm glad Oakey left them alone. Just the day before he had offered to cut her flourishing grass (for a fee), and she had warned him about the wildflowers. She was particularly anxious to encourage the wild roses, which most people preferred to root out in favour of the cultivated variety. In Alice's opinion, cultivated roses were like overbred bulldogs - cumbersome grotesques. She regarded the delicate, pink, naturally occurring variety as infinitely preferable.

Driving down Marshall Street, she passed several culti-vated rosebushes, as well as a number of freshly trimmed lawns. She wondered if Oakey was responsible for their spruce appearance. Certainly it was his custom to mow people's lawns in the spring, though not with the clunky old machine he had been using yesterday. Where on earth had it come from? Was it Maureen's old mower? And where was the lovely big monster on which he had lavished so much care in the past?

Perhaps it had broken down. Perhaps it was sitting in Oakey's cellar, in pieces, like poor old David's television. Alice smiled as she thought about David. He had been in and out of her house quite a lot lately, with stacks of hired videos - *colour* videos. There was no way of connecting Maureen's video player to Oakey's ancient TV, because the TV had apparently been manufactured before the home entertainment revolution. Poor old David. How he suffered without his TV.

Alice was hoping that he would enjoy the evening ahead; if he did, and Lindsay Beaton liked him, he would have access to as much TV as he could handle. Lindsay, after all, had about four television sets - one of them in his ensuite bathroom. Of course it was very hard not to like David: he was such a sweet boy, so funny, so endearing; Alice always felt her spirits rise when he came buzzing around. And he was so decorative, too . . . but then again, his looks were beside the point. If Lindsay did like him, it would have to be for the right reasons. Alice had hesitated before asking Lindsay if she could bring a friend. She had wondered if it would look a bit *tasteless* - two gay men - a bit as if she was trying to play matchmaker, God forbid. For a while she had wavered, mulling it over, but at last she had decided to go ahead and let them make their own decisions. They were, after all, responsible adults. And they were also two of a kind, sharing the sort of urban sophistication which was rather thin on the ground in Kempton County. She believed that they would enjoy each other's company, and that both of them would, to some degree, benefit from the encounter.

But when she picked David up, she tried to prepare him for what lay ahead.

'Lindsay talks a lot,' she revealed. 'He'll talk about anything. His haemorrhoids, his suicide attempt - anything. Don't be surprised. And if he gives you something, he wants you to keep it.'

'What sort of thing?'

'Anything. He seems to like giving things away. Clothes, or whatever.'

'Really?'

'He's very generous. That's how I met him. He made a big donation to the county hospice, and we ran a story about it.' Alice slowly braked as she approached Lindsay's distinctive gateposts. 'People say he wouldn't have missed it - he's already so cashed up - but that doesn't mean a thing. Lots of wealthy people won't give you the time of day, let alone their money.'

'He's got a lot of it, then?'

'Oh, I think so.'

The sound of her engine brought Lindsay out onto the front steps, and Alice noticed that his hair was a different colour, this season: more of a strawberry blond. He also seemed to be cultivating a goatee, although this was still in its early stages. Alice wondered if he would have to dye it to match his hair.

'Hello!' Lindsay cried, thrusting his long, rather vulpine face through the driver's window. He had bright dark eyes, a long neck and a high forehead. Although he had never revealed his age, Alice guessed him to be in his late thirties. 'You can leave the car over there. Under the tree. Hi - is it David? Nice to meet you, David.'

Obediently, Alice parked her car and followed Lindsay into the house, conscious of David's wide-eyed astonishment as they passed under the stained-glass fanlight and into the entrance hall. It was all white-painted panelling and gleaming parquet; a majestic staircase swept up to the bedrooms; eighteenth-century oils were arranged above genuine chippendale chairs and side-tables. Alice knew what these furnishings were because Lindsay had pointed them out to her, on her very first visit. Now he was giving David the same grand tour.

'Excuse the mess,' he declared, waving his hand at the cardboard boxes stacked near the grandfather clock. 'I'm still camping out, as you can see . . . why, thank you. Yes, it's a beautiful house. Turn of the century. They built it around the fireplace - it's an Adam fireplace. Imported, naturally.' The living room was just as Alice remembered it: a treasure-trove of antique furniture, including an inlaid *escritoire*, collections of cameos and snuffboxes, an eighteenth-century pastel portrait and an early American lowboy. The grand piano was draped in a canvas shroud. Lindsay apologised for the tapestry cushions. 'They're my great-aunt's,' he explained. 'Dreadful things. The rug wasn't meant for this room - I ordered it for the master bedroom, but it was dyed the wrong shade of green. So they had to make another one, and I put this one down here. Oh, do you like the shutters? Not a bad effort, are they, for a local tradesman? Originally I was going to have curtains, but the fabric would have cost me $16 000 and I just thought - what's the point? Anyways, they have a bit of a beach-house effect, don't you think?'

Without waiting for an answer, he proceeded to show David the octagonal, wood-panelled library; the state-of-the-art kitchen; the lofty dining room with its Jacobean refectory table and thirteen-piece dining suite. 'Don't ever get anything done around here,' he warned, after drawing David's attention to the Staffordshire figures on the mantel. 'It's just not worth it. I mean, they're very nice people, in these parts, but they have no idea. I took this table to a french polisher up near Watervale - such a wonderful man, Slovenian, salt of the earth - but I mean look at it. Just look at it.' He shook his head as David peered blankly at the glossy surface. 'I'll have to send it to Toronto, and get the job done properly.'

David glanced at Alice, one eyebrow comically elevated. But Lindsay was already on his way back to the living room. 'I haven't unpacked the wine, yet,' he was saying, 'so I'm afraid there isn't much choice . . .' In the end they had to settle for imported French champagne, served with stuffed olives and corn chips; once again, Lindsay apologised for making them 'rough it'. Since he was all by himself, they would have to put up with his lasagne, and a fairly unimaginative tossed salad. 'I've never been much of a chef,' he warned, arranging himself in one of his elegantly upholstered carver chairs, and fixing David - who was sitting opposite - with an intent, quizzical look. 'But since you're Australian,' he added, 'you must be used to the rugged life. Barbies and bushflies and the rest of it.'

David laughed, and coloured.

'Hardly.'

'No?'

'I'm not the Paul Hogan type.'

'Oh!' Lindsay cast up his hands. 'Paul Hogan! Paul Hogan is in a league of his own. But I know what you mean - it's all a bit too much, isn't it? Personally, if *I* want to go camping, I go to a Holiday Inn. That's camping enough for me.'

Smiling, Alice watched as Lindsay unleashed his three-hundred-watt, four-hundred-volt personality. It almost became exhausting after a while: the explosive laugh, the sudden gestures, the way he leapt up like a jack-in-the-box when he wanted to give himself more room in which to declaim. He was quite a small man, but he had the delivery of a rapid-fire machine-gun.

His voice - a nasal tenor - was always slightly breathless, as if with excitement.

'... My sister - she's this voluptuous blonde, she looks like Mae West on amphetamines - she's been down the Amazon and across the Kalahari and it's just beyond my powers of imagination, God knows what she does with all her Lancome and Shiseido - she must get it flown in. Supply drops ...'

Alice had heard about this sister before: about her cosseted childhood, her liposuction and her unerring eye for rare books. But her one-night stand with Trudeau was a new one, as was her (failed) marriage to a Ukrainian engineer. 'The wedding was just miserable,' Lindsay sighed. 'Poor things, they didn't stand a chance. My cousin was standing about two feet away from him, and I heard her say: "Well - it's a short step from the chauffeur's room to the master bedroom." Those were her exact words. About two feet away from the groom! But of course poor Turk didn't speak English very well ...'

Over supper, Lindsay's energy flagged a little, and he began to probe David for personal details. Alice could tell that he was impressed with David. As for David, he laughed a lot - sometimes he laughed so hard that he choked on his lasagne - and handled the nineteenth-century Coalport china with awed respect. But sometimes he looked a bit overwhelmed; Lindsay's undivided attention would have overwhelmed anyone.

' . . . I can take children one at a time - even two at a time - but in large numbers they terrify me. Especially the ones around here, I mean they're tough. People talk about city kids, but I'm telling you, the kids around here . . . is that dressing all right? I'm afraid it came out of a bottle . . .'

The pasta and salad was followed by apple pie and cream, with Lindsay apologising profusely for neglecting to clear away the salt and pepper shakers before serving dessert ('You must think I'm such a ruffian'), after which coffee and Belgian chocolates concluded the meal. On the way back to the living room the conversation turned to local affairs, then to weight-loss and workouts - a subject which left Alice with very little to contribute. She was beginning to drift off, drugged by the wine and the firelight, when the sound of her host complimenting David on his physique jerked her back to consciousness.

She looked up to see David, red-faced, murmuring some-thing about cricket.

'Cricket!' Lindsay exclaimed. 'Now, that's a game I've always admired. So much more elegant than baseball, though I'd be lynched if I ever said so in front of a full-blooded North American male.'

'That sounds as if you don't consider yourself a full-blooded North American male.'

'Well, do *you*? I mean, look at me - am I the John Wayne type?'

'Uh-hmmm.' Alice struggled to her feet. 'I'm sorry, Lindsay, but it's time I went.'

'Oh *no*!'

'I'd love to stay longer, but I have to get up early to-morrow.'

'Tomorrow?' Lindsay sounded appalled. 'But tomorrow's Saturday!'

'There's a fire hall open day I have to cover.' Bracing herself for Lindsay's histrionics ('My *God*, you're so *dedicated*!'), Alice glanced at David, who began to push himself out of his chair.

'I suppose I'd better make a move too,' he said, but seemed quite happy to submit when Lindsay grabbed his arm.

'No!' Lindsay cried. 'No, I won't let you. It's only eleven thirty - don't tell me you've got some God-awful family affair tomorrow morning?'

'No, but -'

'Then you can stay for a sip of my port. I won't take no for an answer. Where do you live - just down the road? Oh, you can spare me another five minutes.'

So Alice left David to fend for himself. Driving back towards Sable Cove, she found herself worrying about Lindsay's intentions, and tried to dismiss these worries from her mind; I have to remember, she thought, that they're both over the age of consent. In any case, it's none of my business. If David likes Lindsay, then David likes Lindsay. He deserves a bit of fun, poor boy.

But it did concern her that David's idea of a 'bit of fun' might differ somewhat from Lindsay's. There could be no doubt that Lindsay lived in a faster lane than Kempton was accustomed to. The question was, would it be out of David's league as well?

* * *

'If there's one thing I've learned,' Lindsay declared, in a loud voice, 'it's that no matter how warm it is on land, it's always cold on the Bay of Fundy. Always.'

They were sitting in the stern of the little boat, wrapped in layers of brightly coloured, waterproof clothing. Some of the other tourists were not so sensibly dressed; they wore shorts and cotton jumpers, and shrieked every time the spray lashed their huddled bodies. There were only eight of them, all together, because it was the first weekend of the season - the last weekend in June. 'It gets too crowded, in July and August,' Lindsay had said. 'There aren't too many whales about, this time of year, but there aren't too many tourists either. Less chance,' he added, 'of being puked on.'

The water was certainly choppy, but the day was bright and the wind fresh, and no one - so far - had succumbed to seasickness. The rocky headlands glided past, grey and mysterious, each of them crowned with a toupee of dark-green fir. Always prepared, Lindsay had brought a hamper full of home-made lemonade, camembert, beer, grapes and crackers, as well as his anti-nausea pills. 'I would have brought a newspaper,' he remarked, 'if I didn't get seasick, reading on boats. You'll find it pretty dull.'

'Boats *are* dull,' David agreed. He had never taken to yachting, except on Sydney Harbour; there, at least, there was something to look at. And Hawkesbury River cruises were all right, too - providing you could stop, occasionally. But the open sea was too dull for words. 'So you don't think there'll be any excitement?' he asked, conscious of Lindsay's arm pressed against his. 'No whales or porpoises?'

'Oh, we'll see a whale,' Lindsay yawned. 'We'll see a whale or get our money back - that's the guarantee. But we might not see much of the whale when it decides to turn up.'

'Look!' The middle-aged blonde woman with the pink nail polish was pointing away from the shore, towards a pair of distant, misty shapes, which - on closer inspection - proved to be a couple of stationary boats, not much larger than the one they were in. Lindsay announced that these boats were also whale-watching vessels.

'Standing room only,' he said.

'It seems like a lot of boats,' David frowned. 'Won't the whales be frightened?'

'Oh, you learn to live with it. Like Princess Diana.'

'I hope something turns up soon.'

At that moment the skipper reported a humpback whale in the vicinity, and there was a murmur of anticipation. But as the minutes dragged by, and no whale appeared, anticipation turned to disappointment. The two children on board began to complain in a persistent, mid-western whine.

'Here,' said Lindsay, rummaging in his hamper and withdrawing an exquisite set of opera glasses. 'Use these.'

But David shook his head. 'It's okay. You use them. They'll get in the way of my camera.'

'There!' someone shouted, and David turned just in time to see the spout. A fin appeared, then very slowly disappeared, as everyone rushed over to the port side. The boat began to swing around, chugging away manfully.

'Damn!' said David. 'I didn't get a picture.'

'It'll come up again,' Lindsay assured him. 'They have to come up every ten minutes.'

'Ten minutes?'

'Yes, I know. It seems a hell of a long time when you're waiting.'

Evidently their movements were being tracked by the other two boats, which immediately set off in pursuit. (It was rather like a hunt, David thought.) There followed a few minutes of slow-motion activity, culminating in another waterspout - this time some metres astern. Focusing his camera, David gasped as a huge, scarred, charcoal-grey back filled his telephoto lens. *Click*. The back disappeared.

'Got it!' he cried.

'Well done.'

'I wish it would show us its tail or something. Something a little more dramatic.'

'Ah.' Lindsay adjusted his hideously expensive, drop-dead Ray-Bans. 'I believe the technical term is "breach". What you want is a "breach".'

'Those other boats must be spitting chips.'

They did not, however, spit chips for long. The whale next appeared not far from the biggest boat; David could hear the whoops and cheers of happy tourists wafting gently across the water. From then on the pursuit followed a pattern: first the spout, then the chase, then the clicking of shutters, then the long, long wait in the broiling sun. Whenever the whale surfaced, the stampede from port to starboard (or starboard to port) nearly capsized them.

After an hour of this, their skipper headed back to dry land.

'Well, that was a bit disappointing,' David observed, as they pulled away from the other two craft. 'How much whale did we see? About four square metres?'

'Like looking at a nude beach through a telescope.'

'I see what you mean about Princess Diana, though.'

'Yes, I thought you might. It's like being a Fleet Street photographer, isn't it? Or one of those tourists who take the bus tours of Hollywood, in case they get to see Sylvester Stallone emptying his trash.'

'Personally, I think it's a rip-off,' said David, who was feeling tired and sun-dazzled. 'Someone ought to complain about those whales. They must be getting a pretty hefty cut of the profits, and they're just not pulling their weight. We're paying them good money for this.'

'Ah yes, but you know where it all goes, don't you? Up their *arms*, my dear.'

David laughed, and the eavesdropping woman beside them turned to her husband. David knew exactly what she was saying to him, though her voice was pitched too low to hear: '*Homosexuals*' – or, perhaps, 'one of *those*'. Stupid bitch.

When they disembarked, he derived great pleasure from telling her that there was a piece of green vegetable matter stuck to her front tooth. As he climbed into Lindsay's convertible, he could hear her berating her husband for not informing her of this fact himself.

'Where shall we go for lunch?' Lindsay asked. 'There's a roadhouse not far from here where they serve Lunenberg fish-cakes. Have you ever had Lunenberg fishcakes?'

'I'm not very hungry.'

'What's wrong?' Lindsay glanced across at him. 'Aren't you feeling well?'

'Just a bit tired.' Looking out at the slowly unfolding streetscape of Shelby, with its sagging shingle fish stores, its Dodge pick-ups and lobster traps and seagulls, David felt sud-denly very far from home. He propped his forehead against the window glass. 'Don't you feel like a freak, out here?' he said. 'I mean - doesn't it get you down?'

'Doesn't what get me down?'

'You know.' David was watching the men outside the gas station. Baseball caps, moustaches, windcheaters - the nor-mal uniform. 'Sometimes I feel like I'm the last queer on earth.'

Lindsay uttered a short, sharp yelp.

'You what?' he exclaimed. 'You must be mixing in the wrong circles, my friend.'

'How do you mean?'

'Oh, David, David, David.' Lindsay crawled down the ramp and on to the ferry. 'You've been walking around with your head up your ass.'

David was in no mood for insults. 'Fuck you,' he said.

'No, I mean it. There's quite a lot of action going down around the bingo halls, if you keep your eyes peeled.' Switching off the ignition, Lindsay reached for the hamper on the back seat - but there was no more beer. 'I've got a friend in Vancouver who owns a porn distribution business,' he continued. 'Specialising in the gay and transsexual markets. Of course his mailing lists are *strictly* confidential - strictly - but he's a *very* good friend of mine, and I've done him a lot of favours -'

'Perhaps you'd better wind up the windows.'

'- and let me tell you, he has some pretty good customers around here.'

'Shelby, you mean?'

'No, Kempton.' Lindsay unscrewed the cap from his Thermos, and poured himself a cup of lemonade. 'Ever heard of Hardie Garron?'

'No.'

'Neither have I. Pity. He's a faithful customer. Walter Rudd? He's another one.'

'Walter *Rudd*?'

'You know him?'

'It can't be. It can't be the same guy.' Walter Rudd! David stared in astonishment. Walter Rudd! It was impossible. Impossible, yet . . . delightful. Fantastic. What a fantastic revelation. He found himself grinning.

'What?' said Lindsay. 'What's the joke?'

'Walter Rudd.'

'What about him?'

'He's . . .' David paused, and shook his head. 'Don't you know him?'

'Nope.'

'He's like the Lord God Almighty, around here. He's like Winston Churchill.'

'As a matter of fact, I've always had the hots for old Winston.'

'God, I don't believe it. *Walter Rudd!*'

Slowly, ever so slowly, the island receded behind them, while David gazed around at the cars and the gulls and the wheelhouse. Walter Rudd! He was still marvelling over this juicy piece of gossip when they reached the wharf on the opposite side of the channel; Lindsay began to tease him about his relationship with Walter. 'It's a dream come true,' he said. 'You're obsessed with the man.'

'I am not.'

'You've got a fetish for Legion ties!'

'Fuck off, Lindsay.'

'Oh no - of course - you must be faithful, ever faithful, to the errant Augustus.'

'Augustino.'

'Whatever.' Lindsay swerved into the left-hand lane, passing a pick-up and two hatchbacks with consummate ease. 'You know, you're fooling yourself if you think he's not out sleeping around.'

'You don't know anything about it.'

'Oh David. So *romantic.*'

'Fuck off!'

'He surely doesn't expect you to stay celibate for a whole *year*? While he's back there screwing his wife and his cricketing friends and whoever else happens to catch his eye -'

'If you don't shut up,' David said, in a shaky voice, 'I'm going to get out of this car.'

'At ninety kilometres an hour?'

'I mean it, Lindsay!'

'Yeah, yeah. My lips are sealed.'

'It's none of your business!'

'I just hate to see you suffer, Dave.' Lindsay peered at him over the top of his sunglasses. 'It's not natural. Especially on your vacation. Get out there and live a little, kid!'

David, who knew exactly what Lindsay was trying to do, remained silent. He was not ready for Lindsay yet. Lindsay was funny, and generous, and pleasingly trim, but he was also a little frightening. Not threatening, exactly, but wild - too wild. A puppy with a tiger's shadow, irresponsible as only the rich can be. And despite his upbringing, David was not all that experienced in such matters. There had been Michael, of course, and Gus, and that silly thing with Raoul, but on the whole . . . on the whole, he was not the promiscuous type.

In any case, he was saving himself for Gus. He had the superstitious belief that if he remained celibate while he was away, then Gus would remain celibate too - at least when it came to the male gender.

Surely Gus was not the sort of man who would sleep around?

'I'm sorry, David.' Lindsay sounded genuinely contrite. 'You're not mad, are you? Don't take any notice of me, I can't help it. You're such a hot piece of ass, and I haven't had a decent fuck since before the Deluge - that's what I call old Dean, the Deluge - but it really isn't good manners. I'm ashamed of myself. I won't mention it again, okay?'

David had to laugh.

'Yeah, right,' he said.

'No, I mean it. If I mention the subject one more time, you can hit me over the head with your handbag. Or better still, put me over your knee and spank me *hard*.'

David rolled his eyes. The man was incorrigible.

'Anyway,' Lindsay went on, 'this is all beside the point. We have a decision to make here - an *important* decision - and I want your advice, because it's too big a problem for me to solve on my own.

'The thing is, Dave: what the hell are we going to do about lunch?'

July

✳

Alice was insanely busy. On top of her usual commitments, such as the Board of Trade, Recreation Commission and Crime Prevention Association, she had to cover the myriad fetes, fairs, parades, open days and sporting events which seemed to blossom on every clear patch of ground during the summer, like tiger lilies. People in Kempton County (indeed, people all over Canada) were obliged to pack almost a year's worth of activities into three or four months of sunshine; they were as busy as bugs - as busy as the blackflies and mosquitoes and earwigs that hatched, swarmed, mated, laid eggs and died in the few short weeks allotted to them, before they disappeared in the fall. Sometimes Alice felt as distracted by all the human activity as she was by the clouds of blackflies that attacked her down by the shores of Sable Cove. Sometimes (although keeping busy was her privately acknowledged aim in life) she felt like slapping the next person who approached her with the date of yet another bake sale, Women's Missionary Society meeting or 4-H Mud Stomp dance.

Worst of all, in the midst of this frenzy, the Hockey Rink laid off three staff - who subsequently decided to sue the Recreation Commission for wrongful dismissal. It was the biggest news in Kempton since the hospital closure. Cursing her deadlines, Alice had to postpone a photo shoot and rush off to interview Mike Wylie, who was stuck in his rinkside office fielding endless telephone calls. He greeted her with less than his usual bonhomie; the humble office, with its worn carpet and fake wood panelling, looked as if it had been hit by a paper-bomb.

'It's a fiasco,' said Mike. 'The order comes down - they're going to be merging two jobs, which is crazy to start with. Then they make both guys apply for the new job, and decide to hire one of their *assistants*, who doesn't have anywhere near the same qualifications -'

'You don't approve of this, then?'

'Hell, no!'

Mike ranted on, stopping every now and then to answer the telephone ('Don't ask me, ask Walter . . . I told him to ask Dell to pass it on . . . well, how in hell should I know?') while Alice jotted down notes and made sympathetic noises. She was very, very tired, and her deadline day was looming. It occurred to her that she was in dire need of a break.

'. . . And I'm going on vacation, tomorrow,' Mike declared, almost as if he were reading her thoughts. 'Driving up to P.E.I. I'm not about to postpone it, not again.'

'P. E. I.,' Alice murmured, picturing her mother's old house behind the apple tree. 'Should be nice, this time of year.'

'I haven't had a day off in eighteen months,' Mike added. 'It's getting so I can't remember where my car keys are.'

185

'I know what you mean.'

Mike glanced at her, curiously. 'What about you, Alice?' he said. 'Will you be taking a holiday, this summer?'

'I doubt it.'

'You should.' He began to lecture her, in a somewhat stilted fashion, about efficiency and statistical analysis and something in the *Reader's Digest*. He had a habit of dropping into ponderous declamations of this sort, particularly at work: Alice wondered, not for the first time, if he read self-improvement literature. *The Efficiency Paradigm; The Six-minute Manager; Joke Your Way to Success.* She glanced at her watch, surreptitiously.

' . . . go with David,' Mike was saying. 'Cut loose. How much longer is he here, anyways? Six months? You should enjoy it while you can.'

'I beg your pardon?'

'Take him to Maine, eh? Take him to Niagara Falls. It's hokey, but it works.' As Alice stared, he began to wilt a little. 'What? What's the problem? It's okay by me. I think it's great.'

'What's great?'

'You and David.'

'David *French*?'

The shock in her voice seemed to take him by surprise. He beat a prompt tactical retreat. 'Hey - it's none of my business.'

'I'm not involved with David French, Mike.'

'Sure, whatever.'

'I'm *not*, Mike!'

'Sure! Sure! I never thought you were!' He averted his gaze, and began to rifle through the papers on his desk. 'I told her it was garbage -'

'Told who?'

'Gwen.'

'Gwen?'

'She said she heard something from Raylene . . .'

Raylene, thought Alice grimly, as she drove back to work. The knowledge that her own name was being bandied about in bars and bedrooms - that people were speculating, insinuating - well, she was used to that. But to have someone tell lies, downright lies, about her . . . it was too much. She swung into the parking lot, stamped on the brake, yanked her keys from the ignition and, after slamming the car door with a satisfying thud, stormed into the office.

'Where's Raylene?' she demanded.

'Out on a job,' Erica replied.

'What job?'

'Eunice Wheelhouse.'

'Oh yes.' Eunice Wheelhouse was being recognised for her contributions to the county hospice society. Raylene had gone along, ostensibly to photograph the presentation; Alice suspected, however, that her motives were mixed. As the writer of the derogatory Animal Shelter article, Raylene was bound to cast a pall over the proceedings. 'Is she coming back?'

'As far as I know.'

'When she does, tell her I want to see her.'

As she shut herself in the darkroom, Alice was conscious of Erica's surprised look, and wondered if the nun believed Raylene's stories. For some reason, it was particularly unbearable to have Erica thinking that she and David were curled up in bed every night. God, and it was all so stupid! As if *David* would be interested in her. Even if he had been heterosexual, David was a catch. A hunk. A pin-up. Well . . . perhaps not a hunk, exactly, but certainly a boy of many attractions. It was doing him an injustice to believe that he could pull nothing more glamorous than a forty-six-year-old country newspaper employee - who was, in any case, supposed to be a lesbian. Hunting around for the fixer bottle, Alice found herself smiling at the memory of that stale old rumour. Questions had always been asked about Alice's sexual orientation. No one knew anything about her husband Bernard, or why they had split up; no one had ever seen her daughter Louise, or received any kind of information about her, beyond the barest facts. It was generally understood that Alice came from Prince Edward Island, had gone to university in Halifax, and had spent some time in Toronto. But beyond that, nothing much was known - and Alice intended to keep it that way. Her reserve had been so absolute that it naturally served to encourage speculation, and a brief visit by her old school friend Isabelle had kindled the smouldering embers of local gossip. Perhaps this so-called husband had never existed? Or perhaps, if he had, his wife's lesbian tendencies had driven him away? Alice had almost welcomed this interpretation of events; the truth, after all, was much worse. In fact it was so much worse that it had prevented her from forming just the kind of relationships that would have silenced the gossips forever.

Of course people had stopped talking about Isabelle after a while, but the doubts had lingered. Until now, perhaps. Now, at least, the new story about David might kill the old.

Alice emptied fixer into a tray. She rinsed out another tray and filled it with fresh water. Developing photographs was a soothing activity, and after forty-five minutes Alice's equilibrium had been restored. Nevertheless, she was eager to talk to Raylene; the sound of Raylene's voice – her insistent, penetrating, ubiquitous voice – brought Alice out of the darkroom just before lunchtime.

'Raylene.'

'Hello. You'll never guess –'

'Could I see you for a minute? In my office.'

Raylene's face fell. She cast a questioning look at Erica (who shrugged), before trailing after her boss. Alice shut the office door behind her.

'Raylene, I just spoke to Mike Wylie. He said you told Gwen that I'm involved with David French. Is that true?'

Raylene blinked, but decided to brazen it out.

'Aren't you?' she said.

'No.'

'But he's been staying over at your house. You said he spent the night there. Four times.'

'Raylene, I don't appreciate this. I don't want you spreading this kind of crap.'

'But I didn't –'

'These are lies, Raylene. Now I know why you've been telling them, and it's got to stop.' As Raylene opened her eyes very wide, in an expression of injured innocence, Alice made an impatient noise. 'Do you think I'm stupid? It's that Linda Tibbett business. You're trying to help her out – well, not at my expense, thank you. Or David's.'

'But he really likes you,' Raylene said stubbornly. 'I know he does. I can say that, can't I?'

'Raylene, you don't know anything! David is gay, you fool! He wouldn't so much as look at me or Linda.' Even as she spoke, Alice's fury was beginning to subside - and she realised that she had made a terrible, terrible mistake. 'But if you tell anyone,' she added, fixing Raylene with an icy glare, 'and I mean it, Raylene - if you tell anyone, you're going to be sorry.'

'I wouldn't tell anyone.'

'I *mean* it, Raylene.'

'Yeah, I know you do! So do I.' Raylene cocked her head, leaned across the table, and lowered her voice confidingly. 'How do you figure he's gay? Did he tell you, or did you work it out for yourself?'

Alice could hardly believe her ears. She was casting about for a scathing rejoinder when the phone rang; picking it up, she heard David on the other end of the line.

'Hello!' he said. 'Have you got a minute?'

'Uh . . . hang on.' Alice covered the mouthpiece. 'We can talk about this later,' she said. 'For the time being just keep a lid on it, will you? I've got enough on my plate as it is.'

Raylene nodded. When she was out the door, Alice permitted herself a sigh of despair, and put her feet up. 'So what's the news?' she asked. 'Is your TV back?'

'No.' It was David's turn to sigh. 'Don't remind me. No, something else has happened. Lindsay's just asked me to go away with him. For a week. He wants to drive around the province.'

'Oh.' This did not come as a surprise to Alice. She seemed to remember other short trips, with other handsome boys. But of course she would never have said as much to David.

'What do you think?' He sounded worried. 'Do you think I should go?'

'That's not for me to say.'

190

'Yes, but what do you think? You've known him longer than I have. Do you think it's a good idea? Do you think I'll have fun?'

'I don't see why not,' said Alice, cautiously. 'It depends what you mean by fun.'

'I mean fun. Not sex - fun. Sightseeing. Photographs. Good food.' Suddenly David laughed. 'I know, I'm being unfair. It's nice of him, though, don't you think?'

'Very nice.'

'Even if he is just trying to get me into bed.' There was a pause; then he added, in shy, confiding tones: 'I'd rather go with you. It would be good, wouldn't it? A trip like that. You could show me Prince Edward Island.'

Alice was touched. What a nice boy he is, she thought. How easily he says nice things. She found herself envying his mother for her lifelong claim to his sensitive, morale-boosting presence. 'I'm afraid I haven't the time right now,' she said. 'Summer is my busiest season.'

'I know.'

'Perhaps in the fall.' It was a pleasant image. 'Perhaps we could stay at my mother's.' But as she put the receiver down she reviewed the suggestion, and found it laughable. Take a twenty-five-year-old boy to the old house? Her mother would flip. Her mother would call Mitchell, and Mitchell would drop his parish duties and come scuttling over to give her some brotherly advice, in his usual ham-handed way. No thank you very much.

Alice stared out at the rising, blue-green tide; at the wheeling gulls and the pier. She wondered if David would accept Lindsay's invitation. If he did there would be trouble, because someone would almost certainly find out sooner or later, and

191

then people would start talking. They were always talking about Lindsay. They talked about the clothes he wore and the car he drove. They talked about his house and his friends and his jewellery.

But surely David must know that by now? If he was keen to maintain a low profile, hanging around with Lindsay was not the way to do it.

* * *

Although a Blueberry Carnival program had been published in Alice's newspaper, David was not one of those people who tore it out and stuck it on a fridge door, or inserted it into a date book. He had received his own annotated program from the hands of the Chairwoman, and was careful to slip it into his pocket before going to meet Lindsay - who was waiting by the letterbox in Calvin Klein jeans, a pink polo shirt and his go-to-hell Ray-Bans.

David was wearing his first ever baseball cap, purchased at Zellers for $2.95 (plus tax).

'Go Leafs!' Lindsay cried, and punched at the air with his fist. David looked bewildered.

'What?' he said.

'I didn't know you were a hockey fan.'

'Pardon?'

Lindsay pulled David's cap over his eyes. 'The Maple Leafs. They're a hockey team from Toronto.'

'Oh.' David took the thing off, and examined the motif embroidered over its brim. 'Really? I just thought it was nice looking.'

'Say that, Dave, and they *will* peg you for a queer.'

It was a beautiful day, warm and sunny and fragrant, with just the occasional light breeze. Flowers blazed along the roadside. A woodpecker tapped on a telephone pole. Cars lined the backstreets of Scotsville, and the main drag was buzzing; David saw that someone (Gordon Blanchard?) had hung coloured flags across the street, from shopfront to shopfront. He decided that the clusters of blue balloons distributed about the place clearly had something to do with blueberries, and pointed them out to Lindsay.

'Looks more like a polar bear convention,' Lindsay replied.

'What?'

'Polar bears. They're people who go swimming in the middle of winter. You see a lot of blue balls when the polar bears are around.'

'Ha ha. Very funny.'

The parade was scheduled for eleven o'clock; all the floats were marshalling in a disused paddock, up behind Raylene's place. They would roll down South Street, do a circuit around the fire hall, and return to the paddock as slowly as possible. David explained all this to Lindsay as they strolled past the post office, taking pride in his own thorough knowledge of the proceedings.

'I can't believe you're not in the parade,' said Lindsay. 'Why aren't you dressed as a blueberry muffin? I think you'd make a fine blueberry muffin.'

'Gee, thanks.'

'Oh, look! Cotton candy. Do you want some?'

'Not for me.' David had spotted Raylene Tibbett, deep in conversation with Walter Rudd; she wore a very professional-looking camera around her neck. Alice had mentioned that

Raylene would be covering the carnival, while Alice went to photograph a provincial badminton champion in Shelby. Poor Alice. It was dreadful the way she never had a free weekend, though sometimes he wondered if her schedule was deliberately planned that way – if her life was so empty of family and close friends that she had to fill it with alternative interests. Whenever this thought occurred to David, he would be torn between a desire to repress it instantly – in horror – and the desire to rush over to Alice's house with a stack of brochures on psychotherapy and penfriend networks and video dating services.

'Look,' he murmured, nudging Lindsay's elbow. 'That's Walter Rudd.'

'Where?'

'There. In the grey suit.'

Lindsay looked, and almost choked on his cotton candy.

'My God!' he spluttered. 'You certainly pick 'em!'

'Shh.'

'I wonder what would happen if I goosed him?'

'Would you please behave yourself?'

They sauntered around for a while, inspecting the beer garden and the auction display, which had been set up under a tent in a carpark; Lindsay made facetious comments about the range of electrical appliances, handyman's tools and cocktail accessories that would be passing under the hammer. Presently they heard a buzz of excitement, and emerged to see a vehicle turning the corner up near Keith's house. It was the Fire Chief's car, and Keith himself was inside it. Then came a firetruck, in the vanguard of the procession, followed by two Royal Canadian Mounted Police dressed in scarlet uniforms, sitting on horseback. Each carried a maple-leaf flag.

David, who had never before seen a Mountie in dress uniform, was hugely impressed.

'Don't they look wonderful?' he remarked, to no one in particular, and heard Lindsay sigh.

'Don't they?' said Lindsay, but fortunately made no further comment. A bullock cart came next, and then the very first float: an Animal Shelter float, featuring a real dog, a real cat, and a lot of people dressed up in zoo costumes. David recognised none of these people. He did, however, recognise several of the children on the second float, which had something to do with fishing. He could see Amanda Burgess and Owen Tibbett sitting in a huge *papier-mâché* clam shell, wearing silver leotards and dried seaweed and what looked like crowns of starfish.

'Amanda!' he cried. 'Owen!' Amanda heard him; she waved shyly as he beamed across a wall of heads. Owen, however, was scowling down at the plastic pearls draped across his torso. David wondered how on earth he had been persuaded to put them on in the first place.

'Shriners,' said Lindsay, as a swarm of large, middle-aged men on almost microscopic scooters swept past. 'You can tell they don't have a problem with the size of their penises.'

'Shut up.'

'They obviously have a problem of some kind, but I haven't worked out what it is, yet.'

There were three brass bands in the parade, one from Kempton Junior High, one from far-off Bridgewater, and one from the military base, C. F. B. Greenwood. There were also any number of clowns, police, and people on horseback. The Legion float elicited gasps of admiration because it incorporated a model cannon, half a dozen military uniforms (past and present), a Canadian flag made entirely of paper flowers, and some genuine antique pistols. The official carnival float was the biggest of all; on it sat the Blueberry Queen, eighteen-year-old Angela Wheelhouse.

'Looks more like the cantaloupe queen, to me,' said Lindsay, and David experienced a sudden surge of irritation.

'Fuck off,' he snapped. 'You're hardly qualified to judge.'

'And Walter is?' (Walter Rudd had been on the selection committee.) 'Maybe *Walter* should be the Blueberry Queen. Why does she have to be a female, anyway? It's downright sexist.'

'If you don't like it, Lindsay, you know where you can go.'

This was a frivolous remark, made in haste, but Lindsay seemed to take it seriously. He vanished. One moment he was standing beside David, the next moment he had disappeared. David could hardly believe it. Had he been rude? Had he been offensive? He watched the tail-end of the procession by himself, feeling faintly worried; as everyone dispersed to the beer garden and fire hall (where various food and craft stalls had been set up), he wandered about unhappily, looking for Lindsay's face among those gathered around the carousel and the greasy pole and the dunking machine. The dunking machine was new to David. He noticed that Dwayne was doing a very good job collecting balls and counting out change.

The standard of marksmanship was unexpectedly high. All that baseball, perhaps?

'David!' It was Gordon Blanchard. He wore a flustered expression, and carried a clipboard under his arm. 'What do you think? Are you enjoying yourself?'

'Oh, it's terrific. I can't believe . . .' David paused, surveying the busy scene in front of him. 'I can't believe it's actually happening. After all that work.'

'We're not through yet,' Gordon sighed. 'I've still got to organise the pie-eating competition. Will you be entering that?'

'Oh . . . uh . . . no. No, I don't think so, thanks all the same.'

'What about the pie-throwing? You've got to enter the pie-throwing - didn't you say you were a pitcher, or something? In cricket?'

'A bowler,' said David. 'I'm a bowler. But I don't think I can bowl a pie.'

'Sure you can.' Gordon slapped him on the back. 'We'll be rooting for you. Show those little shits who's boss.'

So David agreed to enter the pie-throwing competition. Satisfied, Gordon rushed off to greet the Mayor, leaving David to resume his search for Lindsay. He found Gwen Wylie painting children's faces outside St Matthew's church; when the square-dancing started, in the fire hall, he found Paul and Sue Anderson with their three offspring in tow. But there was no sign of Lindsay anywhere.

Perhaps he's gone, David thought. It seemed very peculiar. Lindsay had never sulked before; he was the breeziest of souls, who could take just as much as he dished out. During their trip around the province he had lost his temper once or twice - usually at other motorists - but his outbursts were short and sharp. He could be snide, but never surly. And he always liked company when he did things, even if it was fill-ing the petrol tank. To walk off without a word of explana-tion was most uncharacteristic.

David was beginning to wonder if he should return to Lindsay's house, and find out what was wrong, when he felt a tap on his shoulder.

'Miss me?'

'*There* you are!' Studying the wolfish grin - the raised eye-brows - David decided that Lindsay looked perfectly relaxed. No hint of resentment disturbed the lines of his brow. 'Where the hell have you been?'

'Making a purchase.'

'A purchase?'

'For tonight.' Lindsay adjusted his glasses. 'Nose candy.'

'*What?*'

'Just a sniff. Nothing excessive.'

'For God's sake!' David was astonished. 'Where did you -? How on earth -?'

'Friend of mine,' said Lindsay, in a very low voice. 'Name of Cluny. Reliable *and* reasonable.'

'*Cluny Tibbett?*'

A smile. 'Chill out, Dave. No fuss, no muss.'

'That's unbelievable.' David had never met Cluny, but had seen him from a distance - a slow-moving, well-knit young man. Raylene's brother. 'You mean he's just . . . just walking around . . .'

'With a suitcase full of samples? No, we usually do business in his car.' Lindsay went on to explain, in a quiet, elliptical fashion, that he had met Cluny through a mutual customer named (of all things) Bucky, encountered at Club 66. Lindsay did not know his surname. 'He was a seasonal worker - roads or something. Very funny guy. Hard drinker. Chain smoker. Gut like an inner tube. We had a lot of fun.'

'You hang out at Club 66?'

'Sometimes.'

'Jesus.'

'Don't be such a snob, David. There's nothing wrong with Club 66 that a drag act wouldn't fix.'

It was now half past one, and time (as Lindsay said) for a wiener. They each had a long red wiener on a roll, with ketchup and mustard and relish, followed by ice-cream and a Diet Pepsi. David poked around the craft stalls looking for Christmas gifts, while Lindsay chatted up the young man selling baseball cards. He also seemed quite taken with Keith Hughes, who was manning the lottery booth near the fire hall entrance.

Must be the uniform, David thought.

'Hello, Keith.'

'Uh . . . hi, David.'

'I saw you in the parade. Out the front, there.'

'Yeah. Well . . .' Keith practically squirmed in his seat. 'It wasn't my idea.'

'Have you met Lindsay? Lindsay Beaton?'

'Hi,' said Keith, with a visible effort. He seemed even shyer than usual - in fact he was red in the face. 'How're you doin'?'

'Pleased to meet you,' said Lindsay, shaking his hand. 'What's the prize here?'

'The microwave.' Keith pointed to it. 'Second prize is the hamper.'

'Dollar a ticket?'

'Yup.'

'I'll take ten.'

David also asked for ten, and as Keith recorded names and addresses the conversation turned to pie-throwing, and pie-eating, and rappie pie, and other Nova Scotia specialties like Solomon Gundy.

'I had some in Yarmouth the other day,' said David. 'In a cafe there. It's not really my sort of thing, pickled herring.'

Keith grunted.

'Did you know I'd been away? Just for a week or so. We drove down through Yarmouth and Shelbourne and spent a day in Halifax and then up through Truro to Pugwash and Amherst and then back down here again. It was really great. Terrific weather.'

Keith nodded, smiling in an uncertain kind of way. He was still red - as red as a beet - and David wondered if his tongue-tied embarrassment had something to do with Lindsay. Poor Keith found it hard enough to talk to new people, let alone people wearing mirror sunglasses and solid gold jewellery and a Rolex watch specifically designed to intimidate. Or was it the faintly quizzical look in Lindsay's eye that terrified poor Keith?

Whatever it was, David decided to put the Fire Chief out of his misery, and went off to join his fellow pie-throwing competitors. He had been told to report to the fire hall parking lot at twenty past two; upon emerging into the sunlight he found himself in a great crowd of people, from which he was plucked by the ever-vigilant Raylene. 'Over there,' she told him. 'Gordon's over there.' Fourteen people, ranging in age from six to sixty, were already lined up behind a red ribbon, while Gordon Blanchard stood on the sidelines with his clipboard in his hand.

'There you are!' he exclaimed. 'I thought you'd forgotten. Five dollars, here's your pie, and you're number eleven. We'll be doing it one at a time - longest throw wins.'

'Where do you place your bets?' said Lindsay, and Gordon frowned.

'There's no betting.'

'Why not?'

'There's no betting. Gary! Are you going to do this? We've room for five more.'

David took his pie and his place, wondering uneasily if pie-throwing contests tended to become free-for-alls. He had never liked flour-bombs or water-fights, and was alarmed at the thought of getting squashed blueberries all over his beautiful Country Road shirt. Lindsay, for his part, was not reassuring.

'My God,' he said. 'You're right next to that kid. Maybe you'd better get him before he gets you.'

'Longest throw wins, Lindsay.'

'Wins what? That alarm clock? I'm sure that kid wants an alarm clock. Or do you think he just wants the chance to throw a pie at someone without getting walloped for it?'

'Shut up. You're making me nervous.'

'Oops! Better get off the field.'

Gordon was beginning to call out numbers. Number one was Floyd McNeil, who threw his pie with an obvious lack of enthusiasm. Perhaps Bonnie had forced him to enter the contest. Next was Dwayne Wheelhouse, who received a sympathetic round of applause - despite (or because of) the fact that his pie almost hit one of the spectators. The only female contestant was number three: she was a teenage girl in a halter-neck top, who threw underarm. Number four threw his pie like a discus, number six like a basketball. After each throw, a woman in shorts scurried out with a tape measure, and the distances were recorded. Three metres, forty-five centimetres; six metres, eighteen centimetres; five metres; eight metres; two metres. The little boy beside David was laughing so hard that his pie hit the ground only half a metre or so from the red ribbon. Then it was David's turn.

'Number eleven!' Gordon intoned. David turned to Lindsay.

'I need a run-up,' he said.

'What?'

'I need some space.'

'Oh.' Lindsay swung around, and addressed the people behind him. 'Can we move back, please? Number eleven needs more space. Back, please. Step aside.' His facetious manner helped things along; within seconds he had cleared a five-metre approach.

David removed the pie from its foil dish, and balanced it in his hand. Tricky. Not in the least aerodynamic, and one side was thicker than the other. But he curled his wrist around it, and went in to bowl.

His delivery was good - a fielder's delivery, with a bit of height to it. Splat! The pie hit the concrete, and a cheer rang out. When the woman in shorts announced her measurement, everyone cheered again. Ten metres, sixty-two centimetres.

No one else even matched this result.

'Good work,' said Lindsay, as David collected his prize. 'Very professional. What do you call that, a sinker?'

'A googly,' David rejoined. He was rather pleased with himself. Not bad, for someone so out of practice. He saw Bonnie, and waved.

'Bonnie!' he cried. 'Did you see that?' He had not laid eyes on her since returning from his trip; she had been very busy with the carnival. But when he approached her she smiled awkwardly - crookedly - as if he were a stranger.

'Hello,' she said.

'Were you watching? I hope Floyd's not too mad.'

'No. I don't think so.'

'It's going very well. You should be proud of yourself.'

'Thank you.'

Then her eyes flicked over to Lindsay's face, just for a split second, and everything became clear. David went into shock - he felt as if he had been punched in the stomach.

Lindsay, however, noticed nothing.

'It's the best one yet,' he remarked. 'I've been to four now, and they're getting bigger and better every year.'

'Well . . . we think so.' Bonnie smiled again, in an unconvincing fashion. 'I guess David has to take some credit, lending us his house, and all. Excuse me, will you? I've got to go see Walter. Looks like he's in trouble with something.'

And off she went. David watched her, his spirits somewhere around his knees; when Lindsay urged him to try his hand at the dunking machine ('You've got a magic arm, boy'), he mumbled his excuses.

'I think I'll go home. I've had enough of this.' Suddenly the colours seemed garish, the people loud and uncouth. The sun was giving him a headache. He trudged back up South Street, with Lindsay at his elbow, thinking about the alarm clock he was holding. He wanted to kick it. He wanted to tear it apart. Perhaps he would stamp on it when he got home, just to rid himself of this sick, debilitating fury.

'Mind if I pay a quick call?' Lindsay inquired, on reaching David's letterbox. 'I don't know if I'll make it home, otherwise.' Though faintly suspicious, David could hardly deny him access to a toilet - and sure enough, Lindsay had no sooner emerged (with half his fly buttons undone) than he began to question David about his state of mind.

'What's up?'

'Nothing.'

'Come on, Dave, you look like your mother died.' He sat down on the coffee table, opposite David, and put his hands on David's knees. 'Is it something I said?'

'Of course not.'

'What, then?'

'Don't you know? Didn't you see?'

'See what?'

'Bonnie.' David swallowed the lump in his throat. 'She's obviously come to a few *conclusions*.'

'About what?'

'You. Me.' It was unlike Lindsay to be so dense. 'Me, mainly.'

'Ah.'

'I just don't believe it,' said David, covering his face with his hands. 'I just . . . oh, I don't know . . .'

'Hey.' Lindsay peeled the hands away. 'Don't you dare. Don't you *dare* let her get to you. Screw her, David, she's jealous. She'd love to be in my shoes.'

'Oh, please.'

'Why not? You're a good-looking guy. Come on, don't do this. What do you care what she thinks? She's a dumb bag lady. She wears stirrup pants, for God's sake. Come on, Davey, you don't need that kind of crap. Forget her. Come on, eh? Cheer up . . .'

The first kiss was for comfort, but gradually the patting and stroking became more purposeful. Filled with a kind of weary resignation, David decided that the time had come. After all, where was Gus, these days? The last postcard had been dated March 24. And Lindsay was so nice. And he had a gorgeous little washboard stomach.

And anyway, David thought angrily, as he pulled off his beautiful shirt, I might as well. Everybody thinks I've done it, so why not do it? Why not give them something to talk *about*?

* * *

Alice had known from the beginning that it would be a tough job. But Raylene was at the Shelby Children's Parade, and Gwen had pleaded for coverage - so at two o'clock on Saturday afternoon Alice rolled up to the Royal Canadian Legion Hall with her notebook and camera.

The occasion was a briefing by the Family Violence Prevention Initiative, which had been set up two years before by representatives of the local Crime Prevention Association, the Association for Community Education, and the Ecumenical Society. That, at least, is how Alice had put it when reporting the event in her paper. But the Initiative (as it was called) had actually been the brainchild of Gwen Wylie, Winnie Rudd, and social worker Alberta Belliveau; its purpose, as Alberta had informed Alice more than once, was to

'develop greater awareness and understanding of family violence'. To this end, a briefing was being held for those who
worked in local agencies, businesses and schools - and whoever else might be interested. No bookings were required. No
admission fees were being charged.

To Alice, it seemed like a well-organised little venture.
There was even a pamphlet, which she received at the door.
Gwen, who was distributing the pamphlets, welcomed her
with an eager display of gratitude.

'So good of you to come, Alice. I know how busy you must
be.'

'Where shall I sit? Up the front?'

'Oh, anywhere. Hello, Kendall, how nice to see you. How's
Marjorie?'

Alice made her way to the front of the hall, which was
quite cosy, as halls go, with carpet and flowers and upholstered chairs. A lectern had been placed on a dais under the
Queen's portrait. Plaques and photographs were hung on the
walls at precisely measured intervals.

Alice was surprised to see a familiar head among the touks
and perms and baseball caps in the second row.

'David?'

He looked up, and smiled.

'Hello!' he said. 'I should have known you'd be coming.
You're omnipresent.'

'What are *you* doing here?'

'Oh, I just thought I'd drop in.' As Alice slipped into the seat
beside him, he lowered his voice. 'There are quite a few kids
at school that ... well, you have to understand what the
problem is.' He went on to describe his concern over various

students, whose peculiar combination of aggressive and anxious behaviour was beginning to get worse. Did it stem from conditions at home? He had heard in the staffroom that some parents (one fisherman, in particular) boasted something of a reputation for beating up wives. When David had referred the matter to Gordon Blanchard, Gordon had sighed, and referred him in turn to Alberta Belliveau. Apparently Gordon had been involved in more than one family ruckus, with chairs and bottles flying back and forth. Now he always left it to the professionals.

'Sometimes I feel more like a social worker than a teacher,' David said. 'But I'm not really *qualified* to counsel those poor kids about hygiene and domestic violence and things. That's why I decided to come.'

Alice nodded. She glanced down at the pamphlet, which opened with some alarming statistics: in the previous year, in Nova Scotia, at least 41 000 children, 35 000 women and 4 000 elderly people had been abused in some form or another. One in eight Canadian women . . . one in nine boys, sexually or physically . . . one in four girls under the age of seventeen . . . Alice shut her eyes, took a deep breath, and slipped the pamphlet into the back of her notebook.

Time enough for that later.

'I think we might start, now.' Alberta was at the microphone, a dark, sturdy woman in a navy suit. She carried a thick wad of notes in one hand and a pair of gold-rimmed spectacles in the other. 'But before we do I'd like to thank everyone for coming here today, and giving up some of their precious weekend. We wouldn't be asking you to do this if we didn't think it was important.'

Alice quickly surveyed the room. About thirty-six people – not bad, but not great. Quite a few men. She caught Paul Anderson's eye, and lifted her hand.

'Family violence has many different faces,' Alberta continued, reading from the notes in front of her. 'Physical assault, emotional abuse, intimidation, sexual abuse, neglect, deprivation or financial exploitation. Understanding family violence means understanding its full complexity . . .'

Words, Alice thought. They're just words. All I have to do is concentrate on their arrangement. As she scribbled them down she became aware of a rather nice smell – the smell of David's aftershave. It was not an aggressive aftershave. For some reason she found it comforting.

' . . . Fear, hope and isolation are the three main reasons why women stay in an abusive relationship. Fear of poverty. Fear of failure. Fear of retaliation – research indicates that the most dangerous time for a woman is when she leaves a relationship and sets up on her own.'

Alberta went on to describe what she called the 'cycle of violence' in which so many people are caught: the mounting tension, the fear, the psychological abuse, the manipulation and behavioural changes; keeping the kids quiet, keeping them out of the way, furniture broken, dishes smashed. Then the first punch, the apologies, the promises. 'And the tension begins to build again,' she said. 'The more the cycle repeats itself, the less contrition and remorse you get. In the end, it's just tension to abuse, tension to abuse.'

I should have asked Gwen to tape this for me, Alice decided. But she ploughed on, through child abuse, the abuse of elderly people, the socialising of women, the socialising of men, lessons learned in the home and in the playground. 'Violence begets violence,' Alberta intoned. 'We are learners, all of us - we learn from role models.' By question time Alice felt wrung out. Drained. Exhausted.

'You don't look very well,' David whispered, as Delbert Wheelhouse (an inveterate frequenter of public meetings) asked how a simple slap or smack differed from child abuse. 'Are you okay? Would you like to leave?'

'No.'

'Are you sure?'

'I'm fine. Really. I'll just - I'll just take some pictures.'

Fortunately they were sitting at the end of the row; Alice managed to sidle out and position herself towards the southern wall, where she was well placed for action shots. The business of adjusting her focus and aperture was just absorbing enough to distract her from the topic under discussion. She took several photographs of Alberta, and one or two of intent faces in the audience.

Afterwards, she congratulated Alberta on a job well done.

'Oh, it was Gwen and Winnie who organised everything,' Alberta replied. 'I just stood up and talked.'

'But it was a great speech.'

'Do you think so? I hope so. I hope I got the message across . . .'

At that instant, as Alberta aired her opinions on what should be written in the *Gazette*, Alice heard Gwen remark, very softly: 'That's him. That's David French.' She was talking to Winnie Rudd, who turned and gazed across the room; David was over by the entrance, with Paul Anderson.

'Oh yes. I've seen him before,' Winnie observed. 'You wouldn't pick it, would you? He seems quite normal.'

'They're not all sissies, Win. Anything but.'

'I wonder if the school knows? You'd figure he'd have to tell the school.'

Alice swallowed. She felt the blood rush to her head, and trickle away again. She cut Alberta off short.

'I'm going to have to go,' she declared. 'I'm right on deadline. See you, Gwen. Winnie. Excuse me. Excuse me, Kendall. Thanks.'

Raylene, she thought. It's Raylene. I can't take any more of this. Pushing her way through the clusters of people, she emerged into the open and sat down on a low brick wall. The sun felt warm on her face. She took a few deep breaths: in, out, in, out.

'You *are* sick.' It was David. He had followed her. 'Let me take you home.'

'No, no.'

'Please, Alice.'

'I just need some air.'

'You're an awful colour.' He stood there for a moment, gazing down at her. Then he said, 'It's not cancer, is it?'

'What?'

'You're acting like it's cancer, and you don't want anyone to know.'

Alice laughed. She patted his arm. 'Believe me, David, if I had cancer, I wouldn't keep it a secret.' But he was still look-ing worried, so she stood up to kiss him. Even on the tips of her toes she could hardly reach his jaw.

'It's all right,' she said. 'I'm not sick. I was a little upset, but I'm all right now.'

'Upset?'

'It was the subject matter.' She tapped her notebook. 'I find it upsetting.'

'Oh.'

'I'll - I'll give you a call.' She knew that she would have to tell him, but wanted to do so in private. Tim Horton's was not the place; nor was the Legion Hall parking lot. 'There's something we have to discuss. Are you in tonight?'

'Yes.'

'Then I'll call you.'

But first she would call Raylene. Raylene, who should be at home by this time. Alice went back to the office, and began to transcribe her notes; at half past four she dialled Raylene's number.

Gary answered the phone.

'Hello? Gary? Is Raylene there?'

'Yup.'

'Can I talk to her, please?'

There was a brief delay. Alice could hear Gary's voice, muffled by distance: 'What does she want now?' She could hear the clatter of crockery, and Raylene's approaching footsteps. There was a clunk. A laugh. The sound of breathing.

'Hello?'

'You've got some nerve, Raylene.'

'I'm sorry?'

'What did I tell you? I told you not to tell *anyone* about David. Didn't I tell you that?'

'Alice . . .' Raylene sounded confused. Shaken. 'I didn't -'

'Don't lie to me.'

'I didn't!'

'Gwen Wylie was talking about it. Winnie Rudd was talk-ing about it.'

'Well, that's not my fault! What do you expect, when he goes off with that Beaton guy for a whole week?'

Alice frowned. 'How do you know about that?' she asked.

'Oh, come on, Alice. They drove down South Street, in that fancy convertible. With all their luggage. *Everyone* saw them.'

Alice was speechless. She gazed out the window; there were clouds rolling in over the Bay of Fundy. I knew it, she thought. The Kempton grapevine strikes again.

'I haven't said a word,' Raylene continued, in a sulky voice. 'I can't believe you'd think I would. I *told* you I wouldn't.'

'Well . . . I'm sorry.'

'And in case you're interested, I got some terrific photos of the Children's Parade. And Glen Burgess wants to talk to you about something. I told him to ring Monday.'

'Thanks, Raylene.'

But she had already slammed the phone down. *Clunk!* Gently replacing her own receiver, Alice was filled with remorse. She knew that she had been too hasty - that she had jumped to conclusions. Raylene worked so hard, and for such a pittance; she gained nothing for her efforts *except* the gossip. Doubtless if someone had actually asked her, point blank, if David was gay . . . well, that might have been tempting. A hint here, a hint there. But she would never have brought the subject up herself. Alice believed that, very strongly. She wanted to believe it because if it were true, then it let her off the hook.

With a sigh she lifted the receiver again, and called David.

'Hello?'

'Oh! Hello!' His delight was hard to take. 'How are you feeling, better?'

'Yes thanks.' The gulls hovered. They raked the pier with their beady little eyes. 'Listen - before I forget, there's something I have to mention. I heard some people at the meeting today. They were talking about you.'

'About me?'

'And Lindsay.'

'Ah.' A pause. 'Well, that figures. I already knew there was gossip.'

'You did?' Alice was surprised. 'You didn't tell me.'

Another long pause. 'It didn't seem very important,' David said at last, carefully. 'I mean, it's no big deal. It won't make much of a difference.' He hesitated. 'Do you think?'

Alice hardly knew what to say. 'I guess not,' she replied, in doubtful accents. Certainly it would make no difference to some people. But to others . . . ?

She heard David sigh.

'I'll just take it as it comes,' he said. 'Lindsay's leaving soon, so maybe it'll all blow over. Maybe they'll find out that Eunice Wheelhouse is having an affair with Dwayne, or something.'

'We can only hope.'

'Maybe I'll start spreading that bit of news around myself,' David added, and laughed. 'You know what they say: if you can't beat 'em, join 'em!'

'Mmmm.' Alice wondered if he were joking. 'But I've never regarded that as much of a solution. Personally.'

'No, I guess not.' David's tone was serious; then it brightened again. 'Still, if we're talking clichés, every cloud has a silver lining. At least this means Bonnie won't be shoving old Raylene in my face any more!'

August

❄

'So when are you coming to visit me?' Lindsay inquired. His fingers danced up David's chest. 'Next week? Next month?'

David grimaced. 'I don't know,' he said. 'Don't push me, I'm not sure - ouch!' Lindsay had tweaked one of his chest hairs. 'Don't do that! There are few enough as it is.'

'I'll pay your fare.'

'It's not the money, it's -'

'Augustino.' Lindsay pronounced the name with an exaggerated Italian accent. 'Fuck him. Or rather, don't fuck him.'

'Listen. I've been making plans.' David sat up; around him Lindsay's Jacquard cotton sheets billowed like a white cumulus cloud. 'I'm saving to go on a trip. A long trip, at the end of the year. Across Canada, maybe, and over to Europe.'

'In the winter?'

'I can visit you then.' David did not want to visit Lindsay too soon. He did not want to become inextricably involved with Lindsay Beaton, though Lindsay was nice enough for a fling.

What he wanted was Gus.

'I'll have to go,' he added, glancing at the alarm clock. 'I'm due at the fire hall in half an hour.'

'The fire hall! Why?'

'For a . . .' David hesitated. 'For a pot luck and corn boil,' he said, bracing himself for Lindsay's response. (*A corn boil*, his mother had written. *What the hell's that, some kind of foot complaint?*) Sure enough, Lindsay burst out laughing.

'A corn boil!' he cried. 'Go, Dave! "Thank God I'm a Country Boy!" '

'It's a kind of tribute,' David continued stubbornly. 'For everyone who helped with the Blueberry Carnival.'

'You mean they're going to *eat* with you? But what about the queer germs?'

David grunted; that particular topic was a delicate one. He untangled his legs from the sheets and was reaching for his underpants when Lindsay caught him from behind.

'Wait! Wait, not yet. I'm leaving tomorrow, remember? What about a kiss? Don't I rate a kiss?'

It was like trying to get away from a giant octopus. Lindsay demanded one more kiss, and another, and another; at ten past six, David had to peel him off. 'Look - please - I've got to go, now. Alice will be waiting.'

'Write.'

'Of course.'

'Phone me. Reverse charges.'

'I will.' Pecking at Lindsay's cheek, David experienced a sudden surge of fond regret. Lindsay was all right. He might be a motor-mouth - he might have slightly bizarre tastes, and a somewhat shallow outlook on life - but he was very good company. 'Thanks so much. You've been terrific. In every way.'

'You know, there are people who'd pay big bucks for that ass.'

'Goodbye, Lindsay.'

'Don't do anything I would do!' Lindsay collapsed back onto his pillows. 'Give that woman's husband - what's his name? Lloyd? - give him a big French kiss from me!' As David crossed the threshold he heard the tell-tale sound of a pull-top snapping open; looking back, he saw that Lindsay was draining a can of beer.

They waved, blew kisses, and parted. It was thirteen minutes past six. David hurled himself downstairs, tucking his shirt into his trousers, thinking: that man drinks too much. The furniture in the entrance hall was already under dust sheets; the carpet had been rolled into a long, drab sausage. What a waste it was, really - conspicuous consumption. He clattered out the door, ran down Lindsay's driveway and turned left, conscious of the dinner-time smells in the air. It was a short walk (and an even shorter run) to Maureen's house, but when he turned the corner he saw that Alice's car was already parked outside the back door.

'Shit!' he said. 'Shit, shit, shit!' Alice was sitting in the driver's seat, reading. The sound of his approach made her look up.

'Sorry!' he panted. 'I'm sorry! God - I was just saying goodbye - Lindsay's leaving tomorrow . . .'

'Yes, I know. He called me.'

'I'm sorry, Alice. You haven't been waiting long, have you?'

She smiled, and shook her head. David saw that the book

on her lap was some kind of health report. (For work, he decided.) She put it on the passenger seat and got out of the car; she was wearing a dark-blue dress with pleats, and a white collar.

David had never seen her in a dress before. Normally she wore pants or skirts.

'You look very nice,' he said. 'Elegant.'

'Thank you.'

'I like the earrings.'

Alice touched one of them, gently. 'They were my grand-mother's,' she told him.

'Heirlooms?'

'I guess so.'

'Why are you taking the camera? I thought you said this was purely a social occasion.'

Alice cast him a quick sidelong glance before locking her car door. 'I don't know what this is,' she replied. 'I don't know why they invited me. It was Raylene who did all the work this year - I didn't have much to do with it.'

'But you ran the stories.'

'Yes.'

'Perhaps they're scared that you won't run them next year, if you're not invited.'

Alice shrugged. Together they strolled down the hill, savouring the silky air and the rich evening colours, admiring the last of the lupins and the first of the tiger lilies. Alice could name most of the flowers they passed: bluebells, irises, mallow, myrtle, Queen Anne's lace. She pointed out the chest-nut and apple trees, most of them untended, struggling through tangles of wild rose and blackberry. So many of the orchards and pastures in Scotsville had been left to grow wild. 'You'll have a lot to eat, come fall,' said Alice. 'That's a pear tree over there. That's a quince.'

'But don't they belong to people?'

'People who don't care. The apples fall off the trees and rot. Squirrels eat the chestnuts.'

'Why?'

Again Alice shrugged. 'They're not good apples - they haven't been looked after. You can stew them, or make them into juice, or jelly - ever had quince jelly? - but it's a lot of trouble. People don't bother making jelly any more. They don't know how. They eat chips and donuts and drink pop.'

'Bob Wheelhouse grows his own peaches. He's got a vegetable garden. I've seen it.'

'Some do, some don't.' Alice sighed. 'I don't. I don't have the time. I wish I did.'

'You know a lot about gardening.'

'That's because I grew up gardening. When I was a child, we ate our own vegetables. Potatoes. Cabbage. Pumpkin. The only fruit we ever bought in the summer was oranges.' Alice stopped, and pointed. 'See that? That's a cherry tree. You might get something off that.'

David remembered what Alice had already told him; that she had grown up in a small country town - practically a village - and that her father had been a lobster fisherman. She rarely talked about her past, although it was her recent rather than her distant past that remained the biggest mystery. Sometimes she would talk about her childhood: the wood stove, the well water, summer jobs at the fish plant. (To David it sounded like something out of Steinbeck, or Hemingway.) But she almost never mentioned her husband or daughter, an omission which David could only regard as glaring. Why such reserve? Sometimes it offended him; it made him feel as if he was untrustworthy.

'Do you think you'll miss Lindsay?' Alice suddenly inquired. It was such an unexpected remark that David had to think for a moment before answering.

'Miss him? Yeah, I suppose so.'

'But not very much.'

David looked at her. She was staring at somebody's fretwork tulips, which had been inserted into a marigold bed. Scotsville's gardens were full of wooden adornments of this kind: flowers, ducks, little girls with watering cans. They were the gnomes of Nova Scotia.

'I'm not going to pine away, if that's what you mean,' he said. 'Don't worry - it wasn't a big thing. It was just fun.'

Alice nodded. By this time they were drawing near to the fire hall, which was ringed with cars; David wondered if he and Alice were the only guests who had walked the short distance to dinner. He could see two women arguing beside an open car boot.

'Ida Wheelhouse,' said Alice, 'and Winnie Rudd. I hope they haven't forgotten the ketchup.'

'Winnie Rudd? Is that - ?'

'Walter's wife.'

Walter's wife. David peered at her with renewed interest. I wonder, he thought, if she realises? If she did, her sculptured hair, high heels and flattering summer suit suggested that she had yet to give up hope. Or perhaps she *had* given up hope, and was looking around for husband number two? At any rate, she was still focused on possibilities. On wider horizons.

Unlike her friend, who was evidently living from day to day in a confusion of dirty laundry and broken light switches.

'Ida is Bob's wife,' Alice informed him. 'They're both part of the Ladies' Auxiliary. The Ladies' Auxiliary usually does the catering for these things. In a pot luck, they each bring one dish.' Alice appeared to think for a moment. 'I hope Sally Hughes has brought her coleslaw.'

She led David, not through the fire hall's main entrance, but through a side door that opened on to a flight of stairs. This led up to the second floor, which was devoted to business and bingo; there was a kitchen, and toilets, and a very large room lined with stacks of chairs and glass cases. Two long tables had been set up, covered with plastic cloths, and laid with plastic cutlery, serviettes, bread baskets, ketchup bottles and tubs of margarine.

'How're you doin'?' A voice at David's elbow made him jump; he looked around to see a little grey-haired man staring at Alice. This man had the most extraordinary blue eyes – they were the colour of chemical toilet cleaner.

'Oh. Hello, Delbert.' Alice's tone was flat. Wary. Unenthusiastic.

'Did you get my letter?'

'Which one was that?'

'The one about the bank pullin' outa Shelby.'

'Oh. That one. Yes, we got it.'

'Are you gonna be at the meetin'?'

'I don't know.' Alice was already looking for an escape route. 'Gwen! Hello. You remember David.'

'Yes, of course.'

'And this is Sally Hughes, Keith's wife. Sally, I don't think you've met David French.'

It occurred to David, suddenly, that he was facing something of an ordeal. Many of the people in the room were unknown to him - and the people he *did* know were not particularly easy to talk to. Keith Hughes was painfully shy, Gary Ruggles monosyllabic, Walter Rudd incomprehensible and Bob Wheelhouse your basic, old-fashioned bore. As for Dwayne . . . Dwayne's attention was focused on a fragment of old Christmas tinsel, taped to one of the fluorescent lights.

So David ended up with Gordon Blanchard, who was in one of his sour moods. He spent fifteen minutes grousing about the School Board, then abruptly headed for the punch bowl when he saw Walter Rudd approaching. He and Walter were involved in a low-grade feud about teacher-training budgets.

'Grrffllmmng . . . enjoying yourself?'

'Oh - um - very much.' David felt awkward, knowing what he did. Disturbing images kept flashing before his mind's eye: Walter masturbating, Walter in drag, Walter feeling up a Mountie. They made him want to laugh.

Then a hideous thought occurred to him.

'Fbbllgrph . . . great weather . . . lffmbmmgrrr. You ought to go sightseeing . . .'

'I have,' said David. He could feel himself growing hot. Was Walter trying to establish the truth of all those rumours about David? Or was he - ? Could he be - ?

David shuddered. He could think of no one more unappealing than Walter Rudd.

'David.' It was Alice - she had shaken off Bob Wheelhouse. 'Are you going to sit with me?' All around them, people were suddenly moving towards the kitchen, as if in response to some unseen signal. A series of bowls and platters had been laid out on tables under the serving hatch. 'It's like a buffet. You pick up your plate at that end -'

'Yes, I see.'

There were steaming corn cobs and wieners bobbing in hot water; stuffed baked potatoes; a pile of overcooked steaks; Sally's coleslaw and Ida's chicken wings ('Ida does a terrific honey-glazed chicken wing'); cold sliced turkey and cold pressed ham and cold pressed chicken. The salads were all rather stodgy - rice salad, macaroni salad, egg salad, caesar salad drenched in thick, white dressing and laden with bacon bits. David was interested to see that the chicken wings went far more slowly than the pressed ham. Few of the men ate any salad at all, confining themselves to corn and potatoes.

I suppose they think that salads are for poofters, he thought, but ladelled macaroni onto his plate nonetheless.

He then took a seat next to Raylene Tibbett, noticing as he did so that the Wheelhouses were all at the other table. Obviously a policy of strict segregation was being pursued. Raylene was talking about someone called Ross Reid; at first he identified this name as belonging to a local figure, but gradually realised that it was the name of the Minister for Fisheries and Oceans. Apparently Ross Reid was looking into fishing quotas, and was expected to make an announcement very soon.

'Gary's lucky,' Raylene announced. 'With all the fish stocks going down, it means that the lobster numbers are going up. There won't be as many fish to eat the young lobsters.'

'Is that true?' said Gordon. 'I didn't know that.'

'Well . . . we've had some good seasons,' Gary replied, cautiously. His plate, David noted, was heaped high with rubbery red wieners.

'If the quotas go down any more,' Bonnie observed, 'it's going to get pretty bad, around here. Pretty bad.'

Bonnie. David looked at her as she sawed away at her steak, the flesh jiggling on her plump upper arms. She wore a sleeveless top of white and yellow gingham (from Frenchy's, perhaps?), and a pair of big, round, white plastic earrings. Floyd sat beside her, stolidly cutting all the corn off his cob.

'Things are already bad,' Bonnie continued. 'We can always tell, at work, from the people signing up for pogey.'

Pogey, David knew, was the slang word for unemployment insurance. The conversation turned to such insurance, and whether or not it was working, and how the economy could be improved, and whether tourism was a viable alternative to fishing (with Alice dropping a few tourism statistics, collected from the Board of Trade), and David tuned out. He had a very low tolerance for this kind of discussion. He thought about Gus - who remained stubbornly silent - and Lindsay, and his mother. He thought about Maureen. He had heard very little about her, lately; Clara reported that she was keeping indoors a lot, and was using the winter weather as an excuse. (But surely the winter weather in Sydney was equivalent to summer - or at last spring - weather here?) According to Clara, Maureen was always scuttling away when Clara tried to strike up a conversation, much as Bonnie was always scuttling away from David, like a crab. Scuttling and dodging and squirming. There were no more friendly visits, from Bonnie - no more muffins or words of advice. She would wave to him, sometimes, when he saw her hanging out her washing or backing her car down the driveway. She would greet him at the supermarket: Hello, David, how are you? Good. Well, I'd best be on my way.

He watched her now - watched her rise and go to collect a dessert bowl - and something compelled him to follow her. She failed to notice him, at first, because she was too busy scanning the colourful range of sweets laid out under the serving hatch. When he asked her to identify them she jumped, and looked embarrassed.

'Oh, well, that's pumpkin pie, and that's lemon meringue pie, and those are fudge brownies - chocolate, of course - and walnut muffins, and peach squares. And I think that's snow pudding, but I'm not sure.'

'I haven't had any of *your* muffins, lately,' David said, watching her carefully. She shrugged and smiled, but the smile was not a happy one.

'Those are my carnival muffins,' she replied, with heavy humour. 'Now that the carnival's finished -'

'You don't need me any more? Or you don't need my house any more?'

Bonnie was spooning strawberries into her bowl. By doing this, she was able to avoid his eye.

'I'm always so busy in the summer,' she said. 'Never a spare moment, what with the Animal Shelter and Floyd's mom - she always comes down here to visit - and the Auxiliary and all the quilts and blankets and rugs to be cleaned -'

'Why don't you just come out and say it, Bonnie?' David kept his voice low and even. 'Why don't you tell me what you really think?'

Still she refused to look up, slapping cream onto her straw-berries as if her life depended on it. 'I don't know what you're talking about.'

'Oh, yes you do. You don't want to see me, because you've heard that I'm homosexual.'

'That's got nothing to do with anything.'

'Did it even occur to you to ask *me* about this?' David was trying to remain calm. 'Didn't you think: I ought to go and ask David for his side of the story?'

At last she looked up. Her brow was puckered. Her eyes were concerned. 'You mean it's not true?' she said, and David suddenly lost his temper.

'That's all that matters to you, isn't it?' he hissed. 'Not my feelings or my friendship or anything else – it's what I do with my dick! Well, if you must know, I *am* gay, and I'm not ashamed of it, and if you don't like it, you know what you can do!'

'Not ashamed of it? Not *ashamed* of it?' Somehow Bonnie managed to pack a lot of emotion into a mere whisper. 'If you're not ashamed, why didn't you tell me? All this time, and you didn't say a word!'

'Why should I?'

'Because it's important! How would you feel? One minute I'm warning you about that Beaton man, and the next minute I'm hearing this!' Bonnie's voice rose to a squeak. 'Can't you see how awkward it is? I didn't even know!'

'So what?' David was genuinely confused. 'What difference does that make?'

'It's false pretences,' she snapped, her gaze flicking around nervously. Keith Hughes was heading their way. 'It's living a lie. You were trying to look like something you're not.'

'And what would that be?' David gasped, almost choking with anger. 'A normal human being?'

'Look, this isn't the time or the place.'

'Are you -'

'I don't want to discuss it.'

She turned on her heel just as Keith arrived at the dessert table. He selected a slice of pie and a peach square; glancing at David's empty bowl, he said something about how hard it was to choose.

'Pardon?'

'There's such a big choice. It's a hard decision.'

'Oh.' David heard him almost without understanding. Blindly he grabbed the nearest spoon, and served himself a dollop of pudding. He was sick with rage. Shaking with it. Even his pent-up sense of betrayal was nothing compared to that sudden, horrific insight into the way her mind worked. Obviously one had to *classify* oneself, at the very outset, so people (decent people?) could modify their behaviour in a suitable fashion. In this day and age . . . in a civilised country . . .

He returned to his seat; slammed his bowl down. Beside him Alice turned her head, and he could sense her questioning glance. But he had set his sights on Floyd.

'Oh - Floyd?'

Across the table, Floyd looked up.

'I said goodbye to Lindsay Beaton this evening.' David spoke in loud, carrying tones. 'He told me to give you a big, wet kiss, but I never kiss on the first date. So can I book you for the first dance, instead?'

A deathly silence. Floyd turned white, then mauve. Gwen gave a strangled laugh.

David wiped his mouth on his napkin, and rose to his feet. 'As a matter of fact,' he said, in a trembling voice, 'I'm feeling a bit sick. In the gut. Funny how some things are so hard to stomach.'

There was nothing else to do after that, except leave.

* * *

The Kempton County Exhibition was always held in August. It was fairly modest, as agricultural shows go, because the region specialised in fishing and forestry. Nevertheless, the 'Ex' (as it was called) still rated some sort of coverage in the *Kempton Gazette*, and on the third day of its five-day span Alice devoted an entire afternoon to it, rolling up to the gates at about half past one.

But there were no parking spots within easy walking distance of the grounds. Alice had to drive all the way past the second Baptist church (Watervale had two Baptist churches) before she found a space that was big enough for her generously proportioned Chevrolet. Saturday, she thought – I should have realised. She had brought a hat, and sunglasses; a bottle of water was tucked into her camera bag. On her way back to the Exhibition she heard blue jays fighting, but as she drew closer to the lofty wire fence, the clamour of excited children drowned out every other noise.

At the gates she found Eunice Wheelhouse in the ticket booth, talking to her cousin Delbert. Eunice offered her a watery, reproachful smile.

'Walter told me not to charge you,' she said, and Alice slunk away quickly. She found Eunice an uncomfortable companion, nowadays; Raylene's Animal Shelter story lay like a dead whale between them. As for Delbert, she had seen enough of him to last her a lifetime. If he wanted an audience for his views on local government or the casino issue, he could talk to someone else for a change.

The 'Ex' was divided into four sections: the horse ring, the animal sheds, the big hall and the little hall. Interminable riding events were taking place in the horse ring; the animal sheds were full of cattle and horses - mostly oxen and cart horses, as befitted a logging county. There were a few pens of sheep, one of goats and two of pigs, but these animals were the product of hobby farms, and most of them had pet names. A young boy was selling rabbits.

Alice wandered among the titanic backsides of the Clydesdales, marvelling at their size (and avoiding manure), before moving on to the little hall. This building - dedicated to some long-dead Wheelhouse - contained all the gardening, craft and flower displays. Unfortunately, the flowers were already beginning to wilt: the first-prize zinnia looked like a dead tarantula, and some of the rhododendrons like dirty wet tissues. Alice thought the flower arrangements far more interesting. Winnie Rudd and her crew had excelled themselves, this year, and apart from the usual one-word classifications - 'Fragrance', 'Elegance', 'Tranquillity' - there were several more interesting, complex themes. 'Streets of London' was one of them. So were 'Come Fly with Me' and 'From the Bible', the latter being divided into three subsections. 'Jesus casting out the moneylenders' was the most popular: people had employed a lot of columns, golden coins and peacock feathers to good effect.

'Alice!' It was Adelia McNeil. She was standing near the quilt display with her sister-in-law Bonnie, and Ida Wheelhouse. Alice had never much cared for Ida, but she put on her social face, and greeted them all with a polite smile.

'Hello, Dell. Ida. Hello, Bonnie.'

'We're just admiring Doreen Ruggles' quilt,' Adelia continued. 'Isn't it beautiful?'

'Beautiful.'

It was, indeed, a work of art: all the quilts were works of art. Alice could appreciate that, but was lost when it came to technicalities. She stood mute as Adelia and Bonnie discussed the Jacob's ladder, log cabin, and monkey wrench motifs.

'Of course Doreen designs her own patterns,' Bonnie remarked, and went on to reveal that an American tourist had paid Doreen three thousand dollars for a grapevine quilt. It was agreed that Doreen would have to make many more three-thousand-dollar quilts, after Ross Reid's announcement - which was bound to affect Enos - and all at once Alice was deep in yet another debate concerning the new fishing quotas.

'From 26 000 tonnes to 15 000 tonnes! In the whole of the western province!'

'But that's just dragger fishermen. Isn't that just draggers?'

'It's the cod quota. The pollack quota is something else . . .'

'You're lucky Floyd's not fishing, any more,' Ida sighed. 'He's pretty well settled into logging now, isn't he?'

'Yes.'

'Oh, Floyd,' said Adelia, with a sneaky, sidelong glance. 'Floyd's found his niche, all right.' And she smiled as Bonnie bade them an abrupt farewell, saying that she had to go and look for her son.

'Touchy,' Adelia remarked, as soon as Bonnie was out of earshot. 'Ever since that kissing business.'

'Oh, yes.' Ida turned to Alice, her eyes wide. 'Did you hear what happened? Apparently he kissed that fellow - that teacher -'

'No, no.' Adelia corrected. 'The teacher kissed him. Right on the mouth.'

'No one *kissed* anyone.' Alice struggled to keep calm. 'I was there, at the table. It was a silly joke.'

'Well, we weren't at the table, but Bob said the teacher rushed off, and then Floyd -'

'Nothing happened,' Alice said coldly. 'Believe me.'

'Are you sure?'

'Quite sure.'

Infuriated by Adelia's sceptical stare, Alice checked her watch, said goodbye, and left the building. What a bunch of blackflies they were! Gossip, gossip, gossip. Alice had been fending off inquiries on just this subject for days: it was out in the open now, with a vengeance. People were talking about David all over town, although they were chiefly interested in his relationship with Floyd - and, of course, with herself.

David had not revealed to Alice the motive behind his outburst. She had followed him out of the fire hall, and walked back home with him, but for the most part he had been silent, practically slamming the door in her face. Later, when calling up to apologise, he had laughed, and said some defiant things about what he would do when questioned in public. But he seemed reluctant to talk about Floyd. Or, indeed, Bonnie. 'It wasn't Floyd, it was Bonnie,' he had revealed. 'It was stupid. A stupid argument.' But that was all he would say.

Alice went into the big hall, where the ox-pull was being held. The tiers of seats were packed with spectators; a pair of oxen had been harnessed to a kind of wooden cradle, which was loaded with blocks of concrete. Each time the oxen completed a measured haul of unvarying length, the number of blocks grew. It was a trial of strength which Alice could not enjoy, because every time she looked at the straining beasts, under the cracking whip, she thought of her own workload. Her sympathies were with the oxen.

But she took several photographs, and was about to leave when Mike Wylie hailed her.

'Alice! How's it going?'

'Hello, Mike.'

'Great editorial, last week. Just terrific.'

'Thank you.'

'You're damned right, you know. Can't expect the Tourism Committee to clean up the streets and improve the service at Foodland. Everyone's got to make an effort, if we want to pull in the bucks.'

Since this was, effectively, what Alice herself had written, she could do nothing but agree.

'By the way,' he continued, 'I had a big laugh about what I said to you last time we met. About your friend David.' He grinned. 'Lots of egg on faces now! I was right all along. Didn't think you were seeing him.'

Alice grunted.

'And now Gwen tells me he's having some sort of thing with Floyd McNeil. Floyd McNeil! Not exactly a pin-up boy, I would have thought –'

'That's not true, Mike.' Alice was so sick and tired of the whole subject that she barely had the strength to argue. 'Gwen's got it all wrong – she can't have heard him. It was a stupid joke.'

'Really? But someone said he went off somewhere with that antique dealer –'

'David is gay, Mike. No one denies that. But he's not involved with Floyd McNeil.' Alice pushed past him. 'Now if you don't mind, I've got a lot of work to do.'

And that's no lie, she thought, as she made her way back through the animal sheds. In fact I need a vacation. Perhaps if I take a week off – if I go and visit Isabelle in Moncton, or the family in Georgetown. Or Louise, perhaps . . . ?

No. Not Louise. Anybody but Louise.

She realised suddenly that the man tugging at his cap in front of her was Oakey Marshall.

'Oakey!'

'Alice.'

'How are you keeping?'

'Fine,' said Oakey, who looked anything but fine. He looked thin and exhausted; his face sagged like a bloodhound's.

'You're not sick?'

'No.'

'But you seem tired.'

Oakey gazed at her, reflectively. 'No more'n you,' he retorted, and she laughed.

'Yes. Well, I've been pretty busy.'

'Always are, in the summer.'

'I guess so.'

'You should try and slow down.' He surveyed the scene around him with pale, expressionless eyes. 'Nothin' to see here that hasn't happened before.'

Again Alice laughed. 'Are you advising me to recycle?' she said, and he shrugged.

'Cows are always cows.'

'Yes they are, but if I ran a picture of someone in last year's shirt, there'd be hell to pay. You know what it's like around here, Oakey. They never miss a trick.'

He nodded. 'They sure don't,' he sighed. Then he tucked his hands into his pockets. 'Well,' he said, 'it was good seein' you.'

'Likewise.'

'Take care, now.'

'You too.'

And he walked away. Alice watched him go, feeling strangely comforted. Whatever they said about Oakey, he was a kind man. A kind man and a good neighbour, who would never even *think* of trying to pump her for information.

Thank God, she thought, that someone in this county doesn't give a damn about David's sexual preferences.

* * *

Every year, in August, a meteor shower passes over eastern Canada. For a week or more the night skies are full of shooting stars - more shooting stars than most people, under normal circumstances, would see in a year. As Lindsay had put it, when discussing the phenomenon: 'It's like whale watching. You're guaranteed at least one.'

David had never actually seen a shooting star. Living in Sydney, he rarely even saw stars, let alone shooting ones; the city's radiance - the street lights and the glowing neon - tended to bleach even the darkest sky, fading all but the most robust constellations and turning black into a washed-out, charcoal grey. So the prospect of a star-show made him very excited. He tried not to air his feelings too much (since his enthusiastic comments had been greeted by blank, uncomprehending stares), but he kept an eye on the weather channel, which gave regular updates on the meteor shower's progress. When it was right overhead, and was therefore at its peak, he borrowed a pair of binoculars from Gordon Blanchard and went off to find the perfect viewing space.

But he had not reckoned on the efficiency of the local council. He had not registered the fact that the streets, even in Scotsville, were very well lit. There were lamps everywhere, and in those few areas where there were no lamps there were always trees, overhanging trees, great bushy summer trees that blocked out most of the sky. He drove all around Scotsville without finding the right spot; then he ventured farther out, towards Sable Cove, without success. At last he found a small hill on the Watervale road, where the houses (or were they farms?) stood in open paddocks, and the street lamps were as widely spaced as the trees. He parked a few metres from someone's letterbox, and positioned himself exactly halfway between the two nearest lamps.

Then he waited.

The show, he soon realised, was not going to be quite as spectacular as he had envisaged. The sky was not exactly awash with shooting stars; they did not fall like snow, or confetti. One would fall, and then - perhaps three minutes later - another would follow its example. And they tended to fall at different points of the compass, so that David was always catching them out of the corner of his eye rather than in the lenses of his binoculars.

Still, there was enough activity to keep him occupied. He would have enjoyed himself thoroughly if not for the crick in his neck, and the knowledge that he was providing something of a spectacle for passing traffic. Not that there was very much traffic (because it was, after all, ten thirty) but of the dozen or so vehicles that did thunder by, at least half slowed down as they approached David.

I guess it's pretty late, he thought. They're probably wondering what the hell I'm up to. Then he repeated to himself Alice's well-used phrase - 'Not much excitement around Kempton' - and turned his back to the road, focusing instead on the northern sky, which was only slightly paler than the distant black treetops plastered against it. He could hear nothing but wind, and crickets, and a dog barking. Off to his left, a golden window marked the location of someone's house.

Presently the sound of an approaching engine reached his ears. He tried to ignore it, concentrating on the Milky Way (he had never really looked at the Milky Way), but as it slowed, and idled, he felt compelled to turn around.

A light-coloured ute was sitting on the other side of the road; inside it, two dark shapes were barely recognisable as passengers. David sensed that they were staring at him. But before anything could be said the ute began to move again, very slowly, disappearing over the crest of the hill.

David thought nothing more about it until it reappeared, about five minutes later. This time it was on his side of the road. It stopped near his car, its tyres crunching on kerbside gravel. Someone leaned out of the window.

'Hey!' A male voice. 'What're you doin'?'

'I'm – I'm watching the stars.'

'What?'

'I'm star-gazing.'

There was a pause. The head withdrew. There seemed to be some kind of discussion. Then the ute moved off, slowed, and stopped again. It backed up.

'Hey!' the same voice barked. 'Are you that faggot teacher?'

David froze.

'Because if you keep on hangin' round here, looking for business, you're gonna get your head kicked in.'

There was a long pause. David thought: If I run for the car, will that encourage them? How far is the house? What if I scream – will somebody hear me?

Suddenly the ute roared to life. It swung back on to the road with a squeal of tyres, and disappeared into the darkness. David moved just as quickly. He ran to his car, jumped inside, and had completed a U-turn before the driver's door was even shut. His hands were trembling. His heart was racing. Conscious that he was in a highly emotional state, he tried to focus all his efforts on speed and distance, pushing everything else to the back of his mind. He had to get home. Once he was home, he could think about what had happened. Once he was home, he could collapse into a heap.

It was the worst drive he could remember (and he had

experienced quite a few drunken drag races around Bondi, at three o'clock in the morning). Somehow he reached Maureen's house; as soon as he switched off the engine, he began to feel dizzy. Then he began to feel scared. Would they be waiting for him? Did they know where he lived? Clutching his keys like a weapon, he stumbled out of the car and up the front steps, almost deafened by the pounding of blood in his ears.

As soon as he was inside he sank down, his back to the wall, and moaned.

He was thinking about Terry, in hospital. Terry was one of his mother's friends - not a close friend, more of a friend of a friend, but still one of the magic circle. He had been caught in a park, and bashed until he lost an eye. He had also lost the use of one kidney. According to Terry, the culprits had been teenagers, no more than sixteen or seventeen. Nine in all, though two of them had seemed to hang back. They had shouted insults - 'Ass-fucker! Ass-fucker!' - and other, incomprehensible things. 'I'm afraid my knowledge of the latest cant terms is rather underdeveloped,' Terry had mumbled, through broken teeth, trying to smile.

After seeing Terry, David's nightmares had changed. He could still feel the shock - the visceral crunch - that had deprived him of speech when he first looked at Terry's face. It had changed his habits, ever so slightly: he kept his eyes peeled, avoided certain suburbs, reduced his liquor intake. But he had never encountered his nightmares in real life . . . until now.

Oh, Jesus, he thought. Oh, Jesus, they know who I am. What am I going to do? What if they come here? He went to the phone and called his mother, but she was out. He called

Gus, but no one was there. He called Alice, and almost cried with relief when she answered.

'Hello?'

'Oh, Alice - God - the most awful thing -'

'David?'

'I thought they were going to bash me!'

'What?'

David described what had happened to him. He described what had happened to Terry. Curled up on the sofa, a cushion on his lap, he revealed, for the first time, what Bonnie had said, and how he felt about it. Everything came gushing out, like verbal vomit, bringing an enormous sense of relief.

'She was like: Why didn't you tell me, David? Why wasn't I *informed*? And I'm like: What difference does it make? But it makes one hell of a difference to *her*, you see, because she was treating me like some kind of normal person, right?'

'Mmmm.'

'I mean, it's not that she won't talk to me, but she wants to talk to me in the right way, or something - I don't know - she's fucked in the head, it's unbelievable, and she does all this community shit, this Save the Animals . . .' David could feel the tears rising. 'She said: "If you aren't ashamed of yourself, then why didn't you tell me?"'

'Oh, David.'

'It's such a fucker - God - but I wouldn't even care, I wouldn't even *care* . . .' Suddenly he was crying in earnest. 'Except that Gus hasn't called, he hasn't written, he doesn't give a shit. It's so obvious. He doesn't give a flying fuck about me, never has. I kept writing and he didn't write back and then I thought, Well, two can play at that game, we'll see who cracks first, but it's me! It's always me!'

'I'm sorry. I'm sorry, David.'

'It's so stupid. I can't believe how stupid I am. He's *married*, for God's sake, what was I expecting? All he wants is a quick fuck every so often, and he's probably found someone else for that. Oh, God, I'm just - I just can't -'

'David? I'm coming over.'

'No, no -'

'I'm coming over. I'll be over in a few minutes.'

'You don't have to. I'm all right.'

'Well, I'm not. I'm feeling a bit blue, this evening.' Alice spoke firmly. 'It will do us both good.'

Half an hour later she arrived with her toothbrush and pyjamas. She made him tea and gave him one of Maureen's Valiums; she ran him a bath and filled it with soothing oils (which she supplied herself). Then, after he had cleaned his teeth and crawled into bed, she came to sit with him.

'Don't worry,' she said. 'I'm right here.'

'Aren't you going to sleep?' he asked drowsily.

'Soon. Very soon.'

'The other beds aren't made. The sheets are in the hall cupboard -'

'Shh. I know where the sheets are.'

'. . . pillows . . .'

'Shh.'

He drifted off to the creak of her rocking chair.

September

Oakey went away at the beginning of September. Before he did, he visited Alice one night when she was writing up her journal (. . . *The acorns are out, and the squirrels are busy. Poor David called me yesterday, to complain about rats in his ceiling, but they were squirrels rolling acorns. He said they're driving him mad . . .*), knocking on the door with a diffident little tap that she failed to hear, at first. Absorbed in her account of a squirrel in a pear tree, she was deaf to everything but the human voice, and only noticed him when he began to call her name.

'Alice? Are you there?'

'Oh!' She jumped up, almost spilling her tea, and ran to let him in. 'I'm sorry, I was just - I was down the back . . .'

'It's okay.' He hovered awkwardly, as if reluctant to enter her living room. He was not wearing his baseball cap. 'Sorry to bother you, at this hour, but I wanted to ask -'

'Come in.'

'Oh no. This won't take a minute.' Smoothing his moustache with one bony hand, he said abruptly: 'I'm goin' away.'

'Uh-huh.'

'For two weeks.'

'*Two weeks?*' Alice was astonished. As far as she knew, Oakey had never gone away for more than three days at a time. Not since his brief stint at Dalhousie. 'Where are you going?'

'On vacation,' he replied. 'Just . . . travellin' around.'

'I see.' Alice studied him, but was unable to glean anything more from his gaunt, gingery, unremarkable face. She sensed, however, that something had happened.

'Are you all right, Oakey?'

'Sure. I'm fine. I need a break, is all.' He produced a set of keys from his pocket. 'Could you collect the mail, while I'm gone? And watch the house? In case there's another fire, or somethin'.'

'I'd be happy to.'

'Thanks.'

'What about Tripod? Do you want me to look after him?'

Oakey was already backing out the door. 'Hell, no,' he said. 'I've put him in Ernie's kennels.'

'You have?' Alice frowned. 'When are you leaving?'

'Tomorrow.'

'*Tomorrow?*'

'If you wanna reach me,' he continued, retreating down the front steps, 'just call Maureen. She'll know where I am.'

'But –'

'I'll see you later.'

And he disappeared. Alice was left standing, staring, turning things over in her head – but she could find no explanation for Oakey's peculiar conduct. So she went back inside and wrote it all down, in painstaking detail, just underneath

her description of the sticky little squirrel with its enormous
pear.

*Oakey dropped by a few minutes ago. He was dressed in old brown
corduroys and one of Foster's shirts. No baseball cap. He seemed very
nervous, and told me that he was going away. 'Where to?' I said. He said:
'On vacation.' Wouldn't tell me where . . .*

On reflection, she wondered if 'nervous' was quite the
right word. 'Unsettled', perhaps, was a better one. Or
'disturbed'. At any rate, not happy - not the way a man on
vacation might be expected to look.

Over the next fortnight Alice faithfully observed her
duties, making a quick tour of Oakey's house every evening to
check for forced locks or broken windows. She also collected
the mail, which was all bills and advertising catalogues. Then,
as the third week began to pass, she grew concerned. Where
was Oakey? There had been no message - no postcard or telephone call. If he had decided to lengthen his trip, surely he
would have told her?

'Oh, he's probably up in the Northwest Territories, skinnin'
polar bears,' Fairlie McNeil remarked. 'That's the sort of thing
old Oakey would do for a vacation. I bet there isn't a phone
within three hundred miles of where he is.' A laugh. A wave
of the hand. 'I wouldn't worry. Not yet.'

But Alice did worry. She talked to Raylene, who said: 'He's
probably down in South America. He's probably been shot.'
She talked to Erica, who said: 'Why don't you call Maureen?'
So she called Maureen, who was airily unconcerned. 'Oh, he'll
be back,' she said. 'I spoke to him a couple of days ago.'

'You did?'

'He - he went further than he planned. He's in Manitoba.'

'Really?'

'He should have called you. I guess he forgot.'

'But what about Tripod? Has Oakey called the kennels?'

'Oh.' A pause. 'Well . . . could you take care of that, Alice? Until he gets back? I know he won't be much longer.' And Maureen went on to talk about her life in Sydney: about the beautiful jasmine bush in her garden, and the terrible rudeness of the drivers, and the needle exchange at the local church. She chattered on, with unusual prolixity, about having to test all the cleaning products - which had different names, in Australia - to find something that approximated her favourite Canadian brands. If Alice had not known better, she would have suspected Maureen of trying to distract her.

It was a notion that did nothing to relieve the niggling worry at the back of her mind.

For a few days she let it sit there, like a rat in a box; then one evening, at David's, she finally opened the box, expressing her concerns once again.

'How do you mean she was odd?' said David, referring to Maureen. 'Do you think she was lying?'

'No. That is . . . I don't know.' Alice reviewed the exchange as she remembered it, picking out pauses here and inflections there. 'What I mean is, I don't think she was quite as - as calm as she was trying to appear. That's all.' She shrugged. 'It could have been something else. Something else could have been bothering her.'

'You could be right.' David shook his head. 'I've been talking to Mum, and she says Maureen's changed. It used to be all sweetness and light, over there - tea and muffins from morning till night, with a huge crowd of churchy friends from some choir Maureen goes to. But now everything seems to have quietened down.' He swung his grasshopper legs over the edge of the chesterfield, and leaned forward. 'How long has Oakey been gone now? Three weeks?'

'Yes.'

'Maybe you should report him missing.'

'Maybe.'

'Or we could check inside the house, first.' David's face brightened; Alice knew that he was thinking about his TV. 'Maybe we'll find some clue, inside the house!'

'Either that or your television,' Alice retorted, with a smile, and he grinned back.

'So we kill two birds with one stone. Is that a problem?'

'I guess not.' Alice conceded that Oakey might have left a travel brochure or telephone number which could prove helpful. She also felt that it was time to look for chequebooks and bank statements, because sooner or later she was going to have to start paying Oakey's bills.

Perhaps, she thought, we really should go take a peek.

'Does he have a credit card?' David inquired, as he pulled on his jacket. 'You can tell where people have been, from their credit card bills.'

'Credit card!' Alice was amused. 'You wouldn't see a Marshall with a credit card. They don't believe in credit. Neither a borrower nor a lender be - that's their motto.'

She and David agreed to go in separate cars, so that David could drive himself back afterwards. It was a spur-of-the-moment thing. Through the deepening twilight they headed for Oakey Marshall's house, arriving there just as it began to rain. The dull, restless waters of Sable Cove spluttered and hissed along the shingle. A damp wind blew. A dog howled, somewhere in the distance.

'We should have done this tomorrow,' David said, locking his car door. 'It's too creepy. Don't you find it creepy?'

'You mean the weather?'

'The house. The weather. Everything.'

'You've been watching too many horror movies.' They had parked in Alice's driveway; Oakey's keys were in her dresser. But she fetched them and crossed the yard to Oakey's house, past the site of his septic tank, past the ashy square where his barn had been, until she arrived at his back door, where David was waiting.

She tried several keys before she found the right one. It slipped into the lock easily enough, but was difficult to turn. At last David had to take over, employing a great deal of force and making a great deal of noise.

'There must be a trick to it,' he panted, as the door swung open. 'You probably have to push it back, or pull it forward or something.' A stale, woody smell greeted them – a smell overlaid with dog and oilskins. There were oilskins hanging behind the door.

Alice groped for a light switch, and found it quickly enough. When she turned it on she saw that they were standing in a kitchen, a large kitchen, full of fifty-year-old cupboards. The cupboards were painted pale green, and were built against three of the four walls. There was an old-fashioned range, a pot-bellied stove, and an ancient-looking fridge.

At least it's not an ice chest, Alice thought.

'Wow,' said David. 'Cool.' He flicked through the calendar that hung over the sink, but it revealed nothing. There were

Curling Club dates scribbled through the year, a doctor's appointment ('Significant?' Alice wondered aloud), and several reminders about things like tune-ups, tax returns and vehicle registration. The kitchen table was bare. There were no fridge magnets, with or without notes underneath them. When David began to check in the drawers, he found an impenetrable mess of string, wire, nails, scissors, screwdrivers, tools, plugs, rubber bands, safety pins, cotton reels, pencil stubs and old receipts.

'I don't know,' he said, peering into this confusion. 'There doesn't seem to be anything . . .'

'We'll check the phone,' Alice decided. 'He may have left something near the phone.'

'Where's that?'

'I'm not sure.'

They pressed on, into a room that was probably the dining room. There was no dining suite, although dents in the wooden floor suggested that a table had once stood in the centre of the room, under the hanging bulb. Dark patches on the wallpaper marked those spots where pieces of furniture had once been positioned, shielding the wall from the western sunlight. There was a sense of things missing - of absence and loss. The corners were silted up with piles of old napkins and runners and tea-towels, doilies and tablecloths, coasters, corkscrews, cutlery tied together with faded ribbon. They looked very forlorn, dumped there like rubbish, as if they had been left behind by someone. For some reason.

The living room was the same. It contained a few battered, art deco china cabinets, full of old books and magazines; a collapsing chesterfield; a rug; a bamboo side table; an old meat safe supporting a cheap Sears table lamp. But there were mysterious, flattened shapes on the rug. There was a record player, but no speakers or other stereo equipment. And the telephone was sitting on the floor.

'Does this . . . ?' David hesitated. 'Does this look odd to you?'

'Yes.'

'There's stuff missing. There's got to be.' He opened the door of a china cabinet. 'You don't think he's left for good? Just packed up all the nice stuff and gone?'

'Oh no.' Alice was startled. 'Why would he do that? Besides, he didn't pack anything, except a suitcase. I saw him leave.'

'What about the phone? What about the phone books?'

Alice checked them. 'Nothing.'

'I'm going to look in the basement,' David announced. 'That's where he said my TV was. How would you get to the basement?'

'There must be a door in the kitchen. Or under the stairs.' The door, in fact, was under the main staircase, which divided the enormous house in two; as soon as Alice discovered and opened it, the damp, earthy smell that filled her nostrils told her that the basement was unfinished.

Sure enough, they found a dark, cavernous space with an earth floor and unplastered granite walls. They also found a can of paint, a few rakes and shovels, a roll of black plastic, a pile of kindling and a broken toboggan. But no TV.

'No TV.'

'I don't believe this.' David shook his head. 'If it's not here, where is it?'

'Upstairs, perhaps. In his bedroom.'

'Let's take a look.'

On their way to the top floor, Alice commented on the absence of any furnace. She found it hard to believe that Oakey heated the whole house with one wood-burning stove and a couple of fireplaces. But when they reached the landing, and looked into the first bedroom, she saw that this was, in fact, the case.

The bedroom was built right over the kitchen, and a small hole had been cut in the floor so that the heat could rise.

'Judas Priest,' she said. 'I never knew he lived like this.'

'Couldn't he afford a furnace?'

'I don't know.' She surveyed the room and its contents: the single bed under its faded quilt, the sagging velvet curtains (living-room curtains?), the washstand, the highboy. There were winter clothes in the highboy – shoeboxes full of old shoes and birthday cards under the bed. Alice looked through the birthday cards. (From Maureen, from Foster, from Judith.) 'That's the sister who died young,' she observed.

'Nothing here.'

'No.'

'He would have taken his brushes and stuff with him.'

They searched the rest of the house. There were five bedrooms, but only two had fireplaces. One of the bedrooms was full of kindling. Another contained broken furniture. The smallest was still habitable; Alice wondered, as she examined the three-quarter brass bedstead with its flock mattress, whether it was Foster's old room. She was beginning to get a feel for the house – she sensed that, long ago, someone very neat and houseproud had painted the lavish woodwork and hung the pretty floral wallpaper (now grimy and faded). Oakey's mother, perhaps? Digging through the hall closet, poking around the garage, checking the kitchen cupboards, she registered other possible absences: no electric fan or kettle, no radio, no spare quilts, no washing machine, no dryer. The snow-blower was undoubtedly gone, as were the lovely big lawn-mower, and the shotguns. Oakey had had several shotguns, but they were nowhere to be found.

'Perhaps he's taken them,' David conjectured. 'For hunting.'

'Perhaps.'

'Unless he's *sold* them.' He and Alice exchanged a long, speculative glance. 'Do you think he's sold them?'

'It's starting to look that way.' They were back in the kitchen, among the pale-green cupboards and antique appliances. 'You know what's missing? The things that you don't really *need*. You don't really need a snow-blower - you can survive without it. You don't really need an electric kettle, or a shotgun, or a washing machine, or a television -'

'But that was Maureen's television!' David cried, and gasped as the full implications sank in. 'If Oakey's sold her TV,' he said, 'would he have told her about it?'

'I don't know.'

'There's something strange going on.' David spoke in hushed, uneasy tones. 'The question is, are they both involved, or is it just him?'

They fell silent. The refrigerator hummed. The rain pattered against the windowpanes. The old house creaked.

'I'll ask Maureen if she knows what's going on,' Alice said at last, slowly. 'Then it's up to her. She is his sister, after all.'

'Do you think he's been gambling?'

'I don't know.'

'Perhaps it really is drugs! Like Raylene said!'

'Don't be silly.' Alice was feeling confused and annoyed. She ushered David out of the kitchen and locked the door behind them, struggling (again) with the ill-fitting key. Then they both ran back to her house through the pouring rain, which was blowing straight off the water and tasted faintly of salt.

Her cheap little bungalow seemed warm and welcoming, after Oakey's spartan bedroom.

'I think we deserve a drink,' she said. 'A drop of the Bailey's? Or I've got some port - somebody's Christmas present.'

'Bailey's, please.'

'And some shortbread?' Alice had been stocking up on cookies and candy, now that she was seeing so much of David. He had a very sweet tooth for someone so thin.

'Yum,' he said.

She filled her two remaining liqueur glasses, dumped the shortbread onto a plate, and settled down beside David on the chesterfield. They sat there for a while, sipping and chewing, listening to the wind as it whistled through the cracks in her window frames. Every so often the lights would flicker.

'Nasty storm,' said David.

'Sure is.'

'I hope the driving's not too bad. I hope it calms down a bit.'

'If it doesn't, you can always stay here.' Alice drained her glass, and put her feet up on the coffee table.

She was beginning to feel drowsy.

'Alice?'

'Mmmm?'

'Do you think this business with the television - and the guns, and stuff - do you think it has something to do with Oakey going away?'

'I don't know.' She turned her head, smiling as she saw the mess that David's hair was in. He looked like a drowned rat. 'Oakey's never been away before. But there might not be a connection.'

'I think there is,' said David.

So, on reflection, did Alice.

* * *

David's new class was a sixth-grade class, and it was difficult. It contained three students who had been made to repeat a year - one of them slightly simple, one hyperactive, and one a terror with a shorn head and a deprived background. This child, whose name was Stanley, could disrupt an entire afternoon's work by dropping a single 'fuck' or 'bullshit' into an earnest discussion about rain gauges. He was also violent, and would attack his classmates with a savagery that frightened David. When Stanley was in a rage, nothing could reach him: he was like a wild animal. Even the counsellor called in to address the problem was making very little headway.

For David, dealing with Stanley became his number one chore - something that ate up the greatest proportion of his time and energy at work. Not that he hated the boy. He pitied him, and was moved almost to tears by those odd, infrequent occasions when Stanley would come to him with a request or a query (phrased in that curiously broken, husky voice), and tug at his sleeve, and receive an answer with a shy little smile or a look of awe, the effort of concentration written clearly on his puckered brow. When this happened, David wanted to hug him.

But all too often their exchanges were sharp and angry - confrontations rather than discussions. Most of the time David had the last word. Usually he emerged the victor. Only once, in the boys' washroom, did Stanley strike a blow that left David gasping for breath.

It was at lunchtime, and David was on duty. All morning he had been trying to quell Stanley's talk of deer hunting, and how this year he would be 'doing' the hunters' safety course. Every October, the Fish and Game Association ran a hunters' safety course which enrolled people as young as twelve; small-game licences, however, were only available to those aged fourteen and over. Most of the boys in the school were waiting for the glorious moment when they would be issued with their licences - and Stanley was closer to that magic age than anyone else in the student body. As a result, hunting was his favourite subject. He had accompanied his father on many hunts, which he would describe in gory detail whenever the opportunity presented itself.

So David tried to make sure that such opportunities were few and far between. He found Stanley's descriptions of blood-trails and skinning knives highly disturbing. Most boys are bloodthirsty, but Stanley's relish when it came to steaming guts and braincases worried him. Without undermining the boy's knowledge and prestige in this rather specialised area, he was careful to steer the conversation away from hunting whenever the subject arose. Unfortunately, as October loomed, the topic arose more and more frequently.

It therefore came as no surprise to David that when he opened the washroom door, he heard Stanley's voice talking about bolts and triggers. But he was surprised to see Stanley carrying an air rifle.

'What the hell . . . ?' he exclaimed. 'What are you doing with that thing?'

For a second nobody moved. Then Stanley darted forward, and tried to dodge past, but was too slow; David grabbed the boy and wrenched the gun from his grip. Stanley's two friends stood petrified.

'Now, Stanley,' David said. 'You know the rules -'

'Give it back!'

'No guns on school premises.'

'Give it!'

'I can't give it back to you until the end of the day.'

Stanley kicked out, and missed. His face began to turn an ominous shade of dusky red. 'You better give it to me!' he roared. 'You better!'

'Calm down. It's yours, you'll get it back. But not until the end of the day.'

'Faggot!'

David, who had heard this insult tossed around the schoolyard many times (by children who had no idea of its meaning, or correct application), decided to ignore it.

'I won't report you to Mr Blanchard, as long as you promise not to bring it here again -'

'Sissy! You're just scared of guns, you queer! I know about you, you faggot! Faggot!'

David was so appalled that he loosened his grip, and Stanley charged out of the washroom. In the silence that followed, David could hear the *drip-drip-drip* of a leaky tap. He looked over to where Stanley's friends (Peter and Alex) stood frozen against the wall.

'You know the rules about guns,' he said wearily. 'Don't encourage him.' Then he flicked his hand, and they scampered away - leaving him alone with the air rifle.

He did not report the incident. That afternoon he returned the rifle to Stanley (after removing the ammunition), warning him that if he ever brought it to school again, he would be banned from the hockey team. Stanley responded with a grunt. David knew better than to bring up the 'faggot' issue, but on his way home began to wonder if something should be said at the next staff meeting. The subject of his own sexuality had been studiously avoided since the Floyd McNeil affair, more out of delicacy than disgust. Nevertheless, it was perhaps time to point out that the sex education curriculum was somewhat lacking, in certain areas.

Of course, the problem was really at home, not at school. David was under no illusions as to where Stanley's insult had come from. Stanley was just a mouthpiece - his family was the real culprit. His father . . . good God, his father could have been one of those shadowy figures in the pick-up truck!

David swung Maureen's car into Maureen's driveway, parked it near her back door, and went to collect the mail. There was only one envelope in the letterbox, and it was addressed to him. The stamp was Australian. The name on the back was Gus de Souza.

With trembling hands, David ripped it open. *Dear Dave*, he read. *I'm sorry I haven't done this before, or called you or anything. It's been a complete shitstorm, around here . . .*

Suddenly a horn blared. Looking up, David saw Bob Wheelhouse waving from his big American tank. David smiled, and bolted into the house. He wanted to read his letter in private.

. . . Tina is driving me crazy. She's got some fucking stupid idea in her head – she keeps following me around. I can't go for a slash by myself. And she's such a bore, she bores me shitless, I can't believe I married this woman. I can't believe I've been so good to her, when I had someone like you around. I miss you, Dave . . .

David collapsed onto the sofa. His eyes devoured the large, ragged script.

. . . I think about you all the time. I thought maybe it would cool off, but it hasn't. Maybe I'm not cut out to be married – especially not to such a slag. She's so untidy! Not like you. You even smell better than she does. You fuck better, too. And you're a hell of a lot more fun.

David groaned.

. . . I wish you were here. I wish you'd come back. I keep thinking about your body, and the way you laugh. How long have you got to go? Three months? I can't wait. I'm hanging out. Don't forget me.

It was signed, simply, 'Gus'.

'Oh, Gus,' David whispered. 'Oh, Gus.' He felt as if he were going to die – literally die – of happiness. He felt weak in the joints. Dizzy. Breathless. He headed straight for the phone, rehearsing speeches in his head: I love you. I want you. I need you.

But the voice that answered did not belong to Gus.

'Hello?' It was her voice. Tina's. Bitch, he thought, then: Poor thing. She doesn't know she's lost him.

'Can I speak to Gus, please?'

'He's out. On a job.'

'Can I leave a message? Can you tell him that David called?'

'David?'

'He knows my number.'

I should feel guilty, David thought, as he put the receiver down, but I don't. I've done my best. I left the country. If he still wants me, there's nothing I can do about it. And he wants me! He really wants me!

He had to tell someone, so he called Alice. Alice, however, was also 'out on a job'. It was an hour before she called him back, an hour that he filled with mindless, restless activity: turning on the television, turning off the television, making coffee, drinking coffee, starting letters, throwing letters away. When the phone finally rang he pounced on it, thinking that it might be Gus calling him back.

'Hello?'

'David?'

'Oh Alice! You'll never guess! You'll never guess who wrote to me!'

'Who?'

'Gus! Gus wrote me this unbelievable letter – he loves me, Alice!'

'Did he say that?'

'Well . . .' David scanned the precious lines of prose. 'Not in so many words, but that's what he means. He misses me. He wants me. He doesn't think he should be married!'

Alice made an indeterminate noise; then she fell silent. David could hear some sort of commotion in the background.

'Can't you talk?' he said. 'What's happening?'

'Oh, it's just Delbert. He and Raylene never see eye to eye.'

'What's the matter, Alice?' David could feel her withhold-ing. Disapproving. 'Don't you - aren't you pleased?'

'Yes of course. Of course I am. But don't . . .' She hesitated. Then she said, in a very low voice: 'He's married.'

'He doesn't love her!'

'That's not what I mean. What I mean is that he's in a mess. He's in a great big mess, David, and you're too good for that kind of mess.'

'What?'

'Just think about it. Even if he does do the right thing, which . . . well, I haven't seen the letter.'

David swallowed. 'You think it's all crap,' he said. 'You're on her side.'

'No.' Alice spoke so gently that he could hardly hear her. 'That's not true. I'm on your side. Which is why I don't want you to build too much on this.'

When she rang off, David sat for a while, frowning. Build too much! How could he build too much? Gus loved him - it was as clear as day, and everything else would stem from that.

When we talk, I'll have a better idea, he decided. I'll know where he's coming from. I'll ask him: Do you love me? And he'll say: Yes. And we'll see what happens then.

But no one called that night, or the next morning. And when he came home from work, there was still no message on his answering machine.

* * *

By the end of September, the Department of Fisheries and Oceans had amended the fishing quotas. It had closed the haddock fisheries to western Nova Scotia's fixed gear fleet, and the cod and pollack fisheries to the mobile gear fleet. It had done all this on the recommendation of the Fisheries Resource Conservation Council - which then, with a questionable sense of timing, decided to conduct its hearing on the next fishing season at Scotsville's Fire Hall.

Alice, who was slated to cover this event, prepared for it with a sinking heart. She knew that there would be a lot of raised voices, if not raised fists. But she shouldered her camera and went along, hoping that her presence might discourage the fishermen from lynching any FRCC representatives.

As it happened, the representatives did escape with their lives - but only just. Remarks like 'This council has no part in management; our mandate is conservation' were not guaranteed to smooth ruffled feathers. Enos, for one, was apoplectic with rage. 'This meetin' is a kangaroo court!' he cried. 'I don't know how DFO can expect us to come here and speak to this council when people have lost their jobs and I, personally, stand to lose thousands!' It appeared that Enos had already paid for his percentage of the season's quota, and was now left with $5000 of invested quota that he was not allowed to catch.

'This council,' the chairman began, wearily, 'has exercised its judgement to prevent the collapse of declining stocks -'

'Stocks are only down because of the mismanagement of the DFO!' Hardie Garron exclaimed. 'Small fishermen like us - how can we compete with the big offshore companies? How can we afford to lobby Ottawa?'

It was all very emotional and upsetting. Insults were traded; threats were made. When the hearing finally closed, the FRCC representatives disappeared so quickly that Alice had no time to ask them any questions.

'Scared,' Fairlie McNeil chuckled when she pointed this out. They were standing in the parking lot, admiring the sunset. 'Scared of Enos. Scared he's gonna shoot 'em.'

'Poor Enos. I feel so bad for him.'

'I feel worse for the young fellas. Enos and me, we've had our share. But the ones who're startin' out - they'll be hit the worst.'

'At least they are starting out,' said Alice. 'They're young. They can change. Get other jobs . . .' Even as she spoke, she knew that she was being overly optimistic. For the most part, there *were* no other jobs. Not in Nova Scotia.

Fairlie grunted. 'I'm lucky,' he said. 'I can retire. Got the house . . . investments . . . I can take Dell away. Down to Florida. Hawaii.' He turned his benevolent gaze on Alice. 'Speakin' of which, you heard from Oakey, yet?'

'No.'

'And Maureen . . . ?'

'Says she knows where he is. Says he's just fine.' Maureen, in fact, was growing increasingly reticent. When Alice had told her about the apparent disappearance of her TV, she had lapsed into monosyllables, and hung up. This, more than anything else, had convinced Alice that Maureen knew exactly what was going on.

Pondering once again the extraordinary clannishness of the Marshalls, she remembered an incident that had occurred several days previously, when, on her way to put out her garbage, she had heard the telephone ringing inside Oakey's place. She had rushed into her own kitchen, extracted his keys from her dresser, rushed over to his house and unlocked the back door - but just as she reached his telephone, it had stopped ringing.

'Maureen says he'll be back any day,' she remarked.

'Sounds like he's up to somethin'.'

'What makes you say that?'

'I dunno . . .' Fairlie shrugged. 'Anyways, we can't do much about it. Just sit and wait and wonder.' He began to smile, as the carpark slowly emptied. 'Dell thinks he's found himself a woman. Some woman he can't bring back here. A married woman.'

'Do you think so?'

'Could be. Either that or he wants to find out who burned down his barn.' This time Fairlie laughed out loud. 'I can just see old Oakey, runnin' around like James Bond. Who'd he say done it - some oil company?'

'I don't know,' Alice replied. She was in no mood for such silliness; she was far too exhausted. 'I'm going now, Fairlie. See you later.'

'Take care, now.'

'You too.'

It was inevitable that the county should have begun to talk. Oakey had been gone for almost four weeks, and people wanted to know why. There were even jokes being made about Walter Rudd hiring an assassin. In fact the heavy drinkers were making poor Walter's life miserable, teasing him about his well ('Big enough for Oakey's pick-up, Walter?') and his flower beds ('So, Walter, you been using some new kinda fertiliser for your roses?'). Alice reflected, as she drove down Marshall Street, that when Oakey *did* return, he would never hear the end of this little excursion;

people would still be ribbing him about it in ten - twenty - even thirty years.

Perhaps that's why he's staying away, she thought, stopping in front of his mailbox. Perhaps he can't face all the winks and nudges.

There were three envelopes in the mailbox: one from the *Reader's Digest*, one from Maritime Tel & Tel, and one from Ontario. For an instant Alice's heart leapt; then she saw that the last envelope had been sent, not by Mr T. Marshall, but to him. (Oakey never went by his nickname in official correspondence; he was always Mr T. Marshall. No one seemed to know what the 'T' stood for.) The address in the top left-hand corner of the envelope was that of a hotel - the Hillview Hotel - in Kitchener. Inside, a badly typed letter announced that Mr T. Marshall had checked into the Hillview Hotel some three weeks before, had signed his name in the book, unpacked his suitcase, stayed one night and then disappeared. He had not paid his bill or collected his luggage. *It would be apreciated if contact could be made at the early possible convenience to discharge debt and other matters.*

Alice leaned against her car. She felt almost winded. Oakey had disappeared! From his hotel! And he had left his luggage . . .

Forgetting her own mail, she jumped back into the Chevrolet, parked it near her house, and rushed inside. The Hillview Hotel - there was a phone number on the letterhead. She dialled it and waited. And waited. On the twelfth ring there was a click; a dreary male voice recited something that sounded like a recorded message.

But there was no beep.

'Um . . . hello?'

'Yeah.'

'Oh, good. You are there.' Alice proceeded to explain her problem, as her interlocutor sat silent at the other end of the line. When she had finished, he said, 'Hold on,' and disappeared for five minutes. At last another voice - a female one - addressed Alice from far-off Kitchener.

'Hello? Can I help you?'

So Alice had to repeat herself. This time, however, her words had some effect.

'Oh sure. I know 'bout that. I typed the letter.'

'And you haven't heard anything since? From Mr Marshall?'

'Oh no. We still got his suitcase, out back.'

'What about his truck? Did he leave his truck?'

'Hold on.' There was a brief, muffled exchange. 'No, there's no truck here.'

'Did he leave his wallet? His keys? Did he take anything with him?'

Another murmured discussion. 'He didn't leave no wallet,' came the reply. 'Just some old clothes.'

'Brushes? Shaving gear?'

'Look . . .' The woman was beginning to sound impatient. 'I'm no goddamn detective, eh? I can't help you. The guy left. He didn't settle his bill. Are you his wife, or what?'

'No, I'm - I'm just a friend.'

'Well, he stayed one night, like I said. That's forty-five dollars plus tax. When you find him, you tell him to call here. Because he owes us.'

'I'll pay,' Alice said, and gave the woman her credit card number. 'Keep that luggage,' she added. 'Someone might want to have a look at it.'

Then she hung up, and thought hard. Maureen. Maureen would have to be told. But when she dialled Maureen's number she got David's answering machine, still with David's voice on it. (David had mentioned this; apparently Maureen liked a man's voice on her answering machine, because it discouraged intruders.) So Alice recorded a brief, urgent message and hung up again. She called David, but David was not at home, and she remembered suddenly that he had gone to dinner at the Andersons'. Again she put the receiver down; again she thought hard. Nothing could be done until she spoke to Maureen. Until she *confronted* Maureen. But if Maureen refused to panic – if she refused to report Oakey missing – then what could Alice do? Alice was only his neighbour, after all. Maureen was his sister.

Alice went into the kitchen and made herself a cup of coffee. She went into the living room and stared at her picture of Oakey: a fine-grained black and white shot which had captured his habitual slouching posture, as well as his slow, intent, unreadable regard. Finally she went into the dining room, and removed a couple of cloth-covered notebooks from the dresser. She took them back into the living room, sat down on the chesterfield, finished her coffee and put the cup to one side. The notebooks contained her journal – or at least some of her journal. They covered the last fifteen months. She began to flick through them, working her way backwards. Whenever she saw the word 'Oakey' she would stop and read.

Oakey's telephone was ringing . . .

Not that.

Maureen said Oakey was in Manitoba . . .

Forget that, too.

Oakey dropped by a few minutes ago. He was dressed in old brown corduroys and one of Foster's shirts . . .

Alice read on. She rarely reviewed her journals; it was an interesting experience. So much detail. So much that she had forgotten. The Family Violence Prevention Initiative. The dinner with Lindsay. References to David's missing television - plenty of those. Reference to Oakey's using the old lawn mower. Interesting. Reference to a certain night in May, when Oakey had transferred a great many mysterious objects from his house to his garage.

Loading up his truck, perhaps?

That's it, Alice decided. That's when he started selling his things - his guns and his fishing tackle. May, that was. And in April? Oakey asked for a copy of the paper. Oakey's barn burned down. March: Oakey lost his snow-plough job. February . . .

The guy in the yellow car.

Alice blinked. The entry was stuck between an account of a local house fire and a description of the monthly Board of Trade meeting.

I was washing up the breakfast dishes, before going to work, when I saw Oakey's pick-up drive down to his garage, followed by a yellow car. I hadn't even registered that Oakey's pick-up was gone in the first place. Oakey got out of his pick-up and another man got out of the car. He wasn't from around here - his car had Ontario plates. They both went inside, and then I left for work.

The car was gone when I got home, tonight.

Ontario plates. That was surely a clue. But the journal was frustratingly laconic: no description of the man, no record of the number plates. Alice closed her eyes, and cast her mind back. A man in a yellow car. Some kind of hat. No moustache.

265

That was all she could remember.

Glancing at her watch, she saw that it was ten past ten. Ten past ten, and no supper! She made herself some scrambled eggs, left the dishes to soak, and called David again - but he was still out. So she brushed her teeth and went to bed, setting her alarm for five thirty. She knew that she would have to get up at five thirty, if she wanted to call Maureen.

Maureen, however, beat her to it. At five o'clock Alice was awakened by the sound of the telephone; groping for the bedside extension, she knocked over her denture glass, swore, and began to mop up the water with tissues as she tucked the receiver under her chin.

'Hello?'

'Alice?'

'Maureen!' The sound of Maureen's voice galvanised Alice. She stuck in her front bottom teeth. 'Did you get my message?'

'Yes of course, that's why I -'

'Something's happened, Maureen. I think you'd better call the Mounties.'

'Yes. Well . . . that's what I want to talk to you about.' Maureen spoke haltingly. She sounded upset - almost tearful. 'It's all so complicated, I can't . . . I don't want to . . . I think he's all right, Alice.'

'But he's disappeared! He's left his clothes -'

'But not his wallet. Not his car or his wallet.'

'He didn't pay the bill.'

A long pause. At last Maureen said, 'He might have been in a hurry.'

'A *hurry*?'

'Look, I - I can't give you all the details. It's a family matter.

But I can tell you that he was after someone.' Alice could hear Maureen breathing heavily at the other end of the line. 'The person he was after tends to move around a lot. Oakey might have had to leave quickly.'

'That was three weeks ago, Maureen. And he still hasn't paid the bill.'

'He might have forgotten. He mightn't have had enough time.' Another pause. 'It's not easy, when you don't have a credit card. You have to mail things.'

Alice was speechless. Oakey, chasing someone? It all seemed so far-fetched. 'Is it that guy he's chasing?' she asked. 'The one who was here in February?' Then she heard a sniffle, and realised that Maureen was crying.

'I can't - I can't tell you. I'm sorry, Alice.' Sniffle, sniffle. 'And please don't tell anybody. *Please*. It's all so . . .' She trailed off.

Alice sighed. 'Maureen,' she said, 'I think you should call the Mounties. Report him missing.'

'I will.'

'Because something might have happened.'

'I know.'

'Call the local Mounties. In Kitchener. You should be able to get the number through Directory Assistance.'

Maureen was still crying, very quietly, in a ladylike fashion. For a minute or so not a word was said. Then Alice, moved to pity, asked if there was anything else she could do.

'No,' Maureen said. 'Just don't tell anyone.'

'I won't. I won't as long as you call the Mounties.'

'I will.'

And that, for the time being, was that.

October

David woke in shock. He had been dreaming that he was late for work, that the school bell was ringing, but of course it was only the telephone. He checked the luminous digits on his alarm clock, and saw that it was three a.m. Three a.m.? It had to be an emergency! He threw back his sheets, stumbled towards the light switch, stubbed his toe on Maureen's blanket box (damn her) and finally made it into the hall.

There were two extensions in Maureen's house: one in the kitchen, one in the hall.

'Hello?'

'Is that David?'

'*Gus?*' It had been three weeks since the arrival of Gus's letter; during that time, David had left at least eight messages with various members of the de Souza family and written a six-page declaration that should have melted the polar ice caps. But there had been no response from Gus - until now. 'I got your letter. Did you get mine?'

'Listen.' There was a depressing amount of noise in the background. David wondered if Gus were calling from a bar, or worse still, a railway station phone. 'Letters are fine. You know letters are fine, as long as you post them to my post-box number. But how many times do I have to tell you, David? *Don't ring the house.*'

David swallowed. This was not the conversation he had expected. 'I wouldn't have to ring the house, if you returned my calls,' he said.

'Look - it's not easy, okay? I can't call you on my mobile, and I can't call you at home. What time is it there now?'

'Three o'clock in the morning.'

'See? See how hard it is? Even if I did call you I'd be waking you up.'

'I don't *care* if you wake me up!' David looked around, but there was not a chair in sight. Damn Maureen. 'I'd rather you woke me up than never called me at all.'

'Well, shit. I hate these long-distance phone calls anyway.' (It was either a party or a pub; the roar of voices was interspersed with the clink of glass.) 'They're a bloody rip-off, and my mind goes blank. Too much to say, and not enough time for any of it.'

'What do you want to say, Gus?' David gripped the telephone cord so tightly that it hurt. Oh, please, he thought. Oh, please.

'Just what I told you. Don't ring the house.'

'Is that *all*?'

'Dave, I'm near the bogs here, mate. It smells bad.'

'I love you. I miss you.'

'Yeah. I know.'

'You wrote that letter!' David wished passionately that he could reach down the line, grab Gus by the collar, and shake him. 'You said you missed me!'

'I do.'

'Then why . . . ?' David began, and trailed off. He was too confused - he had been woken too abruptly. He knew that something was wrong, that the situation was not quite as Gus saw it, but was unable to express this belief in a coherent way.

'Why what?' said Gus. 'I wrote to you. Now I've called you. It's not as good as sex, but it's the best I can do. What else do you want?'

'To know that you love me,' David whispered.

'What's that? I can't hear, there's a bloody riot going on.' Gus laughed. 'Some bird's playing strip snooker - you should see all the guys chalking their cues.'

David felt as if he were drowning. All the dry, clear, solid questions that he had been arranging in neat little lines - they had been washed away by the flood of emotion that Gus's voice always released in him. Now he was thrashing around amidst the wreckage of those imagined discussions . . .

He was about to go down for the last time when one lone spar of a question drifted into his consciousness.

'What about your wife?' he said. 'You told me you weren't getting on.'

Gus snorted. 'That's an understatement. If it wasn't for Poppy, I'd kick her out.'

'Oh.'

'Look, mate - I'm going to have to go, this is eating a hell of a hole in my phonecard. Just don't call the house, eh? It's giving Tina more ammunition, she's following me around everywhere. Sometimes I think she's mad. Look after yourself and I'll see you soon, okay?'

'Gus -'

'Gotta go. Bye!'

'I love you!' David cried. But he was speaking to a dial tone; Gus had rung off. Somewhere thousands of kilometres away he had broken the connection, drained his glass, and returned to the bar for another. David realised suddenly that he was standing all alone in a deathly hush.

He went back to bed, where he lay thinking for the next two hours. His heart was leaden. *If it wasn't for Poppy, I'd kick her out.* This was not the response he had anticipated. Gus was battling, all right, but he was not giving up. He was dismayed, but not desperate. David had formed the impression that Gus was locked in an absorbing contest - that everything outside the tangled web of his marriage was in every sense peripheral right now, including David. Especially David. After all, David was at the other end of the world, and Gus had always tended to focus on what was right under his nose: the next job, the next meal, the next pay cheque.

Out of sight, out of mind, David thought sadly. He rolled over and buried his face in the pillow. How had he ever become involved in such a mess? *You're too good for that kind of mess,* Alice had told him. Perhaps she was right. A man locked in mortal combat with his spouse, a man who was focusing all his energies on gaining the tactical advantage, could not possibly provide the romance that his lover craved.

David was still thinking about Gus when he fell asleep at dawn. An hour or so later he was jarred awake by the alarm clock, and had to drag himself off to school nursing a nasty

271

headache. As usual, the day was full of thundering feet and piercing yells and slamming doors, but he was sustained through this torture by the knowledge that he would be eating at Alice's house that night. He knew that Alice would comfort him. Not that he had any intention of bringing up Gus's name, because he was frightened of becoming a bore (David and his endless emotional crises), but he found Alice a soothing companion. He felt so safe with her in that quiet, ugly house - so insulated from life's troubles - so removed from the simmering resentments of the Great Rift (which still affected the school atmosphere, occasionally), from his worries about the obviously neglected or perhaps even abused children in his class, and from the infrequent, veiled references to his homosexuality in the staffroom. Although he had a good deal of energy, which was one of his greatest assets as a teacher, even he found himself drained by the troubles that racked the school. So when the playground fights and staff meetings became too much for him, Alice's house was always a haven of peace.

But soon after staggering home that afternoon, he received a call from Alice, who informed him that dinner might be delayed for an hour or two.

'It's Walter,' she said. 'He's called some kind of meeting about Oakey, at the Legion hall.'

'About *Oakey*?'

'He wants me to come. He wants you to come. Sounds like half the town's coming.'

With an effort, David wrenched his thoughts away from his own problems. He made a little joke. 'Do you think he's going to confess to murder?'

Alice sighed. 'He's going to stick his oar in, that's what he's going to do,' she said. 'I wish he wouldn't. Things are delicate enough as it is.'

Something in her tone made David prick up his ears. 'Why?' he asked. 'What do you mean?'

'Oh . . . I'll tell you later.'

The meeting was scheduled for half past six, so David had ample time in which to buy his weekly provisions on his way home from school. He also bought a frozen cheesecake, thinking (as he hesitated between the cherry and the chocolate) that he should really take another shot at some of Maureen's recipes. Since the disappearance of her television he had mastered most of the cookie doughs, but his enthusiasm had waned, recently.

Time to tackle the puddings, perhaps.

He went home, unloaded the car, showered, changed and treated himself to a bar of peanut brittle. On his way back into town, via a route which took him past several large tracts of forest, he noticed how many of the leaves were beginning to turn: here a touch of red, there a touch of yellow. Soon they would fall off, and the snow would come, and he would be back shovelling Maureen's driveway. He shivered, at the same time reflecting that this sense of encroaching chill perfectly matched his mood. Would the Big Freeze bring more lonely nights? And not a word from Lindsay, of course; all those promises had come to nothing. Doubtless Lindsay had found another 'hot piece of ass' in Toronto. With money like his, he would never have to look very far for anything, least of all sex.

Just a couple of months, David told himself. Just a couple of months, and then I'll be back in Sydney. Where Gus is. He was so busy thinking about Gus that he almost missed the

Kempton turn-off; he had to change lanes rather abruptly, with an embarrassing squeal of tyres, and roll into town amidst a barrage of angry car horns. Shaken, he briefly forgot where he was heading (To school? To Foodland?) and was fortunate that the road on which he was travelling took him directly past the Legion hall.

This hall stood, not on the waterfront, but in the windswept backblocks of Kempton, not far from the ice rink. It was surrounded by fast-food huts and garages and bleak, three-storeyed apartment buildings full of single mothers. David was surprised by the number of vehicles in the carpark; he had not expected such an enthusiastic response to Walter's invitation. The sight of so many people gathered within the building surprised him even more. He calculated that there were at least fifty of them - perhaps even sixty. The entire Blueberry Carnival Executive Committee was present (with the exception of Gordon Blanchard), as were Floyd McNeil, Ida Wheelhouse and Winnie Rudd. Kendall Tibbett was there. Eric McNeil was there. Gwen and Mike Wylie were there, sitting right next to Alice. David also recognised Eunice Wheelhouse, Erica the *Gazette* receptionist, and the little old man from the Blueberry Carnival pot luck - the one with the vivid-blue eyes.

Alice waved, and David slipped into the seat that she had reserved for him.

'Aren't there a lot of people!' he exclaimed.

'Nosy parkers,' said Mike - who had, as usual, been eaves-dropping. 'They're interested in what Walter's up to.'

'So am I,' said Alice. She was studying the three chairs that had been set up to face the audience; they stood on the dais, under the portrait of Queen Elizabeth. When Mike asked if

Alice would be reporting on the event in that week's paper, she frowned. 'Of course not!' she said sharply. 'I was invited as a friend of Oakey, not as a representative of the *Gazette*.'

'And Raylene?' said Mike. 'What about her? Is she here as a friend or as a reporter?'

Alice opened her mouth, but before she could speak Walter Rudd marched up to the microphone. He was dressed in an ill-fitting suit and conservative tie, and his aftershave was so lavishly applied that David could smell it all the way from the fifth row. Beside Walter, Winnie Rudd looked very trim and elegant; she selected one of the three chairs on the dais, sat down, and crossed her ankles. Beside her, on the middle chair, sat a thin man wearing what looked almost like jungle camouflage.

'Ernie Tibbett,' Alice whispered. 'He owns the Sunshine kennels.'

'Oh.'

'Where Oakey boarded Tripod.'

'Grrfflmmph . . .' Walter cleared his throat. 'Thank you for coming . . . pffgrrllmm . . . use of the hall . . .' (Amplification did not improve his delivery.) 'Lffrggrrrn . . . come here to discuss the disappearance of Oakey Marshall . . .'

He went on to explain that several weeks ago, he had spoken to Bill somebody in the something-or-other. ('Bill Garron,' Alice translated, 'Hardie's brother. On the local police force.') He had been airing his concerns about Oakey, and Bill had promised to pass on any information that might crop up. ('Wants to scotch all the rumours,' Mike remarked, in a low voice. 'Wants to prove he didn't bump Oakey off himself.') Earlier in the week, Bill had informed him that Oakey had been something-something, by his sister Maureen.

A murmur flowed through the crowd. David turned to Alice. 'What? What did he say?'

'He said that Maureen has reported Oakey missing.'

'*Really?*'

'Gffffrrmphhlm . . . called Maureen,' Walter continued. 'She says that he disappeared in Kitchener . . . mnnllbbrmfn.'

'Several weeks ago?' Gwen hissed, in surprise. 'Why didn't she tell us?'

'Maureen has no idea what could have happened,' Walter concluded. 'That's why I've called this meeting . . . frrlmphngff . . . if we can lend a hand.' He looked around, as if searching for someone. Then his gaze fastened on Alice. 'I hear you've been looking after his house. Is that true?'

'Yes,' Alice replied, reluctantly. She pushed her glasses back up the bridge of her nose.

'Mmffllrmmn . . . been inside?'

'I have been inside. There's nothing there.'

'Nothing unusual?'

'No.'

David stared at her in astonishment. What about the missing furniture? But she had set her mouth, and folded her arms.

'*Okay*,' said Walter. 'Can anyone else help out? Grmmm-bbmm . . . anything unusual? Before he left?'

'His barn burned down,' someone remarked, slyly. ('Fairlie McNeil,' Gwen observed. 'Oakey's neighbour.') 'That's pretty unusual.'

Walter shook his head. 'We all know about the barn,' he replied. 'Mgllrrrm . . . accident. Is there anything else? Anything he talked about? Anyone he saw?'

'Oh!' A memory had just surfaced in David's mind. He recalled a morning - a winter's morning, because the pipes had frozen - and a man in a yellow car. He put up his hand. 'Um . . . I don't know if this is relevant . . .'

All eyes turned towards him. A whisper trickled from the back of the hall to the front.

Walter peered in his direction.

'Yes?'

'It was late winter, some time. One of my pipes had frozen.' David thought that his voice sounded squeaky, and coughed. 'I - um - I called Oakey, and he came over, and while he was there, a man turned up. A man in a yellow car. He asked for Maureen, but he went off with Oakey.' Why was Alice sighing like that? 'I've never seen him since.'

Walter opened his mouth, but was forestalled by a strident young woman with a round, white face and red hair pulled into a ponytail. ('Isn't that Angela Wheelhouse?' Gwen mumbled, to no one in particular. 'She's filled out a lot in the last year.')

'You say he had a yellow car?' the young woman asked David.

'Yes, that's right.'

'And he was about forty? All beat-up lookin'?'

'Yes!' David gaped at her. 'How did you know?'

'Because he stayed at the hotel where I work. I remember him.' She addressed Walter over the heads of the people in front of her. 'He skipped without payin'. Left a false address. We've been after him for months. Can't find him.' Withdrawing her attention from Walter, she spoke to the room at large. 'The car was a rental, from Ontario. Thunder

277

Bay. He'd left a different address with them, but we still drew a blank.'

'Did he pay the rental company?' Floyd McNeil inquired.

'Oh, sure. They make you pay up front.'

'And where did he return the car?' Mike Wylie chimed in. 'Did you ask 'em?'

'St John. The next day. We don't know where he went after that.'

There was a long pause. David was quite intrigued – even excited – but when he looked at Alice, she was staring glumly down at her belt buckle.

It was Bob Wheelhouse who finally stated the obvious.

'Ontario,' he said. 'Oakey disappeared in Ontario, and this fella was from Thunder Bay.'

'Fggmmllrr . . . disappeared in Kitchener,' Walter objected.

'So? It's still Ontario.'

'What was his name?' Bonnie asked, and the redhead replied: 'Brown. Ryan Brown.'

Brown, David thought. That's no good; there must be a million Browns. Glancing at all the disappointed faces, he realised that everyone else was thinking much the same thing as he was.

'Bmmnnllprrff . . . speak to Maureen,' Walter declared. 'Ask her if she knows this person. Gfflllmmmb . . . anything else?'

Erica raised a tentative hand. 'I've got a cousin who works the St John ferry,' she volunteered, in her soft voice. 'I can ask him if he remembers the yellow car.'

'After all this time?' said Fairlie, in doubtful tones. 'After so many cars?'

Erica smiled. 'They play a game,' she told him. 'They keep score - they even write things down. He *might* remember.'

'Okay. Good.' Walter obviously thought little of Erica's plan. 'Anything else? No? Fggrrlmmfn . . . think about it. If you have any ideas, come to me . . . gsslmbtfrr . . . cooperate with the authorities . . .'

The meeting broke up in a babble of conjecture. People gathered in knots, bright-eyed, exclaiming over this unforeseen development - this first-class, fully fledged mystery. On her way out, Alice said crossly, 'Walter makes me so mad, sometimes. How on earth did he get your number, David? That's what I want to know.'

'What number? Oh - you mean in Sydney.' David glanced at her, overcome with a completely irrational sense of guilt. 'Well . . . I gave it to him. He rang me, and I gave it to him.'

'Oh.'

'Why? Shouldn't I have?'

Alice stopped. They were in the parking lot by this time, and the crowds were dispersing. An autumn chill nibbled at their earlobes. Alice fumbled for her keys.

'Maureen didn't want anyone to hear about this,' she said, very softly. 'According to her, it's some kind of "family affair".'

David gasped. 'You mean you knew about it? About Oakey being reported?'

'Yes.'

'And you didn't tell anyone?'

'She asked me not to.' Looking up at him, Alice adjusted her glasses and lowered her voice until he had to stoop to catch it. 'I've got a hunch that she and Oakey were in this together. I'm not sure what it all means, but I know Maureen does, and she's

terrified that someone else is going to find out what's going on.'
A pause. 'She didn't even want to report him missing.'

'Wow.'

'Anyways, the last thing she needs is the whole of Kempton County baying after Oakey like a pack of bloodhounds.'

'But . . .' David was trying to reassemble his scattered thoughts. 'But do you know what the problem is? Is it something to do with this Ryan bloke?'

'She didn't tell me,' Alice replied, and headed for her car. 'You're coming straight home, aren't you?' she added, over her shoulder. 'If I stop at the store, can you let yourself in? You know where the spare keys are.'

'Yes, I know.' David lifted a hand, and turned to look for his own vehicle. Then he remembered. 'Oh - Alice!' he cried, turning back. 'Alice!'

'What?'

'Don't get any dessert! I've bought a cheesecake!'

She nodded, and shut the driver's door. Then she started her engine. By the time David had buckled up she was out of sight, heading for Sable Cove at a suicidal rate of knots.

Goodness, he thought. She is angry.

* * *

Once again, Alice found herself in the middle of a tumultuous gathering of fishermen. This time she was at the October meeting of the Maritime Fishermen's Union, which was being held in the auditorium of Shelby Elementary School; with the lobster season fast approaching, many lobster fishermen had decided that the time had come to thrash out, once and for all, the issue of lost gear.

'I lost seventeen per cent of my gear, last season,' Gary Ruggles complained. 'We've had boats go down the bay in the middle of the night, bold as brass, to steal people's gear!'

Glen Burgess grunted. 'It's a problem,' he admitted. 'Maybe –'

'And it's because we're all on top of one another!' Gary interrupted. 'We're stickin' knives in each other's backs! This is the last decent fishery left in the bay, and look what we found last year – cages and cages of bagged lobsters, all of 'em planted on the first day of the season. We can't let it happen, not again.'

'Yes,' said Glen. 'Now if –'

'I've lost four hundred traps in the last three years,' Gary continued, 'and I'll probably lose more, because of what I said tonight. We've gotta stop cuttin' each other's throats.'

'You're right,' Glen declared. 'I've been approached before on this issue. Which is why I want to ask members if they support a trap limit. And maybe some way to enforce it, like – I dunno. Marked buoys. Marked traps. Unmarked traps could become illegal.'

A low muttering. Alice sensed that the suggestion was not a popular one. It occurred to her that every one of the members – even Gary himself – might be poaching on each other's territory.

Gary's father Enos put up his hand.

'Trap limits won't do no good,' he pointed out. 'Most of the poachin' happens in summer.'

'And it's all because of them native fishermen!' someone else declared. (Alice was unable to identify him.) 'You let 'em plant traps in the summer, and why shouldn't anyone else?'

Another uproar. Alice's shoulders slumped; she knew that it was going to be a long evening, and wondered - in a fatalistic fashion - if she would miss the last ferry. Fortunately Glen also had his eye on the clock, and at ten p.m. declared the meeting closed. Alice immediately leapt up and made for the door. (Beat the stampede, she told herself.) But as she hurried away from the stately wooden school, crossing its dimly lit, asphalt playground, Glen Burgess suddenly appeared, panting, at her elbow.

'I heard about Oakey,' he said.

'Uh-huh.'

'Fairlie told me he's been reported missin'?'

Alice sighed. The past few days had been perfectly hellish; Oakey's status as a Missing Person had made him the number one topic of conversation. The theories were flying thick and fast, some of them more loony than others. Although a few people subscribed to the belief that Oakey's invention was at the heart of his disappearance, opinion was almost equally divided between the drug-running hypothesis and the sex-crime hypothesis. The sex-crime hypothesis proposed that Oakey had somehow become involved with a prostitute, whose pimp/partner/pusher had shot/stabbed/strangled him.

'Yes,' Alice sighed. 'Oakey's been reported missing.'

'Have you talked to Maureen?'

'Yes, I've talked to Maureen.'

Glen nodded, gravely. 'Well - you tell her that if she needs any help, I'm always here.'

'Yes. I'll do that.'

Though what possible help Glen could provide was anybody's guess. Alice jumped into her car and made her way briskly to the ferry wharf, where at least nine vehicles were already waiting under banks of powerful floodlights. But that was no problem - the ferry could hold sixteen. She would certainly fit on, unlike some of the fishermen behind her, who faced the prospect of hanging about on the wharf until the ferry made its return trip. Alice could almost hear their grumbling when the boom gates creaked shut behind Fairlie McNeil's Mazda.

It was a chilly ride across the water after dark. There was always a stiff breeze, and no sun to warm the damp, salt-scarred deck plates. Nevertheless, as the clumsy craft inched towards the mainland, occupants of all sixteen vehicles on board got out and conferred. Every one of them (except Alice) was a member of the Maritime Fishermen's Union.

'Flounder stocks're gettin' pretty low . . .'

' . . . the offshore quota shouldn't be transferable to the inshore . . .'

' . . . square nets, not diamond-shaped . . .'

' . . . Ruggles . . .'

Fairlie McNeil made a beeline for Alice, and spent the next ten minutes chuckling over various theories currently circulating about Oakey's disappearance. Alice had never welcomed the end of the Shelby ferry ride with such whole-hearted relief. But even then she could not entirely escape him; he followed her all the way back to Sable Cove, waving cheerily as they parted company on Marshall Street, where he turned into his driveway about half a kilometre from Oakey's house.

Alice felt as if she were being pursued. Everywhere she went, people asked her for news about Oakey Marshall, and looked at her sceptically when she said that she knew no more than they did. It would have been easier to handle if she had not been in Maureen's confidence; she hated having to lie. And the pressure would continue to build until Oakey returned - or at least until the passing of the years finally cast him as another unsolved mystery, like Orry McNeil's suspicious death in 1968.

Alice shut her front door behind her with the sense that she was shutting out a ravening horde. It was cold, so she turned on the furnace. Then she kicked off her shoes, pulled on a pair of woolly socks, and heated up some of last night's chicken in the microwave. Kentucky Fried Chicken, it was; she never had enough time to cook, any more. She would turn into a blimp, and Louise would disown her.

Ha.

She was just sitting down with her pathetic, warmed-over scraps when the telephone rang, loudly and urgently. It rang and rang. Finally she could ignore it no longer, and went to answer it (although her mouth was full of food). ' 'Lo?' she said.

'Alice?' It was Maureen. 'Oh, Alice . . .'

'What?' Christ, Alice thought. Christ, he's dead. With an effort she swallowed her chicken. 'Have they found him?'

'No. But they found his car.' Maureen's voice was barely recognisable. It was hoarse, quite hoarse, as if she had laryngitis. 'Someone else was drivin' it. Near Buffalo.'

'Across the border?'

'This man - he said he found it, Alice, he . . . oh, God -'

'Maureen? Take it easy now, I can't hear you.' Alice was trying to speak calmly. Reassuringly. 'Was it him? Was it the guy you . . . the guy that Oakey was after?'

'No,' Maureen sobbed, and launched into a confused babble of words, moaning, hiccoughing, choking into her mouthpiece. Alice realised that she was hysterical.

'Maureen? Listen, dear - listen to me. Go into the bathroom, and get a cold wet cloth, and put it on your forehead. Put it on the back of your neck.'

' . . . he's killed him . . .'

'Maureen? Are you listening?' Alice was trying to think. 'Have you got any Valium? Go and ask David's mother for a Valium.'

'*No!*' Maureen shrieked. 'I don't want anyone - anyone -'

'All right. Don't panic.' Alice was beginning to panic herself. 'What do you want me to do? You called me - what do you want me to do? I'm listening.'

'I - I ca -'

'Take it slowly.'

'*It's all my fault!*'

Another burst of sobbing. Alice soothed and clucked; she sat and waited, hunched over the phone, until Maureen had recovered enough to speak coherently. Even when she did, her message was vague. Disjointed.

'I couldn't believe it,' she groaned. 'I couldn't believe he'd do it. I didn't *want* to believe.'

'That who would do what?'

'Ryan,' said Maureen, and Alice sucked in her breath. Ryan Brown! 'He wanted money. I would have sold the lot, but David was there, and Ryan wanted more. So Oakey - Oakey went to see him . . . to persuade him . . .'

'Ryan was *blackmailing* you?' Alice could hardly believe her ears. 'But why? Oh -' She corrected herself. 'Don't tell me if you don't want to. I'll understand.'

Maureen was crying more softly now. She said that she had to tell Alice, so that Alice could tell the police. Maureen was incapable of telling the police. She had tried, but without success. The words had lodged in her gullet. She had been sick on the floor.

'Ryan's my son,' she said faintly – and, as Alice remained silent, added: 'He was born when I was sixteen. I gave him up for adoption.'

'Oh, my dear.' Alice felt the tears stinging her eyes. 'I'm so sorry.'

'He found out. They can find out, these days. He's such a – he's no good, Alice.' She began to whimper again. 'He said he'd tell everyone. I couldn't stand it. I couldn't believe he'd turned out so bad.'

'But Maureen . . .' Alice hardly knew how to phrase her next remark. 'Times have changed, you know. Look at Linda Tibbett. No one would – I'm sure people would understand.'

'No.'

'They might talk, but only a little. Illegitimate children – they're a dime a dozen, these days.'

'*No!*' Maureen cried. 'It's not like that! You – it was –' She began to make strange noises. Slowly Alice realised that she was retching; retching and gasping. The sound pierced Alice like cold steel. She recognised it. She knew what it meant. Feeling dizzy – disoriented – she swallowed, and filled her lungs with air; then she exhaled, and breathed in again. I have to be calm, she told herself. I can't let go. This is Maureen's tragedy, not mine. I've got to make an effort.

'It's all right,' she said at last, with some difficulty. 'I know. I know what's wrong.'

'He – he's –'

'Your father's son.'

'No!' A despairing wail. 'Foster's!'

Foster's. Alice closed her eyes; she saw Foster as she had known him. Cheery. Convivial. Clean-shaven, with a modest beer belly. Losing weight rapidly in the last year of his life. Now that she came to think about it, Maureen had never mixed very much with Foster. It was Oakey who had always mown her lawns, who had put up her Christmas lights and ploughed her driveway.

Who had looked after her.

Oh, Christ, she reflected dully. This is too much. This is too much for me to cope with. Why do I have to be the one?

'It's all my fault,' Maureen was saying. 'All of it. He's dead.'

'We don't know that, Maureen.'

'He's dead, and it's all my fault.'

'No, it's not.'

'It is! Ryan's killed him, and it's all my fault!'

'But why should Ryan want to kill Oakey?' To Alice, the idea seemed illogical. It shook her out of her shock-induced daze. 'There's no profit in killing.'

'. . . angry . . .' Maureen muttered.

'What?'

'*Angry!*' Maureen shouted. 'He hates us! We sent him away!'

In the end, there was not much comfort that Alice could offer Maureen. Things looked bad for Ryan, and worse for Oakey. But Alice promised that she would talk to the police ('Detective Kinney – Lionel Kinney. I'll give you the number,') and pass on what Maureen had told her.

'They'll want to speak to you, though,' she warned. 'They're going to want more details.'

'I know,' Maureen whispered. 'But I won't have to see . . . hear . . . I mean, I won't have to tell them myself.'

She seemed a little calmer. Alice urged her to have a warm bath, take a Valium and go to bed. Maureen pointed out that it was lunchtime. 'But you're not at school?' said Alice, in consternation.

'No,' Maureen replied. 'I couldn't go to school. I took the day off.' They agreed that Alice should make contact with Detective Kinney first thing in the morning, then call Maureen (regardless of the time) with details of what the detective had said.

'We should keep each other fully informed,' Alice advised. 'If something happens at this end, then I'll call you. And vice versa.'

'Yes,' said Maureen.

'I also think you should try to get hold of some sedatives. You won't do anyone any good if you don't sleep.'

'I know,' said Maureen. 'I will. And . . . Alice?'

'Yes?'

'Don't tell anyone.'

Alice smiled a crooked smile. Tell anyone? Maureen had come to the right person, if she wanted secrecy. 'I won't,' she said. 'Believe me, I wouldn't dream of it. I know exactly how you feel.'

* * *

David was suffering from his very first bout of hay fever, brought on, not by spring pollen, but by autumn winds. The wind blew and blew, all day and all night, and the dead leaves flew about, and the air was full of irritants. David's nose ran incessantly; he was always sneezing. He used up an entire box of Kleenex in just over a day, and had to resort to toilet paper instead. He went to see Paul Anderson, thinking he was ill, but Paul recommended antihistamines. 'Allergic reaction,' Paul declared. 'It'll pass.' Standing in the schoolyard amidst the rattle of tumbling leaves and the shrieks of excited children, clutching his damp handkerchief, David experienced a new dimension of misery.

One night he was so sodden, so wretched, that he called his mother to complain. And it was she who finally alerted him.

'Hang on,' she said, as David recited (in exhaustive detail) his last conversation with Gus. 'What does he mean, you're giving his wife "more ammunition"? What does he mean by that?'

'Well . . .' David paused, disoriented. 'I suppose I'm - I left these messages, you see -'

'But what *else* have you been doing?'

David thought.

'Unless it's what *he's* been doing,' Clara went on, pursuing the point to its logical conclusion. 'Unless he's just been - I don't know - out a lot, maybe. Out with the boys.'

'The boys?' said David, in alarm. What boys? Clara quickly changed the subject, but she had already sewn seeds of doubt in his mind. After hanging up he sat for an hour or more, sniffing, thinking, watching the rain run down the living-room windows. *More ammunition*. What had Gus said, exactly, during that fateful phone call? *It's giving Tina more ammunition, she's following me around everywhere.* As if she were suspicious. As if she doubted him.

David got up, and began to pace the room. How long was it since that dialogue? Two weeks? Three? And not a word from Gus since then (as usual). But the letter - the letter had been a cry from the heart. A testimonial. A declaration. David hurried into Maureen's bedroom, where his wallet was sitting on the bedside table; he extracted the well-thumbed document with shaking hands. *I miss you, Dave . . . I wish you were here . . . I keep thinking about your body, and the way you laugh.* Declarations, all of them. Deafening trumpet blasts that had drowned out everything else. But there, right there; there it was again. *She's got some fucking stupid idea in her head - she keeps following me around.* David had thought that Gus was referring to some domestic disagreement, about the way Gus spent his money, perhaps, or the way he devoted so much time to his work. Alternatively, he had feared that one of his own letters (or one of Gus's postcards?) had somehow fallen into Tina's hands. But now a third, more chilling possibility occurred to him. What if Tina's suspicions stemmed from something else? From some*one* else?

What if Gus was sleeping around?

'No,' David said. Why write such a letter, if that was the case? Why write a love letter to the person you were betraying? Unless guilt was the motive . . .

David's eyes filled with tears. He wiped them away angrily, and read through the letter once more. *I can't wait. I'm hanging out.* Gus's words seemed to glow like embers; they sparkled against that dark, frustrated background of complaints like forked lightning against a cloudy sky. And there were a lot of complaints. David realised this suddenly as he sifted through the paragraphs, noting how Tina occupied so much of the space between those all-important endearments. Her sluttish habits. Her boring company. Her obsessive behaviour. My God, he thought. Don't tell me he was striking out at *her*.

Then it hit him. It hit him with such force that he actually fell back onto the bed, open-mouthed, staring. How could he have missed something so obvious? How could he have been so dense? He had come to Canada for one reason only: to force Gus into realising how much they needed each other. He had believed the old adage 'absence makes the heart grow fonder' and had acted accordingly. Not once - not once, in all this time - had it occurred to him that Gus was all by himself, horny, over the other side of the world. Not once.

He must have been out of his mind.

He clutched his head, grimacing, too astonished to be angry. He had done it himself, for God's sake! He had slept with Lindsay Beaton! But Lindsay was so long ago - Lindsay was nothing. A slight error. An ice-cream on a summer's day, trivial, ephemeral, unmemorable. Lindsay had been Gus's fault, because Gus had neither called nor written. And the substitute had proven to be no substitute at all.

David went to the telephone. He dialled Gus's number. Presently he heard Tina's voice.

'De Souza Pest Extermination, can I help you?'

'I'd like to speak to Gus, please.'

'Gus isn't here right now.'

'Can you tell me where he is?'

She hesitated. 'He's out on a job.'

'Can you give me the number then? Of the place where he is? It's an emergency.'

'Oh, no.' She sounded almost shocked. 'I couldn't do that.'

'Please. It's urgent.' David was suddenly filled with a reckless courage. 'It's his lawyer.'

'His *lawyer*?'

'I have to speak to him. Now.'

'But –'

'I can't tell you why. He'll have to tell you himself. Just give me the number, please!'

She found it for him, and recited it in a dazed voice. David rang off. He then dialled the number she had given him, and asked for Gus de Souza. Gus's greeting, when it came, was slow and cautious.

'Hello?'

'Gus?'

Dead silence. David ploughed on.

'I have to talk to you,' he said.

'What the *hell* do you think you're doing?'

'I want to know if you're seeing someone else.'

'You're mad.' Gus seemed genuinely appalled. 'How did you get this number? You didn't get it from *Tina*, did you?'

'You never call me, Gus. You never write. What am I supposed to think?'

But Gus's anger had finally flared.

'You fucking idiot!' he roared, and slammed the phone down.

Stubbornly, David dialled again. A stranger answered, and told David that Gus refused to speak to him. So David replied that if Gus did not come to the telephone, he, David, would call Tina and tell her everything.

Gus was back on the line in seconds.

'Listen,' he said, his voice almost cracking with the effort of keeping a level tone, 'if you say one word to Tina, I'll break your neck. I mean it. A friendly warning, Dave.'

'Who are you sleeping with?'

'Fuck off.'

'Who are you sleeping with?'

'For fuck's sake!' David heard a door slamming, somewhere on the other side of the Pacific Ocean. 'What is this? I don't need this! I can get it from my wife!'

'Yeah - because she knows you're sleeping around.'

'With *you*, mate.'

'Bullshit!' David could feel his anger rising. 'Do you think I'm stupid? I've been over *here* for the last ten months!'

'Jesus Christ -'

'You'd better tell me, or I'll ask her myself. I will.'

'Ah, Jesus,' Gus sighed, as if he found the whole topic irksome and disgusting. 'What are you, a schoolgirl? What's the matter with you? Can't you just enjoy a good fuck, now and then, without turning it into a three-act opera? You're not bloody Madame Butterfly, you know. Neither am I. You're going to mess this up, carrying on like a drag queen - it won't be worth the punishment.'

'You've already messed it up!' David cried. 'You don't even give a shit!'

'Yes I do -'

'I'm nothing to you. I'm just a fuck, like all your other fucks! Well, I've taken a page out of your book, mate! I've followed your example!' David wanted to hurt. Maim. Destroy. If Gus had been present he would have attacked him physically. 'While you've been chasing ass down there, I've been making friends up here. A certain millionaire antique dealer called Lindsay Beaton - he's promised to pay my fare to Toronto any old time. Money to burn and a washboard stomach, what else could a schoolgirl want?'

'You've had sex with some *antique dealer*?'

'He owns a house up the road. Only spends two months a year there. A holiday house, full of antique paintings -'

'You fucking *whore*!'

And that was that. There was no more discussion, only shouting and abuse. Gus called David a whore. David told Gus that he was the whore, not David, because he slept around even though he was married. Gus said that he would wring David's neck. David told Gus that he made love like a block of concrete. They hurled names at each other, every vicious name they could think of, and trampled on each other's morals, tastes and habits.

It was Gus who finally broke the connection. David knew, when he heard the dial tone, that there was no going back. It was finished. Pulverised. Gus had broken the connection in more ways than one.

He replaced the receiver and burst into tears.

An hour or so afterwards, when he was thinking back, David could remember very little about the next few minutes. He knew that he must have rampaged through the house, because he seemed to recall that some of the tables had been upended, and one of Maureen's ugly porcelain figures had been smashed. He knew also that he had somehow located his car keys, because he eventually found himself bowling along the highway at one hundred and forty kilometres an hour. The sight of his speedometer had calmed him, somewhat; he had slowed, and changed lanes, and swung on to the St Andrew's Ferry turn-off.

Then he parked his car and sat for a while, as the waves of despair and rage washed through his body. For a few seconds he would think in a serious, detached sort of way about the upset tables, or the possible cost of replacing the porcelain figurine; then he would hear Gus's voice, abusing him ('You're a real poofter, you know that? A real fucking poofter of the worst possible kind!'), and he would double up, gasping, as if someone had stabbed him in the heart.

But he knew that he would not be allowed to sit by the side of the road forever. If he stayed too long those foul-mouthed gay-bashers would turn up again, with their shotguns and pick handles. So he took a few deep breaths, and wiped his eyes, and blew his nose. Then he turned his key in the ignition, and was about to change gears when he remembered Alice McDonald. Alice. She lived down the road, just a few minutes away. What time was it now - eight o'clock? She would surely spare him a few words of comfort. He had to talk to someone, and she was always there for him. Always.

Feeling slightly better, he headed for Sable Cove. It was only a ten-minute trip, and when he turned into Alice's drive-way he saw that her kitchen light was on. Thank God, he thought. Her car's here. *She's* here. Still clutching his clammy handkerchief - which had remained wedged in his hand throughout his entire ordeal - he ran up her front steps and knocked on the door. He felt as if he was going to fall across her threshold; as if he would choke on the words that were piling up behind his front teeth.

But when Alice appeared, her pale, distraught face stopped him like a cliff. He felt his impetuous greeting wither on his tongue. His mouth dropped open.

'Oh. David,' she said. 'What are you doing here?'

'I'm just - I wanted to talk to you.' He peered into her shadowy eyes. 'Is something wrong? You look terrible.'

Alice hesitated. Then abruptly she turned. 'Come in,' she said, over her shoulder, and led him into the living room - where there was an uncharacteristic sense of disarray. (Dirty cups on the floor. Papers on the chesterfield.) She sat down and said, without preamble: 'They've found Oakey.'

David caught his breath. He looked at her.

'Maureen just called,' Alice continued. 'They found him in a hospital, in Toronto. He'd been attacked.'

'Attacked? You mean -'

'Kicked. Punched. He was in a coma for two weeks. When he woke up . . .' Alice paused. She shook her head, and studied her hands. 'He wasn't functioning properly. Still isn't. He's having a hard time remembering anything - including his name. He was left in a park, with no wallet or identification.'

'Oh my God.'

Alice straightened her back; inhaled; continued. She sounded very tired. 'Apparently he's lost a lot of his motor skills. Can't walk. Can't feed himself properly. Maureen's flying out there in a couple of days, to be with him.'

David sat down. He was appalled. Visions of Oakey in a wheelchair, Oakey's head drooping as someone wiped custard off his chin, made him flinch and shudder. Oakey Marshall! The man who could fix anything!

He gazed at Alice.

'Do they know who did it?' he inquired.

The pause that followed was so long that when Alice finally said 'No', David knew that she had reservations.

'They do, though, don't they?' he said.

'They can't be sure. Oakey doesn't remember.'

'Was it anything to do with that Ryan bloke?' David was watching her profile carefully; he saw her lashes flicker and her lips purse. For someone with such fine features, she had a very strong profile.

'If he is involved,' she said at last, 'then it's not my place to say. You'll have to ask Maureen.' And she looked up to meet David's stare, studying his face, which must have borne the marks of recent emotion. After a short interval she said to him, very gently, 'What about you? What did you want to talk about?'

But David shook his head, and waved the matter aside. Somehow, after her news of Oakey, he felt as if he were making a big fuss over nothing.

November

November had never been Alice's favourite month. She found it ugly and melancholy, with its brown, leafless vistas, its fogs, its damp chill and lowering skies. It was a rotting month, too, pulpy with rotting windfall apples, rotting leaves, rotting Halloween pumpkins left on people's doorsteps. And it was also a hunter's month; the woods were full of orange jackets and deafening bangs (not to mention fleeing ducks and deer). A month of death, she always thought. Depressing.

She preferred the clean, white, bracing months of winter.

At work, the weather seemed to affect everyone; even Raylene lost her enthusiasm for committee politics, as she wrestled with the issue of kitchen cupboards. (Lobster season was almost upon them, and Gary still had not completed her bi-fold doors or her microwave cabinet.) The atmosphere seemed stuffy, the news stale. Erica yawned, and made coffee, and flicked through the obituary columns in *The Chronicle Herald* and *The Mail Star*, in search of anyone who, although they might have died elsewhere, had nevertheless been born around Kempton – and could therefore be claimed as a local. Alice found herself taking a very desultory stab at her report on the latest School Board meeting. *It was explained to the School Board that a fuel oil tank had been replaced at Watervale Consolidated School,* she wrote. *The work had started on October 28 and there appeared to be some contaminated soil involved.* God, but it was dull. Would anyone bother reading it? She could barely stay awake long enough to write it. *The education department has also approved a $20 000 emergency grant to pay for ventilation in the school's industrial arts department.*

Alice heard the front door slam, as someone entered from the street; she heard heavy footsteps, and a cheery greeting. She recognised the voice instantly.

It belonged to Delbert Wheelhouse.

'How's it goin'?' he said.

'Good afternoon, Delbert.' Erica sounded resigned. 'How can we help you?'

'There's a meetin' on. I wanna put this ad in the paper.'

'I see.' Rustle, rustle. From the shelter of her private office, Alice deduced that Erica was reading through Delbert's bulletin. There was a pause. Then Erica said, in thoughtful tones: 'Just wait here, will you? I have to run this past Alice.'

She shut the door behind her after penetrating Alice's cubbyhole.

'What is it now?' Alice muttered. 'Improved bus routes? The high cost of sesame bagels?' She took the slip of paper from Erica's hand, and read: *CONCERNED PARENTS – November 13 at 7 p.m., St Andrew's Christian Centre, St Andrew's Ferry. To discuss the moral guidance provided by teachers in our schools. Are they setting a bad example? Everyone welcome.*

She and Erica exchanged looks.

'Do you know anything about this?' she inquired softly, and Erica shook her head.

'It's not something we'd support.'

'Then I guess you'd better send him in. I want to find out exactly what this means before I make any kind of decision.' While Erica was fetching Delbert, Alice studied the notice again. It smelled like a witch hunt, but who was the witch? Reading between the lines, she could sense that Delbert had something very specific to convey, and wondered at his cautious wording. Usually he was more straightforward, unabashedly blaming banks, businesses, government departments and anyone else who might have aroused his ire.

She put the notice aside when he walked in.

'Hello, Delbert. Sit down, will you? I just want to ask you about this ad you've brought us.'

Obediently, Delbert sat down. He stared at the mess on Alice's desk, and on the floor beside it. His innocent blue gaze travelled from wall to wall, snagging on the filing cabinet and the broken typewriter. He was wearing a hand-knitted touk pulled down low over his ears; it made his head look like an egg in an egg cosy.

'Now, Delbert,' Alice began, tapping the bulletin with one finger, 'I have to know what this meeting is actually about.'

'Oh. Sure.'

'So what *is* it about?'

Delbert looked surprised. 'The moral guidance provided by the teachers in our schools,' he quoted.

'Yes, but what do you think they're doing wrong? The teachers, I mean.'

'Oh.' He nodded. 'Sure. I getcha. Well.' He hitched up his trousers and stuck out his chest. 'It's all these homeosexuals,' he offered.

'Homosexuals?'

'Teachin' kids. Now, I don't care what they do to each other, but they oughta stay away from the kids.' Delbert seemed to think for a moment. 'No wonder they're teachin' all this sex education crap, nowadays. With all these homeosexuals around, they'll be givin' demonstrations next.'

Alice eyed him pensively. The phrasing of his last few comments had sounded slightly odd - as if he were reciting someone else's words. 'Demonstrations', for instance, was a surprisingly sophisticated term for Delbert to be using.

'Who told you that?' she asked. 'I mean, who have you been talking to?'

'Huh?'

'Who's been helping you out with this, Delbert?' Alice spoke very slowly and patiently. 'You've been discussing this with someone. Who is it?'

'Oh! You mean Walter,' said Delbert, and Alice blinked.

'Walter Rudd?'

'Sure, he's worried. We all are. It's an important issue.'

'Hmmm.' Alice was genuinely taken aback. Walter and Delbert made an odd sort of pair, and Walter was generally so caught up in other, more legitimate concerns (boards, councils, committees) that he never had time to worry about discredited affairs like Delbert Wheelhouse's meetings. Treasurer's reports and attendance rosters, yes; Delbert's meetings, no.

'Well . . . thank you, Delbert,' she said carefully. 'But I think I might just have a word with Walter, before running this. There are a couple of things I have to straighten out.'

'Uh-huh.'

'If we do run it, we'll run it before the thirteenth. You want it in the Community Bulletin Board, don't you?'

'That's right.'

'Then we'll do our best. Goodbye, Delbert.' Alice almost pushed him out of the room. Then she waited until he had left the building before knocking on Raylene's door.

Raylene was using the telephone; she raised an eyebrow by way of inquiry.

'Is that important?' Alice whispered.

'Hell, no. It's Gary, is all.'

'Can I ask you something?'

Raylene bade Gary a brusque farewell, and hung up. Not for the first time, Alice knitted her brows over the great heaps of old newspapers balanced precariously on the filing cabinets behind Raylene's chair. This room, she thought, isn't fit for human habitation. I'll have another word with the General Manager, next time I'm in Bridgetown.

'Could you cast an eye over this,' she said, 'and tell me what you think? It's one of Delbert's, but he says Walter Rudd put him up to it.'

Raylene took the notice and read it, while Alice gazed out of the window at Kempton's waterfront. It looked particularly bleak in November, its overall greyness (grey sky, grey stones, grey water) relieved only by the vivid colours of parked or passing motor vehicles. The tide was low.

'Ha!' said Raylene. 'You know what this is, don't you? This is the condom machines.'

'What?'

'You know. His thing with the School Board, about the school condom machines. He's trying to put pressure on the Superintendent.'

Alice nodded; it certainly made sense. 'But Delbert was talking about homosexual teachers,' she pointed out. 'That seemed to be the main issue. Condoms weren't even mentioned.'

Raylene shrugged. She looked faintly embarrassed, as she always did when David French cropped up. 'I still think it's the condoms,' she replied. 'Maybe not for Delbert, but definitely for Walter. He's trying to get certain people thrown off the board.'

'You think so?'

'Oh sure. He's been trying for years.'

Alice bowed to Raylene's superior knowledge. She picked up the notice, and turned to leave the room. But Raylene stopped her.

'If you want,' she said, 'I can have a word with Dad about this. Delbert shouldn't be allowed to go around bagging people.'

'Oh.' Alice stared at her, perplexed. 'But -'

'If Delbert's involved, it's bound to be a sell. That's what people will think. And St Andrew's Christian Centre - Father Boudreau is a friend of ours. Dad could ask him to withdraw permission. He probably doesn't know what Delbert's doing, anyways.'

Alice appreciated Raylene's offer. But she sensed that it might lead to yet another battle in the Tibbett versus

Wheelhouse campaign, and was reluctant to become involved. Her policy was that as a representative of the press, she should try to remain neutral.

'I think I'll have a word with Walter myself,' she decided, 'and we'll take it from there. Thanks, Raylene.'

But when she returned to her desk, and called Walter, neither he nor Winnie were at home. So she called David instead.

He was cleaning the bathroom, he told her, in a languid voice. He had also been trying to rent a colour TV: did she know how difficult that was, around here? Oh, and Gordon had asked him about Oakey's water pipes - something to do with 'draining' them. Did Alice know what he meant?

Alice did know what he meant. She explained that if a house was not heated during the winter, its pipes had to be drained before the first freeze. Otherwise it would end up with burst plumbing.

'As a matter of fact, I've been thinking about that myself,' she confessed. 'If it's going to be done, it will have to be done soon.'

'So you don't think he'll be back this winter?'

Alice sighed. Her latest report from Maureen suggested that Oakey was progressing, but at a very slow pace. He was still in a wheelchair, and his speech was still distorted.

'Even if he does come home,' she said, 'he won't be living in the old Marshall place. He'll probably be staying with Maureen, so she can look after him.'

'Oh.'

'And if that happens before you go,' Alice continued, conscious of David's alarm, 'then you can stay with me. I'll be happy to have you.'

'Oh,' he said again. He seemed touched. 'That's very kind.'

'As long as Maureen doesn't want you there,' Alice remarked, qualifying her earlier statement. Although she knew little about nursing invalids, she did know that a lot of lifting was generally involved. 'It depends whether Oakey's able to get up.'

Then, dismissing the subject, she went on to tell David about Delbert, and Walter, and the proposed meeting for concerned parents. He listened quietly, showing remarkable restraint. Only when she had finished did he allow himself a snort of derision.

'Walter!' he exclaimed. 'That's a joke.'

'Raylene thinks it has something to do with Jack Dobbs. He and Walter have this ongoing disagreement about school condom machines –'

'Well, don't worry about that,' he interrupted. 'I'll speak to Walter myself.'

'Oh, but I was going to see if I could do something –'

'You don't have to. Please.' He seemed determined. 'I know exactly what to say. He won't dream of making waves once I'm through with him.'

Alice hesitated. She was somewhat unnerved by David's tone. 'You mustn't threaten him, David,' she warned. 'Violence will only make things worse.'

'Violence?' He laughed. 'What do you think I'm going to do, tread on his false teeth?'

'I don't know –'

'It's all right. I won't touch him.' A disgusted noise. 'Believe me, I wouldn't *want* to touch him.'

And that was all he would say about Walter. Instead he returned to the issue of Oakey's plumbing, for which he felt personally responsible. ('Oakey was always fixing my stuff,' he explained. 'The trouble is, I don't know anything about pipes.') Alice suggested that they enlist Fairlie McNeil's help, and wondered if they should set a time in the next few days. Saturday morning, perhaps? Or maybe she should check with Maureen first. But then she caught sight of Erica, waving at her – someone was on the other line – and told David that she would call him back.

'Okay,' she said, after hanging up. 'Put 'em through.'

It was Floyd McNeil, with a news story. Floyd had bagged a six-point buck with an antique, muzzle-loading rifle. He had used a CVA Powder River percussion cap and ball rifle, which was styled after the Western version of the Pennsylvania .58 calibre. Such a weapon required pin-point accuracy, because the smoke from the powder meant that you only got one shot. 'And there's no time to reload anyway, because you're usin' a muzzle loader,' he said, before going on to explain that he had always been interested in antique weapons. Other people might be interested too, especially when they heard about his 'black powder' club. The buck was hanging in his garage. Would Alice like to come and take a photograph?

Alice sighed as she dragged out her notebook. More damn trophy stories. But there was a kernel of interest in this one; an antique rifle club was something new. She would have to run an item, even if it was only small.

God, she thought. How I hate November.

＊　＊　＊

David found it difficult to get hold of Walter Rudd. The first time he left a message, Walter was not at home. The second time, Walter was in the bath. On neither occasion were David's phone calls returned. But luck favoured him at last, because one afternoon he dropped into the Scotsville convenience store, to pick up some milk, and found Walter pondering the limited choice of breads on display. (Scotsville convenience store tended to specialise in chips, sweets, soft drinks, magazines and microwave TV dinners.)

'Walter!' David cried. 'Just the man I wanted to see!'

Walter started, and mumbled something about meaning to call back, but other things had cropped up – Winnie's sister's operation, for example. In his brown polyester pants and cloth cap he cut a slightly pathetic figure, although the range of pens in his breast pocket (he was wearing a tweedy-looking jacket over a yellow shirt) hardened David's heart, somewhat. Pens displayed thus were the badge of a committee man, in David's opinion.

'I'd like to have a word with you, if I could,' David said. 'In private.'

Walter hesitated.

'It won't take long,' David continued. 'We could drop into my place, if you like.'

'Er . . . no.' Walter's heavy features remained static, but there was a trace of alarm in his voice. 'Grrblmnfbb . . . my house is closer . . .'

David agreed; Walter's house *was* closer. He followed the older man out of the store, noting with satisfaction that he had forgotten to buy his bread. He also noted the questioning looks of both staff and customers, who always watched David's every move whenever he ducked in for a carton of milk or an ice-cream. Were they surprised to see him picking up someone of such advanced years? Or were they astonished that it had happened in broad daylight?

Perhaps they were simply amazed that Walter Rudd was the target, Walter being what he was (at least in the public eye). No wonder he's scared to set foot in my house, David thought. He knows what kind of gossip it would lead to. Though all things considered, and in other circumstances, someone like Walter would be *lucky* to be invited home by someone like David.

The two men climbed into their respective cars, and David followed Walter back up South Street, towards the Baptist church. Walter lived in an immaculate blue house near Lindsay's; it had neatly kept lawns, a weathercock, a carport and one large tree in the garden. Out front, the mailbox - identical in every respect to the house it served - had been restored to its rightful place, months after that mysterious shooting had deprived Scotsville of one of its finest landmarks. The mailbox was, David had to admit, an extraordinary achievement. Every gable, every stair tread, every fretwork window box had been lovingly reproduced in miniature.

When David approached the full-scale version, Winnie Rudd came to the front door to greet him.

'Hello,' she said. She was nicely dressed, as usual. 'It's David, isn't it?'

'Hi.'

'Blffmngrrrlm . . . quick word.' Walter pushed past her into the living room. 'We'll use my den.'

'Wouldn't you like a drink?' Winnie inquired, her brow puckering. 'Coffee? Tea?'

'Gnnrffll . . . a minute.'

'Did you get the bread, Walter?'

But Walter had disappeared into his den, which lay off the central corridor and had been built, undoubtedly, as a bedroom. David decided that the decor of the house was mostly Winnie's doing - unless Walter had a taste for flowered wallpaper and ruffled armchair valances and fluted silk lampshades - but when he entered Walter's study, he saw that Winnie's influence had stopped at the door. Panelled in rather hideously varnished maple, the room was all leather and tartan: there was a leather sofa, and a tartan armchair, and a reproduction antique desk (with leather blotter), and a brass pen-holder set that featured a heavy, cut-glass inkwell. The walls were covered with photographs and certificates, all of them pertaining to Walter's community service. An old-fashioned rifle was mounted over the window.

'Now,' said Walter, as he closed the door and retreated behind his desk, 'gffflmbrr . . . see me for?'

David was wondering if Walter kept his pornography in this particular room. Behind the bookcase, perhaps? Under the rug? 'It's about this meeting,' he replied, his gaze flitting from corner to corner. 'This meeting for concerned parents. You've heard about it, haven't you?'

Walter made an enigmatic noise.

'It's the one in St Andrew's Ferry,' David went on. 'Delbert Wheelhouse informs me that you had a lot to do with it.'

'Frrrbrmmbll . . . Delbert's doing. I merely advised him -'

'Then you can advise him to call it off, please.' David spoke firmly. 'The whole thing sounds like an exercise in prejudice, and it won't do anyone any good.'

Walter was sending mixed signals, leaning back in a confident manner as he nervously toyed with the edge of his desk. His fingers were like uncooked sausages; his small blue eyes were almost lost under the fleshy pouches that weighed down his eyelids. He cleared his throat and spread his hands.

'Mmmmbflgmm . . . public opinion,' he mumbled. 'I can certainly advise him, but . . . fbblrgfnn . . . guarantee. In any case, what do you mean by "an exercise in prejudice"? I wasn't aware . . . ggrnglfmbmm . . .'

'You know exactly what I mean.' David leaned forward. 'And if that meeting goes ahead, Mr Rudd, I'm going to stand up in the middle of it, and point at you, and say that people in glass houses shouldn't throw stones. If you get my drift.'

Walter looked puzzled. Then he looked startled. Then his face went blank, wiped clean by shock.

'You're - you're not making much sense,' he stammered.

'Your preferences are your business, Walter. Just as mine are my business.'

'I don't know what you're talking about.'

'Yes you do.'

Walter was turning a dull, unhealthy shade of purple. But he grinned (with a ghastly attempt at nonchalance) and shook his head.

'Frrlymmbffgrr . . . I'm afraid,' he said, in breathless tones. 'Are you accusing me of some sort of misbehaviour?'

'No. I'm saying that your tastes in pornography are identical to my tastes in pornography.' As Walter's gaze flew to the bookcase, David thought: Aha. So that's where he's hiding it.

'Fbbgrnfff . . . better go!' Walter spluttered. 'I don't have to sit here -'

'On second thoughts, maybe I won't wait for the meeting. Maybe I'll just wander out and tell Winnie.' David smiled. 'Unless, of course, she already knows - in which case I might tell Raylene, instead. That should do the trick.'

Walter said nothing. He sat frozen, like an ice sculpture. At last, with an effort that made the veins stand out on his brow, he said, 'This is a lie. You can't prove this.'

'Oh, yes I can. I can prove it with one simple mailing list from a specialised publishing house.' David got up, and leaned across the desk until he was almost nose to nose with Walter. 'Lindsay Beaton's friend owns that publishing house. Apparently you subscribe to certain magazines.'

Walter closed his eyes. Then he covered them with one hand, as he bowed his head. David could not help feeling a trace of compunction; the poor old bugger was so *ashamed*.

'Listen,' he continued, 'I'm quite happy to keep my mouth shut. Like I said, your preferences are your business. But if this meeting goes ahead, Walter, I'll have to defend myself against all those bloody idiots who have no idea what some people have to cope with.' He straightened up, and folded his arms. 'I'll have to say: Of course homosexuals can provide moral guidance. Just look at Walter Rudd! He's an example to us all, and he's gay!'

Walter emitted a strangled croak.

'So it's up to you, now,' David finished. 'Are you going to call off that meeting, or not?'

'Grrfflmmbrrr . . .'

'Pardon?'

'I can't guarantee *anything*!' Walter looked up, wild-eyed. 'It's Delbert's - he might not - even if -'

'But you'll try.'

'Yes! God, yes!'

'Even if you have to stand up at the meeting and say it's a bloody disgrace.'

'Yes!'

'All right.' David nodded. He felt drained, and not entirely proud of himself. Walter was damp with sweat; his hands were shaking and his colour was dreadful. God, David thought. I hope he doesn't have a heart attack.

He came around the desk until he was standing at Walter's side, then stooped and laid a hand on one slumped, defeated shoulder.

'Listen,' he said quietly, 'this isn't the end of the world. You're not a pervert. The only thing you did wrong was to try and get *me* branded as one. Don't for God's sake go and shoot yourself, just because I happen to know. I won't pass it on.' Feeling a certain responsibility, he added: 'If you want to talk to me about it, you're welcome. Or there are other people you can talk to. Professional people.'

Suddenly Walter pushed his hand away. 'Are you finished?'

'Yes –'

'Then get out.'

David hesitated.

'Go on! Get out!'

Shrugging, David headed for the door. But before he could reach it, Walter stopped him.

'Wait.' The older man stood up. 'Grrngkllm . . . might look odd,' he said, and wiped his face with his handkerchief. 'Mustn't let Winnie think I'm . . . bffrngrrflmm . . .'

So it was Walter who showed David to his car, fending off Winnie's suggestion that David stay for lunch and making scattered, jovial comments that David found very encouraging. ('I'll look into it . . . don't worry . . . Delbert gets some funny ideas in his head . . .') Knowing that Winnie was in earshot, David deduced that even she was not aware of her husband's peculiar interest in Delbert's meeting; it sounded as if Walter's explanation for David's visit would be one in which Walter himself played the hero, having agreed to help the poor, beleaguered homosexual defend himself against the attack of mindless bigots like Delbert Wheelhouse.

It was all rather funny, in a tortuous kind of way.

'And have you heard anything from Maureen?' Winnie asked, as David fastened his seatbelt. 'How's Oakey faring?'

'Not bad,' David replied. 'He's feeding himself now, and he's beginning to remember things.'

'Oh, good.' Winnie raised her voice over the roar of the engine. 'You give her our regards, won't you? Tell her if she needs anything, she should give us a call!'

David nodded. Driving back home, he was assailed by a desperate desire to ring Alice, but managed to fight it off. He had promised not to tell anyone, and he would keep his promise – just as long as Walter kept his. He would give Walter a week or so, and then ask Alice. Alice would know if the meeting was still on. And if it was, he would just have to do what he had threatened to do: drop a little bomb with Walter's name on it.

But it seemed that Walter was as good as his word. A couple of days later, when David and Alice were settling down in front of *The Magnificent Seven* (one of their all-time favourite movies), Alice suddenly remarked, during the open-ing titles: 'Oh! Did I tell you about Delbert? He's called off that meeting of his.'

'You mean the –?'

'Yes. The concerned parents.' Alice began to nibble a peanut. 'Raylene told me. She said that Kendall had a word with Father Boudreau, and Father Boudreau had a word with Delbert. Father Boudreau runs the Christian Centre.' Watching the evil horsemen ride into the Mexican village, Alice uttered a little sigh. 'Trust the Tibbetts not to let the Wheelhouses get away with anything. You'll see. Delbert won't find another venue to stage that meeting in. The Tibbetts will close ranks, and the Tibbetts are on a lot of committees.'

David smiled. He had his own ideas about the cause of Delbert's defeat, but said nothing. Instead he leaned back and waited for Charles Bronson to make his appearance. (What a physique that man had!) It would be some time yet, he knew; probably half an hour until the famous wood-chopping scene. Meanwhile he would have to make do with Yul Brynner, and Steve McQueen, and that spunky little German whose name he could never recall.

Boots and chaps and Charles Bronson. What else, he won-dered, could a guy possibly want?

* * *

Louise would not be coming home for Christmas. She had turned down her mother's invitation, pointing out that Kempton was hardly her 'home' – that her home was in Ottawa, if anywhere, and that she had made plans with her

314

friends. Wandering along the shore of Sable Cove, Alice tried to imagine who these 'friends' might be. College friends? Work mates? Embittered young feminists, or well-groomed yuppies? She thought about David, and wondered how David would get along with Louise; in her mind's eye she could see them earnestly discussing their troubled relationships. Both quite fragile, in their different ways. But of course David had a great capacity for joy - you could see it on his face - whereas Louise . . . Louise could never let go. Never.

Except through the agency of drugs, perhaps?

Alice walked with her head down, her hands plunged deep into her pockets, her boots sliding on the round, loose rocks of the shingle. Beyond the rocks lay the mud (quite a lot of it, because the tide was low), and beyond the mud, the grey-green water. Opaque water. In just a few weeks, this water would have turned to ice along the shoreline, and there would be no more strolling about among the bleached shells and old fishing buoys. Alice could feel winter approaching, swiftly, on the northern wind. She could also smell fish, and decided that the smell must be drifting across the cove, on that same northern wind, from St Andrew's Ferry. Doubtless some fisherman was unloading his catch: she could hear the frantic, high-pitched squawks of excited seagulls. But how many more catches were left to that fisherman? How much longer would the fisheries survive? It was impossible to enjoy anything, nowadays, without gloomy reflections drifting into one's head. Another touch of November: death, decline, deterioration.

Glancing at her watch, Alice saw that it was half past four, and decided that she would have to retrace her steps. No point getting stuck down here after dark. Besides which, of course, there was the tide to think about - for when the tide turned in the Bay of Fundy, it turned with a vengeance. No one with half a brain ever messed with the highest tides in the world.

Alice stopped. She gazed westwards, towards the bay, squinting as her hair whipped against her cheeks. Then she swung around and headed home, picking her way across the pebbles, skirting the rockpools, climbing through the belt of spruce trees that grew some distance above the tidemark. Beyond the trees lay her garden, its grass still green but its shrubs and bushes now withered brown stalks. The light was on in her living room - a beacon for the homeward bound.

She went inside, took off her boots, and dressed for the party.

Every year, the Remembrance Day party was held on the first Saturday following the eleventh of November. It was sponsored by the Royal Canadian Legion, which provided the hall, the food, the drinks and the band for just a small cover charge. The guest list was generally hand picked. Alice was always invited, and always went, although she sometimes wondered why; pulling on her pantihose, she told herself that it would be something to put in her journal, because the day had been blank and eventless - just the sort of day that led to tortured nights - and she needed the distraction. When her day was full, when it tired her out and gave her plenty to write about, then she was able to sleep. Otherwise her bed became a rack, and the dawn a merciful release from unwelcome images of Bernard.

She put on her red woollen dress, the one with the mandarin collar. She also put on lipstick, of a similar if not a matching shade. Her grief felt like a dense and matted lump, like a fur ball lodged very low in her windpipe; occasionally she caught her breath on it, and then she would scold herself. Louise had never spent Christmas at Sable Cove in the past. Why should she do so now? Alice's hopes had been built on sand, and she had known that from the beginning. There was no excuse for self-pity. No reason to expect anything more. Clenching her teeth, she combed her hair and turned away from the mirror; she found the bleak, grey view of Sable Cove more comforting than her own reflection, nowadays - although the evening ahead wore an even grimmer prospect. If only David were coming! David would have provided the sort of witty, supportive, affectionate company that was normally so lacking at events like this. He would have laughed about it with her afterwards, and kept her amused with his smiles and jokes and slightly drunken imitations. She realised, with a little shock, that she had come to rely on his presence when she was feeling down.

But David had not been invited, and the Legion had never asked her to bring a partner - because everyone knew that she had none. Besides, with Walter there, and perhaps even Delbert . . . doubtless it was all for the best, really.

At half past six she put on her black, double-breasted coat, turned on her answering machine and set off for Kempton's Royal Canadian Legion Hall, where the revellers were already gathering. Under a cheerful display of Christmas lights (which were always put up on Remembrance Day), guests were ushered through the front door. Inside, a dozen or so large, circular tables had been arranged around the main hall, with the head table - long and rectangular - set upon a dais.

On this dais also was the band, a country music band called The Roger Dodgers, which played everything from Nashville classics to Cape Breton reels.

They were playing something twangily morose when Alice entered; she stood surveying the crowds for an instant, wondering where she should sit, but the choice was not to be hers.

'Alice!' It was Gwen Wylie. 'Alice, over here!' Gwen was sitting at what appeared to be a community service table: instead of veterans like Bob and Delbert Wheelhouse, or retired army officers, or even elected representatives (like the mayor, who had been placed at the head table), her fellow diners were Bonnie and Floyd McNeil, Walter and Winnie Rudd, Kendall and Marjorie Tibbett. The usual crowd, Alice thought sourly, as she slid into the seat beside Gwen. She exchanged rather stiff greetings with Walter and Bonnie, knowing what she did about their treatment of David. Floyd produced a nod, and a grunt. Mike grinned.

It was Marjorie who extended the warmest welcome.

'Alice!' she cried. 'How are you?'

'Fine thanks, Marjorie, you're looking well.'

'Oh, I am. I'm just great.' She was a pretty woman, with Raylene's big brown eyes and Cluny's striking features. Like Raylene, she carried some extra weight, but her preference was for bold, cheerful, almost tropical prints - palm trees and zebra stripes and Mexican motifs - rather than Raylene's domesticated florals and farm animals.

She was the subject of some gossip around Kempton, because of her flirtatious manner.

'Three guesses what they'll be serving up tonight,' she said, and Alice smiled.

'Turkey supper?'

'Either that or turkey supper.' Marjorie laughed; the professional catering in Kempton was not very sophisticated, and nine times out of ten the menu consisted of turkey supper, followed by sponge cake or fruit salad and ice cream. Sure enough, as the Mayor stood up to make his welcoming speech, the first course was served - and on each plate was arranged the standard portion of turkey, peas, corn, pumpkin and mashed potato.

Fortunately, the rolls were hot.

'So,' Marjorie said, at the conclusion of the Mayor's address, when the lengthening silence had everyone wracking their brains for a conversation starter, 'how's Oakey, Alice? I hear you're the one who's been keeping in touch.'

'Oakey's better than he was.'

'Raylene says that he's learning to walk again,' Kendall remarked, and sighed as Alice nodded. 'It's tragic,' he said.

'It is,' Gwen agreed.

'Do you think he'll be back soon?' said Bonnie, but received only a shrug in reply. 'If he isn't back soon, someone'll have to drain his pipes for him -'

'I've organised that.'

'And the snow-clearing,' Bonnie continued. 'We can't let his driveway ice up.' She shook her head, sadly. 'When you think about what a self-sufficient kind of man he was ... it's a shame.'

'He'll find it hard,' Gwen pointed out, 'if he can't do the things he used to. He'll find it hard to adjust.'

'And so will Maureen.' Bonnie was speaking through a mouthful of potato, in her eagerness to convey her opinion.

'Oakey did so much for Maureen. He mowed her lawn. He put up her Christmas lights. Who's going to put up her Christmas lights this year? That's supposing she's *back* by Christmas -'

'I would have thought David could do it,' Gwen observed, and silence fell across the table. Alice looked up sharply. She saw that Floyd and Walter were both deeply absorbed in their food.

'I don't think so,' Bonnie said at last, with a noticeable degree of reluctance. 'Besides, he's leaving soon, isn't he? Alice? When's he leaving?'

'On the sixteenth of December.'

'Oh, then he'll be much too busy to worry about Christmas decorations.'

'Hold on.' Marjorie lifted her fork. 'You've lost me. Who's David? What's he got to do with Maureen?'

'He's the teacher,' said Bonnie, before Alice could open her mouth. 'The one she exchanged with. He's living in her house, right now.'

But Marjorie frowned. 'I don't think I've met him. Have I met him, Ken?'

'He was at the dance.'

'What dance?'

'At the school hall. You know.' Kendall pulled a face. 'Raylene's always talking about him. The guy who visited Linda -'

'Oh, *him*!' Marjorie's brow cleared; a dimple appeared in her left cheek. 'Oh, I've heard all about him.' (I bet you have, Alice thought moodily.) 'He drives that flashy car, doesn't he? Wears that little beard -'

Mike guffawed. 'No, that's his boyfriend.'

'His boyfriend?'

Mike began to explain, as Alice sat fuming. Marjorie had heard of Lindsay Beaton, but knew very little about him except that he was rich and gay. She knew nothing of his habits, or his house, or his visitors. She was fascinated by Mike's account of his flamboyant gold jewellery and his strange purchases. ('A whole box of pills and cosmetics, practically every week – he buys 'em from Gwen's drugstore. And cotton wool. Bags and bags of cotton wool.') Then Bonnie joined in with a story about Lindsay's alleged purchasing of illegal drugs, and Alice could restrain herself no longer.

'Lindsay is a friend of mine,' she declared. 'He's a nice man, and he's given a lot to this community.'

There was a pause. People exchanged glances. Then Gwen said, 'Of course he has', and Bonnie returned to the subject of Maureen's Christmas lights. Who was going to put them up this year? Floyd would be glad to, except that his back was bothering him. As for the boys, it was going to be hard enough to make Eric and his brother put up their own Christmas lights, let alone Maureen's.

'I don't know why they hate it so much,' she added, mournfully. 'They used to love helping Floyd, when they were kids.'

Winnie suggested that perhaps Gary Ruggles might oblige. He was, after all, a neighbour – and a vigorous young man, to boot. 'Do you think Gary would do it, Marjorie? I know he would if Raylene asked him. Why don't you get Raylene involved?' But Marjorie smiled a crooked smile, and looked at her husband, who looked at the tablecloth.

'Seems to be trouble, on that front,' she said.

Everyone stared. Even Alice stopped chewing. Gwen was the first to break the stunned silence.

'Don't tell me they've split up? After so many years?'

'I don't know about *split up*,' Kendall replied. 'Bit of a dis-agreement, that's all.' But Marjorie, with a frankness that positively undermined her husband, said, 'He's moved out. Gone back to live with Enos.'

'I *thought* so!' Bonnie cried, irrepressibly. 'I knew something was wrong - his car hasn't been in the driveway.'

And they began to discuss the split, from every angle: Gary's compulsive television watching, Raylene's community involvement, the ever-controversial kitchen cup-boards. Listening to them, Alice felt sorry for Raylene. It was the kind of thing that Raylene would have done herself - this sifting through of intimate details - but surely no one, not even Raylene, deserved to have her unusual domestic com-promises aired in public.

'He complained that her legs were too short,' Marjorie growled. 'Every time he forgot to do something, every time he made a mistake, it was always: "What in hell have you done to your hair?" or "We don't need no bread, you're too fat as it is." He'd undermine her.' Watching Marjorie's bright, malicious, outraged expression, it occurred to Alice that there had never been any love lost between Marjorie Tibbett and her daughter's boyfriend. 'She'd come crying to me, and I'd say: "Raylene, there are other men in the world. There are other ways of living. You don't have to put up with this." '

'Of course she doesn't!' Bonnie exclaimed. 'She's a lovely girl! I've always said she could do better for herself.'

'She doesn't think so. She thinks she's ugly. Gary put that idea into her head, and it's hard to shift.'

'Oh, dear,' said Winnie.

'Oh, my,' said Gwen.

Alice said nothing. She was profoundly saddened, but knew that any kind of comment was pointless. Bonnie dabbed at her mouth, angrily, with a paper napkin.

'I always knew that boy was no good,' she declared. 'I always said so. He was always getting Eric into trouble, and his father just let him run wild . . .' She went on and on about Gary's poor school record, and his father's drinking, and how she had told Raylene, over and over again, that she deserved better - that Gary was a dead-end - until Alice was moved (by a sudden flash of malevolence) to say, 'Why should Raylene take your advice, Bonnie? You were wrong about David.'

Bonnie flushed. Everyone else looked startled.

'As I recall, you recommended David as a good prospect for Raylene,' Alice continued. 'Several times.'

'Yes . . . well . . .' Bonnie attacked her turkey with a set mouth. 'That wasn't my fault,' she said, after a moment. 'He was very secretive. He wasn't frank with people.'

'And does that surprise you?' Alice's tone was grim, her mood angry and jaded; the little ball of grief in her throat was getting bigger, and a tiny pinprick of a headache was beginning to throb above her right temple. She was aware of Gwen's puzzled glance - of the general embarrassment. *What's wrong with Alice?* was written on all their faces.

Mike cleared his throat.

'Getting back to Oakey Marshall,' he said, in a hearty voice, 'has there been any progress on who did it? On who beat him up, I mean.'

'No,' said Alice.

'He still can't remember?'

'Probably not.'

'Either that, or he's not saying,' Marjorie cut in. 'I've heard that he might be too scared to say anything.'

'Oh, that's garbage.' As usual, Bonnie was quick to defend Oakey. 'You've been listening to Raylene. He was mugged, that's all. They took his wallet.'

'But what about that Ryan fellow?' Mike objected. 'Anything more on that front?' He turned to Walter, who mumbled something about exploring every avenue, and also mentioned that Bill Garron had been trying to find out if the police in Ontario were looking for any particular suspects. Apparently they were.

'Gffrrlmmm . . . no details, yet,' Walter concluded. 'He said he'd tell me the minute they came in -'

Alice stood up. She did it so abruptly that her chair fell over. Half the room turned to look at her.

'You know,' she said, in shaky accents, 'there's a lot of things happening in the world. It beats me why you people can't find something else to talk about.' Suddenly the closed, stuffy atmosphere was unbearable; the sight of the half-eaten turkey made her feel ill. She restored her chair to its upright position, retrieved her purse from the floor, and added: 'You'll have to pardon me - I'm feeling a shade unwell. Don't think I can face dessert.'

Then she staggered out into the clean, fresh, slightly clammy November air. There, she thought, as she inhaled lungful after lungful. Now I've done it. They'll be talking about me for the rest of the night, after that little outburst.

And she wondered, as she reflected on her own surprising conduct, whether it might be time to make a change.

December

❄

The first snow began to fall at dusk, large flakes drifting gently down in the stillness. David found himself standing at the window, watching it; there was something remarkably soothing about the slow, monotonous descent of so many icy white feathers. Like watching goldfish, he thought - and then the phone rang.

Alice was on the other end of the line.

'Maureen's coming home,' she announced. 'Has she told you?'

'No . . .'

'She's bringing Oakey with her. They're due Friday.' As David absorbed this news, Alice went on to explain that Oakey still needed a lot of care, and that he would be staying with his sister for the time being. Meanwhile David could live with Alice. 'It's only for a couple of weeks,' she said. 'You don't mind, do you?'

'Not as long as you don't.'

'She wants us to fix a few things before she arrives. A

handle next to the toilet. An electric heating pad. Clear out the wardrobe in the second bedroom . . .'

'A handle next to the toilet? Like in a hospital?' David was appalled; everything was moving far too quickly. 'But how are we going to do that?'

'With help,' Alice replied. 'Don't worry. We'll work it all out.'

And they did. Paul Anderson found a handle, which Keith Hughes installed. Gwen Wylie ordered (and donated) an electric heating pad. Fairlie McNeil cleared Oakey's driveway - though it was doubtful whether Oakey would be using it for some time. 'Just to show that we're lookin' out for him,' Fairlie observed. 'He might want to drive past the old place.' As Friday approached, more and more people turned up on David's doorstep bearing cookies, cake, flowers, frozen blueberries, pickled herring, woolly socks and, in Bob Wheelhouse's case, a bedpan. 'Might be needin' it,' he pointed out. 'I did once. If he don't, just give it back to me.' On Thursday afternoon, Gary Ruggles even helped David to put up Maureen's Christmas lights, dangling off eaves and ladders with a disregard for the laws of gravity that was frightening to watch.

'My first ever time on a roof,' David confessed afterwards, as he and Alice changed the sheets on Maureen's bed. 'Another first.'

'You didn't have to wind them around the chimney, you know.'

'Oh, yes I did. Gary practically forced me to do it, at gun-point. Everyone else has lights on their chimneys. It's a matter of keeping up with the Joneses.' David laughed. 'Only I did draw the line at having "You can't spell Christmas without Christ" plastered across the front of the house.'

Alice grunted; she too had seen Bonnie's new Christmas message. Apparently the spirit of the season had softened Bonnie's heart, because David's presence in Maureen's house had not prevented her from delivering - in person - two large Tupperware containers full of clam chowder, as well as an apple pie and a little tray with fold-out legs, specially designed for serving meals to bedridden invalids. 'I bought it for Floyd, the last time he did his back in,' she explained. 'I thought Oakey might want to use it.' David sensed that she would have liked to direct the homecoming preparations herself, and probably would have, if not for the fact that David was involved in them. Even when making her delivery, she had advanced no further than the doorstep. But for once he was not offended, because if Bonnie had decided to take charge then she would have had to fight Alice for the privilege, and Alice had very definite ideas about Oakey's return. She wanted to keep it as quiet as possible. There would be no visitors, no questions, no friendly advice - not until he had recovered from his journey. It was she who transferred all his winter clothes from the old Marshall place to the wardrobe in Maureen's second bedroom; she who asked the post office to redirect Oakey's mail, and who fetched the unhappy Tripod from Ernie Tibbett's kennels, and who helped David to move his belongings from Maureen's house to her own.

Finally, it was she who drove to Halifax, to meet the plane from Toronto. Because the flight was due in at one forty p.m., David's school commitments prevented him from accompanying her. But he was ready and waiting when she arrived back in Scotsville at four forty-five; the sound of her engine brought him stumbling from the bathroom, adjusting his trousers, as Tripod barked hysterically.

'Tripod! Calm down, boy. Tripod!' Tripod had to be leashed before David could open the door. He was a powerful little dog, despite his handicap, and he nearly dragged David down the front steps in his frantic effort to reach Alice's car. Eventually David had to wind his leash around one of the porch balusters, right away from the stairs, so that no one would be knocked down by his impetuous greeting. For it was, without doubt, a greeting; by some unfathomable instinct, Tripod had managed to identify his master from the vaguest, most faceless of silhouettes.

David advanced towards the driveway. About three centimetres of snow lay on the ground, and the sky was heavy with tumid grey snow-clouds, their bellies brushing against the tops of the highest trees. There was no wind. By the time David reached Alice's car she was already out of it; she had opened one of the back doors, and was wrestling with a pair of steel crutches. David stood well back as slowly, carefully, she and Maureen helped Oakey to emerge – first one leg, then another, then a bowed head in a baseball cap. Oakey had lost weight, David noticed. His jeans hung loosely. His limbs shook, and the right side of his face was a mass of knotty red scar tissue. (The biggest scar ran from his ear to the bridge of his broken nose.) When he blinked, his right eyelid moved more slowly than its counterpart. Someone had shaved his moustache off.

'Hello, Oakey,' said David, stepping forward. But Oakey was staring at Tripod, who stood on his hind legs, straining at the leash. Maureen touched Oakey's arm.

'We should get you inside first,' she suggested. 'Sit you down. Otherwise you'll get knocked over.'

Oakey said nothing.

'He's walking real well, now,' Maureen continued, turning to David. 'It's just his right leg's a little weak.' She looked exactly the same: same hairstyle, same twin-set, same long, immobile face. Her recent experiences had left her completely unmarked. 'There's no ice on those steps, is there?'

'No,' said Alice. 'We put salt down.'

'Good.'

'Do you want a hand, or –?'

'Oakey can manage.'

David began to unload the suitcases. There were a great many of them, and a collapsible wheelchair as well; he spent half an hour dragging all the luggage indoors, conscious that Bonnie was observing him from her living-room window. Inside Maureen's house the heat was turned up, and Oakey was inserted into the snuff-brown recliner chair, from which David had hurriedly removed the quilt that had been placed there (in an effort to conceal the drab upholstery) some twelve months before. Shuffling in and out with the bags, he caught snatches of conversation: '. . . I see he's rented a new TV . . .', 'These cookies are Adelia's', 'So nice to be back' – and finally, as he dumped the last bag in the vestibule, 'We've decided not to press charges.' It was Maureen who made this last comment, in a low voice, from the kitchen. Oakey had not yet uttered a single word.

'. . . been found, then?' Alice inquired, and Maureen said, 'No. We think it's better if he isn't . . .' David would have liked to hear more, but realised that he was eavesdropping, and sat himself down with the intention of trying to communicate with Oakey - who was regarding him in an intent, cockeyed sort of way.

'Hi.' It was difficult to know where to start. 'You must be glad that you're back.'

No response.

'A lot of people told me to say hello.'

Oakey muttered something.

'Pardon?' David leaned forward. 'I'm sorry, I didn't quite -'

'Tripod,' said Oakey, and David leapt to his feet.

'Oh!' he exclaimed. 'I'm sorry, I'll get him. Poor dog.' Struggling with his snowboots in the vestibule, he added: 'I can't think how I left him - he must be freezing, out there.'

Tripod was certainly keen to get inside; he pulled David all the way up the front stairs, nearly choking himself on the leash, and when David finally unhooked him he shot straight across the living room like a bullet. David made a clumsy attempt to grab his collar, but relaxed as Oakey welcomed the dog with open arms. 'Good dog. Good old dog. Thataboy.' Maureen returned from the kitchen with a cup of tea, which she set down on the coffee table.

'Here's your tea, Oakey.'

'Uh-huh.'

'We should leave it to cool, some.'

Oakey nodded. Then Alice came in, carrying a tray, and he cocked his head to peer up at her. (He seemed to have difficulty moving his head.)

'You done a good job lookin' out for this dog,' he said, very slowly.

'Ernie looked out for him.'

'You done a good job with the house, too.' A pause, as if he was husbanding his strength. His hands moved jerkily over Tripod's coat. 'Thanks for bein' such a good neighbour.'

Alice set the tray down. There was a teapot on it, and a plate of cookies, but instead of collapsing onto the couch to sample them she straightened, and announced that it was time for her to go. 'You both need a rest. You've had a long day. If you need anything else, just give us a call - but I don't think you will. The fridge is stocked up. There are fresh towels in the bathroom.' To David, she sounded particularly arid; she seemed to be using her office voice. 'No one'll bother you. I made sure of that.'

'Thanks so much -'

'You ready, David?' She turned to look at him, cutting Maureen off in mid-sentence. 'I want to get home before the snowstorm hits.'

'Oh, yes. Of course. I'll get my stuff.' David scurried into the bedroom; by the time he returned, toting his gym bag, Alice had disappeared - and the front door was standing open. He and Maureen exchanged embarrassed smiles.

'See you later, then,' she said.

'Bye, Oakey.'

'Take care, now.'

'You too.'

It was a strangely awkward leavetaking; Alice had spoiled it, somehow. When David reached the car he found her sitting in the passenger seat, furiously blowing her nose on a shredded tissue.

'Do you think you could drive?' she said, and this time her voice was not arid, but husky. 'I've done too much driving today.'

'Yes of course.' David threw his bag onto the back seat. When she dropped her keys into his open palm, he saw that her eyes were suspiciously moist. 'Are you all right?' he asked gently. 'Is there anything you want?'

She sniffed, and shook her head. But as they coasted down South Street, past the fire hall, she suddenly said, 'It's sad, don't you think?'

'You mean about Oakey?'

'Yes.'

'He'll improve.' David spoke cheerfully, though he was far from optimistic. 'Look how much he's improved in the last month.'

Alice sniffed again. They drove for a while in silence, beneath the heavy, brooding, watercolour clouds, along roads frosted with salt and lined with banks of hard, dirty snow. They passed lighted windows and crossed dark estuaries. They plunged into scrubby woods. As the Sable Cove shoreline unfolded before them - all misty and grey, with monochrome rocks, like an etching - the first tiny flakes of snow began to settle and melt on the windshield.

'Alice?'

'Mmmm?'

'You've been told, haven't you?'

She wrested her gaze from the scenery, and fixed it on David.

'About Oakey,' he continued. 'About what happened. They've told you, haven't they?' Flicking on the indicator, he turned carefully into Marshall Street. 'I heard you talking to Maureen. In the kitchen.'

Alice sighed. 'It's not my secret,' she said.

'I know.'

'I've made a promise.'

'Of course.'

'I'm sorry, David.' The car juddered as it hit the trench at the mouth of her driveway. Snow whirled about in the light of the headlamps, like a million frantic insects. The windows of the house were all dark. 'I can't tell you. It's a sad little story. Depressing. You wouldn't want to know.'

She got out of the car, and began to trudge down the drive-way, hunching her shoulders against the cold. David followed, carrying his bag and her keys; the snowflakes dissolved on his face with tiny, frozen kisses. Together they went inside, and took off their boots, and turned on the lights, and then Alice drifted over to the living-room window. David joined her there.

'You mustn't let it get you down,' he said, hesitantly.

'What? Oh . . .' She shrugged.

'Whatever happened, it's not - I mean - you've done your best.'

'Believe me, I'd like to tell you what happened.'

'Oh, I know -'

'But I can't. It wouldn't be fair. It's not my secret.' She took off her glasses, and rubbed the inner corners of her eyes. Her hands were unsteady. 'I know what it's like, you see - when you confide in people, and they talk.' (She swallowed.) 'I was working in a small town when I found out about my hus-band. He was abusing my daughter. Sexually abusing her. It's not something you specially want people to know.'

David caught his breath. Oh my God, he thought. Oh my God.

'I can't give you Oakey's secret, but I can give you mine,' Alice continued, in dry, almost rasping tones, as she put her glasses back on again. 'My secret is mine to give. But if I transfer custody, you have to keep it safe. I know you understand that.'

'Oh, Alice –'

'Other people don't. I had to leave that town. I had to leave my husband, of course, but I had to leave town as well. It was very hard.' She was staring out at the tumbling snowflakes, her arms folded across her chest. 'That happened in New Brunswick, when Louise was ten years old. We moved to Toronto. You can lose yourself in a big city, and I wanted everything to be different, although it never really was. It was never much good, after that.'

David was speechless. He wanted to hug her and kiss her and make horrified, sympathetic noises, but her composure prevented him from expressing himself. Her imperturbability was like a fence.

'Louise got very wild,' Alice went on. 'She ran away twice, and went through a drug stage – which is understandable. She seems all right now. Not *happy*, you know, but all right. She doesn't want anything to do with me, though. She's too scared.'

'*Scared?*' David blurted it out before he could stop himself. 'Why should –? It wasn't your fault!'

Alice looked at him, calmly. She seemed to think for a moment. 'It was, to some degree,' she replied. 'There was a pattern there. When I thought about it afterwards, there was a pattern there. Only I'd missed it. I hadn't been concentrating.' Once more her gaze turned to the window. 'That's one reason why I started keeping a journal. It helps me plot the patterns. But Louise,' she said, suddenly changing tack, 'Louise isn't scared of me, she's scared of my guilt. She's scared of my feelings. They're too much for her, poor thing – she doesn't want to know.'

David wondered if he had missed some vital point. Alice's feelings were nowhere in evidence; her restraint was remarkable. 'But surely . . .' he began, and hesitated. 'You seem to have them pretty much under control,' he said at last. 'All this time, and I've never even . . . well, you're so strong. You're so together.' He laughed a shaky laugh. 'All this time you've been comforting me about Gus, and Bonnie, and Lindsay, and now finally I get to return the compliment, and you don't even need a hug!'

For the next half a minute, or thereabouts, Alice neither moved nor spoke – she was perfectly still except for the slow pulse of her breathing. Her expression was thoughtful, her gaze fixed. Then she began to nod: a slight, almost imperceptible movement.

'I think I could do with a hug,' she said, in a very small voice.

So David hugged her. He felt her small, brittle bones relax against his body. When she buried her face in his chest, he dropped his chin onto her scalp, and rocked her back and forth as he watched the falling snow.

After a while she broke away, and went to fetch her handkerchief.

* * *

Oakey made his first public appearance at David's farewell party. He had insisted on coming, much to everyone's

335

surprise; although he was a welcome visitor, he was also an unexpected one. Why should he wear himself out, when he and David were mere acquaintances? Maureen seemed to feel that he was unhappy about forcing David to move.

'But David doesn't mind,' Alice protested. 'David would feel much worse –'

'I know. Oakey just gets these ideas in his head. Still, I think it'll be good for him – he's gettin' pretty restless, stuck inside all day.'

So Oakey came to David's farewell bash, along with Maureen, and the Andersons, and Gordon Blanchard, and Jill Comeau, and Sam Peck, and no other members of the Kempton Elementary teaching staff whatsoever. ('They've never invited me anywhere,' David remarked. 'Why should I invite them?') Raylene came alone, as did Erica and Ian; Gwen brought Mike, and Keith brought his wife Sally. Neither Bonnie nor Floyd had been invited.

The party was scheduled for a Friday night, at Alice's house. In her five years at the *Kempton Gazette* she had never before thrown a party; six for dinner was as far as she had stretched herself, and by Wednesday she was beginning to panic about the arrangements. There would be a buffet supper, of course: cold turkey, salads, bread, cheese, fruit, wine, beer and perhaps a cake. (Should she have it made specially? With a farewell message inscribed on the top, in blue icing?) She had to borrow crockery from Maureen, and music from David. She had to borrow extra chairs from Fairlie, because he lived nearby and drove a pick-up – and then she had to invite him, as payment for his trouble. But Fairlie plus Adelia made twenty guests, so she had to go and buy more beer, just in case. 'Alice, please,' David moaned, 'you're getting yourself in a tizzy. Let *me* do all this. I'm used to parties. My mother has one almost every weekend.'

Alice, however, was determined that David should not have to organise his own party. On Friday night she left work at three, went home, cut up fruit, made tossed salad, carved poultry, changed the towels in the bathroom, washed dishes, laid the dining table and hung up a large sign, which was made from sheets of copy paper fluttering like pennants from a piece of string. The sign said *Bon Voyage*, and David arrived home (late, after farewell drinks at school) just as she was fastening one end of it to the big curtain rod in her living room.

'Oh, Alice,' he said. 'You didn't have to do that.'

'I didn't. Erica did.'

'It's beautiful.' David looked around. 'You've done everything. I told you to wait for me.'

'The chairs aren't done. You can arrange the chairs.'

Then all of a sudden it was half past six, and Alice had run out of time. She scampered about putting film in her camera, changing her clothes and emptying packets of peanuts into wooden bowls, as David slowly, methodically, blew up twenty-five pink balloons. 'Always have balloons at a party,' he declared, when questioned. 'They're very useful.' After tying them to various strategic doorknobs and picture frames, he retired to his room and put on a brightly coloured, festive shirt, tight black jeans and a gold necklace.

Alice wore her red dress with the mandarin collar, because it was too cold for her navy pleats. She only possessed two formal outfits: one for summer, one for winter. It occurred to

337

her that she would have to go shopping, one of these days, and buy something else – something black, perhaps. If only David had been staying a little longer! She sensed that he would be a good person to take shopping, especially clothes shopping, because he wore such beautiful things himself.

When the first knock came Alice was standing in the middle of her living room, biting her thumbnail and wondering if she had given everyone the right time. She glanced at her watch – six forty-five, for God's sake! Had she told someone six thirty, instead of seven? But it was Maureen on the doorstep, and she apologised for arriving so early.

'I thought if Oakey could fix himself up before everyone else came,' she said, in a low voice, 'then he wouldn't have to do it in front of people –'

'Yes, of course. I should have realised.'

'He's gettin' out of the car now. He won't let me help, any more. He has to do it alone.'

Alice was touched to see how thoroughly Oakey had groomed himself for the occasion. He wore grey trousers and a tie; his sparse hair was slicked back, and he smelled of aftershave. When he reached the front door he took the pot plant that Maureen was carrying and gave it to Alice.

'This is for your trouble,' he said.

'Oh . . . you didn't have to do that.'

'Better get it inside, or the cold'll kill it.' To David, who was hovering in the background, Oakey presented a whole case of beer. 'It's in the trunk,' he said, pointing. 'Moosehead. Real Nova Scotia beer.' His speech, Alice noticed, had improved a little; when she remarked on this (very quietly) to Maureen, Maureen nodded.

'It's because he's had to talk. In Toronto he didn't talk much - there was no one there to talk *to*. But since he came back, people have been callin' him up all the time. He's got a lot of practice.'

And he got even more practice that evening. As the guests arrived, one by one, they gravitated to Oakey's side - Fairlie and Raylene and Gwen and Mike and Keith and even Paul Anderson, who had never been introduced to Oakey, but who was interested in what had happened to him. Raylene and Gwen almost fought each other for the privilege of serving him supper. Sally Hughes was so upset by his slurred, hesitant speech that she retired to the bathroom with a box of Kleenex.

David was driven to remark, as he helped to peel Saran wrap off the refrigerated bowls of salad, that he was being completely overshadowed at his own party.

'Oh, my.' Alice looked up at him, stricken with guilt. 'I never thought. But he probably won't be staying much longer -'

'Alice, don't be silly!' David laughed, and kissed her temple. (He had already downed several cans of beer.) 'You're such a little worry-wart. As if I cared! I'm having a great time.'

'Are you?'

'Of course. Just look at all the goodies I'm getting!'

Most of the guests had, indeed, turned up with unsolicited presents: a Toronto Blue Jays baseball cap, a cassette tape of Cape Breton fiddle music, a pair of lobster-claw salt and pepper shakers, a packet of maple sugar fudge, a Pugwash pewter Christmas decoration, a snow-shoe fridge magnet, and four bottles of real maple syrup. Many jokes were cracked about the maple syrup. In fact Alice was surprised at how well everything seemed to be going; she suspected that David's heavy hand with the alcohol (for he had insisted on serving the drinks) may have had something to do with this festive atmosphere. David's two teacher friends were young and energetic, and after supper they joined Raylene and Sally and the Andersons in demanding a limbo contest. A broomstick was fetched, but never used, because David suddenly suggested balloon dancing as an alternative. He made Paul and Sue Anderson demonstrate, and by ten o'clock even Fairlie and his wife were up on the dance floor, a pink balloon wedged between their swaying stomachs. People stamped and laughed and screamed until the foundations shook. David's compilation tapes were played: he put on all of his fifties, sixties and seventies compilations, together with a somewhat startling eighties compilation that he called his 'Sex Change house party' tape. Then he danced a two-balloon tango with Paul Anderson, occasioning howls of laughter as well as a few raised eyebrows, and it occurred to Alice that he was rather smitten by Paul. Oh dear, she thought, I hope Raylene hasn't realised. Fortunately David was being kept very busy directing the frolics - for which he seemed to have a natural talent - and hardly had the time to follow Paul around.

Not that he would, Alice decided. He's far too sensible for that. He just needs someone to shine for, that's all. She was watching him trying to organise a step dance ('Who knows what they're doing? Adelia, you must. Raylene, what about you?') when she realised that Oakey had disappeared.

Over the course of the evening, Oakey had faded into the background, somewhat; unable to dance, even if he had wanted to, he was gradually abandoned by everyone but Maureen, who sat beside him watching the fun from a safe distance and fielding the odd question about Australia. (She was, as usual, maddeningly uncommunicative, even when pressed). Silent, faintly smiling, Oakey had followed the progress of the party with an incredulous look on his face. Then all at once, in the interval between a disco number and a Cape Breton jig, he had vanished.

When Alice asked Maureen if he was in the bathroom, she shook her head, and sighed.

'He's gone to look at the house,' she said.

'Next door, you mean?'

'Yes.' Maureen had to raise her voice to be heard above the music. 'We've decided to sell it. He's not fit to take care of a house that size, not any more. I guess he wanted to look it over.'

Alice nodded. For a few minutes she sat in Oakey's seat, thinking, but the music was so loud that she found it hard to think. So when David invited her to join the step dancers she declined, and got up, and went to the vestibule, where she put on her coat and scarf and snow boots. Outside, the air was damp, and the sky was clear; in the light of a full moon she could see Oakey leaning on one crutch, as he prodded at the ground with the other. He was standing behind the Marshall house, where his barn had once been.

The sound of Alice's rubber soles, squeaking on the crystalline snow, made him lift his head.

'Hi,' she murmured, joining him. 'It's only me.'

Oakey grunted. Even with the light from Alice's porch illuminating his face, his eyes were pools of shadow. He looked back down at the snow-encrusted earth, and turned some of it over with the heel of his crutch.

Alice watched him for a while. Then she said, 'Did you burn it down yourself? For the insurance?'

Prod, prod. Scrape, scrape. He neither spoke nor raised his head. The silence stretched out, growing more and more dense, until at last Alice smiled. She had her answer.

'How much did you get?' she asked.

'Not much.'

'Not even for your invention?'

A snort. Alice folded her arms, and gazed at him. She was already feeling the cold on her exposed ears and fingers.

'It was a big sacrifice,' she remarked. 'To destroy that invention . . .'

But Oakey shrugged, stiffly. 'It never had a chance,' he said, in his halting, indistinct way. 'I told you it never had a chance.'

'So you think some oil company might *really* have tried to destroy it? If you hadn't got there first?'

Oakey laughed - a short, sharp, husky sound. 'Oil company!' he exclaimed. 'Hell, no. I mean that nobody would ever have got interested. People like me don't change the world. You should know that.' There was another pause; he swung around, clumsily, to look at the old Marshall place. His breath emerged in great clouds of steam. 'I didn't know,' he said abruptly. 'When Ryan turned up, that was the first I ever knew. Didn't believe him, at first. Maureen always said it was some logger done the job.'

'I'm sorry, Oakey.' Alice's heart went out to him. 'It must have been tough.'

'If I'd known,' he went on, but stopped right there, and swallowed. Alice saw the light shift on his Adam's apple.

'I'm sorry,' she repeated. From her house came the throb of dance music, and the babble of excited voices. There was no other sound. 'Maureen tells me you're selling up. Moving in with her.'

Oakey nodded. Again, he seemed to find this simple manoeuvre extremely difficult. 'I wouldn't live here any more,' he replied gruffly, 'even if I could. It's a bad-luck house. Always has been.'

'It's big, though. A big property. You should get a fair price.'

'If it sells.'

'I guess.' Alice knew what he was getting at. The real estate market in Kempton was standing still; poor economic prospects made buyers cautious, and the Marshall place was lacking in such basic comforts as an oil furnace and a finished basement. It was a cold, old house - the worst kind of house to get rid of.

Alice looked at it, and shivered.

'You're cold,' said Oakey. 'You should get back inside.'

'So should you. You don't even have a coat on.'

'I'm used to it,' Oakey replied. But he began to head for Alice's porch, swinging his crutches with long, easy movements as his right foot dragged in the snow. Alice walked beside him, keeping pace, wondering if he would ever regain full use of his limbs. Wondering if he would ever curl or mow lawns or shovel snow again. What was he going to do with himself, if not?

'Maureen says you won't be laying charges,' she observed, before they reached the front steps. 'Is that smart, do you think?'

343

'We don't want no more trouble.' Oakey was panting. 'So long as he keeps away, we'll keep our mouths shut.'

'But Oakey – look what he's done to you. It's not just the money, it's . . .' Alice stopped, aware that her voice was trembling. Oakey regarded her with expressionless eyes. He spoke softly, so as not to be overheard.

'Ryan Brown was hard done by. He's an angry boy who wanted to get his own back.' Oakey frowned, and shrugged, and winced as something went *crunch* in his neck. 'I guess I don't blame him. Foster's dead, so he took it out on me.'

'But it was nothing to *do* with you!' This was the point that Alice found unbearable. 'You just said you didn't even know! Why should *you* be the one to suffer?'

Oakey looked confused. He scratched his chin and peered at Alice as if he could hardly believe what he had just heard. 'We've all suffered,' he said slowly. 'It's a family thing.'

Then he began to drag himself up the stairs, step by step, towards the light and the music. Alice followed him like a shadow, wrestling with the irony of it all. Who was she to advise Oakey? Do what I say, not what I do, she thought.

They were two of a kind.

* * *

David's flight was due to leave Halifax at one p.m. Since he was required to be at the airport one hour before the scheduled departure time, and the trip to Halifax was an easy three hours on top of that, he and Alice had to be out of Sable Cove by nine o'clock in the morning. Both of them were slightly concerned about possible delays; Alice set two alarms (one for her, one for him) and David packed everything – except his

344

toothbrush and pyjamas - the night before he left.

As it happened, however, they need not have worried. Because neither of them slept very well, they were up by six, and on the road by eight. David insisted that Alice take him on a last tour of Scotsville, and they also completed a quick circuit around Kempton before striking out for the highway. It was a wet, misty sort of morning; the roads were all sand and slush. Chimneys smoked peaceably, and cars trundled along in a torpid fashion, steam billowing from their exhaust pipes. From the top of the hill behind Kempton David could see Kempton Gut receding into the haze, its fishing boats moored, its mudflats encased (here and there) in sheets of dirty brown ice. Alice mumbled something about a thaw. 'I hope it doesn't freeze again, before I get home,' she remarked. 'The roads will be a nightmare.' Then she headed for Halifax.

David watched the passing landscape, making one last attempt to commit it to memory; the granite headlands, the low, dense forests of pine, the boxy shingle houses and majestic barns - soon they would all disappear, to be replaced by sandstone cliffs, gum trees, highrise units, harsh sunlight and vivid colours. Sydney in the summer. He could barely remember what it felt like.

'And I never did get to Prince Edward Island,' he said mournfully. 'I wish we'd made that trip, don't you?'

'Yes.'

'I didn't get to Cape Breton, either. I'd have liked to go there. Someone said they still speak Gaelic.'

'My grandmother spoke Gaelic.'

'Really?' David looked at her, startled. 'You never told me that. You mean she spoke it *all the time*?'

345

'Oh, no.' Alice changed lanes. 'We wouldn't have understood her. No one else in the family could speak it.'

'How incredible.' David pondered the mystery of Alice's background – her strange, primitive, Celtic background on that fog-enshrouded island. He felt a powerful urge to visit her ancestral home. 'Maybe if I came here again,' he suggested. 'For a holiday . . .'

'You'll always have somewhere to stay if you do,' she replied.

They bypassed Middleton and Kentville, skirted Windsor, and hit the dull stretch of road that cuts straight through mile upon mile of tedious scrubland. But before they reached Sackville, and the straggling outskirts of Halifax proper, Alice turned on to a road marked 'Airport'. 'This'll take us to Fall River,' she said. 'Are you hungry, at all? Do you want something to eat?'

David checked his watch; it was ten forty-five.

'We're early,' he said.

'I know.'

'I could do with a donut.'

But strangely enough, they could not find any donut shops in Fall River. So they proceeded to the airport, through a fine drizzle, and parked within a short distance of the front door. David had three suitcases and two large boxes to check in; he had to pay a hefty overweight baggage fee, but was not obliged to queue for the privilege. 'This is such a civilised airport,' he commented, as he left the check-in counter with his sheaf of boarding passes. 'It's so little and cosy.'

'There's a cafe down there. We'll go and get you a donut.'

'I'll have a really fancy donut. It might be my last chance.'

But the airport cafe barely ran to iced donuts, let alone the fudgebusters and maple dips of a Tim Horton's outlet. David was forced to buy a very plain example of the donut maker's art (cinnamon sugar) and an ordinary apple muffin. Alice bought a piece of carrot cake. They sat down on chairs which had been fastened to the floor - perhaps to stop delayed passengers from hurling them around in a fury - and were suddenly lost for words. The cafe was noisy and bright. The view from the window was of rain-lashed tarmac. Children screamed, plane engines roared, and disembodied voices announced departure times at far too regular intervals.

'I hope I bought enough presents,' said David. 'I haven't been keeping track.'

'You can always check out the souvenir store.'

'I should have got some American money, for that stopover in Honolulu - in case I want to buy something.'

'How long will you be there?'

'An hour and a half.'

'Oh, you should be all right. They won't charge you to use the bathroom.'

'I've got a chocolate bar. And some fruit. That should tide me over, don't you think?'

'Just remember to keep drinking. Don't let yourself get dehydrated.'

It was all empty talk, designed to fill in the lengthening pauses. David felt curiously tight in the chest. He found himself glancing at Alice, noting the shape of her face, the lines around her eyes, the way her glasses would keep sliding down the bridge of her nose and the way she would have to keep pushing them back up again. She had such neat, blunt, pale little hands.

'You will write, won't you?' he said. 'I'm relying on you to keep me informed about what's going on.'

'Yes, of course.'

'I want to know what happens with Raylene and Gary. And whether Oakey manages to sell the house. And Walter - keep an eye on Walter, won't you? I don't want to lose track of him.'

Alice smiled, and nodded, and glanced at her wrist. It was twelve fifteen. 'You'd probably better go in now,' she said. 'They'll be boarding any minute.'

David rose. He picked up his gym bag. Together he and Alice walked over to the security barrier, through which they could see an escalator leading up to the departure gates. Alice said something about his in-flight movie - how she hoped it would be a good one - but David was speechless. He put his bag down again, and tried to swallow the lump in his throat.

'Well . . . I guess this is it.' She was smiling. 'You take care, now.'

He nodded.

'I hope you have a good flight, and . . . I hope things go well. I'm going to miss you.'

If David had spoken, his voice would have cracked. So he hugged her instead, very tightly, and felt the pressure of her arms around his ribcage. They clung to each other, as he fought back the tears. God, he thought - God, this is terrible. How I *hate* goodbyes. There were so many things he wanted to say, but he could say none of them.

'Thank you,' Alice murmured. 'Thank you so much.'

He kissed her and let her go. Then he shouldered his gym

bag and carried it to the X-ray scanner, emptying his pockets of all keys, small change and foil-wrapped cough lozenges.

His last glimpse of Alice was through the security door; he saw her standing there in her drab blue anorak, very small and tired-looking, her glasses slightly crooked on her nose. As he turned to wave, she lifted her camera: the flash almost blinded him.

On the plane he opened her farewell present. It was a photograph in a frame. The frame was of maple wood, hand carved, highly polished.

The photograph was of an old cart wheel, almost hidden by snow.

EPILOGUE

December

Sydney airport was a shambles. The immigration staff were on strike, and a handful of ill-trained airport employees had been forced to replace them. As a result, six planeloads of people were piled up behind the barriers, slowly inching their way through, growing crosser and crosser, hotter and hotter - because there did not appear to be any airconditioning. At the carousels, suitcases were pouring on to the moving belts before their owners had even had their passports stamped; this meant that there were too many bags, and not enough space. One Qantas steward had to leap on to the edge of the worst affected carousel and pull bags out of the heap for some of the weaker passengers, who were not capable of reaching up so high. 'Sydney Airport,' he said, in his flat, Australian drawl. 'There's nowhere else like it.' His accent sounded strange, after so long.

The customs officials were waving almost everyone through, reluctant, perhaps, to aggravate the traffic jams. There was hardly a clear inch of floor space; every corner was packed with trolleys, luggage, railings and exhausted children. Someone had vomited somewhere close by. The moving belts clanked and squeaked and rumbled.

When Alice finally emerged into the arrivals hall, she felt as if she had passed from purgatory through the gates of heaven.

'Alice!' It was David's voice. 'Alice, over here!'

Alice scanned the rows of eager faces before her. There were so many! People were shouting and laughing and embracing. The noise was terrific.

So was the heat.

'Alice!' And there he was, pushing through the crowds, tall and slim and unmistakable. He wore jeans and a T-shirt, and did not seem to have changed much in the year since Alice had seen him last. He was smiling. When he reached her, he swept her off her feet in a hug so fierce that she protested.

'Sorry,' he said. 'Sorry.'

'Can't breathe -'

'You poor thing. You look *dead*. Do you feel dead? It's appalling, isn't it? Literally like hell. Here - I'll take those. I'm afraid we're parked *miles* away, but I brought you a hat. Do you like it? It's a real Akubra. Oh, it looks terrific on you! Oh, it's so good to see you, Alice. I can't believe you're really here!'

Neither can I, thought Alice. The contrast was almost too much to cope with. But she told herself that she had wanted - needed - a change of scene, and this was about as different as you could get. Fresh horizons. New challenges. There was certainly nothing here to remind her of Nova Scotia, or any of its attendant problems.

David relieved her of her trolley, took her by the arm, and guided her gently out of the tightly packed multitudes towards a pair of automatic doors. Beside these doors a large, dark-haired young man suddenly straightened, and lifted an eyebrow. He stepped forward.

'Oh,' David said, a little shyly. 'I forgot about Nick. Nick, this is Alice. Alice, this is Nick. He insisted on coming.'

Alice adjusted her glasses. She saw that Nick had a wide, genial face and even wider shoulders; his hair was cut very short at the sides, but was reassuringly long and tousled on top. He had a slow, sweet smile and a warm, resonant voice. He wore an earring.

'Hello,' he said, sticking out his hand.

'Hello.' Alice shook it. 'So you're the wonderful Nick.'

'And you're the wonderful Alice.'

'I've heard all about you.'

'Oh, God. Not all about me, I hope.' Nick laughed. 'Some things are better left unsaid.'

Then they all laughed - not because they were amused, but because they were happy - and strolled out into the fierce Sydney sunshine.